GUINEVERE
EVERMORE

THE GUINEVERE TRILOGY

Guinevere
The Chessboard Queen
Guinevere Evermore

To Dr. John Yunck
whose inspiring and inspired classes both sent me
on my search for Guinevere and gave me the tools
with which to find her. With love and gratitude.

Library of Congress Cataloging in Publication Data

Newman, Sharan.
    Guinevere Evermore.

        1. Guenevere, Queen—Romances.   2. Arthurian romances.
I. Title.
PS3564.E926G83   1985   813'.54   85–1709
ISBN 0–312–35322–7

First Edition

10 9 8 7 6 5 4 3 2 1

GUINEVERE EVERMORE

By Sharan Newman

ST. MARTIN'S PRESS, NEW YORK

GUINEVERE
EVERMORE

Chapter One

Lancelot of the Lake, son of Ban of Banoit, and most illustrious knight of the Round Table, squatted by the campfire, polishing his armor with casual grace. He had been aware for a while that someone was watching him from the woods; someone who could hide as cleverly as a wild animal. But Lancelot knew it was human, or close to it, and he waited for whoever it was to make his move. He hoped it would be soon, as he was tired and there was still a long journey to Camelot tomorrow. He was sorry now that Gareth had left that afternoon, to spend some days at Tintagel with his mother, Morgan le Fay. It would have been easier if one man could have slept and the other watched.

He laid the armor on a blanket and picked up his sword, running the cloth up and down the steel blade with a kind of caress. He kept his right hand on the hilt as he spoke.

"You have been sitting there for nearly three hours. Wouldn't you rather come out and share the fire?"

There was a rustling in the bushes for a moment, and then a boy crawled out. He stayed on his hands and knees until he reached the circle of light from the campfire. Then he lifted his hands, arms stretched, palms up in the Christian attitude of prayer.

"Please forgive me, my Lord," he bleated. "I was overcome by your glory. I saw you and the other angel pass by this afternoon, and I followed you. Never in my life have I seen anything so radiant!"

Lancelot set down his sword. He shifted uncomfortably. He had been called many embarrassing things in his life, but "angel" had to be the worst.

"Look, boy," he replied with some sharpness. "I am a man, just like yourself." *May I be forgiven for that!* "My friend and I are not angels, we are knights."

"I never heard of knights. My mother never mentioned them. Are they a kind of priest? Mother doesn't want me to be a priest, but she thinks they are good men."

"Where have you lived, child, that you have never heard of King Arthur or his knights?" Lancelot was affronted by such ignorance. By now everyone knew of Arthur. "He rules almost all of Britain and we are his lieutenants. We see that his laws are enforced and that evildoers are punished."

"And what do you do with that long metal stick?" The boy pointed to the sword.

Lancelot could not cope with such stupidity. He turned his back on the boy, wrapped his armor against the night air, rolled up in his cloak, and went to sleep. When he awoke, the boy was gone. He felt a little guilty for his impatience.

"He was probably some poor farmer's son, never more than a mile from his own pigsty. I should have been kinder to him."

He had loaded his horse, Clades, when he became aware that the boy was back. His face was dirtier than before and his nose was running, as if he had been trying not to cry. He carried a leather bag over his right shoulder and from his left hung a scabbard and sword. The work on the metal was delicate as lace.

"I'm ready," he announced. "I told Mother about meeting you and that I wanted to be a knight too. At first she cried and said she would never let me leave her. But I said I had to go and that was that, and so she gave me this thing. She said it was my father's and love of it killed him. She told me to find a wise man to learn from and to be dutiful, obedient, and honorable to women. Then she cried some more and hung on me and made me promise to come home if I didn't become a knight. So here I am."

Lancelot felt his sympathy for the boy disappear.

"You left you mother in tears to come after me? Who said you could become a knight? You don't have any idea of what a knight is. You can't just appear and say that you're joining us and be accepted. It's an honor that must be earned."

The boy's jaw set. "I want to be a knight. I'll do anything you say."

"Very well." Lancelot mounted his horse. "You may come with me, if you can keep up. I see you brought nothing to ride on. How fast can you run?"

The boy smiled. "I can outrun the deer!" he boasted.

"Then we'll see if you can outrun Clades."

He set off down the road at a gallop. With barely a hesitation, the boy started after him.

An hour later, Lancelot looked back. Even though he had kept Clades to a trot, that idiot child was still following. He was falling behind now. Sometimes, when the road bent, it was a full five minutes before he came in sight again. But he hadn't lied. He could run. Even with the sword slapping his side at every step, he kept up the pace. He would have some colorful bruises tomorrow.

With a sigh, Lancelot reined in and waited. When the boy drew even with him, he leaned over.

"Clades cannot carry two and our gear, but I will take your baggage on behind me. You needn't fear. If you should change your mind and decide to return to your home, I will return it to you gladly."

He tied the bag and the sword on with his own equipment and set off again. The boy took a deep breath and started running.

It was high summer at Camelot. The air was warm and a soft wind teased its way among the buildings and over the practice field where the clash of sword and shield was accompanied by cries of laughter and good-natured joking. Laundry hung drying between the Great Hall and the women's quarters. The flapping of the linen and the clank of the metal blended with a hundred chattering voices as the inhabitants of Camelot went about their work.

The smell of roasting meat wafted across the courtyard and filtered down to the practice field, where the men began wiping their blades and removing the padded mail they wore. Soon, they joined the rest of Camelot at the midday meal.

The dining hall was crowded and the doors and windows had all been thrown open to let in the light and let out the odors. The food had been set on the tables, but no one took any. They stood waiting. King Arthur tapped his knife handle against the back of his chair as he chatted with his seneschal, Cei.

Queen Guinevere rushed in, a little breathless. "I'm so sorry I'm late." She smiled at everyone in the certainty that she would be forgiven without explanation and hurried to her seat.

As soon as she sat down there was a great clatter as everyone reached simultaneously for the meat and bread and pitchers of ale. Arthur's favorite hunting dog, Cabal, curled himself around the table legs, his eyes following every flick of the knife, prepared to catch his share of the meat before it hit the floor.

It was not a particularly elegant group. Most of the people were going back to work after eating. Their clothes were not their finest and their faces and hands not all that clean. The unmarried knights all sat in one corner, laughing at ribald jokes and poking each other for emphasis. Fosterlings hovered around them, serving the meat, refilling the pitchers and dreaming of the day when they would be knighted, too. The ladies sat in their own section, some balancing babies in their laps as they daintily carved their meat into tiny pieces and soaked bits of the bread in gravy to stuff into the children's mouths at frequent intervals.

There was a sudden commotion at the doorway. Everyone turned to look. Arthur craned his neck to see what it was.

"Good Lord!" He stood up in his chair, knocking over the water pitcher. "Lancelot! What are you doing riding your horse in here, and who is that with you?"

The room had suddenly become more crowded as Sir Lancelot, silver armor shining and white plumes waving, pulled his panting horse up in front of the dais. Hanging onto his ankle, nearly in a state of collapse, was a young man. He was wrapped in a rough woolen tunic and his shoes were coming apart. As he stood gasping for air, he raised his shaggy head and looked around. He breathed more deeply and a slow grin of delight appeared. Lancelot dismounted. He climbed up to the table, bowed to the King and Queen, looked back at his companion, and shrugged.

"Arthur, this is Percival. He followed me home. May I keep him?"

Percival couldn't believe the place he had come to. His mother had not given him any clues about the outside world. She had hated any mention of what might be beyond their gates. Now there was so much to learn that the days weren't long enough for him to ask all he wanted to. At first, he spent his time trailing behind Lancelot.

"Why is the road up here so twisty?" he asked.

"To keep out invaders," Lancelot told him. "Not that we have any trouble now. Arthur has put the Saxons in their place and the Irish raiders, too."

"Then why must we practice fighting?"

"In case they forget or some new foe attacks us."

"I want to help. When can I learn to use my father's sword?"

"When you stop tripping over it."

Percival thought it was time to change the subject. "Who is the little boy who is always with the Queen? He looks like her; is he her son?"

"No, he is my son, Galahad. Guinevere has taken him to foster."

"Your son? I thought you weren't married. Are you married? Where is his mother?"

"I'm not married. His mother is dead. I think you've asked enough questions for now."

The look on Lancelot's face told Percival that he had.

"Poor Sir Lancelot," he thought. "He must miss his dead wife very much."

He wandered around, bemused by the wonder of it all, his eyes everywhere but where he was going. There was a chapel decorated with paintings in bright new colors. Brilliant pennants flew from all the towers, and roses and ivy climbed the walls. Even more awesome and unnerving was the small building behind the Great Hall. In it were great stone basins, sunk into the earth and filled with hot and cold water. He was expected to remove all his clothes and wash there, even if other men were present. It took both coaxing and threats to get him in there the first time, and he never was able to feel at ease among the splashing bodies. He usually huddled in a darkish corner away from the others so that he wouldn't be noticed.

Still, it was a good place to find things out. He found he could ask more there, before he was told to go away. One day he caught Gareth, one of Arthur's nephews. Gareth had only recently become a knight and seemed willing to talk. Percival didn't know that Lancelot had told his friend especially to be kind to the feckless newcomer.

"The King and Lancelot must be very good friends," Percival opened.

"Of course. After all, Lancelot is the greatest knight at Camelot; the strongest, the bravest, the most religious. Arthur depends on him. And they also go hunting together and play chess and that sort of thing."

"I thought Sir Gawain was the strongest knight," Percival ventured.

Gareth frowned. "Only in the daytime. Old Gawain can't stay awake past sunset and even before then, he's almost too weak to crawl to bed."

"What happened to him?"

"Nothing. He's always been like that. We used to play some great tricks on him when we were boys, but he was a rotten sport."

"Did you grow up with him?"

"For a while, until Mother sent him away to Cador. He's

really nothing special; just one of my brothers. Are you going to wash or just sit there, Percival?"

But Gawain fascinated Percival. He was so energetic. And he had the courage to walk right up to Queen Guinevere and pick her up and swing her around, or pull her braids loose, or steal a comb so that she had to chase him all over the gardens to get it back. They were just like children together and nobody seemed to mind. Gareth said it was because Guinevere had been fostered with Gawain, so that they felt more like brother and sister. But Percival still couldn't understand it. He was in awe of both of them, but especially Queen Guinevere. She glistened in the sunlight as she walked, her silk skirts shimmering about her. He doubted that he would ever have the courage to speak to her. He noticed that even Lancelot was different around her. Once Percival came upon them as they stood watching Galahad at play. Her hand was on his arm. She spoke and Lancelot looked down at her. Something in the stillness or something in their faces made Percival shrink back against the wall, hoping he hadn't been seen. He wondered about it for a long time.

Autumn was early that year and the roads had iced over before everyone was safely transported to the winter quarters in Caerleon. There were more people than ever, and the old Roman fort, though large, was hard put to hold all those who had now become indispensable to the running of Britain. Arthur had started to consider creating several mini-capitals in which he could leave regional administrators all year round. There were men holding such positions now, unofficially. The trouble was that the very men strong enough to be left to do a job on their own were also the ones who might decide it was unnecessary to answer to a High King. And the good men he trusted were too useful to have them gone nine months of the year. Still, the congestion was breeding petty animosities that got on everyone's nerves. Every day, it seemed, there was some sort of argument brought into the hall at dinner. The seating arrangements had been changed so many times to accommodate the feuding that Arthur wasn't sure anymore where he sat, himself.

Percival didn't notice any of the bickering. Caerleon was even more fascinating to him than Camelot. It was so old and the stones of the walls were so large. Giants must have lived in Britain to make such a fort. There was more work to do here, too. He had to clear out after the animals and spread hay and rushes on all the floors. He helped in the kitchens and carried hot ale to the shivering guards. One day he was sent to curry the horses. But after a few minutes he threw down the brush and swung around, aching to punch something.

"And what war are you in, boy?" The harsh voice stopped him cold. Percival looked up. Caet, the horsemaster, was staring at him with disdain. Slowly, he opened his fists. But his anger wasn't stilled.

"I came here to be a knight and they have me doing slave work. Lancelot said he'd teach me, but all he does is stare at the Queen," the boy muttered.

Caet was a small man, but he caught Percival up in hands of iron and shook him until his ears rang.

"No man here is a slave! But my horses have better sense than the likes of you. Get out of here and don't ever let me see you around them again. And watch your tongue, young gossip, or you'll never be a knight. What do you know about the Queen? She's far above anything you've ever seen. Now, get out!"

Stunned by the force of the man's anger, Percival scurried out and hid for the rest of the day behind the storage bins. He was found there by one of the serving girls.

"What's the matter with you? Seen a ghost? They say the old soldiers still march up and down the watch by night." She laughed at his face. "Well, you can't stay here anyway. Come on, what's wrong?"

She smiled encouragingly. Shyly, Percival smiled back. Stumbling a little over the words, he told her what he had said to anger Caet.

She shook her head at his ignorance. "Now look, just so

you don't make any more mistakes like that, I'll tell you what I know." She became abruptly serious. "It goes back to before I came here. But they say that Lancelot and Queen Guinevere have always been, well, very fond of each other, but she's the King's wife, you see, and we all love Arthur. I mean, he's not to be hurt. Do you understand? We don't talk about it much, even among ourselves. I don't think even Guinevere and Lancelot want to hurt him. It's more like they just can't help themselves. You can't hate them for it, really. It just seems so tragic."

She sighed at the romance of it all.

Percival shook his head. "I thought Lancelot was still grieving for his wife."

The girl's eyes widened and she looked carefully around, to be sure no one else was near. Her voice dropped.

"I know about that; I come from Cornwall. Lancelot never had a wife. He was tricked by Morgan le Fay and her sister, Morgause, into sleeping with poor Galahad's mother, Elaine. There's some that say he thought she was Guinevere. Anyway, he accepted the son, but cast the mother out, sent her back to Morgause." Now she was whispering hoarsely. "She killed herself, because of him, they say. But Lancelot didn't care. He only loves the Queen."

She stopped. She looked at Percival, waiting to see what he thought of such a story.

"It doesn't make sense to me," he said finally. "You must not have it right. I'll ask Lancelot."

The girl grabbed him with razor-sharp nails. "Are you mad? Don't ever breathe a word of this to anyone. I'll be sent home to my father if you do. You must promise me." The nails dug harder. "Swear!"

Percival nodded as he tried to pry her fingers from his arm.

She relaxed a little, then smiled. "If you truly promise, then you must seal it with a kiss."

He leaned away from her. "I never kissed anyone but Mother. Is that the custom here?"

"It certainly is, and, if you like, I can teach you some of our other customs."

Percival thought. His mother had said to be dutiful to women. It occurred to him that this one was very pretty. He nodded and smiled. She smiled back.

For Arthur, the winter was a time to go over plans and study the problems for the next year. He tried to get men from all over Britain to come and tell him about the concerns in their lands. The north worried him. There were too many independent kings there whose tribes had never really been under Roman control. They needed careful treatment before they would agree to submit to Arthur. But who to send to them and what should they promise? He studied a list Gareth had compiled during his last journey north. But his train of thought was broken by the abrupt arrival of his seneschal, Cei, with his wife, Lydia, at his heels.

"Arthur, you've got to do something about that Percival!" Cei bellowed. "He just tried to attack Lydia!"

"What? Lydia, dear, are you all right?" Arthur looked from one to the other. Cei was red with fury but there was a look of exasperation about him. Lydia was clearly not damaged and seemed more as though she were about to burst out laughing.

"I'm fine," she assured him. "Although Percival may be a bit sore for a few days. My husband saved me with more energy than was really necessary. But Arthur, dear, we really have to do something with the boy. He doesn't know the first thing about how to behave around other people."

"All right, tell me what happened."

Cei began sputtering, but Lydia intervened.

"It was nothing, really," she insisted. "I was trying to show Percival how to mend that tunic of his. I can't imagine what his mother was thinking of, to send him away with such ragged clothes. He had just managed a rather crooked seam and I praised him; he seems so eager for approval. Arthur, I swear, I just gave him a sisterly hug and a pat on the back when, all at once, he was all over me. He grabbed me and started kissing my hands and arms and on up to my face. He seemed to think it was the custom here. I tried to push him off and explain that it just wasn't done, but then my gallant husband showed up. Poor Percival, I don't think he knows yet what hit him!"

"Poor Percival!" Cei exploded. "Arthur, he was slobbering all over Lydia, ripped her dress and everything."

"It was just a tear in the sleeve," Lydia added. "I'm sorry, darling. If it had been anyone else, I would have been more than grateful for your magnificent defense, but Percival . . . he's no more danger than an overgrown puppy. He is as much nuisance, however. Someone really must take him in hand. Isn't he supposed to belong to Lancelot?"

Arthur nodded. "Do you really want Lancelot to teach Percival how to behave?"

Cei and Lydia squirmed. They had grown to love Lancelot dearly, but there was no denying that he was still inclined toward some strange viewpoints and actions. Bringing Percival home with him, for example.

"There must be *someone* who can do it?" Cei broke the awkward silence. "What about Bedivere?"

"He's a good man, but he hasn't the patience," Arthur answered. "Never understood that; he's wonderfully tactful in negotiations but absolutely unforgiving of ignorance. What about one of the women?"

"We've done more than our share already," Lydia insisted. "It was bad enough that he suddenly decided he was in love with me. But when Risa helped him get settled in the boys' quarters and made sure he didn't get into any fights about precedence, do you know what he said to her? That idiot child told her she was almost as pretty as his mother. His mother! You can imagine what Risa thought about that."

In spite of himself, Arthur chuckled. "Especially when her eldest isn't much younger than Percival. Well, we have any number of people here who are free for the winter. Suppose I ask for volunteers?"

"Do you really think anyone would take him on?" Cei was more than doubtful. "We need someone with considerable patience as well as manners. I can't think of anyone here with both."

"You know," Lydia said thoughtfully. "Palomides could do it. He has exquisite manners. He's traveled all over the old empire, and he doesn't have any specific job to do this winter. He could civilize the boy to the point where the rest of us could take over and teach him about what we do in Britain."

"I don't know." Arthur would never admit it, but he was somewhat in awe of Palomides, who had come from Constantinople via Africa, Greece, and (it took his breath away even to think it) Rome. The fact that the man had made his way to Britain specifically to put his mind and his sword at Arthur's service abashed him still more. He was so damned elegant. It had been a long time since anyone could make Arthur feel like a country lout, but watching Palomides at dinner made him aware that his hands and face were greasy and his clothes were rumpled. Arthur wasn't sure he could stand it if Percival became like that, too. One could tolerate it in a foreigner, but not in a raw recruit. Still . . . "He could probably teach the boy well. Do you think he would?"

"I'll ask him." Lydia was glad that the matter was settled. "He's really very kind about doing favors. Now, don't worry any more, darling. You have enough to do around here."

"That's true enough," Cei grunted. "But if that snot-face bothers you again, he'll be breathing out of the back of his head."

"Don't be crude, dear." Lydia kissed his cheek lightly. "If that's taken care of, I must be going. Cole found mildew in the vegetables this morning and it will take all afternoon to empty the bins, clean them, and refill them with the sound food that is left."

"That won't affect the food supply this winter, will it?" Arthur asked.

"No, we caught it early enough. And we always have an abundance of turnips. There will be plenty left as long as your men make sure there is fresh meat all winter."

"That we can do. It's the best way I've found to get the men out and keep them active in the cold weather."

"Then don't worry. You certainly have better things to do than fret about mildew."

Arthur nodded and she left. Cei remained to go over reports from the east and south, where Britons were living in uneasy proximity to the Saxons. Although there was a truce of sorts between the old people and the new, it took constant and delicate diplomacy to keep it going. Messengers crisscrossed the kingdom in every weather to keep the High King informed. Even in winter, Arthur felt submerged in the paperwork. But, in a way, that was what he had been working for. People knew now that they had someone to turn to. They no longer needed to fight their battles alone or suffer unjustly from their neighbors. Even the priests were coming around. Oddly enough, it had been Guinevere who had remembered the line about rendering unto Caesar. But then, she was much more well read than he was. He let his mind drift to his wife again, a ridiculous thing to do, considering they had been married nearly thirteen years. She still enchanted him with her elegance and mysterious, distant allure. She was like a spirit who had kindly consented to remain for a bit in human form, something never touched by mundane worries or needs.

As Arthur tried to focus his thoughts on the paper before him, the door was blown open by a small gold and green whirlwind, shrieking at the top of its lungs.

"King Arthur! Sir Cei! Save me! She's going to catch me!" It dove under the table, scattering loose rolls as Guinevere entered the room. She was panting hard from running, and her face was red. Her hair had caught several cobwebs in it when she had crawled through a storage room seeking her prey. Now, with a whoop of delight, she pounced on the little foot sticking out from beneath the table.

"I've got you fairly now, Galahad. You're going right down to the baths. You're going to be cleaned from head to toe whether the other boys laugh or not. And, when you've done that, you can consider yourself promoted to dinner at the high table with me, your father, and Arthur. But only for tonight!"

She pulled him by the ankles out from under the table. As soon as she let go, he threw himself on her in a bear hug.

"At the high table! I'll even wash between my toes for that!"

"Cheldric will be there to see that you do. I'll race you there."

With a wave to her husband, the spirit wiped her face with her sleeve and ran.

Chapter Two

The winter afternoon was already dark. Guinevere sat in her rooms, a codex in her lap, her mind on nothing at all.

"Guinevere?"

Her heart constricted at his voice, and as she reached out to him through the gloom, there was a radiance in her eyes.

"Lancelot! Why aren't you down in the Hall with the others?"

"Arthur suggested you might be lonely up here by yourself."

"You are here because Arthur asked you?" She knew it wasn't true, but the idea nettled her all the same.

For answer he caught her up from her chair and kissed her so fiercely that her breath went and her heart seemed to expand so that she could feel it pounding at her throat and wrists. She pressed against him.

"It's been so long." His breathing was ragged also.

"Sometimes I can't remember that you love me," she whispered. "We walk and talk and laugh like old friends and then you go away for months and we only hear rumors of your passing, as if you had gone beyond this world. And I sit in my rooms here or at Camelot and wonder if you've been enchanted by some nymph of the forest or your Lady of the Lake, or if you've simply learned to live without me."

He pulled her down beside him to the pillows on the floor and settled her snugly against his shoulder, both his arms still circling her.

"Each time I go," he told her, "I pray that you will forget me, that I may discover a charm or potion that will keep me from wanting you every moment. I don't think such prayers rise at all; I never mean them. If you forgot me, I would not want to live. And if I stopped loving you, I would die all the same, because you are more a part of me than my soul."

"I know that now, when I am with you," she sighed. "But sometimes, when you are gone, it slips away from me. If only I were as free as you to leave when I wished. It would be nice to go someplace where no one ever heard of Arthur, where we could be together like this in the daylight."

His hold on her tightened and he closed his eyes, imagining what it would be like to come to her every night instead of standing aside as Arthur entered her room and shut the door.

"We could not dishonor him so." He kissed her again.

"Honor is something you men have invented because you can't do the right thing just for love's sake." She pushed away from him, but only a fraction. "I have given Arthur no children. He could put me aside but for his sense of honor and pride. And so we stay on, all politely pretending and each one of us aching for love or sorrow. Is there more dignity in meeting like this than in running away?"

"I have no dignity left where my love for you is concerned, but I would not take Arthur's also. Would you really want to run and hide somewhere, leaving him alone for his enemies to laugh at and his friends to pity?"

Guinevere wanted to scream, "Yes, of course! Anywhere, if we could be together!" But she involuntarily thought of

Arthur. He was as strong as ever and ruled Britain with a firm hand. Everyone knew that he could still lead his knights and soldiers into battle if he had to. But she thought of the new lines on his forehead and the streaks of gray around his temples, and the nights he lay awake, half from worries of the day and half from the pain in his teeth. He dreaded losing them, especially the front ones, which would make his speech strange and less commanding.

She had no sense of honor; it was a word men played with when it suited them. But she had learned to love her husband, and she knew that somehow she was important to Arthur, even though she couldn't give him the kind of love she should. Even through the happiness she felt whenever she was with Lancelot, the thought of leaving Arthur, hurt and alone, was more than she could face.

She buried her face in Lancelot's shoulder. "I wish I had been his sister and your wife."

She got up and lit the candles from the little oil lamp by the window.

"You have been here long enough to coax me to come down. Tell Arthur that I would rather eat alone tonight, but that I will wait up for him. I will join the others tomorrow."

She took his hands, conscious that now their outline could be seen through the window.

"Someday, I would like to be able to love you without wondering who is watching us."

When he had gone, she sat down again upon her couch and hugged a pillow to her breast, brushing her cheek against the wool. Some days it was too much to be near him and feel everyone averting their eyes so they would not witness anything. It was better to be alone; or with Galahad. She thought of Galahad; her child, as much as if she had borne him. Didn't everyone comment on how alike they looked? Elaine could not have been his true mother, only a vessel used to carry him until he could reach her. Morgause's sorcery had arranged it all, whatever her intentions had been. Morgause had let Lancelot think he was making love to Guinevere; therefore the child conceived was Guinevere's. She believed that with all her heart.

Her face softened as she imagined him, asleep now in his corner in the pile of fosterling boys. His face would be dirty no matter how often she had had him clean it. He had finally explained to her, very gently, that it just didn't do for him to look so cared for when none of the other boys did.

"Some of them are awfully homesick," he said. "And Lydia just can't love each one of them, not the way you love me. So I don't want to remind them about it by being too clean."

Arthur had laughed when she told him about it. "He's got round you again, love!" But Guinevere wasn't so sure. Galahad seemed to have been born with the sensitivity that Guinevere was only beginning to know existed. He knew who was sad and who was angry and who was surly because of shyness. He knew who needed kindness and he gave it to them, not from a sense of duty or religion, the way Lancelot did, but just because he could do nothing else. Sometimes Guinevere feared that he would learn of her love for his father and hate her for his mother's sake, but that was only her own guilt speaking. Galahad judged people by their hearts.

Lancelot walked slowly through the torch-lit corridors of the old fortress. He needed time to arrange his expression. Despite the years he had had to make a hole in his conscience for his love for Guinevere, he still had not learned to look at Arthur with unclouded eyes. Even when they had not been to bed, the intimacy they shared alone was adultery enough.

When he got to the hall, Durriken, the poet, was regaling the audience with the tale of Gawain's adventures with the Green Knight. It had happened about five years ago, and Gawain had been furious about the whole thing.

"There I was, thinking I was nobly risking my life for the honor of Camelot, laying my neck on the block, when all the time the whole thing was just another stupid allegory!" But he had told the story and endured the laughter with a shrug. Durriken was already introducing some heroic elements into the tale, and it was just as well that Gawain could never be awake at night to hear them.

Lancelot skirted the room quietly and reached Arthur.

"She'd rather wait in her rooms for you," he whispered.

Arthur merely nodded, his face turned toward the poet, but Lancelot could see the release of tension in his arms. Another dart shot into his conscience. Lancelot sat down next to his friend, wishing he had never left his home under the Lake. He waited until Durriken finished and then excused himself to lie awake in his bed, wrestling with demons until dawn.

Percival was not in the hall that night. He was in his room, practicing manners with his tutor. Palomides had taken the request seriously and had moved the boy into his own room to take on his education. Percival was sorry for anything that tore him away from Lancelot, but Arthur had taken him aside and explained to him kindly that Palomides would make a far better teacher, having a greater knowledge of the world. Percival agreed. He had noticed the touch of awe in everyone's attitude toward the man who had been born in Constantine's city.

Just now, there was awe in Palomides' eyes as he studied the boy before him. How could anyone have reached the age of reason and still be so woefully dense about interacting with his fellow human beings? He would give a great deal to meet the mother about whom Percival was so rhapsodic.

"All right, boy, once again," he said wearily. "You are traveling alone in strange lands. It is growing dark. In the distance you see a great house, with many small farms around. What would you do?"

Percival scowled in hard thought.

"Is it summer or winter?"

"What difference does that make?"

"In summer, I would sleep in the fields."

"And wake up naked with your horse gone, if you woke up at all. Try again."

Percival sighed. He had spent many nights in the fields. The worst that had ever happened was being awakened by a goat who thought his hair was fodder. He concentrated. What had Lancelot done on their short trip to Camelot?

"I would go to the big house and announce myself to the lord and ask for lodging." There. That sounded good.

"A strange lord? In an unknown country? Percival!"

"Well, what then? I can't think of anything else."

"You would go to a farmer's hut, or, even better, a herdsman's. You would let him think you were a poor stranger, perhaps in the service of a great king, but not very important. He is the one you would ask about a place to stay and the temper of the lord; what neighbors he has and how he deals with them. About some men, you won't even need to ask. Look at the condition of the huts and then the width of the castle walls."

Percival only looked blank. Palomides gave up. With any luck, no one would allow the boy out on the roads alone.

"Well, then. How are you coming in making conversation with the ladies?"

Percival looked even more glum.

"I've been trying to remember everything you said, Sir, but they never seem to answer the way I expect them to. I was talking with the Queen the other day and I was doing fine, I thought. I told her about meeting Sir Lancelot and about my mother and our horses at home. Then she suddenly started laughing and couldn't seem to stop. Gawain had to pound her on the back."

"What were you telling her about the horses?"

"Only about Glisten, my favorite. He's beautiful, but a little skittish, especially around mares. Anyway, it suddenly struck me that her hair was the exact color of his coat. So I told her. You said to compliment ladies whenever I could!"

This was given in a tone of anguish as Palomides' face twisted. What could he say? Percival always gave the highest compliments he could, and he meant them. Could he help it if most women did not want to be compared to his mother or his horse?

"Sir Palomides?"

"Yes, boy."

"How did you learn what to say and do? Is it true that you've even seen the Emperor?"

"I've seen greater than that, young Percival."

"Tell me." The boy sat cross-legged on the floor, his eyes

begging for a story. Palomides composed himself to recite his history, as he had done his first evening at Camelot.

"I was born in Constantinople, in the shadow of the Emperor's palace. My father was a member of the Nubian guard and my mother a Thracian slave of the Empress's household. He saved his earnings for seven years to buy her freedom. But the Empress would not release her, so he stole her away—and, with her, myself, a child of five. He fled with us to Jerusalem, where they were married in the church as good Christians should be.

"Throughout my childhood we traveled, to Syria and Egypt and south to the land of my father's fathers. I have been to Hippo, where the blessed Augustine lived, and to sorrowful Rome. I have been to Dalmatia and the lands north, where men still worship stones and trees. As I grew, I began to feel a calling within my spirit, a need that I could not ignore. My parents found a home at last in Thrace, but I could not stay with them. I wandered farther, to Babylon and to the mountains that hold the sky away from the world. Finally, I returned to Jerusalem. I knelt one dawn before the very place of Our Lord's sepulchre. And, as the gray night was pierced by the first rays, I thought I heard such a voice as Mary Magdalene heard: 'He whom you seek is not here; you must seek him among the sons of men.'

"It was there that I first heard the tale that old Joseph, whose tomb it should have been, did not remain in Jerusalem, but sailed away, through the Lake of Rome, past the gates and out into the endless ocean. And he did not die there but came to a wondrous land, unknown to Rome. There he built himself a small house and planted seeds from the trees of his garden. And there he left a great treasure to those of our faith."

He stopped. Percival's eyes were big and his breath came fast. "And then?"

Palomides smiled. "He died. That is all the stories tell. They do not say what the treasure was, only that it had been touched by Our Lord, Jesus. So I sailed through the gates and out to an island that was unknown to Rome in those long-ago days. I found other stories there, about a man who was creating a better land than Rome had known since the days of the Republic. The closer I came the more I learned about him, and it seemed to me that if someone in these hideous times was succeeding in building a society based on honor, it could only be with the help of some strong power. And what power could be stronger than this?"

He held out the symbol on the end of the chain around his neck. Percival had never seen it before.

"Is it Christian?" he asked. "My mother is a good Christian, but she never showed me anything like that. Where is the fish, or the pomegranate or the *chi* and the *rho* put together?"

Palomides smiled. "It is more Christian than any of them, and a better reminder of Our Lord. It is a cross. They are very common now in the eastern Empire."

Percival made a look of disgust. "But that is so shameful, a criminal's death. I don't want to think about things like that. It's not the way I was taught to think about religion."

"Ah, yes. Your mother, no doubt, only told you of the glories of heaven and the wonders of redemption."

"But we must be noble, honorable, faithful, and good to deserve them," Percival intoned.

"Of course. Can you read, Percival?"

He shook his head.

"Then find someone who can, and have that person tell you the true story of our faith, of the times of persecution and the days when it was considered a fairy tale for slaves, and of the man who was spat upon and beaten and died forgiving his tormentors. There are those who feel, even today, that we must emulate Christ's passion and pain in order to enter his kingdom. But I believe we should only remember it with thanks. And how better than with the symbol of his greatest suffering? Don't you understand the symbolism of the Mass you attend every morning?"

"I never thought about it; the Latin is not like ours. I don't follow it very well. I'm sorry, Sir." Percival shrank inside himself, as if expecting a blow.

Palomides sighed and tucked the cross back inside his

tunic. "Never mind, boy. I've been here long enough to know what passes for ceremony here. Who's to say that you have less religion than those in Constantinople, who argue the nature of the trinity in the taverns while they are waiting their turn with the whores upstairs? Our lesson is finished for tonight. Go get yourself something warm to drink and then come back and sleep. Tomorrow morning we will work on the military side of your training. How old are you, boy?"

"Almost fifteen, Sir."

"At your age I could wield my father's sword and shield against any man but him. We will spend the morning in the upper court working on your reflexes and ability to aim and avoid projectiles."

Percival shivered. "But the courtyard is full of snow!"

"I'm well aware of that. Sir Gawain and Sir Gaheris and perhaps others will meet us there. They will be our opponents."

"We will fight all of them, even Sir Gawain?" Percival swallowed hard and tried not to think of what Gawain could do to him.

"The Queen will be on our side also."

"The Queen? She's going to fight?"

"Certainly. I understand she throws a very accurate snowball. Now hurry! And bring some warm ale for me, too."

Chapter Three

The knocking was growing louder as the messenger pounded more heavily on the thick wooden door.

"Lord Modred! I am sent by your mother and the Lady Morgause to bring you to supper. I must not return without you! Please open the door!"

Modred rolled over lazily and began cutting the ropes that bound the girl to the bed.

"You see, I told you no one would care if you screamed. Now you have a sore throat along with everything else, and I'm not going to give you a present. Remember that next time. There. Clean up in here before you go. All right!" he yelled at the door. "I'm coming! I'll be out in a minute!"

The noise stopped as the messenger realized he had finally been heard.

Modred took his time about dressing, adjusting the drape of his tunic, cinching his belt a little tighter, drumming his fingers on the table as he selected a brooch for his cloak. He paid no further attention to the sniffling girl as she worked behind him. Yet he was instantly aware when her sniffling stopped, and he whipped around in one smooth motion, nearly in time to catch the knife she had thrown. The expression on his face never wavered as he picked it up and reached for her where she stood, too frightened to resist him. He pulled her close to him, pinioning both her arms in one of his, and then drew the knife across her face, cutting it deeply from the right temple to the chin. He stepped back quickly to avoid getting the blood on his cloak. Then he wiped the knife on the bed clothes and put it back under the mattress.

"That has just ruined your chances for advancement here. Tonight you will take yourself back to your father's hut. I can't wait to see what kind of husband he will be able to find for you with that face. If I think of it, I may send someone for you, myself. Now, finish your work and get out."

Calmly, he turned his back on her, unbolted the door, and left.

Morgan Le Fay and her sister, Morgause, were nearly finished with their meal when Modred entered, but they did not chastise him for his tardiness. His mother rose to greet him with her arms open, and Morgause smiled tenderly and offered her cheek to kiss.

"Such a busy afternoon you must have had, darling," Morgan cooed. "I'm so glad you aren't bored at Tintagel the way all your brothers have been. It would break my heart if you should abandon me, too."

"Now, Mother. Why should I be bored? Tintagel has so much to offer by way of diversion. But I am a grown man now, and it would be better if you gave me some idea of why I've stayed here instead of going to Camelot with Agravaine, Gawain and the others. You always said there was something special for me to do, and I believed you. Don't you think it's time you told me what it is?"

Morgan raised her eyebrows. "What do you think, Morgause? Should we tell him?"

Morgause shrugged. "I've been saying for the last year that he was our best hope. We should never have waited so long to see about Galahad. Even though it was our potions that made Lancelot beget him, he just isn't one of us. It was clear by the time the child started talking that he would never be turned to our side."

"Clear to you maybe, sister," Morgan snapped. "And how many sons have you raised? Galahad is totally unlike any child I've ever known, but he might have been convinced to help us, if only for love. He does love us!"

"Morgan, the child loves everybody! He's as unjudgmental as a new-born calf. But he is incapable of understanding the simplest motives of revenge and he always will be. It's some sort of flaw in his makeup."

"I, however," Modred interrupted, "am quite willing to go along with your little plans for power and revenge as long as it's fully understood that I intend to be the next ruler of Britain."

Morgan smiled lovingly on her son.

"Of course, my darling. I always meant you to be, from the time you were a little boy. It's your right."

Modred shrugged. "I don't know about that. Lacking a son, Arthur could choose almost anyone he liked to succeed him. But, for the same reason, a nephew could easily be selected. Especially if he already had support from the Saxons and the lords of the North. And I haven't been totally idle. I've made friends in both camps."

Morgan hugged her secret a little closer in her heart. How thrilled he would be when she told him! He was always the most precious of the five, twice hers, and the tool she had prayed for to destroy her dear half-brother.

"My dears, have I ever told you about the fathers of my sons?"

Morgause groaned. "Not again, sister. I know it all. Agravaine is Lot's. Nice of you to let him have the first, he being your husband. Gaheris belongs to one of those hermits we have perching on the rocks below us. Gareth, although you hate to admit it, looks just like that half-idiot guard of your husband's . . ."

"It was a very long winter!" Morgan protested.

"It must have been. And if I hear that story again about Gawain being conceived by a shaft of sunlight, I'll scream!"

"Do you have another explanation for Gawain?"

"Would you like me to make a list?"

"Ladies!" Modred interrupted. "May I point out that in her narrative, my mother has never mentioned which of her illustrious lovers is responsible for me?"

"Exactly, my dearest." Morgan settled back on her couch. "I never told anyone, not even the man himself. Of course, I didn't know who he was, then. He was just a boy, really, and totally inexperienced. But he was so eager to learn. I never even reminded him of it when we met again at his wedding. I thought that showed great delicacy on my part. You came with me, Modred dear, don't you remember? And I didn't say a word. But, after all, he is your father and he has no legitimate sons. I see no reason for him to deny you his throne."

She arched herself like a preening cat, stretched out her arms and gave the other two a satisfied grin.

They stared back in horror.

Modred spoke first. He seemed to be choking.

"You stupid bitch! Are you telling me that Arthur, your own brother, is my father! That's just wonderful! Do you have any idea what people think about incest? I'll be lucky if I'm not burnt at the winter fires along with the other unclean things!"

Morgan sat up in indignation.

"When did you start being a prude? I've certainly heard some interesting goings on in Morgause's room between the two of *you*."

"I certainly don't go about getting pregnant by my relatives," Morgause sniffed. "Anyway. What we think is not the point. It's what Arthur thinks and all the other devout morons he gathers around him. Do you suppose for a minute that he would acknowledge Modred openly and make him his heir?"

"Of course not," Modred said slowly. "He couldn't do that; it would ruin him. But he might be convinced to accept me privately, very privately. If we went about this the right way, he might very well be persuaded. I can work on his guilt. Poor Modred! Doomed by his father's sin! Cheated of his birthright. It won't be easy, though. It might have helped if you'd sent me for fostering at Camelot. Then he would know me, at least."

"You have a point, Modred, dear," Morgause answered. "Your mother was always such a fool about that. She couldn't bear to have any of you parted from her, except Gawain, of course."

"He always gave me the shivers. At least you others were all human. I never knew what he might turn into. But I wanted you all here at Tintagel with me, where our strength lies. Think how much more soaked in magic you are than the others. I'm sure it will help. Do you think we can blackmail Arthur into leaving Britain to you?"

Modred shrugged. "From what I've heard, he might be brought to it. He has a strong sense of justice. But my birth could work against us, if I'm not careful."

· 26 ·

He strode across the room, his boots kicking the rushes aside and hitting the stones with angry beats.

"Now I will have to go to Camelot. I had hoped to organize opposition to Arthur among the kings of the old tribes and get support from the town bishops whom he's taxed against their will. There are many in Britain who are not in favor of Arthur's 'new Rome.' I could have done it legitimately that way! You see what you've done? I can't ignore this; it's an edge I must try to use. But now it will be that much fouler. You've taken a clean victory from me. Now I will need to be treacherous and fleeting. But, of course, under your tutelage I've become expert at that. Don't worry. This way the victory will be all that more certain. I will enter Arthur's untarnished, shining court and breathe decay upon it. But that was what you always dreamed of, wasn't it? God damn you, woman! Why did I have to have a whore for a mother!"

He stretched his hands, talonlike, toward her throat. She cringed back as they trembled closer to her. Then, with a cry, he spun around and ran from the room. Morgan crumpled onto her couch, her wool and linen robes sagging and bunching around her body.

"What have I created?" she wailed. "I loved him more than all the others, twice our mother's child. He should have been the one most willing to revenge the degradation Arthur's father forced on her. I should have told him Arthur raped me."

"He wouldn't have believed you." Mogause looked with disgust upon her younger sister. "You idiot. Uther Pendragon has won again. That is not your son, or Arthur's, but Uther's own grandson and as like him as any man could ever be. He's right. He could have conquered Britain without once entering Camelot. It will be twice as dangerous for him now. I've been there. You don't know what it's like. Arthur wields a kind of enchantment. Lords like Meleagant think he does nothing but sit in his rooms all day and send out laws to anger them. They don't know the hold he has over his knights. Have you ever heard of one of them being bribed?

They may fight and carouse and game on their own, but when he orders them to settle a dispute or mediate a claim, they become everything he expects them to be. Even your sons do. Modred will have to find a way to break that, or he can never hope to destroy Arthur."

"He wanted to strangle me!" Morgan caressed her throat, half expecting to feel bruises.

"At the moment, I'm sorry he didn't. By Maebdh's own wrath, sister! I've told you often enough that you can't play on the fringes of sorcery. Look at yourself. You're three years younger than I am and you look thirty older. You've used your little bits of magic to seduce and cajole and shape pillows around your life. You can't hope to control anyone that way. You must take the risks. I have looked into the fires and the mists. I have been burnt and scalded, but I hold power! You are nothing more now than the little slaves Modred plays with. You'll get no more love from him."

Morgan's wail rose at that and she buried her face in her couch and sobbed, beating her fists on the soft headrest. Morgause watched a few seconds, then sighed and went about her business.

Modred was shaking by the time he returned to his rooms. He threw out the barber waiting for him and told the guard to keep his friends away.

Little light came through the thick windows. The oil lamp sputtered and died as Modred sat before the hearth, staring at his hands as the firelight played over them. Modred thought he had long ago abandoned the old taboos of his Celtic sires and the new ones of his Christian grandmother. He had never thought of his games with Morgause as incest. She hardly looked old enough to be his aunt and she was so inventive . . . But the nausea in his throat told him that his sophistication was an elaborate veneer. It was one thing to feel delightfully sinful in his aunt's bed and another to find he was the product of such sin. From deep in his childhood came tales overheard about monsters conceived in unnatural lust. He wondered if he might have been born with horns or the tail of a pig, thoughtfully removed by his mama. His lips whitened.

What bizarre deformity might still be within him?

He gripped the arms of the chair until his nails broke and bled. Very well. They had done this to him, his mother and the too-pure Arthur. If he had been born outside the pale then there were no more cords binding him to it or its rules. He was free. Whatever weakness they had given him was not in his arms or his wit. He was stronger and more agile than any of his brothers but Gawain, and more attractive to women. He had the gift of seeming friendship, too, and the wisdom to keep his own counsel.

"Damn them all!" he roared. "I will be the greatest king since Constantine! You made me, Arthur, and you cannot stop me!"

Chapter Four

Spring had arrived at Caerleon. The courtyards were muddy, the practice fields were muddy, the paths down to the shops were muddy. Children soon discovered that it was easier to run barefoot than to scrape wet mud from boots over and over. The water in the baths was tinged with red and ochre earth despite the constant draining and refilling.

Guinevere and Risa, her maid, climbed the hill from the town, their arms full of packages and their toes squishing happily. Below them they could hear cheerful blasphemy as a carter and four helpers tried to dislodge the wheels of his cart from the mire. Above them, Caerleon was hung out for all to see as bedding and hangings were washed and aired before being folded up for the trip to Camelot.

Risa laughed at the sight of the multiform pennants.

"They flap about in the wind like wild birds. I can almost hear them squawking."

"That's probably Cei yelling at the children to get off the lookout towers. As soon as the sun comes out, they're up on the roofs, spying for messengers and visitors. There is some sort of prize to the one who spots them first."

"Really? I had no idea you kept in such good touch with all the children at Caerleon."

"Galahad told me. He explained that it was a matter of honor that he take his turn with the others, even though he knows how it worries me. He promised to be extremely careful, however, and not hang over the edge."

"Well, if it's a matter of honor . . . Some days that boy sounds just like his father." Risa laughed at the thought of a miniature Lancelot.

"They are much alike, only Galahad never worries about right and wrong. He just seems to know. I think he is the way Lancelot might have been if he hadn't been raised so oddly."

"It was not the usual sort of family life," Risa agreed. "Very few people are kidnapped by immortal . . . whatever the Lady of the Lake is, and wet-nursed by an outcast afflicted with religious melancholy. No wonder he worries so much about sin. Of course lots of us were raised by religious fanatics. It's just the combination that seems odd."

"I don't recall your family being especially religious." Guinevere panted. The hill was growing steep near the end.

"My parents weren't; wrong generation. But Grandfather was a Pelagian and ridiculously proud of his heresy. I never understood a word of it."

"I hope it's the mud that's making this climb so hard, today. I would hate to think I was getting old."

"You!" Risa laughed. "You look the same now as you did twenty years ago when you came to Cador for fostering. I don't know how you do it. But I am certainly older, and these pots grow heavier with every step. I hope there's someone at the gate to help us."

As they aproached, they saw that Cheldric, one of Arthur's guards, was there. He saluted them and then scooped all Risa's parcels up in his one arm and motioned for someone to take Guinevere's things.

"My Lady, I will have these taken to your rooms," he said. "The King wants you to come to him at once. There has been a message for you."

He spoke so stiffly that Guinevere was alarmed. Cheldric had known her as long as Risa had, and his arm had been lost protecting her. He knew he did not need to be formal when they were together.

"Where did the man come from?" she asked.

"The King will tell you," he answered.

"Go on, Guinevere," Risa urged. "I'll see that everything is taken care of."

Guinevere hitched up her skirts and raced across the slippery walks to the Great Hall where Arthur received guests and supplicants. She stopped at the door to catch her breath and smooth her hair. Her hands were cold and she tried to warm them in her skirts. Then she pushed the door.

The hall was dark and formless after the brilliance of spring outside. She hesitated and then made out the group around the high table: Arthur, Cei and his wife, Lydia, Gawain, Lancelot, and a man who seemed familiar. She couldn't place him, but he was clearly the one who had brought the message. As she approached, they all turned to face her and she knew him. It was Aulan, one of her father's men. She tried to smile.

"Aulan! What brings you here before the roads have dried? Do you have a letter for me from Mother?" She held out her hand.

He drew a leather pouch from a pocket of his cloak and handed her the scrap of vellum inside. Guinevere read it slowly, seeing her mother's face as she sat at her table. Some words had smeared before they dried.

"Aulan, was my father still alive when you left?"

"Yes, Your Majesty. He is very weak, though. We should hurry."

Arthur put his arms around her, for support. Her eyes closed and she leaned against him a few seconds. Then she took a deep breath and made herself stand alone, gently pushing him away.

"Lydia, call your brother here, please, and ask if he will come with me. He was fostered by my father. Cei, can you possibly spare Caet this journey? I know he has charge of the horses, but he was born in our house and he belongs with the rest of the family. Aulan, has anyone sent for my brother?"

The guard nodded. "Your mother said nothing to us about it, so Pincerna sent the best horsemen for him at the same time I left to come here."

"That was right." She looked around, suddenly bewildered. Lydia took her and led her from the room.

"Come, my dear. We'll find Risa and get your things together. I'll have her warm some wine for you, too. Then I want you to rest. This evening I'll come back and let you know what is happening. Don't worry about anything but your father. Let me take care of it all."

Alone in her room, the cup of wine next to her couch, Guinevere tried to piece together what was happening. Her mother's letter, laid upon her lap, was only a jumble of words. "Leodegrance not well. Please come to us." She had not had the heart to write more. Writing it would make it come true. Guinevere tried to picture her father as he was now, as she had seen him last. He had never recovered fully from his last battle and had remained drawn and old even after he had been able to leave his bed. But she couldn't see him so. Instead she saw him on horseback, pounding into their courtyard just behind her, letting her think she had won the race, or swinging her high on his shoulders when she was still too small to keep up with her brother's games. On his strong back she was mistress of all the world, and she never felt so omnipotent or so safe as then. He was what kept the world glued together. In all the years she had spent away, she kept the certainty within her that she could always return home and it would not have changed. Whatever happened outside, her father and mother could hold away the darkness and the evil. What would rush in if Leodegrance were gone?

There was a soft tap on the door. Guinevere sat up and tucked the message under a cushion.

"Foster Mother, can I come in?"

"Of course, Galahad!" She held out her arms to him.

"My father told me you were sad. He wanted to make you feel better but didn't know how. So I've come to ask."

"You can help me. I need you now, just to hug me."

She scooped him into her lap and asked him about the things he had done that day and what he wanted to see at Camelot and what he wanted to do when he grew up. Slowly the burning cord in her throat faded as her fear ebbed and all the world became less important than the golden boy encircled by her arms.

Arthur was wrapped in a blanket, as the morning was chill. He had not slept well. He did not know his father-in-law well, but Leodegrance was part of the legends Arthur had grown up on. Leodegrance had seen Ambrosius and had dined with Uther Pendragon. As boys, he and Merlin had hunted and raced together. His father had been one of those who received the last message from the Emperor, telling Britain no help was coming, that they must maintain Roman tradition alone. "Now," Arthur thought, "I'm becoming the old one. And I don't know the old ways anymore. I can only guess what things were like when Britain was a part of Rome. Damn it! I don't want to do this by myself. I feel so groping."

Guinevere didn't care about the passing of an era. She wanted only to get home to her father and hold back mortality from his door. It wasn't fair! No one had the right to die while she still needed him. She barely felt Arthur's good-bye kiss or Lancelot's arms as he lifted her onto the horse.

"How long will it take?" she asked Aulan.

"If you can keep the pace, we'll be there tomorrow afternoon."

"Don't hold for me," she answered. "Why are we still here?"

In another moment, they weren't.

Arthur and Lancelot stood at the gate until they were out of sight. Then Arthur gave a rueful smile.

"I needn't have gotten up at all. She didn't know we were here."

Lancelot smiled back. "She didn't, at that. But, you know, I feel somehow jealous of her, even though it aches to see her hurt. I just keep wishing I had known my father long enough for his death to matter to me like that."

Arthur nodded.

"Old Uther was a bastard, they say, but I still would have liked to have known him, to see what of him is kept in me. Christ's teeth! It's bloody freezing out here. Let's go see if anyone's left a pot of ale by the kitchen fire."

They found their ale and some warm bread and meat and took them to a corner out of the way of the busy cooks and kitchen servants. Arthur laughed as they clinked cups.

"We'd not be taken for a king and counsellor just now. More like two old soldiers trading lies about campaigns they never were on."

"Don't believe it, Arthur. You'd never be taken for anything but a leader, a great leader."

"I wasn't looking for flattery, old friend. It's spring, and it's chill as a witch's heart in here, and dank and gloomy. And, if we don't sneak out in a hurry, someone is going to find work for us."

Lancelot grinned suddenly. "I happen to know where the boys keep their fishing gear. We could borrow some and follow a stream I know of just to see where it goes. Isn't it part of our duty to explore the terrain? We might even catch something to help feed your people."

Arthur stood up and stretched, feeling the years slide off his shoulders. He grinned back.

"As King, I think it is essential that we set out on this dangerous journey at once. I'll meet you in the stables in five minutes.

Morgan le Fay stood in the center of her room at Tintagel. It had never seemed so empty before. Everything was as it had always been: bed, clothespress, chests, sofa, chairs, the elegant mirror her father had given her, thick hangings covering the harsh stones, thick glass covering the tiny windows, animal skins on the floor. It was hers, along with the towers and the halls and the rock below. She had always drawn her strength from Tintagel. Now, it seemed, it would give her no more. Empty. Modred had been her favorite, her truest son. All her dreams had crumpled when he turned on her.

She looked in the mirror. A face looked back, wrinkled and worn, with tear-swollen eyes. It was no one she knew.

For the first time in her life, Morgan felt that she had to get away from Tintagel.

"I shall go visiting," she said to herself. "I shall go see all my friends."

Calmly, she went to her jewelry box. She picked out the best pieces and wrapped them in a woolen shift. Then she selected a few good gowns and some slippers. These she bound up in a leather bag. Then she sent for her horsemaster and informed him that she would be needing his services.

"We will leave at once," she told him. "I wish to be well on my way by nightfall."

"To where, my Lady?" the man asked. He had been at Tintagel for fifteen years and never once had his mistress traveled more than an hour from the place.

"Tell them in the kitchens to get enough food ready for several days' journey. Nothing difficult; bread, geese, dried fruit, and wine will be enough. I should have a party of four or five guards. Be sure they're sober."

"Yes, of course. At once." Still bewildered, the man stumbled out to face the wrath of the cooks who wanted to know just how they were supposed to kill, drain, pluck, singe, and roast geese to be ready at once. He made some suggestions, none of which were practical, and then went to the guard rooms to spread the joyous news further.

Morgan called her maids to lay out her riding clothes and arrange her hair. They rubbed perfumed oils into her skin and dressed her. She hardly spoke to them. Before they left, she gave each one something from her jewelry box. Not the good bits, of course, but more than they had ever expected from her.

The horsemaster returned to say that all would be ready in an hour. He waited.

"That will do, then," she said. "Have everyone in the courtyard to bid me good-bye."

When he had gone, she went to the window and tried to peer through the thick green glass. From here she had first seen that horrid king, Uther Pendragon, come to steal away her mother. Her husband, Lot, had ridden from that direction, too, but not for a long time. She wondered if he were even still alive. From this window she had watched her sons come home to her, but the one she wanted most had said he would not come again.

"Good-bye, Tintagel," she whispered.

She gave her directions to the guards but would not tell them the destination. Her strange manner had started all kinds of speculation. It was even rumored that she was leading them into the lair of Gwynn ap Nudd, hunter of death. The hands of the guards shook as they mounted their horses.

They journeyed several days. Morgan chatted and flirted with her escort as they rode. She told them about her childhood and the excitements of the old days. At first they took the main roads and stopped at inns or country houses where, as ruler of Cornwall, she was honored. She began to wake up a little and smile as if her face had not been stretched.

One night she overheard the guards playing dice.

"Loser sleeps with her hagship!" one laughed. They all joined in.

The next morning she left the road. There was no trail at all that any of them could see as they floundered after her.

She heard them cry out as branches whipped across their faces. She wished she could remember how to turn foliage into snakes.

About noon they stopped on the shore of a wide, still lake. The forest around was entirely silent as they ate their cold goose and bread and uneasily stretched out for a nap.

Morgan was not tired. She watched the snoring men with contempt. Idiots! She never should have bothered to bring them with her. Nothing would have happened to her if she had gone alone. But it was unthinkable for a woman of her station to travel without proper escort. And she had tried very hard to preserve the outward status. Morgause had never understood that. But perhaps she was right in relying on sorcery alone. Attempts at conformity had not helped Morgan at all.

She picked up her bag and started walking around the lake. About fifty yards from the camp, Morgan noticed a large outcropping of rock jutting into the lake. It started out only a few feet from the ground and sloped upward so that from the edge of it one could look into the water.

Morgan slipped off her shoes and stepped onto the stone. The sun radiating off it warmed her chilled skin. She opened her bag and rummaged in it for a comb. Leaning over the edge of the rock, she saw only her reflection in the water. She smiled in sudden delight. That was the face she had been searching for these past few years, still fresh and unlined. That was what she really looked like. She leaned farther over, clutching the bag to her. Yes, her arms and body were young again, too. It was as if her old self were waiting for her in the lake. She reached out to it and the bag dropped. It barely created a ripple as it slipped into the water. Morgan's young self smiled again and seemed to beckon her. Yes, of course. I'm coming! Happily, Morgan stepped off the rock.

Her guards wakened at the splash and came running. But, by the time they arrived, they could see only the disturbed water and, floating on the surface, an empty leather bag.

They fished it out with a branch. No one had the courage to dive into that strange water, which only reflected images, never showing anything beneath its surface. After much debate, it was decided that two of them would take the bag and Morgan's horse to King Arthur and hope he would believe the story of his sister's death. The others would return to Tintagel and break the welcome news that Lot's son Agravaine was now Lord of Cornwall.

Deep within the Lake, in a palace of diamonds and orchids, the Lady lounged on her couch. She was only moderately bored. Lillith had composed a new piece for lute and pipes and it was quite tolerable. There was a report that a griffin had been seen in the woods. That might provide some diversion. She had managed to keep Damion from reciting all seventy-four verses of his latest saga. But it was hours yet until dinner and she wished fiercely that *something* would happen. Again, she regretted letting Lancelot leave her. Kidnapping him as a baby has been the most interesting part of her eternally long life. Raising him had kept her amused for years. If only he hadn't gotten those strange ideas from that nurse and insisted on charging out to help King Arthur save the world.

"Lady! Come quickly!"

"What is it, Torres?" She wasn't unduly stirred. Torres was human and young enough to get excited about almost anything. He ran into her rooms and grabbed her by the arms.

"Come see what we fished out of the lake! She even brought her own clothes!"

The Lady decided that this sounded different enough to be of interest. She followed Torres out to the side garden, where several of her people were gathered around a rather plump, bedraggled, middle-aged woman who was trying to talk and cough up lake water at the same time.

"Bring her in to me!" the Lady ordered and two of the men scooped her up between them and carried her in to the main hall where they set her gently on a low divan.

She stared about the room in wonder, her mouth slightly open. Then she turned to the Lady.

"If this is the afterlife, someone's been giving it a bad name," she said.

Torres laughed. The Lady hushed him.

"If you meant to die, we must disappoint you. This Lake is my realm and, now that you are here, you will never be allowed to age or die."

Morgan's eyes lit up. Why had she never known about this place?

"I don't suppose you could make me look just a little younger first?"

"Well, of course! We could also do something with your hair. What color was it when you started out? But you must understand that, now that you are here, you can't change your mind and go back. I tried letting someone do that once and it worked out very badly."

Morgan fingered the wet folds of her gown. She hadn't really wanted to die when she leaped into the lake. But she was sick of the machinations and the hurt in her life, disgusted with what the years had done to her body. She looked at the men out of the corner of her eye. This, yes, this would do very well, almost too well.

"What would I have to do, to earn my keep, I mean?" she asked.

The Lady looked blank.

"What kind of service would you expect from me?" Morgan clarified.

"Service? I really don't need anything from you. I'm served quite well." She smiled at the ladies and gentlemen around her. "However, if you happen to know any good gossip, that would be fine. I haven't heard any since Torres here came back from Arthur's court. Is Arthur still King? Does he still have the sword that Master Merlin won from me? Did he ever discover the secret of it? And my stepson, Lancelot, I haven't heard anything about him for a long time. Do you know him? Is he still trying to suffer for everyone's sins? Oh, I'm sorry, my dear, you're still wet. Never mind all that now. Go make yourself presentable and then come join us at dinner. You have years and years and years to tell me about it all."

Chapter Five

"So, old Leodegrance is finally dying." Modred's striking profile was outlined in the window as he watched the rain through the glass at his aunt Morgause's home. "He was the last one, wasn't he? Now no one can stop us. There's no one left who saw Uther."

"No one who matters," his aunt Morgause agreed. "Cador might remember, but he can barely see anymore. He's no threat. This will still take time, you know. You mustn't let anyone suspect us. Anything blatant will only get you thrown out of Camelot, even killed."

"My dear, when have I ever been blatant about anything?" He ran his knife idly under his fingernails.

"Don't be so smug, Modred. Leodegrance would have seen right through you. He was the only man who ever got his wife out of Uther's clutches without a war. I wish my father had been half what he was."

"Why, Morgause, such sentiment! It sounds as though he never came into your clutches, either."

"Never mind that. Have you told Agravaine to expect you at Camelot? Perhaps you can win your way into Arthur's heart on your own. Blood calls to blood, they say."

"In this family it certainly does." And Modred laughed as he left the window and rejoined Morgause in bed.

At Camelot, Modred's brothers were upset enough to call a family meeting, something only done in dire circumstances. None of the sons of Morgan le Fay resembled her in the slightest, so, of course, they were nothing like each other. Agravaine was tall and brawny, like his father, Lot. The responsibility of being the oldest of the brood weighed on him, and he was balding rapidly. Gawain had always been almost unbearably handsome, with his golden hair and lithe, effortless strength. He would have taken more advantage of his looks if he could have stayed awake past sundown. Gaheris was the mystic of the clan; he spoke rarely, but his deep blue eyes saw everything. His intensity rather awed his older brothers, who did not speak much to him of worldly matters. Gareth was slight and beige. He blended so unobtrusively with the background that many people never noticed him at all. It was a trial to him, but Arthur took advantage of it, sending him places where it would not have been politic for a knight to be. His main characteristic was his steadfast devotion to Lancelot.

Agravaine stood facing the other three, who were seated on the bed in his tiny room. He folded his arms and cleared his throat. Gareth's eyes were red. He hadn't believed the guard's story about an accident at the Lake any more than the others had. He was awash in guilt. Agravaine's pomposity was grating on him to the point of screaming.

"You all know that under Cornish law, Tintagel passes to me. I don't suppose Mother would have liked that, but there it is. I'll do my best to take care of things there and, of course, you should all consider it your home."

"You'll have to get married now, Agravaine," Gawain chuckled. "The Duke of Cornwall must have an heir."

"How can you make jokes with our mother newly dead?" Gareth cried.

Gawain was unapologetic. "She never cared for me. We all know that. She sent me away as soon as it was decent. All she ever cared about was Tintagel and, maybe, Modred. The rest of us were merely unavoidable miscalculations."

"Well, I loved her anyway!" Gareth couldn't deny Gawain's statement. "And you should at least have some respect!"

Gawain shrugged. "Did you want to get us together just to tell us you're in charge now?" he asked Agravaine. "Because you can have every rock in Cornwall for all I care. Just don't try to lord it over me here."

Agravaine glared at him, then subsided. "When did I ever try to do that? No, how you act away from Cornwall is your own business. It's Modred I'm worried about. He's coming here now. With Mother gone, there's no one to stop him."

They forgot their bickering at once. Against Modred they had to be united.

"Do you think Aunt Morgause is sending him to kill Arthur?" Gaheris asked.

"Nothing so clean, I'm sure." Agravaine chewed his tongue. "If only he weren't so damn oily! You think you have him and he's slipped across the room. He's going to make friends here, you know."

They all nodded. Modred had a knack for making friends.

"We ought to warn Lancelot and Guinevere," Gawain said.

Gareth rose up. "You ought to warn *Guinevere*! It's all her fault; it always was. Lancelot is just too good to refuse her."

"Not again, Gareth," Gaheris sighed. "It's none of our business, anyway. I don't think it would be worth it, Gawain. If they can't stay apart for love of Arthur, they won't for fear of Modred."

"Modred might convince her to forget about Lancelot," Gareth suggested with a leer. "He's got more of a following among the women than you do, Gawain. And a woman who would betray Arthur ought to be easy for him."

The shot went home and the next minute, Gawain was picking his brother up and shaking him until his teeth rattled.

"Stop it!" Agravaine yelled, pulling at Gareth from behind as Gaheris tugged at Gawain. "Gawain, you'll kill him!"

"I c-can t-take c-care of m-myself!" Gareth glared defiantly at Gawain, who dropped him with a look of shame.

"Sorry," he muttered. "But you shouldn't talk about the Queen that way. You know very well she's not like that."

In the ruckus, none of them had heard the door open.

"All of us together again! How jolly!" Modred gazed at them in mock delight. "And beating up on Gareth still? It will be like old times. Well, brothers, aren't you going to welcome me to Camelot?"

They all gaped at him. Gareth wiped his chin. Gaheris sighed and began to recite *Pater Nosters* in his head. Gawain wondered if fratricide were sometimes justifiable, and Agravaine forced a smile and held out his hand to Modred, wishing again that he had been an only child.

They had hardly stopped at all in their race against death. The horses were almost spent when they pulled themselves up the last hill to the villa. But it was too late. Guinevere knew it as soon as the gate opened. The stillness told her. Even the air was muffled with grief.

Pincerna, their ancient butler, met her in the courtyard. His gnarled arms eased her to the ground. Tears slid easily down the furrows of his face.

"He went yesterday," the old man whispered. "My Lady Guenlian was the only one with him."

"My brother?"

"Perhaps the message never reached him."

Guinevere nodded. She wanted to believe that. Whatever angry words had been shouted when Mark ran away with the daughter of his Saxon enemy, she did not believe that he would abandon their father on his deathbed.

Inside, they were greeted by Rhianna, widow of Guinevere's eldest brother, and her daughter, Letitia. Caet hung behind, mindful that his place had always been in the stables. But Constantine was hugged and welcomed as one of the family.

"Guenlian is sleeping, finally," Rhianna told them. "We moved your father to the chapel for now, but she won't let us remove the bedding. She just lies there, clutching the blankets as if he were still there. Perhaps, when she sees you, it will be better."

"Take me to her, please." Guinevere's nails caught in her riding cloak as she twitched it nervously. She had no idea how she could comfort her mother. She had no comfort even for herself.

Pincerna took the men to their rooms. Constantine was lost in grief, or so the butler thought, but as they parted, the younger man took the older aside.

"Pincerna," he asked. "That girl with Rhianna, that wasn't Letitia, was it? I thought she was a scrawny little thing with tangled hair."

"You've been away a long time, Sir Constantine. Letitia is nineteen. She has been eating much better lately and has learned the use of a comb."

He then left Constantine with his thoughts, and turned to Caet.

"So, you run away from your master and now come back as a lord, you think!" He snorted in disgust.

"I am horsemaster to King Arthur." Caet looked him full in the eyes. "I am not a lord, but I am no man's slave. Leodegrance and I made our peace years ago. You have no right to sneer at me now."

"So why are you here!" the old man blazed.

Caet shook his head. "*She* wanted me to come."

Pincerna looked at him closely. "I see. It was always like that, though, wasn't it? You took her punishments more than once, I remember. True enough, Caet, you're no *man's* slave. I love her as my own, lad, but even I can see that you'll only bring yourself grief."

"And when, Pincerna, have I ever expected anything else?"

They went together to the butler's quarters and shared a pitcher before the long night of watching in the chapel. That night, also, there were fires along the fields. The shepherds and farmers wanted to be sure the old gods would light the way for their master even to the new heaven he sought.

Mourning was getting on Guinevere's nerves. Her father was dead. He was buried. They had said Masses for his soul. They had torn their clothes and beat their breasts until the blood came and then they had rubbed ashes in the wounds. It was enough. Caet had insisted on leaving as soon as he could. He complained that the horses would be neglected if he didn't watch over the stable boys. Only Constantine seemed in no hurry to go, but he spent all his time comforting Letitia, leaving Guinevere and Rhianna to cope with Guenlian's deep mourning.

"Rhianna, I can't stay here much longer," Guinevere said one morning as they went over plans for the day. "I must be back at Camelot soon. Arthur needs me."

But it was the music of summer she was thinking of, more than Arthur, and laughter and the jugglers and magicians and the games and dances at Solstice Eve. She had thought she loved this villa more than any place on earth, but it was so empty now, and dim, like the ripples of a reflection in a lake. It belonged to the past, with the evening reading from Vergil or Diodorus and the lush meals served to reclining guests. Guinevere felt that, if she turned her back on it, the house would vanish and, when she turned again, only a peeling shell would remain, roofless and ghosted.

"You're very tired, Guinevere. Your mother is resting now and Pincerna is going to bring her a long list of decisions to make when she awakes. Why don't you go for a ride?"

Rhianna was gray with grief and exaustion, Guinevere noticed with guilt. "Come with me. You need to get away more than I do."

"No, I don't care for riding. Anyway"—there was a glint of humor in her tired eyes—"I think I should stay close enough to be a proper chaperon for my daughter. And to think that I always remembered Constantine as such a blood-thirsty, girl-hating little boy."

So Guinevere went alone. She crossed the creek, still rushing with melted snow, and, without thinking, headed for the woods. Long ago she had found something precious there, but she couldn't remember any more what it had been. Perhaps she had some idea of creeping up on it, for she left the horse at the hut of one of the framers and took the footpath among the trees.

She wandered in the dappled, green light, not caring where she went, until she was deep within the forest, part of the great one that the Romans had sliced through to make way for civilization. They had missed this corner.

She came to a great tangle of bushes in white and lavender blossom. Her hands brushed the tiny petals and she tried to remember to tell Rhianna so they could get the berries in the fall. Then she stared at it, puzzled.

"There is something on the other side of this. I was there once. I know it."

She began to walk along the edge of the bushes. They had grown wild until they were over her head. They wrapped around trees and clambered into the branches. Halfway around, she noticed that the leaves were not the same. There was a space where no bushes grew, only long, thornless vines which curtained the other side. She spread them with her hands and stepped in.

It was only a clearing, about twenty feet across, covered with wild flowers. Other than that, it was completely empty and perfectly still.

Guinevere felt as if she had found the key to heaven.

Slowly, she walked to the gentle rise in the center of the clearing. Violets were blooming there and alyssum. She slipped off her sandals and felt the soft velvet against her toes. The sun was warm and she pulled off her tunic and let her skirt fall on the grass. After a moment, she pulled off her shift, too. She reached out to the sunlight pouring onto her winter-pale body. The warmth curled into her bones and expanded, releasing her. Her hairpins dropped onto the pile of clothing as her braids fell to her knees and unraveled.

"I have done this before," she thought. "I was waiting for someone. Was I a priestess then, or only a child?"

She lay on her back on the hillock, eyes closed but still seeing the orange glow overhead. Her arms stretched out along the grass, bruising the flowers so that their fragrance burst into the warm air. Her fingers pressed into the earth and old incantations came into her mind, arcane syllables intoned to her from the cradle by her nurse. They belonged here. A faint breeze started up and blew her hair across her face and shoulder, brushing against her breasts. There was only one thing missing to complete the enchantment. Guinevere concentrated.

The vines at the edge of the clearing rustled but she didn't move.

"Guinevere." He had thought he was going to shout it, but he could barely whisper.

She smiled. "You heard me calling. It must be a strong magic to bring you to me so quickly."

"Arthur sent me to see how you were. I was not far when I felt it. I did not know it was you. I didn't want to follow."

She opened her eyes and sat up.

"It's too warm for all that riding gear," she said.

He looked around at the entrance, hesitating.

Guinevere laughed. "No one will come. I've put a spell on this place."

Lancelot nodded. He knew about spells. All the women of his childhood had used them as a matter of course. He began to remove his clothing.

She waited, watching him, contrasting the brownness of his face and hands with the whiteness of his body. It was an abstract thought, for his appearance no longer mattered to her. He could have been pocked and scarred from shoulder to thigh and still she would have thought him beautiful.

He walked slowly to her and knelt between her knees. Her hands rested on his shoulders and eased down across his chest. Then, finally, he looked into her eyes. They said more than she ever could. She leaned back and wrapped her legs around his hips, guiding him to her.

"In the daylight," she exulted. "At last!"

His lips were against her throat. The soft gusts of his breath beat a rhythm on her skin. "Without shame," he whispered.

And even the most shadowy corner of her soul blazed with joy.

· 47 ·

Chapter Six

"The man murdered three of my messengers, including Gereint, who was a knight. Then he ran north of the wall and *Saint* Caradoc won't send him back because he's been granted sanctuary!" Arthur roared at the unhappy man who had brought the news. "Ligessauc Longhand would shrivel into cinders if he ever touched a gospel book. It is his father's jewels, donated to the Church, that Caradoc is protecting. Go back and tell them that I will have Ligessauc and the man-price of my messengers or Caradoc will see an army at the door of his precious church! I'll not have my authority in Britain flouted by a self-styled bishop. Tell him to offer sanctuary to the Christian slaves Eliman is selling to the Picts. But then it would be no use; slaves have no gold."

He grabbed the cup before him and drained it as if trying to quench his wrath.

"What else do you bring me today? It's summer, there must be a plague somewhere." The messenger cringed and Arthur's face changed "Oh no! I didn't mean it. Where?"

"In Cirencester, Sir. They think it may be scarlet fever, brought in by a returning pilgrim. They only sent word for everyone to keep away."

"All right. Cei, see if there are any volunteers to take food and supplies to Cirencester. They can leave the bundles outside the town limits. Now, has nothing *good* happened anywhere in Britain?"

"Yes, Sir. Gwynlliw reports that he has successfully eloped with the Lord of Brecon's daughter. They would like you to pay them a visit when the lady has had enough new clothes made and their castle is cleaned to her taste."

Cei gave a faint cheer and then remembered his position. "The only obstacle to the marriage was that Brecon wanted Gwynlliw's prize brood mare in trade for the daughter, Olwenna," he explained. "Gwynlliw wouldn't part with it and the lady found the whole idea repellent. She's a very good horse breeder, herself. I only hope she had the sense to elope on that fine stallion of hers."

Arthur looked at him in astonishment. "Why Cei! How did you come by such a fund of gossip?"

"Lydia was fostered in Armorica, with Olwenna's brother. She felt a family interest in the matter."

"No doubt. Well, then, is that all for today?"

"All of any interest. Will you call the Table together tonight?"

"Yes, now that everyone is here. There should not be an empty seat for long. Also, there are several things we need to discuss. I'm especially worried about the kingdoms in the North. Between the Dal Riada, the Bannauc lords, and the Picts, it's a constant battlefield up there, and those blasted bishops don't help a bit. Every one of them wants to rule Britain himself, or give one of his relatives the job. The priests I know are fine men; even most of the wandering monks, but make a man a bishop and he thinks he can take God's place in the world."

Cei listened with only half an ear. Arthur had been having run-ins with the bishops in the North for years. They resented every innovation in government Arthur had suggested. They had delusions, too, about the extent of their own power. Less than half of the people outside the towns were even nominally Christian. The Picts had only been baptized to hedge their bets. It was a hard life north of the wall. And when they lapsed, Arthur wasn't about to charge up with an army simply to punish them for paganism. This matter of Christians selling Christian slaves to them was another thing, though, and something that had to be taken care of.

There was another matter that Cei didn't like to bring up. However . . .

"Gereint's name is gone from the Table." He didn't look at Arthur. Magic made him nervous.

"I know. He's dead. That's what always happens when a knight has gone. Have you looked to see if another name is there?"

"Yes, the wood is as smooth as if never written on."

"There is a full moon tonight. It will be decided then. Those boys of Meleagant are both panting for it."

"I can't believe any seed of his would be worthy."

"Maybe not. They have a fine mother, though, and the younger boy has a quality about him. What about Modred? He's the only one of my nephews without a place at the Table. Even Gareth finally achieved it."

"He hasn't been here long; perhaps that's why. It's odd, though. He's the one I'd pick. He's strong and quick and could talk circles around any half-brained bishop."

Arthur considered. "He is all that, and more. I don't understand it. Gawain keeps dropping dark hints about him. Gareth won't sit near him. Even Agravaine seems uncomfortable around him. They're his brothers. What's the matter with him?"

Cei shrugged. "Maybe some childhood quarrel never settled. Modred is the youngest by quite a bit. The others could feel that he got too much of their mother's attention."

"Are you speaking from our own past?" Arthur prodded. Cei drew himself up with dignity.

"We always fought it out like men, Arthur. My father wouldn't let anyone have favorites."

"I know. Ector was a good father to me, too," Arthur smiled. "And he gave me a good foster-brother, even if you did rub my nose in the dirt more than once."

Embarassed, Cei shuffled some papers and changed the subject.

Guinevere had spent the morning properly engaged in a trip to the woods to search for herbs and mushrooms. She had been accompanied by most of the other ladies and all of the younger children. The conversation on earlier such trips had of necessity excluded her, since, after herbs, the main topics were children and the vagaries of husbands. She had no children and common sense forbade her discussing her husband with the wives and mistresses of those he commanded. But now that she had Galahad, the circle had opened to her. Much to her surprise, she found that she liked it, and the women who had been just a pregnant and nursing mass to her before became people with whom she shared more than she could have thought possible.

Still, there were areas that were forbidden. She knew by the discreetly lowered voices, the curious, sideways glances. She pretended that she didn't notice, but it was a relief to be back in her own room with Lydia to report on the domestic arrangements and Risa to bring her cool cider and gossip.

"What do you think of the last of Arthur's nephews?" Lydia asked Risa. "Oh, don't look surprised. Everyone knows he was in your room last night."

"I'm not surprised," Risa answered. "There are no secrets here. It seems he had overheard Gawain and Agravaine talking about me and he wanted to find out for himself."

They waited.

"He's very talented, but I don't trust him. I think he wants to use me to find things out about Arthur."

"But that's silly, Risa," Guinevere protested. "What could you tell him that he couldn't find out elsewhere?"

"Nothing, of course. And even if I could, I wouldn't. But why should I tell him that? It's rather amusing. Men are so odd. Modred is just like most of them. They assume that if I'll go to bed with them, I'll do anything else they want out of sheer gratitude."

"Cheldric doesn't," Guinevere interrupted.

Risa grimaced. "I know. He's good with the children, too. Never even asked which ones were his, just loves them all. When I think of what a swaggering bore he used to be, I can't believe it. Losing his arm did wonders for his personality. But I'm not going to marry him, so stop hinting."

·51·

Guinevere subsided. "But I do think you are mistaken about Modred. Arthur likes him."

"So does Cei," Lydia added. "He seems to be the most normal of the bunch."

Risa shook her head. "All the same, I consider it my duty to continue meeting him until I know what he's up to."

"Well, by all means, you can't shirk your duty!"

"Go on, laugh if you like. Just wait and see. There will be a formal dinner tonight, you know, and a meeting of the Round Table. Which jewelry would you like me to lay out for you?"

Lydia got up. "All right. We won't tease you anymore. May I borrow the opal brooch, Guinevere? I'm going to wear my new blue tunic tonight."

"Yes, of course. Risa, will you get that out, too? I think I just want the pearls and the Saxon bracelets. And the comfortable shoes with the fur lining. They'll be warm for summer, but I'll be standing so much this evening that I'll forgo style."

Arthur knew how to feed his guests. In the side court, two whole venison were roasting, lathered over with a basting of wine and cinnamon, basil, rosemary, thyme, and cumin. In the kitchens, huge trays of birds were browning—curlew, partridge, woodcock, and snipe. Trencher loaves of bread, colored with saffron, waited at the tables to be used to soak up the meat juices. Then there were five kinds of fish and eels boiled in almond milk. Lydia had been overjoyed at the recent arrival of a trading ship from Damascus, and so there were also several kinds of dried fruits in clove-and-ginger sauce. With this there were huge pitchers of beer and flagons of wine enough to drown all Camelot.

The meal began as soon as the evening breeze made it comfortable for so many people to crowd into the hall. No serious conversation was allowed and this was enforced through constant entertainment, singing, tumbling, and story reciting. The tumblers had not been to Britain for several years and had perfected amazing new feats of balance that caused people to forget for whole minutes the food before them.

"Arthur, this is magnificent," Lancelot told him. "But are you sure it's a good idea to have this feast before the Table?"

"You and I and the other knights will spend one hour in the chapel as usual before we meet. Those who are eager for the empty place will also be ready."

"I should have known. A man who can't stay sober at a feast like this can't be relied upon to keep his wits about him on a mission. I am very glad that I joined this assemblage before you learned such trickery."

"It doesn't seem fair, but I can't get to know these men the way I did you and Cei and Gawain. I need to resort to deviousness. It wouldn't have worked in your case, anyway. You never touched wine in those days. And you don't fool me now. You fill your cup once an evening, drink it half down and add water. You haven't had enough tonight to make a baby tipsy."

Lancelot fiddled with his knife. "I just don't like the feeling. I want to stay alert. I didn't think anyone noticed. I get laughed at enough for my ways."

"Don't worry. I'm grateful for one man I can always be sure of."

Arthur went back to his meal. Lancelot swallowed and tried not to look at Guinevere, seated next to Palomides. He drained his cup and sat back, focusing all his attention on the bawdy song Durriken had just begun.

Guinevere knew the moment Lancelot glanced at her and away. She tore off a small piece of the meat-soaked bread and nibbled at it. She smiled at Palomides.

"Perhaps when you finish with Percival you will teach the rest of us how they behave at the Emperor's court."

"I see nothing to correct," Palomides grinned back at her. "And by the time I finish with Percival, I will be an old man, gumming my gruel by the fire."

"Nonsense! He is so much better lately. He hasn't compared me to his horse in weeks."

"I'm glad to hear it. He tries to remember my dictates, but he doesn't seem able to apply one situation to another. He has no judgment. I'm afraid it will cause him great harm some
day. And yet, there is something about him. I often wonder if he may not be one of God's chosen, one of His innocents."

"Perhaps." Guinevere wriggled herself to a softer spot on her cushion. "But I think it more likely that he is just a fool. Still, one more at Camelot won't hurt."

Palomides laughed softly. If only he could make the people here see what they had. He looked around the hall. It was a special evening and everyone was dressed in their finest robes. The babies had been left with the nursemaids and the older children served the food and wine. Sometimes they would trip on a dog and there would be a momentary uproar, but on the whole it was orderly. Those at the high table ate off Samian plate and drank from gold cups while those at the lower tables had pewter or silver. To them it was perfect elegance. To Palomides, after the ritual coldness of Constantinople and the lush opulence of Babylon, it was comfortable, simple, and warm. Here the servants were held in esteem; people were still few enough to have worth. No, he had no intention of teaching them to behave with the callous thoughtlessness of the Emperor's court. Someone tapped his shoulder.

"Would you like some of the fruit, Sir?" Galahad smiled at him. "Figs and dates from Damascus. They are very good."

His sticky face and fingers testified to it. Guinevere glanced up at him and laughed.

"We should be glad they aren't any better or no one else would get any tonight. Here, love, let me just wipe your face before the dogs lick you clean."

"I don't mind the dogs."

"Nevertheless." She dampened her napkin and Galahad resigned himself to martyred embarrassment.

When the song ended, Arthur rose. Quiet spread slowly to the end of the hall. When all had stopped, he spoke.

"Tonight we must select a new member of the Round Table, to take the place of our brave Gereint, who was wickedly slain by Ligessauc Longhand. It is our custom, as most of you know, for all of the knights to spend the time before in the chapel, praying for the soul of our lost comrade and for guidance in the choice of his successor. But no choice will be accepted unless the name be written on the Table. We will meet again at moonrise. Until then, please, the rest of you continue with the feast."

Palomides rose also, bowed to Guinevere and left with the others. There were a few moments of silence after they went, punctuated by sighs of envy from the young men who remained. Then Durriken signaled the tumblers to begin again and they did another routine, this time to the beat of a tabor. When they finished, the pipers joined the drummer and the ladies got up to dance.

By moonrise, the tables had been cleared and the children sent to bed. Guinevere waited with Lydia for the knights to arrive from the chapel. They must be the first to enter the Great Hall, where the Table rested.

"I never get used to it," Lydia murmured. "All of this by night and the name appearing on the Table all by itself."

"It's only magic," Guinevere answered. "You shouldn't be afraid."

"Yes, but *who* writes the name?" Lydia shivered.

"I don't know. I never thought about it. Perhaps one of the old gods. The Table was built in their time." Guinevere was unconcerned. She was grateful that she had had the sense to wear her soft shoes. The night was cooler than expected. Brisane was probably dying in those open-lattice things with the high heels. But she always did prefer fashion to comfort.

The candles in the chapel windows flickered as the knights passed out of the building and returned to the hall. Their faces were stern, as if preparing for battle. Without speaking to the waiting group, they entered the hall and took their places as the Table. There were three empty seats. One was that of the knight Gereint. One was the mysterious Siege Perillous, of which they had never discovered the meaning. The last was clearly marked "Sir Gawain." But Gawain was, as always, sound asleep and would be until dawn. Lancelot looked at the space and wondered what it would be like never to have seen the moon at night, or the stars. Poor Gawain! He missed all the enchantment.

Modred's fingers curled into fists at his side. It was too soon. He knew it. But Gawain had been one of the first. He had more right to a seat at the Round Table than anyone, certainly more than that half-wit, Gareth. Why shouldn't he be chosen? Idly, he wondered how Arthur wrote the names. It was a perfect method. Who could complain about the choice of some supernatural hand?

The place at the Table was still blank. Arthur bowed his head, his eyes closed. Suddenly, someone cried out and they all craned to see.

Under the pouring moonlight, letters were being pressed into the wood. Arthur did not move or open his eyes. But he knew when it was finished and signaled Cei to read it out. Lydia stepped up silently behind him, to read the name first and whisper it in his ear. Cei still had trouble with unfamiliar words and names were the most difficult.

"The Table has chosen," he intoned. "The newest Knight of the Round Table is Sir Dyfnwal!"

"Me!" came a squeak from the back of the room. It was the younger of Meleagant's sons. "But . . . but . . ."

Arthur relaxed. "Come forward, young man. We do not question the choice."

He drew his sword, Excalibur, and the light caught it, flashing upon the upturned face of Dyfnwal as he knelt before the King.

"I question the choice!" a voice blared. "He has no right to be a knight before me. I'm the eldest! I'm the one who should have been picked. Let me read that."

Dyfnwal's brother pushed his way to the Table, ignoring the arms that tried to hold him back. His jaw clenched as he made out the letters.

"It's a mistake. He doesn't know how to keep his own ass safe, much less watch out for someone else's. There must be a place for me. What about that one? There's no one there."

"That belongs to my brother Gawain," Agravaine said

clearly. He knew how the man felt; both Gawain and Gaheris had been chosen before he was. All the same, Mallton would get nothing by making a scene. "We all know that his infirmity keeps him from being here at night."

"Then what about that one? No one sits there. Why shouldn't I?"

"Your name is not 'Siege Perillous,' is it?" Arthur's voice held a threat, but the man didn't heed it.

"My Lord, please," Dyfnwal said urgently, "let him have my place. He's right. I'm not worthy."

"*I* think you are." Arthur was a king now. His eyes were hard. "Mallton, you will return to your father in the morning. No one can stay at Camelot who questions my decision and that of the Table."

Mallton had been drinking too much to listen to orders. He was accustomed to being deferred to as Meleagant's heir. He grabbed a chair, set it in front of the Siege Perillous, and, defiantly, sat.

There was a gasp in the room and a shuffle as several men rushed to drag him away. Mallton leaned back with an exultant smirk, which suddenly changed to a look of horror. His eyes bulged and his veins knotted. He gave one hideous, drawn-out scream and slumped forward.

"My God!" Guinevere shrank back in her chair, her fingers making the sign against evil. This was a sort of magic she would rather do without.

Father Antonius, who had followed the knights from the chapel, stepped forward and gently lifted Mallton's head. He looked into the dead face. Those behind him turned away. He closed the man's eyes and straightened.

"He has paid the price for his blasphemy," he said softly. "I will take him home to his father."

Dyfnwal threw himself on his brother, weeping bitterly. Father Antonius drew him away and signaled for someone to remove the body. He then half-carried the shattered newly made knight from the hall.

"There'll be hell to pay for this," Cei murmured to Arthur.

· 57 ·

"Hell's been paid. It's Meleagant I'm worried about. He won't believe his oldest son died without my conniving it."

No one could think of anything more to say and everyone wanted to be away from the Table as quickly as possible, so the ceremony ended abruptly. Arthur let Guinevere lead him to their rooms, where he sat up the rest of the night, trying to understand what had just happened. Lydia stopped by the kitchens and made a strong cup of hot herbed mead for herself and Cei. She wasn't the only one.

Constantine and his father, Cador, were nearly the last to leave. Cador moved slowly now, his legs weak and his eyes blurred. But his mind was still clear and one thing puzzled him.

"Who was the man standing in front of me?" he asked. "He was close enough for me to make out his face, but I think my brain must finally be going."

"I don't remember who it was, Father. Why?"

"I could have sworn that it was Uther Pendragon."

"Uther's been dead for over thirty years, Father. Let me think. Yes, the man you saw was Modred, Morgan le Fay's youngest."

"I don't see how it could be. He was even standing like Uther, his hands opening and closing on his thighs, just as Uther's did when he was waiting to take something he wanted."

"You must have been mistaken. He wasn't even born when Uther died."

"No, of course not. You're right. I'm getting old. Yet, they are enough alike for the boy to be Uther's ghost."

Chapter Seven

Sir Percival, at last a knight of the Round Table, was heading, not too quickly, toward Camelot. He slumped in the saddle in a way which would have horrified Palomides. He sighed deeply. He scratched at a flea in his tunic. They were going to laugh at him. And, if they didn't laugh, they were going to be angry. He sighed again. How could he have known? "It's rude to ask questions." Palomides had told him so a hundred times. "If people want you to know something, they will tell you. If they don't tell you, then use your eyes and brains and find the answer yourself." Well, he had tried, but none of it made any sense to him. From the time they welcomed him to the castle on the river island to the minute they threw him out, he had not understood a single thing that happened. Sir Lancelot had told him that there were many strange places in the world. He had not lied.

Well, he would have to tell someone about it. It was too strange to keep to himself. But who? Lancelot would share his curiosity and Galahad would sympathize but only Palomides would try and explain it all. And Palomides was sure to yell at him.

Sir Percival sighed yet again. This being a knight was not exactly what he had expected. Considering that he had had to work nearly five years before the Table, if not the other knights, accepted him, it was awfully disappointing. He had daydreamed of honor and glory and a certain reverence on the part of those he helped. He hadn't thought that his first job would be to mediate between two blustering farmers on the matter of fouling the communal drinking water. Arthur had prepared him fully before he left and he had handled the matter quite well, he thought. He had even politely rejected the offer of the winner's niece as reward. But it wasn't really dangerous or exciting. Still, everything would have been fine if he hadn't stopped at that castle. Well, there was nothing for it but to confess to Palomides and then try to forget the whole thing.

The walls of Camelot had recently been whitewashed, and they gleamed in the sun like snow. The maze leading up to the fortress was overgrown along the top with wild flowers and herbs. From all the towers pennants flew, and the armor of the guards glistened from the lookout posts like jewels. It was no wonder that those approaching it for the first time often stopped to give a prayer or sacrifice of thanksgiving for the privilege of coming so close to such unearthly splendor.

Percival paid no attention as he threaded his way up to the main gate. He saluted the guard, dismounted and led his horse to the stables. Then he squared his shoulders and went in search of Palomides.

In the small courtyard Guinevere was playing hoop and ball with Galahad and listening to the complaints of Constantine.

"I'm sorry," she panted as she reached the hoop to pass it around the ball as it went by. "If Letitia won't marry you, I won't have her forced."

"But she loves me; she says she does. But since your father died, she's had this perverse idea about being needed by her mother and grandmother. She doesn't want to leave them. I even said she could bring them with her. Cador Castle is gone, but we have a fine villa farther inland where they could be perfectly comfortable. What is the matter? Do I have two heads or warts or what? You've got to do something."

Guinevere changed her tactic and swirled the hoop in a ragged arc over her head, to keep Galahad from getting through it. But he judged her movements so well that he never missed.

"That was a good one, Love," she told him when he had run out of ammunition. "Now pick up all the balls and put them in the basket and then fetch me something cool to drink. You've worn me out."

She sat down, fanning herself, and turned her attention more fully to Constantine's problem with her niece, Letitia.

"I must say that you deserve some consideration simply for your fidelity these past few years. And I don't think that Rhianna or my mother want Letitia to spend her life caring for them. They have plenty of servants, and the farmers and shepherds all owe duty to them and pay it without trouble. I'll try to help you. Perhaps I can get her to come here for a few weeks. You will have time to court her, and when she finds that everything goes well at home while she is gone, she may change her mind."

"Thank you, Guinevere. I don't know how much longer I can wait. I'm past thirty now. Letitia is twenty-five. We don't have much time left. Please help me make her see that she is wasting all our chances for a life together."

"Certainly, Constantine, I'll do my best. Now, can you see what's keeping Galahad? I am exceedingly thirsty."

When he had gone, she closed her eyes and leaned back against the wall. Although Constantine was handsome and loving as well as intelligent, she felt a sympathy for Letitia. It was hard to leave a safe quiet home for the bustle and cacophony of the court. She smiled. Each shriek and quarrel and clank and chuckle outside her windows meant home to her now. It would be the same with Letitia when she overcame her shyness. Yes, she would do her best for her niece. Letitia, at least, could not complain of being given too little time to discover where her heart lay.

Palomides was lying in the sun at the edge of the practice field. His sword and shield lay next to him. His tunic and trews were still damp with perspiration. His eyes were closed and Percival considered slinking away rather than disturbing him. But as he did a hand flashed out and grabbed his ankle.

"Well, young Percival, you would pass by and not greet your mentor? And how did your mission prosper? Did you resolve the dispute?"

Percival sat down next to him. He began fiddling with the thatch, pulling it out and separating the strands of dried grass.

"It went well, Sir. I saw it was as the King suspected, that the farmer upstream was guilty of fouling the water, but that the farmer on lower ground drove him to it by not allowing the first man free use of the common midden. It was settled amicably enough. Both wanted peace, but not at the cost of pride."

"You succeeded, then. I'm proud of you." Palomides gave

· 61 ·

him a wallop that would have taken the breath out of him a few years earlier. But Percival had grown and toughened. He merely coughed lightly.

Palomides gave him a sharp glance.

"What is it, then? If nothing more had happened, you'd not look so morose. Did you have a problem with a woman?"

"Me? Oh, no! She didn't mind at all when I declined. It was later, on the way back."

"Go on; you might as well tell me now. You'll not rest until you do. We have some time before dinner."

Percival took a deep breath and began.

"I was halfway here. It was growing dark and I knew there was no good habitation or village near, so I looked around for a spot to camp or a farmer's hut to find shelter in. I was following the river and chanced upon an old man, fishing. I asked him where I could go for the night, and he told me that farther upstream there was a castle where the lord would make me welcome.

"I had heard of no such lord, but there are so many things yet I don't know. So I went on a mile or more until I came to a place where the river widened. On an island in the middle was a great castle in good repair. There was a drawbridge down and no guard so I crossed it and went in search of someone to ask lodging of."

Palomides groaned. "What were you thinking of, lad?"

"But it was all right. No one attacked me. I found a group a people who welcomed me royally. Cundrie, the daughter of the house, gave me a room and a place to bathe and escorted me to the great hall with honor. The lord was a terribly old man. They called him the Fisher King."

"Why?"

"They didn't say. He was very feeble, though, and seemed to be in some pain from a wound to his leg or groin. He ate very little, and reclined through the meal. Everything was fine, I swear! Then, after dinner this strange procession came through the hall. First came a girl with a towel about her neck and two silver plates in her hands. Then came a man carrying a spear and from it, truly, blood was dripping! Then came a boy holding up something covered in a cloth high above his head. As they passed through, everyone bowed their heads and struck their breasts so I did, too. You told me always to respect the customs of my hosts."

"Yes, of course. Then what happened?"

"Then? Nothing. They simply bade me good night and I went to my room and slept. But the next morning, when I prepared to leave, no one would speak to me. They wouldn't even give me breakfast. My horse was saddled and waiting at the gate and so I left. But Palomides, that wasn't the strange part. When I crossed the bridge and looked back, the castle was gone! There wasn't even an island. Palomides, where was I?"

"Didn't you think to ask your host?" Palomides' voice rose.

"Yes, I wanted to, but you always said I should not ask questions!"

"I didn't mean that sort of question. *You* ask people why they have a red nose or whose room they slept in the night before. You ask their age or how they can be so fat and still mount a horse. Those are questions that manners forbid one to ask, but there are others one is *required* to ask as well, you dolt. I have told you that, also. You didn't inquire as to the man's health? You didn't ask the meaning of the ritual? How will you gather information for Arthur if you don't learn *how* to ask the proper question?"

"I know. I made a mistake. There are so many rules to remember! But why did the castle disappear?"

"Now you're asking the right question but the wrong person. How should I know? Perhaps it was sorcery or a dream or a trick of light. All right, never mind. You did as you thought best. I don't suppose any harm will come of it. Don't worry. I don't see any need to mention this to anyone else. Just try to learn from it."

"Yes, Sir. But I do wish there weren't so many ways to offend people."

"There are though, Percival, and I do believe you may discover them all."

* * *

· 63 ·

That night was a more formal dinner. Arthur was entertaining emissaries from one of the Armorican kings. He was doing his best to impress them with the wealth and stability of Britain, since these men were descended from those who had fled when the Romans left and it looked as though anarchy or barbarians would rule. Now times were changing and the Armoricans were being threatened by the Frankish kings. Arthur hoped to convince them to re-emigrate or at least to start sending their children to him for fostering. They were negotiating for military help. They had brought casks of good wine from their homeland. The evening was certain to be a success.

But the fish had hardly been served when there was a commotion outside the hall. Arthur motioned Cei to see to it. He came back almost at once and, leaning over, whispered in Arthur's ear.

"You'll never believe what is outside. Come, see for yourself."

Arthur gave his foster brother a look of doubt but started to rise. He sat down again, though, as through the open doors came what was without a doubt the ugliest woman he had ever seen. Her eyes were red and glowing and her skin wrinkled and of an unhealthy green tint. Her nose was too small, her chin and ears too large. Her hair was dark but thin and wispy. By contrast, she was riding a lovely white mule.

There was a clatter as everyone dropped their knives to stare at the visitor. Then there was a soft flutter of fingers moving against whatever evil she brought. No one spoke. The woman started to dismount but seemed to be having some trouble with her legs. All the knights were too stunned to move at first. Then a few made half-hearted moves to help her. They were too late. Galahad would not have been startled by the looks of the devil himself. He was at the woman's side in an instant and gently assisted her down.

"Let me get you a stool, Lady," he smiled. "Then shall I take your mule to the stables for the night?"

The thought of her spending the night at Camelot sent a collective shudder around the tables.

The woman gave a black-toothed grin and patted Galahad's cheek.

"That's a good lad," she crooned. "If such a one as you had come, I'd not have had to worry my bones making this ride. Na, na. If you'll but hold the reins while I have my say with this assembly, I'll be on my way again."

"Surely not so late, and with no meal!"

"There's a kind heart in you, boy, but never mind. I've eaten my bit and I'd just as soon sleep in my own bed tonight."

By this time Arthur had recollected his position and rose in greeting.

"Whoever you may be, Lady, and wherever from, you are welcome to Camelot. What is it that brings you here, so near to nightfall?"

The woman straightened as best she could and they could see that her spine was bent. She held out her arms to the court.

"A great grievance against one of your knights, my Lord. That wicked, cruel, thoughtless man known as Percival!"

All heads turned to Percival, sitting with the other unmarried men. He jumped and blushed from his toes to his hairline. A couple of his friends coughed down laughter. Sagremore nudged him.

"Now that I know your taste, it's no wonder you've found no woman here to your liking," he whispered.

Percival jabbed his heel on Sagremore's foot as he got up.

"King Arthur, I swear I have never seen this woman before! I don't know what she is talking about."

"You will when I have finished, wretched man!" The woman wailed above the sibilance. "My name is Cundrie, daughter to the Fisher King."

At this both Percival and Palomides started.

"But four nights past, this selfish knight received the hospitality of my father's home. We fed and housed him as a royal visitor, but he cared only for his own comfort. Even though my poor father's pain was obvious, never once did he ask him what illness made him so weak and groaning. Although we passed three times before him with the patens, lance, and Grail, he did not concern himself enough to ask what they were for or what god they served. And for this great sin, has he been punished? Not at all! It is we who must suffer even more than we had before. Father is condemned to bear his wound, which cannot be healed, and I to carry this hideous shape until another knight find the Grail and discover its secret. And he must be a far better man than craven Percival. We have guarded the Grail and its regalia for nearly five hundred years now, since it was brought into Ireland by our holy ancestor. We took it with us when our tribe settled in Britain. We had hope then that our stewardship would soon end. We have no hope now unless it be that some other man of your court will search us out, ask the questions, and release us. And lest you doubt the truth of my story, I have been given one miracle to show you the power we have been denied."

She bowed her head. The court was silent, waiting for a bolt of lightning or a whirling wind. For a few seconds, it seemed that nothing was happening, then gradually a light filled the room, like that of morning before the mists are entirely dispelled. It grew until some among them covered their eyes from the brightness. Then there was a distant sound of small bells and laughter. A host of blending aromas caused people to look down at their plates. To their amazement, they found put before each one of them the things he or she liked best to eat and drink in the world, from new bread with honey and eggs to rare meats and fish and even all the fruits together regardless of season. Guinevere could not resist reaching out for a full, ripe grape. Without thinking of danger, she ate it.

"Ahh!" she sighed. "There have not been any so sweet grown in Britain since I was a child."

At that, everyone turned to their plates and no one spoke until everything was gone. By then, the light had grown even more intense so that it seemed it should be possible to touch it and weave it into patterns in the air. Now it was clear that it radiated from an object floating above the woman. It appeared to be some sort of dish, but it was covered by a cloth so that only the shape was evident. The woman pointed up to it.

"That is the Grail, which is cloaked and hidden. Uncovered, it can do far more than give food to the body. Whoever finds it will know such peace and understanding of all the universe that his soul may outgrow its vessel and wish to be free of it. It may be more than any man here would dare. But it is only through the Grail's power my father and I may be saved. I can tell you no more."

With that, she took the reins of the mule from Galahad and vanished.

Into the shocked silence came a rush of noise as everyone began talking at once. The emissaries from Armorica gulped down the last of their wine and begged to be excused but no one heard them. Cei shouted for order but it was several minutes before anyone paid him any attention and several more before order was restored.

"Uncle! Please let me go search for this thing. It may be what I have been seeking all my life!"

Arthur's eyes widened. "Gawain! What are you doing up?"

Gawain still stared at the spot where the Grail had been. "It was so bright. I could feel energy coming from it into me. I know it could tell me why it is that I am the way I am. Please, Arthur, I must go!"

But at that moment, either the energy from the Grail died or the last ray of sunlight left, for Gawain toppled over, asleep again.

"This was all my fault, my Lord." Percival faced the high table. "I am the one who must go and find the Grail so that I may repair the damage I have done. She . . . she was a lovely girl before."

Palomides put a hand on his shoulder. "I wish to go with him, Sir. I believe that this is what I have been searching for, too. It has been five hundred years since the death of Our Lord. This must be the treasure that Joseph of Arimathea brought to safety 'to a land unknown to Rome.' Was not Ireland outside Rome's influence? What else could have such power for goodness? I beg your permission, for you have been a kind host to me, but I think I must go, even without it."

Then Lancelot rose. The look in his eyes terrified Guinevere. She knew that Palomides' words had been enough to set him off on another of his frenzied quests for Truth. She cursed under her breath as he spoke.

"Arthur, I do not know where this thing is from, nor what it is. All my life I have been tormented by what I did not understand. I may not be worthy of finding it, but I must go, too. Please allow me to search for the Grail."

"I will go with you!" Gareth blurted out.

At this more that half of the other men stood up and demanded that they also be allowed to seek the Grail, even some of those with wives and children. The room was loud with accusations and replies and the weeping of women who felt they were being abandoned. Cei had to pound his cup upon the table for several minutes before he could make himself heard.

"Are you all mad?" he yelled.

That set everyone off again. Arthur edged down to the end of the table where the priest sat.

"Father Antonius, what do you think of all this?"

The priest was a young man, not much over twenty-five. Arthur had chosen him as much for his laugh and his openness as for piety and learning.

"I don't know, my Lord," he answered. "There were stories such as Sir Palomides tells in the margins of some of the Gospel books at Llanylltud Fawr, where I was taught, but St. Illtud did not credit them. And my grandmother used to tell of a platter owned by the kings of Ireland which had the power of providing each with what he most liked to eat and drink. It vanished long ago. Perhaps it was stolen and brought to Britain. Yet, there was more to what we saw than simple conjuring. Could you not feel it?"

Arthur nodded. "There was a great power with us tonight, but what purpose does it serve? And who will maintain my laws in Britain if all my knights are out hunting phantom tableware? Where will my people look for help?"

Father Antonius swallowed nervously.

"We were taught, my Lord King, to look to God."

"Of course, of course," Arthur replied. "Perhaps he will send the answers."

So, chastised, but not convinced, Arthur returned to his chair. By this time, Cei had finally succeeded in focusing attention on the high table.

"Let the King speak!" he shouted. Red-faced, he motioned for Arthur.

"Nothing can be decided tonight!" Arthur told them all. "Let us finish our meal and go to our beds. In the morning we may all decide that this was no more than a fantasy. But those who are set upon leaving Camelot, come to me after Mass and we will discuss the matter."

He would not hear any more, but extended his arm to Guinevere, who rose and left with him. The whole thing seemed completely bizarre to her, but no more so than many other things that had happened. Lancelot might go, but he would return to her; he always did. Thank God, Galahad was too young to think of such nonsense!

Chapter Eight

"You aren't really going to let them go, are you?" Cei was so angry that he couldn't stand still. He paced the wooden floor before Arthur, the thumps echoing throughout the building. "It's insane. That thing was just an illusion. No one is going to find it, and if somebody does, what difference will it make?"

"We'll have to wait and see when that happens." Arthur spoke calmly, but Guinevere could sense the excitement in him. He hadn't slept at all last night. He had tossed about with each change of mind until Guinevere had been driven to sleep on the couch on the other side of their room.

"I want to speak to each one of them alone," he continued. "No one must be pressured to go on this journey. And no man must leave unless he has made provision for the care of his family while he is gone. Now, give me a few minutes to wash and eat and then send them in."

Cei snorted his opinion and left.

Guinevere knew that Arthur was furious, but not with the Grail or the ugly Cundrie, nor with Percival or any of the knights. What was the matter? He even seemed to have forgotten his worries about keeping the government running. He rubbed his face raw and then threw the towel against the wall. He stopped, looked at his wife, and gave a sheepish grin. Suddenly, she knew.

"You want to go with them!" she accused. "How can you, Arthur!"

All the anger slipped out of him and he sagged into his chair.

"Oh, Guinevere, how can I *not* want to go?"

Alarmed, she went over and knelt by the chair, putting her arms around him.

"Have I made you so unhappy that you want to leave?"

"What? Of course not! It's not you, how could it be? You've been very good to me, Guin."

Her lip trembled and she buried her face in his lap. He ran his fingers across her braids as he spoke.

"It's only that it seems as if at last adventures are beginning again. The last few years have been so horribly dull! With Merlin gone and St. Geraldus killed I had begun to think that true magic had gone from Britain. If it hadn't been for you I might have stopped believing in enchantments altogether. You can't know how much I hate this petty drizzle of childish accusations and stupid brutalities. The constant watching and conniving and playing one side against the other in the hope that somehow justice will come out of it drives me mad. To go forth again, freely, in search of truth . . . Can you imagine it? At last a quest in which no one need harm another. And I must sit here like a dotard and hope that news of it trickles back to me! Do you wonder I want to tear something apart?"

She smiled at him and shook her head. But she didn't understand. She didn't want to. The Grail was a pretty trick; it gave food and light, good things to have. It would be a handy thing to have around in time of winter famine. All this "truth and understanding" though . . . well, really! Guinevere understood all she wanted to, and as for universal truth, she wasn't in any hurry to find out about that, either. Her theology was uncomplicated. If God wanted her to know something, he would tell her. She had read the church fathers and they seemed remarkably clear to her. If she wanted anything else, the old gods were often very thoughtful to those who left a bracelet or a bit of meat at their shrines. Even her mother had not been so cruel as to destroy the lares and penates of the house. They had simply been removed to a small room near the servants' quarters for storage. The door had not been locked and she had often gone in to ask about matters such as a new gown or less nagging from Flora, her nurse. Guinevere believed in letting the deities each do what they were best suited to. To her, the Grail quest was just another one of those things men did to keep themselves occupied.

She was, therefore, unprepared for the storm she discovered among the women that afternoon.

"Well, I can't go, of course," Lydia said firmly. "I have too much to do here, and Ectoris and Aurelia are too young yet to be fostered. Anyway, Cei says it's all nonsense."

"You saw it yourself," Brisane interrupted. "It was as real as we are, and that poor woman! Why should we stay here while they go out and have all the fun? It's not a war they're going to."

She had already dressed in her riding clothes, pants under a long tunic. Her boots had been stained bright green. She would not be mistaken for a knight.

"They don't know where they're going or how to get there," one woman answered. She held her arm crooked to shield her sleeping child from the sun. "It doesn't sound like fun to me. And while my husband is gone, I must be expected to depend on the kindness of my friends. We have no great lands to support us."

"You needn't worry, Tertia," Guinevere said quietly. "We will not change your status here."

Tertia smiled her thanks. "But that's not the worst of it. You know that."

They all nodded.

"It was like this before, you know." The woman who spoke was the oldest of the group. She was grandmother to Bedivere and had come to Camelot when his father died. She had meant to stay only a week or two, but the place had drawn her in and now she was part of it. They looked at her expectantly.

"I remember thirty years ago and more, when a young man swept through Britain like a torch, setting the men afire to follow after him. Only then they took their swords and spears. My man did not come back. He fell at Mons Badon. It's been a long time since then. The soldiers who returned have grown old. Even Arthur is growing old, and I thought at the time that he seemed not much more than a boy, to be leading such an army. But they had the same look about them then that your men do now. You'd have thought the millennium was approaching. It didn't come, though to my mind Arthur has brought us closer than I ever thought I'd live to see. But the young men today never knew that kind of excitement. Life under Arthur has been too calm. For an old woman, it is joy, but not to these young knights. There is nothing now to challenge them, no battles as their fathers waged. They have to seek out something."

"But this is not a battle. There is no reason why a woman could not find this thing. I want to know the secrets of the world as much as any of them." Brisane set her jaw and glared at them.

Tertia looked down at her son. She had had four, but only this one had lived. Yes, she had questions for the universe, also. But she would not leave her child to find the answers.

Risa started to laugh.

"If you set off alone in that getup, you'll find the secrets of the world fast enough. It's all very well for us to make grand talk. But every one of you knows that nothing Arthur can do will keep any woman safe outside of her own lands. That's the way the world is and I don't see much hope of its changing soon. So it's nonsense to go on about it. The only way we go anywhere is tied to some man or other. I'm not saying I like it. I want to go, too. When I saw that light last night, it seemed as if everything I'd ever done were reflected in it . . ."

"That must have been quite a show," someone murmured.

With an angry gesture, Risa continued.

"It was as if none of it mattered. For just a moment I realized that I had been looking at everything the wrong way, from the wrong direction. All the things that I thought important really weren't, and there were other things I had not known of which were more wonderful than anything I had imagined. But before I knew what they were, the Grail had gone. Did none of you feel it?"

Brisane nodded. She rubbed her fingers hard into her boots, as if to erase the dye.

A voice seemed to come out of the air. "You're right, Risa. I felt it, too."

"Galahad! how long have you been here?" Guinevere looked up, startled.

His long legs swung from the tree branch above her. The resemblance to his father was pronounced. He didn't answer her question.

"I think the knights all have it wrong. I was listening this morning. Everyone is going in a different direction. They are thinking of places where the Grail might be; holy or hidden places. But I don't think it will be found that way, like a lost ring or buried treasure. It's not that sort of thing. Cei said it was all an illusion. I believe it's a symbol, like Gawain's Green Knight. To find it, I must be something more than I am now. I will need to study and to suffer. There must be tests for worthiness. Those are what we should be seeking."

Guinevere stood up, using the boy's legs to help her rise. Her eyes were wide, her skin tight with terror.

"What are you talking about? This has nothing to do with you. You're a child! You're only a child!"

He slid down from the tree. With a shock, Guinevere realized that he was as tall as she.

"I'm almost fourteen, Foster Mother," he said quietly. "Others my age are going as squires to the knights. I am going with Percival and Palomides."

"This is insane." Guinevere spoke softly but her words pierced the air. "It will not be allowed."

"What other boys?" Risa asked sharply. The women waited.

"Almost all of us. Everyone wants to go. But I'm the only one who chose Percival. They all think that since he failed once, he won't find anything. I wanted to go with my father first, of course, but he wouldn't let me. He and Gareth are going alone."

Guinevere thanked Lancelot in her heart. He knew what it would cost her to give them both up. He would see that their Galahad stayed where he belonged.

The women's section of the hall was empty that night. Anger and bitterness are poor sauces. The men pretended they did not notice and were all the louder and more boisterous. But more than one of them excused himself early and the lamps of Camelot burnt late. When they went out that night, not every woman cried herself to sleep. Tertia held her spent husband gently and smiled. For all her wanton behavior, Risa had given good advice. Men, she had explained, cannot be reasoned with. They don't have the minds for it. But even a fool will think twice before he gives up a treasure in his own house to seek one far away. One simply needs to remind him of the value of the treasure at hand.

Still, of the knights of the Round Table, nearly half remained determined to seek the Grail. With them were forty or so of the men-at-arms and older boys. When it was certain that nothing could dissuade them, Arthur declared a day of fasting and prayer, followed by a solemn meeting of the Table, since no one knew when they would all meet again.

Arthur's eyes dimmed as he regarded the men about him that last night. Some had been with him almost from the beginning: Bedivere, Gawain (asleep now, but leaving at dawn with the others), Agravaine, Cei, Lancelot. Only Cei and Agravaine were not going. Of the others, Sagremore, Percival, Morvid, Perredur Map Eridur, Kinlith, Meleagant's son Dyfnwal, Gerontius of Dumnonia, Cunorix and Ebicatos, who had come to him from Ireland, and Palomides, who had come from the other end of the world, were now leaving. Arthur couldn't help but feel that they were abandoning him, even though he knew the conflict in their hearts. But he would not send them away with harsh rebukes.

He gave them all his blessing for the venture and assured them of their right to welcome whenever they chose to return. He asked only that they remember their honor as knights as well as the splendor of their quest and conduct themselves accordingly.

"And now, we will break with tradition and drink one cup of mead here, to those who are leaving and those who remain, that neither may forget the other or fail to help them in need."

They raised their cups in solemn stillness. Galahad, who, for Guinevere's sake, had been firmly forbidden to join the quest, watched from behind his father. But he could not see well and surreptitiously inched around until he came to an opening. Oh, how he longed to go with them! He tried not to be jealous of those who had been permitted to accompany their cousins or friends. If what he felt were true, then it shouldn't matter at all where he were. If he made himself worthy, the Grail would come to him. But what could he do around Camelot to make himself worthy of anything? Galahad was growing light-headed. He had spent the night before in the chapel, praying for guidance, and had not eaten all that day. Perhaps he could just sit down a moment. It was weakness. The desert saints would not have succumbed to a mere one day without food. A true knight wouldn't either. But he felt so dizzy! There was a stool nearby, he could pull it over for just a minute and sit down, just till his head stopped spinning. There. He sat.

"Good God! Stop him!!" Lancelot knocked over three men in an effort to reach the boy. Someone else cried out, and all steeled themselves for the worst.

Frightened by this reaction, Galahad jumped up again too quickly. Lamplight on the armour and cups glittered and blurred as he slumped in a faint onto the Table. He did not feel the carven words under his cheek, *Siege Perillous*.

Hands shaking with grief, Lancelot lifted up his son and leaned the body against his shoulder. Galahad stirred and blinked.

"He's alive!" Cei breathed the obvious. "How can that be? Since Mallton, five men have died for sitting at that place."

"He had no evil intention," Father Antonius said cautiously. "Perhaps that makes the difference."

Someone gasped and stood away from the Table. Lancelot looked down and slowly lowered his son to the floor. Galahad swayed a little and steadied himself on the edge of the Table. Then he saw it, too. He tried to swallow but could only choke. There must be something the matter with his eyes, the moonlight was suddenly so bright . . . and warm. He felt wrapped in love and security. Without realizing it, he smiled.

Even in his fury, Modred was not untouched by the radiance in the boy's face. More than one man knelt before it.

The light grew less intense. Galahad turned to Lancelot for direction and was horrified to see tears pouring down his face. "Father?"

"I cannot guide you in this, my son. I am not worthy."

"King Arthur?"

"If you still wish to seek the Grail, Galahad, no one here will stop you."

They all stared at the Table. There, still glowing like flame, were the words. Modred refused to believe them. It was another trick. But he saw no doubt in the faces about him. Lancelot got a proper chair and sat Galahad down again before the words:

SIR GALAHAD
WHOSE COMING I HAVE AWAITED SINCE I WAS MADE

Guinevere had heard the stillness and then the commotion. She hoped that Lancelot would be able to slip away for a few minutes before it was over. She had said good-bye to him many times before, but that made it no less hard and she preferred saying it to him alone, instead of politely, before an audience. Risa sat on the balcony, thinking and watching.

"There was a strange light over the hall again, Guinevere," she called. "What could it be for?"

Guinevere shrugged and didn't answer. She went on with her beadwork.

"It must be over. They're coming out now. No, only Galahad, I guess. Maybe they sent him away since he's not going. I know how you feel about it," she added, coming inside. "But I don't know how you could have held out against them. I couldn't. Domin is going with Bedivere."

"But you have other children."

"Do you think that would make the loss of one any easier?" Risa had anguished over letting the boy go; he was only twelve. But she thought Bedivere was probably his father and, in any case, would care for him. "Children are not like coins. One can't replace another."

"Galahad is all I have, Risa. All I'll ever have. Would you risk that?"

Risa was prevented from answering by a timid knock on the door. She rose, gratefully, and answered it.

"Why, Galahad, I thought you had gone to bed!"

Galahad was very pale. "I need to speak alone with my mother. Would you mind, Risa?"

"Of course not, dear. I was just going, anyway. Good night, my Lady."

Risa wondered about it all the way down to her room. "Mother," he called her, not "Foster Mother." Something's happened. Somehow, the boy has convinced them to let him go and the cowards sent him to tell her himself.

Guinevere never told anyone what Galahad said to her that night. Arthur came up to their room cautiously, expecting to be greeted with either tears or crockery. But he found only his wife, sound asleep, and, if she had cried, there were no traces left on her face.

In the morning all the court, all the landsmen, all the visitors, and all the dogs and cats were at the lower gate to send the knights off on their grand quest. No one knew exactly what they were after, but rumors and dreaming had made it something marvelous, which would change all their lives when it was found.

Lancelot was surprised to feel a twinge of jealousy as he realized that Guinevere was more concerned with Galahad's departure than his own. She gripped his hands tightly, though, when he made his farewells, so that her own came away red. He wished he knew what she was feeling, if it were anger or sorrow or merely resignation. Galahad clung to Guinevere as if he regretted his decision, but, when all were ready, he did not hesitate. He kissed her once more, mounted his horse, and left, just as men had done for all time.

Arthur put his arm around her.

"He will be all right," he said. "They'll all be back by winter; you'll see."

Guinevere smiled. "He made me a promise. I know he will keep it. But I think the days will be very empty here."

As he watched the others ride away, leaving him behind, Arthur totally agreed.

Chapter Nine

"So, Arthur's little knights have all gone off Grail-hunting!" Morgause smiled. "Why didn't I think of something like that?"

"You mean, you didn't?" Modred was astonished. "Who else is there left in Britain who can do that sort of magic?"

"Don't say 'left' as if I were some sort of relic." Morgause ran her hands through her fiery hair. "And don't believe that Christian claptrap about all the 'demons' having been driven from the land. There's magic everywhere. It can't be killed, only stilled for a time. But I never heard of a Grail in our lore. It sounds more Irish to me. They like to blend mysticism with a good, hot meal. We were more ascetic in our day."

"It doesn't matter," Modred answered. "It's left the way open for me. I'm fast becoming Arthur's right-hand man. Cei is busy with the army and household, and Constantine can't think of anything but that granddaughter of Leodegrance's. So Arthur trusts me with all sorts of jobs. He even lets me take his precious wife on trips to the countryside. If it goes on like this, I may even get him to retire in my favor, without ever striking a blow."

"You're not starting to like him, are you?"

"Of course not! But why start my rule with blood?"

"The best sacrifices are blood. And the most powerful sorcery is rooted in it."

Modred shrank back a little from his aunt. He always felt

uncomfortable when she talked that way. It wasn't . . . decent.

"Well, if I can do without it, I will. And, while all the favorites are out beating the bushes for this Grail thing, I am weaving myself through the heart of Britain. Meleagant has never forgiven Arthur for the death of Mallton, and he's just as angry at him for taking Dyfnwal's affection, although I can't see that there was much to take. Meleagant was never too thoughtful with any of his children, even the legitimate ones. But he doesn't want to leave his lands to the most likely bastard. His wife's family is too powerful. He'll support me to get his son back.

"I went to the coast just before I came to see you. Cerdic is another one we can have. He has more Saxon men than British in his control and has no faith in this return to Roman ways."

"And Maelgwn?" Morgause studied her left eye in her hand mirror. Perhaps a bit more kohl around the lashes.

"Maelgwn I may leave to you, my love. He won't fight Arthur, although he won't help him more than necessary. He prefers to wait in the mountains until it's all over. Then he'll favor the winner, or, if the winner has been made weak enough, devour him. But you may be able to offer him something he will snap at. He has, I have heard, most unusual cravings."

"From what *I* have heard, nothing terribly uncommon, only more elaborate than most." She stretched.

Even though it was still late summer, fog lay on Tintagel and oozed in at the cracks. Modred shivered in his furs.

"I have to be getting back soon, before Agravaine comes home. Arthur has decided, for some bizarre reason, to winter in London this year. The whole place is in an uproar since all the winter supplies are at Caerleon. He has asked me to find a suitable place for the people he is bringing with him. There is a wonderful chance to bring about resentment. 'The High King demands your house, my Lord. You may have it back when he is finished.' Of course, London is all merchants and bishops; split down the middle already. I wish those 'men of

God' were half as powerful as they think they are. They forget how few Christians dwell outside the towns. And I don't know what I can promise the merchants that Arthur hasn't given them already."

"Never mind. Something will come to you."

She crossed the room and put her arms around him. As his fingers slipped through her hair, he found himself wondering if Guinevere's were as soft and if it were really as warm as it looked in the summer sunlight. He thought he could hear her laughing again, as she urged her horse past him and ahead. He came to himself with a start.

"Cold, Precious?" Morgause slid onto his chair and pressed her body closer.

"In this place? Of course." He must be insane! Whatever made him think of that . . .? He knew better than to succumb to her the way everyone else around Arthur did. It was an obstacle that drove him mad; even though everyone knew she and Lancelot were lovers, no one said a word about it. It was as if she had bewitched them. Yes, that was it exactly. Meleagant had muttered something about witchcraft in his ramblings against her. But it was preposterous. She wouldn't have the brains. Unless her innocence was all a pose.

"Morgause, when did you last see the Queen? Stop that a minute and answer me."

"You know very well, when I brought Galahad and Elaine to court, when he was a baby."

"How old was she then?"

"I don't know, about twenty to twenty-five, I suppose, nearer the latter. Why?"

"That was fourteen years ago. You look as you did then, I imagine."

"No, I've added a few touches. I changed my eye color and . . ."

"Yes, but you haven't aged, have you?"

"Of course not! What an awful thing to say! What is the matter with you?"

"Well, neither has Guinevere."

"That's impossible. You're exaggerating. She probably has

some good creams and hair dye and covers up a little more in the sun, that sort of thing."

"Not according to her maid. And I've seen her standing in bright sunlight with her head and arms bare. She doesn't look more than eighteen."

"Why, that bitch! How dare she!"

"You see what I mean? Is that natural?"

"You think she traffics with the old ones, too? The daughter of Leodegrance and Guenlian, those paragons of Roman Christianity? The fog here must have gotten into your brain."

"Think about it! She doesn't age, doesn't bear children, and we know, don't we, that neither her husband nor her lover is impotent. She does nothing special, and yet everyone adores her. I've seen perfectly sane men practically come to blows over who will escort her to dinner. Even the women have nothing bad to say about her. And I know that envoys have come to Camelot determined to win concessions from Arthur and, after one evening with Guinevere, have given him anything he wanted. Is that natural?"

"No, I suppose not. But it doesn't seem possible that she could be doing it herself. Do you know," Morgause added with rising excitement, "it sounds like something entirely different. It's the sort of spell that the old priestesses used to put on the children they intended for sacrifice, so that they would not be damaged before it was time for the offering. If that's so, then somehow the time passed without the sacrifice being made. This is fascinating! I never really believed that they worked. Although, certainly it should not last so long after the appointed time. It must be wearing thin by now. Yet, it might account for her looking so young."

"Do you think she knows about it?"

"I doubt it. Innocence in the victim is necessary for that kind of ritual. Something has gone askew. I really must contact some of my friends about this."

"Yes, and ask them what we can do about it. It may be the way to deliver the final blow to Arthur. If we can remove Guinevere and her influence . . . ah, my dear, I'm beginning to get an idea." Modred rose with a suddenness that sent Morgause to the floor.

"Get up from there!" he snapped. "We have work to do."

Gawain and Lancelot had decided to travel together, at least at the beginning. Gareth had taken it with bad grace. He said that Gawain's infirmity would slow them down, especially as summer waned, and that he wasn't serious enough about the quest anyway. But he really meant that Lancelot and Gawain were such good friends that Gareth would be left out, relegated to building fires and fetching water. However, Lancelot's decisions were unquestionable in Gareth's mind so he endured his brother's good humor and flamboyance as best he could.

They set off into the western mountains. Among them were hundreds of uncharted valleys. If one wanted to hide a castle in one of them, it could stay hidden for centuries.

Late one afternoon, they entered one of those valleys. It was lush with summer growth. There was a cluster of huts at one end and a large stone-and-wood castle at the other. In between were small plots of grain, roped off to keep out the horses which seemed to be free to graze anywhere else they wished.

"What beautiful animals!" Gareth exclaimed. "Arthur should know about this place. Perhaps we can do some trading here."

"It looks pleasant enough," Lancelot agreed. "Shall we risk asking for a night's lodging at the castle?"

"Why not?" Gawain yawned. "The worst they can do is turn us away. But let's hurry; I don't want to spend another night sleeping in a nettle patch."

Gareth cringed. "I said I was sorry. It was so dark when we stopped that I couldn't see what kind of plants they were. I tried to put you someplace comfortable."

Their welcome at the castle was more than they hoped for. Arthur's fame had spread far, and even the names of Lancelot and Gawain were well known. To Gawain's embarrassment, the story of the Green Knight had been told there recently, by a wandering bard.

"Of course, of course!" their host chortled. "Goodness! You're even bigger than the stories say! Well, have your slave take the horses to the stable and I'll show you to the dining hall."

Gareth stiffened and looked to Lancelot for aid, but Gawain was even more indignant. It was one thing to ignore one's brother in the family but quite another to have him insulted by a stranger.

"We have no slaves!" he thundered. "This is my brother, Sir Gareth, a most respected and worthy knight of the Round Table. You should beg his pardon immediately, before we are forced to take umbrage!"

As Gareth gaped in amazement at his brother's sudden defense and wondered what the hell umbrage was, the startled lord bustled around wringing his hands and stammering his apologies. Coming to himself, Gareth graciously forgave him and amity was restored.

The food was excellent, fresh game and vegetables with honey-dipped fruits and breads to end the meal. Their host was eager for news of the outside world and their quest for the Grail. But he shook his head sadly, when asked if he had heard of it.

"We know little of what happens outside the valley. Traders and storytellers pass through in the summer and we learn what we can from them, but no one has mentioned anything like that magic. And if anyone less distinguished than yourself had told me of it, I would have dismissed it as just another tale."

At the end of the meal, as was the custom, the lady of the house showed the knights to their rooms. Gareth and Lancelot were left in a small room near the main hall. Gawain was barely able to stumble after the lady as she led him to a richly furnished corner room, with elaborate wall hangings and large windows, facing east. He mumbled his thanks and fell onto the bed, leaving the poor woman to assume that, for all the tales told about his feats, the great Sir

Gawain could not hold his liquor. She mentioned it to her husband.

"Why couldn't we have chosen Sir Lancelot?" she demanded. "I don't like sending her in there with a drunk."

"There's no way he could harm her," her husband remonstrated. "And Sir Lancelot insisted on staying with Sir Gareth. He seemed afraid that we would board him with the animals otherwise."

"Well, I might have. That Sir Gareth certainly doesn't look like a knight. And I don't believe for a moment that he's really related to Sir Gawain. Oh, I do hope it works this time! I just hate the mess of it all. And it would be nice to be connected to the rulers of Cornwall."

Dawn touched the windows of Gawain's room the next morning. He opened his eyes, knowing there was no way he could sleep a little longer. But he was sure that no one but the kitchen drudges would be awake so early. He sighed and stretched, wondering why his host had chosen to decorate the room by hanging a three-foot sword directly over the bed. As his arm came down, he struck something soft. There was a muffled yelp.

Cautiously, he turned his head to see what was lying next to him. His brothers and friends had put some odd things in with him before, from a suckling pig to a snake. Slowly, he peeled back the covers.

"Hello!" The girl smiled at him, but it took him a moment to notice. The first thing that caught his eye was the fact that she was stark naked. It didn't look like one of Gareth's tricks. The girl made no effort to cover herself but went on talking.

"You certainly are a heavy sleeper. I've been trying most of the night to wake you up. I got all your clothes off and you didn't even blink."

Gawain sighed. That was the way things had been going for him, lately. There was no point in explaining.

"Well," he said. "I'm awake now."

"That's true," she replied, and pressed against him. Gawain's eyes lit up. Perhaps his luck was changing.

He had only just rolled on top of her when he heard a snap. Grateful, for once, for his morning strength and agility, he managed to deflect the falling sword with no more than a gash on his arm.

"Oh, are you hurt?" the girl asked calmly. "That was very good. Why don't we tie up your arm and finish what we were doing before my father comes?"

Gawain started to protest and then shrugged. Good offers didn't come his way as often as they used to.

He became so enthusiastic that he didn't hear the door open an hour later.

"My God! Alia! What are you doing?"

Gawain looked up. He looked down again.

"Are you Alia?" he whispered. She nodded.

Yes. Life was going normally after all.

In a few seconds it appeared that everyone in the castle had heard the news and managed to squeeze into the room with them. Alia had cravenly taken the blanket to wrap around herself and so Gawain was left trying to get into his pants and answer the outraged questions of her father and mother. He got a glimpse of Lancelot, looking embarrassed and highly confused, and Gareth, looking smug.

"My poor baby!" the lady moaned. "How could you come here and take our hospitality and then seduce my sweet child? Oh, how awful! Her virgin blood all over!"

"Wait a minute!" Gawain hollered. "That's my blood! She certainly wasn't any . . . And that reminds me. What do you mean by hanging a whacking great sword over the bed where it could fall and kill someone?"

"Gawain, how could you complain? After all those things you said to me?" Alia started to cry.

"Lancelot! Help!" Gawain yelled.

Lancelot was trying to understand what was going on. At first, knowing Gawain's reputation, he was inclined to believe that he had brought this on himself. Then he remembered the accusations which had followed after he had been drugged and lured into bed with Elaine. Gawain had taken his part then. He could do no less.

"My Lord." He pushed through the crowd to Alia's father. "I'm sure there's some misunderstanding here. Sir Gawain could not have . . . ."

"Oh, yes he could! I saw him, myself. Furthermore, the sword didn't kill him the way it did all the others, so, clearly, he was meant to marry Alia."

"Marry!" Gawain yelped.

"What others?" Lancelot asked at the same time.

"It's a family tradition. If a man can lie all night with my daughter and not molest her, then he's worthy to be her husband. But if he tries anything, the sword immediately falls upon him and kills him. Sir Gawain is the only one who survived. And, since it is clear that he and Alia have already consummated the match, it only remains for me to marry them, this afternoon, in the main hall."

The next moment everyone, including Alia, had left to prepare for the wedding. Lancelot and Gareth looked at Gawain, who was still struggling back into his clothes.

"This is worse than the Green Knight," he said flatly. "Then I only thought I would lose my head."

"Look, I can sneak around to the stables, get the horses, and we can be gone in half an hour," Gareth offered.

"What do you think?" Gawain asked Lancelot.

"You know very well that's what I did in the same situation." Lancelot was profoundly uncomfortable. "I think you've been tricked here as cruelly as I was then. You got the horses for me, as I remember."

"It isn't the same, old friend." Gawain swung his boot from hand to hand as he thought. "I made no vow of chastity and no one drugged me. I woke up. The girl was there. I had an hour before breakfast. It was nothing that hasn't happened before. Hell, she seems nice enough, and I'm getting old for this. If I can take her back to Camelot with me, I guess I may as well marry her."

He laughed at the dropped jaws in front of him.

"Come on. See if you can find me something proper to wear and then some food. I want a last meal."

Even though Lancelot assured the people of the castle that

their prize was not going to run, they hurried through the fastest wedding ever devised. Gareth and Lancelot stood dumbfounded as they watched Gawain and Alia take their vows. Afterwards they were persuaded by the happy couple to wait until the next day to continue the search for the Grail. Gawain, of course, had to take his bride back to Camelot before he could go on.

The next morning Alia's parents wept as she bade them good-bye.

"I thought we could keep you forever," her mother sniffed. "The sword seemed invincible."

"Mother! Do you know what it was like having men sliced to death on top of me? Some of those stains never came out. You should be happy for me, married to practically the greatest warrior in Britain."

Gawain mentally vowed to visit his in-laws as little as possible.

"Gareth and I are going to Llanylltud Fawr, to see if St. Illtud knows anything about the Grail," Lancelot told him. "If you decide to follow us, go there first. We'll leave a message for you there. Good luck, Gawain! And to you, Alia!"

After they left the valley, Gawain noticed that his new wife seemed preoccupied. She couldn't seem to keep her mind on what she was doing when they made love after the noon meal. She kept looking around, as though expecting something to jump out at her.

"Poor thing," he thought. "She's never been away from home before. It must all be very frightening for her."

But, late in the afternoon, a horseman appeared, riding from the opposite direction and galloping toward them. He carried a very sturdy-looking spear and had a sword at his side. Alia screamed as he came closer, his arm raised to launch the spear at Gawain.

The spear didn't worry Gawain; he could tell from the way the man threw it that it would go wide. He drew his sword reluctantly, though. He didn't really feel like killing anyone today.

The man made the mistake of waiting to see where the

spear went and Gawain was on him at once. He had wanted only to disarm his attacker, but he was stronger than Gawain had anticipated and he had to parry a few clumsy strokes first, before the man was unhorsed. From the ground, he continued to make a determined, if inept, effort to skewer Gawain. But, finally, the sword clattered down and Gawain raised his to demand surrender. He started to bring it down when Alia, whom he had completely forgotten, threw herself in front of the robber. With a wrench, Gawain managed to turn the blade.

"What are you doing?" he asked her reasonably.

"How dare you try to hurt him! You horrible bully! You think because you're one of Arthur's knights that you can do anything you want!"

Gawain shook his head to clear it, but still nothing made sense. Alia was trying to remove the man's helmet, to check for bruises. Gawain's opponent was trying to get up.

"Stop it, Alia! He didn't hurt me!" The man brushed her away. He reached for his sword, but Gawain's foot was there first. He tapped it against the metal as he considered the pair.

"All right. What's going on?" His jaw was set and the man took a few steps back. Alia, however, was not intimidated.

"This is Rintuidd. He and I have been trying for years to get my family to let us marry. But there was that damned sword always stopping us. I was beginning to think I'd never get away. Finally, you came along and I'm very grateful. Now Rintuidd and I will just be going and you can get back to your Grail-thing."

She remounted her horse and Rintuidd got back on his.

"Wait a minute!" Gawain yelled, trying to keep control of the situation. "You married me!"

She had already started off, but she paused to smile and wave.

"That's all right; I married him first. Thank you again! Good-bye!"

And they galloped off as quickly as their horses could take them.

Gawain sat down in the road. He found a piece of rock under his hand and ground it into powder. He was too angry to move. That was enough. He had been duped again and this time it hadn't even been an allegory, just a featherhead who wanted to run off with her lover. Slowly he rose and dusted himself off. He was giving up the quest and going back to Arthur. What difference did it make if he searched for a Grail or just a nice girl? Something always happened to make him look ridiculous. There was no point in trying any more. Damn! He had pulled a muscle in his shoulder when he swerved to avoid hitting Alia. Well, it could have been worse. He could have had to live with her the rest of his life.

Chapter Ten

"Isn't it wonderful, Letitia? Aren't you glad we convinced you to come to London?"

Guinevere leaned far out the window and gestured at the view of the city. All around were gleaming white stone buildings, interspersed with later, brightly painted wooden ones. The Basilica loomed impressively to the north, the bronze statues of the emperors and praetorians shining as if they still looked out on the vastness of the old empire. To the left was the old Mithraem. It had been cleansed of the influence of the sun-god and rededicated to Christ, but there were rumors that the old rites of Mithras still occurred there from time to time, especially during the longest of the winter nights.

"It's all just beautiful," Letitia answered. "But, Aunt Guinevere, London is so big! Doesn't it scare you a little? Why, just within the walls, there must be five thousand people living!"

"More than that, Arthur says. And, on the south side of the river are all the farms and even some villas like ours. Now you must come and see what my room overlooks; there is an old Roman garden in the courtyard with pools and fountains, and the water is still running!"

They scampered like excited children through the palace built for a long-ago governor, investigating all the rooms and trying to guess their various purposes. Guinevere was enchanted. The last time she had been to London had been for her wedding, over twenty years before, and the confusion at the time had made her memories a blur. This time they would winter here and have the freedom to wander all over the town.

"Isn't this better than being snowed in all season at Caerleon?" she asked Letitia as they went back to the balcony looking out over the city. "My wedding procession went along the Walbrook, there."

She pointed to the stream that bisected the town. "The streets were lined with people cheering, and, just to confuse me more, St. Geraldus had his choir sing a prothalamium for me. It was the only time I ever heard them. I don't know why he always complained about the sound; I thought it was beautiful."

Letitia gave her aunt a sideways glance to be sure she wasn't teasing.

"You *heard* St. Geraldus' voices? But grandmother told me they were a heavenly choir. He was so good and saintly that God sent him the voices of the angels!"

"Well, yes, that is what people said. And he was a very good man. He always took care of me as best he could. I'm sorry you're too young to remember him well. He told such wonderful stories! But as for the singers being angels, he didn't think they were, and, I must say, they didn't look very angelic to me, especially the lady in the green dress!"

"You saw them as well?" Letitia wasn't sure if she should genuflect or run for help. Aunt Guinevere looked sane enough.

Guinevere laughed at Letitia's expression.

"I always saw them. It was a long time before I found out no one else could, even Geraldus. He was a very dear person, Letitia. If people wanted to believe he heard angels, why shouldn't they? He earned his keep at every house he visited, with his stories and songs and the news he brought."

"But, if they weren't angels, what were they then?"

Guinevere shrugged. "Some of the Others, I suppose, the Old Ones like Lancelot's Lady of the Lake. I never thought about it, really. There are so many different beings around, you know."

Letitia shook her head. She did not like her childhood saints made mortal. And she definitely did not like to think about invisible "beings" wafting about her. She preferred to change the subject completely.

"Do you know what I would like to do here?" she asked. "I want to go eat at one of the inns. And I want to have my dinner in the hall with everyone else, not up in my rooms like a lady!"

She glanced at Guinevere to see if she were shocked. Her aunt laughed.

"I think that would be fun. Arthur certainly doesn't want us to become too elitist. Although you may not feel much like eating when you see the table manners of some of the Saxon traders."

"Saxons! You mean they're allowed inside the gates?"

"London is a trading town. The merchants will allow anyone in if they have something to exchange. But you have nothing to fear. Their axes are left at the gates. The city would not have survived so long if the shopkeepers here were stupid."

Letitia's eyes were wide. "I've never seen a real Saxon. After all that Grandmother has said about them, I'd just like a peek at one, but I never dared tell her. I know they killed my father, but that was in battle. He was a soldier. Mother does not hate them."

"I know. But I can't really feel comfortable around them, myself. Of course, if it hadn't been for the Saxons, I wouldn't have met Arthur."

"I never heard that story!"

"You were only a baby, and there wasn't much to it. A Saxon band kidnapped me for a few days and Arthur and his men rescued me. That's all. That's when the gatekeeper, Cheldric, lost his arm."

"But that's so romantic!"

"Is it? It didn't seem so at the time. I just remember being cold and dirty and having to eat very badly cooked meat. But if you really want to see Saxons, there are plenty in London. Some of them even speak British. But don't you get any ideas about them, my dear. It took poor Constantine long enough to make you agree to marry him. If you suddenly fall in love with a Saxon *eorl* I don't know what he'd do."

"Don't be silly, Aunt." Letitia smoothed her dress and hair as she went back into the room. "I just want to see what they're like."

"Certainly. As a matter of fact, you don't even have to go to the inn. There will be some as guests at dinner tonight."

"What! Why didn't you tell me sooner? What should I wear?"

"From my experience, I'd say that their taste was for leather and lots of gold bangles, but that really doesn't suit you. Why don't you just wear the green-and-red check with the yellow trim?"

Dubricius, Bishop of London, ran his hands through his thin, brown hair. He grimaced. Hardly enough of it left to be worth tonsuring, he thought. He spared an idle moment to wonder if it were merely a coincidence that the hair should be shaved at just the places men first go bald. But no, that was unworthy. Why should the fathers of the church have cared? Most of them didn't live long enough to worry about it, what with all the persecutions and martyrdoms. Dubricius, however, had managed to live in less dangerous times and had lasted into his fifties, an old man by most accounts. Although, he reminded himself, he wasn't much older than King Arthur. He just looked it. Lucky man, the King! Gray, of course, one couldn't expect him to avoid that, but still as shaggy as a winter ram. He could afford to shave every day, Roman fashion, without looking naked as an egg. Ah, well! God made His decisions and it wasn't the place of His servant to question them.

Dubricius returned to his records and tried not to reflect upon the wisdom of a deity who would take away a man's hair just when he needed it most to keep the cold out. He had work to do. He had to record the names of all the men he had ordained this past summer, most of them at Llanylltud Fawr. Illtud taught the boys well. Now, there was Samson, from a very devout family, and Paulus Aurelius, from a traditional one. Then there was Gildas, what was his background? Ah, yes, a son of Caius, as he remembered, not wealthy now, but good stock. The boy had a sound classical education, first from St. Docca and then St. Illtud. He should be kept in mind for advancement, perhaps for further education in Armorica.

Dubricius unrolled the scroll a little further and started recording the marriages. He hoped that his dating was right; the twenty-fourth year since Arthur's victory at Mons Badon, that everyone knew. But Dubricius wanted to go beyond Britain, show a link with the rest of Christendom. Now, was Hormisadas still Pope? The last men he had questioned had said so, but they were nearly a year out of touch with Rome. And what about that Gothic, Arian, illiterate, upstart king, Theodoric? He must be close to seventy by now. One would think that God would have rid the earth of him long ago, but those sailors had been certain that he still lived.

The bishop shook his head and dipped his quill again. It was not his place to question the ways of God. He brightened suddenly. There were, though, plenty of men he could deal with.

The knocking at the door was far too insistent to be one of his acolytes. He would have to answer it. It was his duty to minister to those who needed him, even when they arrived inconveniently. With a sigh, Dubricius put the weights on the scroll to keep the ink from smearing and then got up to admit his visitor.

"Sir Modred!" he exclaimed in surprise. "Welcome! How is the King? Does the old governor's palace meet his needs? Some parts had to be repaired last summer and you know how hard it is to duplicate the work of our ancestors."

Modred ignored his pleasantries.

"I came because of your sermon yesterday," he said. "You seem to feel that we are living in a time very dangerous to the Faith. I have been pondering your words."

Dubricius blinked. A penitent? He hadn't thought Sir Modred the type. He had been all business and little religious awe when they had planned the winter accommodations.

"Well, of course," he hedged. "Any age in which there are still people who do not profess the true faith and live by its creed is a dangerous one. But I was speaking generally, really. I had nothing specific in mind and I certainly don't agree with some of my northern brethren about King Arthur. The churches should help to pay for their own protection. And all that nonsense about his tolerance of the old religion. If we can't convert men by example and reason, then they will never be truly won. King Arthur has always been a fine example. He attends Mass almost every day, carries the image of the Holy Mother on his shield. Everyone knows that Christianity is the source of his greatness."

"Bishop, I am not accusing you of slandering the King," Modred snapped with impatience. "I seek your guidance. You spoke of the danger of our becoming contaminated by the old ways, of Christians falling back into pagan sorcery."

"Ah! Yes. That is another matter. Do you know that there are still women who make small sacrifices to the Mother Goddess in the hope of conceiving? We had the old temple to her torn down, of course, years ago, but they make little altars in their homes. And, just last month, there was a man whom I was certain was a devout Christian. We caught him and some of his friends in the church, the old temple to Mithras, you know, trying to dig out some idols that had been buried under the floor. There were statues of Mithras, Minerva, Serapis, and Mercury, and even a sacred knife, used to slaughter the sacrificial bulls. I buried them all again, put the stones back and reconsecrated the spot with the strongest of prayers. Eventually, those pagan gods will be so steeped in Christian presence that their power will be completely ended."

Modred tried not to show his contempt. "Dreadful! And what did you do to the men?"

"I chastised them very strongly and we prayed together all night. Then I ordered them to give fifty chickens and three bags of pepper each to the church as atonement for their backsliding. I was really very outraged."

Also low on pepper, Modred thought. He schooled his face to concern. "But, my Lord Bishop, what would you do if you thought someone were using the powers of the old gods to insinuate themselves into the governing of Britain, perhaps even trying to lead us all back into the darkness of those pagan times?"

He opened his eyes wide and looked pleadingly at the old man, the image of tortured uncertainty.

Dubricius ran his tongue in and out of a tooth socket. It had been pulled only recently and was still tender. It made him think before he spoke.

"That would be a very serious accusation, young man," he said slowly. "Do you have reason to believe that someone close to King Arthur is trafficking with the Old Ones *for the purpose of evil?* That is a very important distinction."

Modred bit his lip and hesitated. "I . . . I don't know. There are things about the court that I don't understand. Perhaps it is nothing, but I could never live with myself if something happened and I had done nothing to prevent it."

"Do you have any proof of your fears?"

"No, not yet." Modred was annoyed. He had expected the

old man to be panting after the heretic with little urging. He would have to contrive to get St. Caradoc down here and some of the other militant bishops.

"Then, my son, there is little we can do. If you can bring me some evidence of sorcery, then I could convene a synod of the few bishops left in Britain and some of the other saints of the church. We would then have the perpetrator brought to trial. But it is a very grave accusation. You must have proof."

"What would be the penalty for malignant witchcraft?"

Dubricius brushed up against the writing table. The paper and vellum crackled at his touch. He jumped away from it.

"It would be treason against the state as well as the church, if the old magic were invoked to aid the enemies of the King. The penalty for treason is always death."

Modred drew his breath in sharply. Dubricius assumed his reaction to be shock and patted his shoulder.

"So you see, Sir Modred, you must be very sure before you make any accusations."

"Yes, I understand. I may be mistaken, anyway. It all seems so impossible, and yet . . . I will continue my vigilance. I only hope I can be strong enough."

"The Lord will protect you."

"Thank you. I will remember that, Sir."

After he left, Dubricius tried to go back to his work. But he couldn't get the matter out of his mind. The poor boy! He was so upset. It must be someone he was fond of, but who? Not Sir Cei, certainly. Now, who else was close to Arthur? Sir Gawain and Sir Lancelot were both unusual men, but, in the case of Lancelot at least, Dubricius was sure of his religious fervor. And Gawain was Modred's own brother! Was there anyone else who could influence the King? I really don't know the people of the court that well, he mused. This winter I'll have to spend more time with them. Have a few talks with Father Antonius, too. Nice boy, though I was rather surprised when he decided to stay on at school and be ordained. I always thought he had such a rare talent for handling pigs.

Modred was not really disappointed by his first encounter

with the bishop. These things had to be done slowly. It might be a year or more before he could set the final trap. But the seed had been planted. Perhaps, if Dubricius asked him about it later, he could feign reluctance, make it appear that he was too noble to betray a friend. He had to stay in the background as much as possible or Arthur's anger would ruin his chances. It was essential that the King continue to need him.

Arthur wasn't working when Modred entered. He was sitting at the window, watching the river flow beneath. He must have known the step, for he spoke without turning.

"Do you think, Modred, that the Tamesa cares whose land she flows through? Are the Saxons less pleasing to her than we are? They used to throw bronze statues into the river as offerings, sometimes even living men. Do you think she is upset that we have stopped propitiating her?"

"Uncle, I don't think what we do matters to the river at all," he laughed. "And neither do you. The gray weather is making you morose. Let me send for some spiced apples to elevate the choler in your blood."

That broke the mood. Arthur laughed, too. "No, no. I don't need any such remedies. I was really wondering if the Grail had been found yet and sulking like a baby because I couldn't go look for it, myself. I thought coming to London would take my mind off it, but it still rankles to be left out of such an adventure. But you have nothing holding you here. Why didn't you go?"

"I prefered to stay with you, Sir." Modred was surprised at the mixed truth of the statement. He sternly repressed any liking for Arthur, but his emotion kept slipping loose.

"You needn't be so formal with me, Modred. None of your brothers are, not even Gareth, who used to jump when anyone even cleared his throat. You're not so much younger that you have to treat me like a patriarch, I hope. I don't remember, exactly. How old are you?"

"I was born in April of your seventeenth year, Sir."

"What an odd way to put it! Yes, that was just before I became leader of the armies. I didn't know, then, that I was the son of Uther Pendragon. And Merlin had me prove my-self by pulling Excalibur out of the stone. I yanked that sword out a hundred times, I think, with great, strapping men straining themselves dry to get it out in between times. It took all afternoon before everyone was convinced. It must have been more than a year later before Merlin gave me the scabbard and told me he had arranged the whole trial in the first place."

"I don't remember Merlin." And a good thing he isn't around now. "He must have been a very skillful wizard."

"I don't know. They say he did magic for my father, Uther Pendragon, but he was certainly chary enough of it with me." Arthur smiled at his memories. "He made rainbows, you know, with sunlight and pieces of glass. Except for the night he moved the Round Table into the hall, they were the closest he ever came to wizardry at Camelot. I wonder where he went."

Arthur looked at his hands as the cold light from the win-dow struck them. They were growing spotted by age. He tried to fight his depression. After all, he had done a tremen-dous amount of work in his day. There were those who in-sisted that it was only the power of his name that even now held the invaders at bay. But what use was it if the peace lasted only for his lifetime? What would become of Britain when he was gone?

"If only I had had a son," he murmured.

For a moment, he had forgotten that Modred was there and was startled when the young man knelt at his side, grip-ping at his hands as if Modred were drowning and Arthur were the shore.

"What would you say if I told you that you *do* have a son?"

Arthur tried to release him. "I would probably laugh, nephew. I have been ridiculously faithful to my wife. No one could convince me of what I haven't done."

Modred was shaking. "This is just part of the plan," he insisted to himself. "It means nothing to me!"

"There was another time, Arthur, before Guinevere. My mother told me. You stayed with St. Docca your sixteenth summer. Merlin left you there to be educated. But sometimes you became bored and wandered off on your own, into the hills. You met her there, she said, many times."

Arthur tore away, pushing the chair over as he backed off.

"How could she tell you that! I didn't know she was my sister, Modred! I was very lonely and she was just a nice woman who was lonely, too. That's all!"

"That's not all! I am what came of your loneliness!"

Arthur stared at him with dropped jaw and frozen eyes.

"I don't believe it. Morgan lied to you. You know as well as anyone what she was like. There must have been dozens of men for her that summer."

"How dare you!" Modred raised his fist to strike. Arthur's hand automatically went to his knife belt. Then he drew it away. Modred lowered his hand.

"I'm sorry." Arthur's voice was quiet. "She *was* your mother. But what you're telling me cannot be true! It was bad enough to learn she was my sister. Do you know how I've suffered for my unwitting sin?"

"You!" Modred choked. "Do you know how *I* have suffered for your sin? To know my father and not be able to name him? At least here, alone, you could acknowledge me. What have I done that you should deny me? I was not an accomplice to my conception. Look at me!"

He moved to the window. The winter clouds diffused the light so that it was clean and sharp, etching his features clearly.

"Look at my face, Arthur, and tell me again that I'm lying! Look at my hands, at the cut of my nose. It's not from Morgan that these come. They are in your image, my Lord. You may close your eyes but they are still the same color as mine. I am your only begotten son!"

Slowly, Arthur moved toward him. He looked at Modred a long time.

"Yes, yes," faintly. "I can see it. It's true. Oh, my son! I'm so sorry. She never told me. For your sake, as well as my own, I can't give you the place of honor you should have. I'm sorry! But here, now, I do own you mine. Modred!"

He reached out and clasped Modred in his arms.

With disgust, Modred thought, "Good lord! The old man's crying."

Then, with horror, he realized that he was, too.

"You're very quiet tonight, Arthur." Guinevere was washing her face in almond milk. "Did anything go wrong today? You haven't heard anything about Galahad, have you?"

"No, nothing from any of the Grail knights yet. I was just thinking. I'm growing older. There's no one now prepared to follow me as king. I should be training someone to take my place. I shouldn't think I'll live forever."

"I don't see why not." Guinevere rinsed her face and groped for a towel. "I can't imagine us dying!"

He looked at her, damp curls about her face. She was as young and beautiful as she had been on their wedding night. Old? How could he be with a wife like that? He laughed, putting aside until tomorrow his fear and his thoughts of Modred. He picked Guinevere up by the waist and swung her around and around until they fell dizzily to the bed.

"I can't imagine our dying either, my love. I don't think we ever will!"

Chapter Eleven

"This ought to be the right road to Llanylltud Fawr," Lancelot grumbled. "If 'road' is the word for it. The hermit was very clear about it."

"If you mean throwing rocks at us and yelling 'Just follow the trail, you idiots!' was clear, then I guess so." Gareth rubbed his shoulder. He couldn't duck as quickly as Lancelot.

As if to confirm this, a branch slapped him in the face as they picked their way down the overgrown path.

"We'll probably get there and find a wide, Roman highway running up to the gate, just to the left of this rabbit track," Gareth complained. "You can be sure that all those lords and bishops don't come this way when they visit their children there. Do you really think St. Illtud can tell us anything about the Grail?"

Lancelot took out his sword to slash through a tangle of morning glories, looked at the frail petals and changed his mind. He wormed his way around them, instead.

"Father Antonius said St. Illtud had books which mentioned it. That could help us. He also knows more about the world than most of the saints. He was a soldier under Uther Pendragon and then Arthur before he decided to forsake earthly satisfaction. Anyway, we have to start somewhere."

It was an unarguable statement. But Gareth wished they could find a better road. He was beginning to feel like a wild man of the woods, with leaves and bark sticking to his hair and skin.

"Gareth, do you hear that?" Lancelot stopped and looked around. Gareth cocked his head.

"The wind in the trees . . . Wait, is that someone *singing?*"

It might have been; it was a kind of high, irregular keening, really. It could have been a bird or cat, but there seemed to be words to it. Gareth shuddered. It was the sort of sound one of his Aunt Morgause's creatures would make. He tried to decide which direction the noise was coming from, with the firm intention of going the other way, when he remembered that he was a knight.

"It's coming from over here." Lancelot's voice sounded somewhere to his right. "And here's a footpath. This way, Gareth!"

Gareth tied his horse next to Lancelot's and followed him. The singing surrounded him, and with every step he grew more terrified. But he had vowed never to desert Lancelot, whatever happened, and this promise kept him moving.

They rounded a bend and Lancelot stopped, causing Gareth to stumble into him. He righted himself and made to draw his sword when he realized that Lancelot was laughing. He looked around his friend's shoulder.

There was a tiny clearing that contained a proportionally small daub-and-wattle hut. Outside the hut was a large dome oven. From the oven protruded the clothed legs and bottom of a woman. And, from the woman, echoing through the stone, came the noise.

Lancelot rushed forward and dragged her out. Her arms appeared, waving a scrubbing brush and ineffectually trying to hit out at her rescuer. Lancelot set her gently on the ground.

"I've nothing for you to steal, young man, not even virtue." She scowled at the tall knight. "And I warn you, if you're the sort who takes delight in tormenting an old woman, I'd make poor sport. And I can still scratch and gouge with the best!"

She backed off a step and lifted her clawed hands in defiance.

Gareth was choking on his laughter. This old stick-figure of a woman facing up to the greatest warrior in Britain was too much for him. But Lancelot's face was grave. He bowed to the woman.

"I beg your pardon, Lady. We thought you were in need of our help. I did not mean to insult you with my touch."

The woman inspected Lancelot warily, then lowered her arms.

"I daresay that from a man like you, it would be no insult. Ah! If I were only fifty again. Well, it's not about to happen in this life. So, what brings two men from Arthur's court to travel on this end-of-everything road?"

"You know of Arthur?" Gareth doubted she knew her own name.

"Know of him! I wiped his bottom before he learned what a privy was for! Such a howling, red-headed baby he was.

There was never any doubt who sired him! Don't pretend you believe me. I see it in your faces you think I'm lying. It's all one to me. I suppose you've come to see that bastard husband of mine, Illtud. Well, you've taken the wrong road, but I'll put you on the right one. Come along!"

She started back up the path but the two men stood in the clearing, rooted by surprise.

"Lady, wait!" Lancelot called. "Please, could we have a cup of water before we go? I have some figs in my pack I would be honored to have you share."

She turned around with a grin and came back.

"You don't fool me with your figs. You want to hear my story. Go on! Go and get them and you'll hear it. The more as know about old Illtud, the better, as far as I'm concerned."

She settled herself on a tree stump and waited while Lancelot fetched the fruit and Gareth the water. When they were all seated she tore off a piece of fig and popped it into her mouth, where it squished from side to side on her toothless gums throughout her tale.

"Illtud was a soldier when I married him, a fine lad in Uther's army, and I was a servant to the Queen Igraine. Poor, dear lady. When the baby was born, Master Merlin had it put about that he had died at birth and the tiny thing was taken from his own sad mother and given to me to suckle until he could be spirited away. I had lost my own child in the usual way, a fever and then a fit. I kept him hidden six long months while Illtud was off fighting. Then Merlin came for him, and it wasn't until years later, when I saw Arthur again, at the head of his soldiers, that I knew what had happened to him.

"But you wanted to know about Illtud, didn't you?"

Gareth was still trying to digest the first part of the tale but Lancelot nodded.

"We only know of him because of his school. I had heard he was a soldier from Armorica but I know little else of his history."

The fig switched sides again. The woman continued.

"He was trained in Armorica, but came to Britain as a

young man. He was a fine soldier, and in my ignorance I thought he was a good husband, too. Didn't he get me with child in our first month? Such a fool I was!

"After Uther died and before Arthur, Illtud fought for whoever would pay. He went back to Armorica for a while. It was there he turned Christian." She spat out the husk of the fig. "I'd like to wring the neck of the man who converted him."

"Lady!"

"Don't take that tone with me, young man. I know what I say. At first he was content to give away our property and have me tilling the fields like a common slave. That was shameful enough. Then one day, he just decided to leave the court at Caerleon with a few of his friends and wander into the mountains in search of true enlightenment and 'Christian' denial. Well, I was a good wife. I set out with him. The very first night, though, I learned just what he had decided to deny himself. In the middle of the night, mind you, he wakes me up and tells me to get him some water. So, simpleton that I was, I went. When I got back, he was rolled up tight as an oyster in the blankets and wouldn't let me back in! Called me filth and temptation and ordered me to leave him! There I was, alone on the edge of nowhere in the dark, wearing nothing but my shift. He relented enough to allow me to stay the night at the edge of the camp. Then he announced that he was going to live a holy life and devote himself to the contemplation of God and the education of young boys. So, finally, I began to understand. And all that time I had just thought he was a wonderfully faithful husband!"

"Surely you wrong him, Lady," Lancelot protested. "He may have only come to a realization of the decadence of his old life and wished, though cruelly to you, to be rid of all of it."

She gave him a contemptuous stare. "So you're another one of them, are you?"

But one of what she didn't say.

Gareth was more sympathetic. He had never been ensnared by religious worries.

"Why do you stay here, then, so close to him? Surely there must be somewhere else where they would take you in."

She looked at him for the first time.

"Goodness, I thought you were his shadow! You can speak, too, can you? Yes, I suppose I could have gone to friends, but I was too proud to show myself after having been treated so badly. I was angry, too. I still am. I vowed to sit on his doorstep and remind him every day of the wrong he'd done me. After a few years, that became too much bother. I felt like a leper at the gates. So, I got a few of his students to build me this hut and I kept bees to make honey for them. Oh, does that irritate the old goat! When they're sick of dried peas and water, the boys sneak down here for a treat. Poor lads! Some of them are as little as seven when they're left here. How could a mother do it? If my son had lived, I'd never have let him away from my arm's reach. So, I give them a little cosseting and some sweets and they're the better for it. And I do so love to make my Illtud mad!"

She laughed and slapped her thighs. Gareth laughed too.

"It doesn't sound, Lancelot, as if *Saint* Illtud will be able to tell you about the Grail, after all," he said.

But Lancelot was grave. His thoughts were not at the moment on the Grail.

"Lady," he asked. "After all he did to you, do you still care about St. Illtud?"

She grinned at him. "You think I'm still pining for his love? No, dearie, I still miss the man he once was, or what I thought he was. But, no, the man he is now is nothing to me. I think I even hate him for killing the Illtud I did love. Now do you want to go meet him and find out if he's as wicked as I said?"

"I only wish to seek information about the Grail," but Lancelot couldn't look at her directly.

"Of course, of course." She got up and motioned for them to follow. "I'll put you on the right path. It's not far. If you're meaning to stay there long, come back and see me. I'll see that you get some decent food. A grown man will starve on what those boys have to eat."

They thanked her and, after getting the horses, set off in the direction she pointed. The road became smoother and better-kept and soon they were in sight of the cluster of huts and halls that made up Llanylltud Fawr. From the larger building came the chanting of recitations as the youngest boys struggled with the Old Latin necessary to understand the Gospels and the Commentaries. Older boys were tilling plots of land around the compound and others were running races around the church. If wealthy parents were pouring gifts into the place, it didn't show.

There was no gate, but a young priest stopped them as they entered the area and directed them first to the stable and then to the hut of the saint.

They were announced by the priest and entered the small building. The only light was from a hole cut in the wall and covered with waxed linen, giving the room a soft, beige tint. Against one curving wall was a narrow straw-mattressed bed covered with a thin blanket. At the foot was a battered wooden chest. The rest of the room was taken up by a large table, overflowing with books, scrolls, and loose vellum. Wedged next to it was a tall writing table and, behind that, sat St. Illtud.

Gareth had not decided what he should expect the saint to look like, between the tales from his former pupils and the story his wife had told. He wasn't ready for a mild-eyed elderly man, with white hair falling to his shoulders behind the tonsure which went across the top of his head from ear to ear. Illtud was emaciated from long fasting but still straight. He held out his hands to them.

"Sir Lancelot! I am exceedingly pleased to welcome you! Your pilgrimage to the shrine of St. Martin is well known here. It is good to know that a man of strength can also be a man of God!"

Lancelot knelt and kissed the old man's hand. Gareth waited, as usual, to be noticed. Illtud smiled at him.

"And you, I think, are one of Morgan Le Fay's sons?

· 107 ·

Gareth is it? I was there when you and your brother Gaheris were baptized. A very brave thing for you to do, considering your family."

He had had more to fear from the weather that day, Gareth recalled. Even with the curtains around the font, standing naked in a freezing pool of water while more was poured over one's head was an insane thing to do in the middle of January. He tried to remember how Gaheris had talked him into it.

But he only mumbled, "Thank you, Sir."

Illtud continued beaming on them. "I can't believe that you have come to me for instruction in holy orders. Have you brought a message from my old master, Arthur?"

Lancelot rose. "No, Father, we are on a quest for an object called the Grail. It has an ancient and mysterious past and we are hoping that you can tell us more of what it is and where we can find it. Have you heard of it?"

"Perhaps." Illtud's wrinkles drew together in thought. "It sounds familiar; something known but not orthodox. I will have some of my students consult the writings. It's not Arian, is it? I'll have none of that sort of heresy in my school!"

"No, Sir. It is British or Irish, we think." And Lancelot went on to explain about Percival and Cundrie, the Fisher King and the overwhelming experience of the covered Grail.

"Very well. Father Samson!" he called to a man outside. "Please take these knights to a place where they can wash and rest. It may take a few days, Sir Lancelot. I hope you will be content to abide with us that long. Perhaps you and Sir Gareth would enjoy a different, simpler life for a time?"

"Thank you. We would be honored." Lancelot bowed and they left, following Father Samson to another wattle building, only slightly more comfortably arranged than Illtud's.

Gareth looked around. "You know I want to help you find the Grail, Lancelot, and this isn't the worst place I've ever slept. But if we have to live on dried pea soup and water for very long, I may gladly disavow that baptism."

Fortunately for Gareth's faith, the meal that night contained bread, cheese, eggs, and wine, as well as fish in a sauce of beans and herbs. Illtud sat with them, but ate only a little bread and sipped a cup of watered ale. He had no information yet on the Grail but was happy to tell them of the school and how it had grown over the years, what fine scholars they had and how many of them had decided to stay on and become priests after the term of education was finished. He said nothing about his life before Llanylltud Fawr, and Gareth, though bursting to ask, found no good point in the conversation to do so.

They prepared for bed in the late summer twilight, the wind in the trees reminding Gareth of the sound of waves on the rocks at Tintagel. He wondered how Agravaine was managing in his effort to reorganize the place and if old Lot had bothered to come back, now that Morgan was gone. Or perhaps Lot had died. Gareth had had no word from him in years, but then, that was no surprise. Not many people thought to send messages to Gareth. He lay down on the straw mattress and reflected that he indeed had known worse. As he fell asleep, he imagined the mighty adventures they would have as soon as St. Illtud found something in his books for Lancelot to follow.

Lancelot lay stiffly on his bed, waiting for Gareth's breathing to deepen into snores. He listened to the gradual silencing of voices about the school; a short exchange between two of the priests, some muffled laughter from the boy's hut followed by a sharp admonition; an atonal singing from a man checking the animals for the night. It was so orderly here, so calm. In a place like this, a person might find a kind of peace within himself. A person might even begin to unravel the confusion and discover the true reason for his life.

The stars were out as Lancelot slipped from under the blanket and out of the hut. Inside, Gareth was happily engaged in vanquishing five Saxon warriors and a small dragon.

The glow of the oil lamp by the altar guided him to the tiny church. He slipped in and stood in the darkest corner, his hands raised in submissive, lonely prayer.

When he finished, it was deep into night. The moon was

new and the stars glittered on him like splinters of glass. His eyes burned under their gaze, and he nearly tripped over St. Illtud, sitting on the ground by the door.

"I beg your forgiveness, Sir." Lancelot stepped back. "Would I be intruding, if I sat awhile with you?"

The old man shook his head.

"I have wanted to talk with you for some time, now. We are not so out of the world here that many rumors about Arthur and the people around him have not found their way to our gates. You are mentioned quite frequently, and I have long wanted to meet the man who left the enchanted realm of the Lady of the Lake. It is a place many men would happily trade their souls to visit, they say."

"I was not suited to the Lake," Lancelot replied with sadness. "I came searching a salvation which my foster mother cannot understand."

"So the Lady truly did raise you! How incredible!" Illtud smiled. "And yet, if the gossip is true, you would throw away your hope of salvation in an adulterous love."

Lancelot froze at the mild voice. He wanted to strike the man. What business was it of his, of anyone's? He lashed back:

"What kind of salvation did you find, abandoning the woman lawfully bound to you to starve or be enslaved?"

"Ah, I thought you might have met her. I have no doubt that she told you the truth. I did not treat her kindly. At that time I was ablaze with the fervor of my calling and I was harsh with her, as with myself. In order to find God, my son, one must put aside the temptations of the flesh and cast away those things which turn one to this insignificant life."

"But do you never long for her, not even in the night when there is nothing between the memory of her and your heart? Don't you ever wake up suddenly, believing you felt her breath on your shoulder and her hair across your body? How can you see God, when she stands before you, so radiant that you are blinded to everything else?"

His voice had risen to a point close to hysteria, and Illtud laid his hands on Lancelot's shoulders.

"If she keeps you from finding God, then she is evil, and must be ripped from your life as one would cut out a malignant growth! Your lust for this woman has bewitched you! As long as you are too weak to break free of her, you will be stained, no matter what good works you perform or how perfect your devotions may be. If you continue this liaison with your lord's wife, even in your heart, you will never find the Grail!"

"You do know about the Grail!"

"A little. Enough to know that it will not be revealed to a man who places the desires of his body above his immortal soul."

"You don't understand. I did not ask to love her, nor did she seek me out. I have tried for years to destroy what I feel. My journey to Tours, to the shrine of St. Martin, was only one attempt. If I lived a hundred years without even hearing word of her, I would still hold her with me, always in my heart. How can you renounce your own heart?"

Illtud absently patted the hunched shoulder. He knew what he ought to say, but the truth was, he had not found it so hard to cast his wife out. It was no more trouble for him to abstain from sex than from strong drink. And it had been easy to lose the little affection he had for her when she taunted him constantly at his very door. He had more trouble finding the charity to forgive her than the strength to renounce her.

"It has been said, Sir Lancelot, that the more difficult the task, the greater the reward. It appears to me that a great many things come easily to you. You may pride yourself on denying your body rest and sustinance. But these are only outward forms of inward submission. And there is no place for any sort of pride in Our Lord's house. You must train your thoughts to God or you will be forever shackled to the earth with no more soul than that Lady who raised you. Cast this Guinevere from your life and welcome in the Faith which is greater than all earthly love!"

Slowly, Lancelot raised his head. Tears ran down his cheeks as he gripped St. Illtud's arms as if they were the only things keeping him from falling into an abyss. Illtud winced, but did not attempt to throw him off. Lancelot's eyes bored into the old man as he made his vow.

"With your help, good Saint, I will!"

In her elegant room in London, Guinevere cried out in her sleep and clung to Arthur, who held her softly, whispering assurance, all the while knowing her fear was not for him.

Chapter Twelve

Gawain arrived in London well before winter set in. He was the first of the knights to return and had to suffer the indignity of failure as well as the laughter at his misadventure with the sword over the bed and the girl in it. Durriken was already hard at work composing a tale with a rollicking enough meter to convey the outrageous silliness of the episode. Added to this was the undeniable fact that Gawain in the winter was never terribly alert. Even the allure of the city women was not enough to cheer him. Therefore, he spent most of the short afternoon hours sitting with Guinevere, the two of them seated on cushions on the floor, staring at the gray sky and wondering.

"He was well when you left him?" she asked for the thousandth time.

"He was well and eager to be off on the search. He told me he need not send you his love because all he had was left in your keeping," Gawain replied for the thousandth time.

"Gareth seemed pleased that I was not going with them," he added.

"Gareth doesn't like me," Guinevere said. Her voice was puzzled. Everyone liked her.

"He is a strange man. I don't understand what he wants. I think he is simply jealous of those who might take something of Lancelot from him."

"Then he should hate us all—Arthur, you, me, Galahad."

Gawain shrugged. "Perhaps he does." He thought a moment. "No, I'm being unfair to him. Gareth really is unhappy with himself. He wants to be a great knight. And, if he can't be, then he wants his hero to be perfect."

"Lancelot is perfect. Where do you think Galahad is now? Is he warm and fed and safe? Palomides wouldn't let anyone hurt him, would he?"

And the pattern of responses started again.

The London winter was not as exciting as Guinevere had planned. Even the pleasure of arranging the wedding between Constantine and Letitia was not as enjoyable as she had thought. There was something going on which she couldn't understand. People seemed to edge away from her when she sat by them. Whispers followed her through the corridors. The indulgent smiles which had always greeted her were thinner, as if painted on at the last minute. Only her oldest friends were the same: Cei, Lydia, Risa, and Gawain, of course. There weren't so many now. Time and the Grail had moved them from her. But why? What was happening? She hurried to the dining hall one evening, late again. The blank stares which greeted her as she entered frightened her. She stumbled as she climbed the dais. Modred caught her by the arm and smiled encouragingly. She took a deep breath and smiled back. At least he was unchanged. Such a nice man! And so good for Arthur! They had been almost inseparable lately.

The first snow was settling on the city that night and Arthur, Cei, and Modred were having a friendly game of dice by the fire, with Constantine watching. Letitia was comparing fabrics for her wedding robes with Risa and Lydia. Guinevere was staring into the flames, longing again for word of Lancelot and Galahad. There was a knock at the door, which she ignored. Someone was always coming to Arthur or Cei for advice. Risa looked up.

"Why, Gareth! What are you doing back?" she cried.

Guinevere froze. She couldn't find the courage to turn and look. Arthur leapt up.

"You look half-dead, man! What happened to you? Where is Lancelot?"

Gareth dropped into the chair Cei brought. His face was gray with fatigue and his cloak filthy and soaked with melting snow. He bent over and hid his face in his hands.

"Lancelot sent me away!" he said to the floor. "Can I have some wine? I'm so awfully cold."

"What did you do?" Modred asked. "Run at the first sight of danger?"

Gareth straightened at the sneer.

"I did nothing! It was that Illtud. And even more than St. Illtud, it was her!"

He pointed stiffly at Guinevere, who still hadn't moved. Arthur brought the wine and gave it to Gareth.

"Drink that and then tell us what you mean," he said sternly and Gareth remembered that Arthur was a warrior even more than a king. He gulped down the contents of the cup.

"Lancelot can't find the Grail because *she* is holding him away from it. Illtud told him that until he renounces everything of the earth, he will never be pure enough to find it. So he's staying the winter at Llanylltud Fawr, doing penance for his sins, he says. Then he's going out to seek the Grail and, whatever he finds, he's never coming back. It's all your doing, Guinevere. He has nothing to repent of, nothing! You seduced him and now he's sitting naked in the snow and living on crusts to pay for it! You drove him mad once before, wasn't that enough? Now you've driven him away forever! He doesn't dare even look at you again! How can you sit there and . . ."

It was Arthur who hit him, but only because the other men were too far away. The chair tipped over and Gareth lay sprawled on the floor, weeping out his anger and grief. If only Lancelot had let him stay. He wouldn't have minded the cold or the long hours of prayer or even the dismal food. But Lancelot listened only to Illtud, now. He had no need of insignificant Gareth. He had spoken so kindly, telling him to go on with the search. "I am not worthy, yet. I should not keep you from the quest because of my sinfulness." As if Gareth cared a damn about the Grail!

Cei and Constantine lifted him up and dragged him from the room. He could see that Guinevere had still not even looked at him. What did she care? She had a husband. She could have a hundred other men. She had only taken Lancelot because he was the best of them all, and she had destroyed him.

Guinevere still stared into the fire, now broken by her tears into a million searing points. She felt Risa's arms go about her, gently urging her to rise. She was too numb to do more than succumb to the pressure. Her mind was whirling. She looked to Arthur.

"Is it true?" she whispered. "Do you believe I have done this?"

"Never," he answered firmly. But she noticed the second of hesitation. It stabbed her with a suddenness that nearly felled her.

"Risa, will you help me prepare for bed?" she asked. "I think I will say good night now."

They all stood as she left and then looked at one another. There seemed nothing safe to say. Constantine took Letitia's hand. She leaned against him, burying her face in the folds of his tunic. Lydia and Cei went to either side of Arthur, as if to protect him. Modred stood by the table, apart from the others, watching through narrowed eyes. It was as if the gods had planned it all for him. Now he only had to be wise enough to take what they offered and shape it to his own ends.

The floor in Guinevere's room was warm. It was an old building, with hypocausts at the corners to send hot air under the buildings. Ordinarily, she luxuriated in the heat, unknown at either Camelot or Caerleon, but tonight it stifled her. She sat at the dressing table as Risa combed and braided her hair for the night. With great effort, she managed to hold still, all but her hands, which cupped each other over and over as if something precious were contained in them and in danger of slipping away.

Risa combed slowly, watching the pure gold of Guinevere's hair glitter in the lamplight. That Gareth! Always needing to blame someone when he couldn't have his own way.

"You mustn't believe him, my Lady, dear," she emphasized with a tug on the braid she was plaiting. "Lancelot may be overly zealous in his search for God, but he could never abandon you and King Arthur for it. He'll be back in the summer, just as he said."

"No." Guinevere dropped the word into her hands. "Something is wrong in the world. Everything is coming undone. I've felt it ever since we came to London. He won't come back."

Risa said no more as she finished the braids. She was worried. Guinevere was right about something being amiss. There were rumors crawling around London, tales with distorted faces that whispered lies about Guinevere, lies just close enough to the truth to make them believable.

"My poor lady," Risa thought. "What's she ever done but be beautiful and innocent and fall in love with a man not her husband? As if they've had more than a night or two together in fifteen long years! And now they're saying she lured Sir Lancelot with black magic and holds Arthur captive with it, too. If she were anyone but the Queen no one would care at all. I've had five children by three different men." She paused and counted on her fingers. "Three? Yes, I'm sure Liagh is Cheldric's, too. And there was hardly a raised eyebrow about the court. It's that Modred's doing! I know it, even if they won't believe me. He wants me to meet him again tonight, and won't I work on him until he tells me what he has planned to hurt my dear Guinevere!"

Her resolve comforted her and she finished her work briskly and left. Guinevere remained on her stool, staring into the hand mirror and wondering wistfully why people didn't seem to like her anymore.

Percival was not having the quest he expected with Palomides and Galahad. Like Gareth, he had hoped for a dragon or hideous monster to slay, thereby winning the praise of the people and the glory of the heavens. At least they could have ridden heroically through the countryside, armour shining and plumes waving, as Lancelot had when Percival first saw him. At the *very* least they could be actively searching for the Grail, grimly following up every slender trail and clue.

So why was he out in the autumn wind, with only his tunic and trews on, straddling the point of a decrepit old hut, owned by an even more decrepit old man, waiting for Palomides to toss up fresh thatch bundles to mend the roof? From below, he could hear Galahad's laughter as he slipped in the mud, sending the reeds flying. The old man grumbled and Galahad laughed again.

"Have patience with me, Father! I'll learn this craft yet and we'll have you dry and warm for the winter, won't we, Palomides?"

"For certain!" Palomides grinned at the boy's filthy clothes. "Another day or two, at most, and we'll be finished. If we had not had your good teaching, Father, we would still be wondering how such thin pieces of stem could hold off the rain and snow. Our thanks to you!"

Percival shivered. Thanks! Little thanks he would get for slicing his fingers and freezing his rear off up here. How could those two stay so cheerful? From the very beginning they had acted as if they had been just set free. They began by overpaying everywhere for their meals and lodging. And, when the money was gone, they gave away their rings and cloak pins. Then, as it began to grow colder, they gave away their cloaks. And always with delight, as if casting off chains instead of throwing away the most precious things they owned.

When Palomides' sword broke as he tried to pry up a stone to fix a wall, he and Galahad exchanged a look of excited glee. The shorter lever proved better at dislodging the stone.

"Brilliant!" Galahad cried, and proceeded to break the tip off his sword and continue with the work.

"How can you do this?" Percival asked them one night as the three of them huddled in an abandoned stable eating an inadequate dinner. "We're going to starve or freeze to death at this rate, and there's no way we'll ever find the Grail."

"But, Percival!" Galahad gestured with his loaf. "We're getting ready to find it now. In another week or two . . ."

"Or year or two," Palomides added. They both laughed.

"I'm sorry, lad," Palomides continued. "Galahad and I are not taking this quest as seriously as we should. I know how important it is, not only for the wounds of the Fisher King and the enchantment on his daughter, but for all the world. And yet, every day we've been on this journey, I've felt closer and closer to something wonderful. We're doing what we should be and I've never been so happy and contented in all my life."

Galahad, chewing on the dry bread complacently, nodded his agreement.

"Just think of all the things we've learned and all the roofs and walls we've mended and wheat harvested between here and Camelot. And since we gave our horses to that poor trader we've been completely free! Can't you feel it, Percival?"

"All I can feel is cold, wet, hungry, and thwarted," Percival burst out. "We have a mission to follow and we've done nothing so far. It's all very well to play at charity, but . . ."

"Charity?" Palomides and Galahad looked at each other. "Do you think we shouldn't have taken any?"

"It seemed to make those people feel good to give us some food and a place to sleep while we fixed their homes." Galahad scrunched his face in thought. "I don't see that there was anything wrong in it. Perhaps he means that we shouldn't have burdened others with our possessions."

"No!" Percival shouted. "Can't you understand?"

Apparently they couldn't. They settled down into their sodden sleeping spaces as happily as if in their mother's arms. Percival spent the long night counting the drips as they thunked onto his blanket and wondering why he couldn't decide to leave these madmen to their delusion.

For the next few days, Palomides and Galahad were eager to defer to Percival's wishes. When he offered a suggestion for an area to search, they agreed and followed along, almost as if they were humoring him. They continued until he suggested that they stop and then waited for him to make ready to start again. Percival knew that this couldn't be the right way to go about it and that someone else was sure to discover the castle of the Fisher King long before they did. Yet, slowly, the joy radiated by the other two was beginning to warm him and he could not go out again on his own.

It was a dark afternoon in late winter. They had eaten nothing that day. A sharp wind sliced through them as they made their way along the road. Galahad was shivering and his lips were blue, but he seemed not to notice. Palomides had given the boy his blanket to wrap around his shoulders and now walked with his hands in his armpits in an effort to keep warm. Percival brought up the rear. His father's sword still hung at his side. In his present state, the weight of it was draining him and he wondered how much longer he would last.

Over the wind, they could hear the roar of an angry river. Percival's heart sank. They could not ford it; they had no payment for the ferryman, even supposing there was one. He was so worn that he didn't even realize that tears were sliding down his face, leaving brief trails of warmth on his cheeks.

The other two saw the water before he did. Galahad threw the blanket high in the air, leapt up after it and landed in Palomides' arms. As Percival approached, they were jumping up and down and hugging each other. The bewildered Percival was swept up in their excitement.

"Is it the castle?" he cried as he struggled to get free enough to see what had set them off.

When he saw it, he blinked several times and then rubbed his eyes.

Sitting calmly upon the raging river, riding gently in place as the current dashed against it, was a delicate boat. It was shaped of dark wood, highly polished and carved. On its deck was a tent of tanned leather and silk and the single sail billowing over it was of bright blue satin. If Percival had known anything about boats, he would have noted that this one had no rudder. At the moment, he was thinking only of how nice it would be to get out of the wind. He wondered if the owner of the boat would let them rest there a while.

Palomides and Galahad were already racing down to the riverbank. The boat lay only a few feet out in the water. They stood admiring it until Percival caught up with them.

"Isn't she beautiful!" Palomides roared over the wind.

"Better than anything I imagined," Galahad agreed.

"Wait a minute!" Percival panted. "Is the owner there? Do you think he can hear us if we call?"

"Oh, there's no one aboard the boat," Galahad told him. "It's for us, to go find the Grail in."

"Galahad!" Percival exploded. "Even I am not that unworldly. We can't steal a boat, especially one like this. Explain it to him, Palomides."

"Do you think it will come closer if we ask it?" Palomides wondered.

Percival stared at him. Then he gave up. Better all be mad together than face the loneliness of solitary sanity.

"Boat! Oh, Boat!" he called, feeling a complete idiot. "Will you allow us to sail in you?"

Obligingly, the boat glided in until it was almost touching the bank. Galahad looked at the pristine elegance of it and carefully removed his muddy boots before he stepped aboard. The others followed.

Once they entered the tent, they felt the shifting as the boat began to move. Percival had a second of panic but the sight of a table surrounded by soft cushions and piled high with warm food blotted out any other consideration. The three of them sat down to eat. Before they began, though, Galahad called out to the air.

"Our thanks, kind benefactor. We place ourselves at your disposal and will go wherever your pleasure is to take us."

They thought then that they heard the sound of small bells and laughter, but it faded quickly and they settled in to the dinner. Afterwards they lay down where they had sat and slept.

Percival woke first. He could feel the swift flow of the water beneath him. Light the color of autumn grain suffused the tent and warmed his body. He did not want to roll over and get up. This was the most comfortable he had been since they left Camelot. He burrowed farther into the cushions.

"Good morning, Cousin."

The gentle voice set him bolt upright. Seated on a little stool near the entrance to the tent was a smiling young woman.

"Shall we wait for Sir Galahad and Sir Palomides to awaken before we eat, or are you too hungry to wait? It makes no difference. I can summon more hot food for them later."

"N-n-no," Percival managed. "I can wait. Who . . . who are you? How did you get here?"

The woman laughed. "I was sent for all of you, Sir Percival. I am Claris, the daughter of your father's elder brother. Cundrie is my aunt. Your companions, by their deeds and by the love in their hearts, have proved themselves worthy of the Grail and, by staying by them, you have earned your patrimony. Therefore, I shall take you all to the castle of our grandfather, the Fisher King."

Chapter Thirteen

Lancelot of the Lake, son of King Ban of Banoit, adopted child of the rarest lady of fantasy and the most illustrious knight of the Round Table, lay in his hut at Llanylltud Fawr and tried not to think of the woman he loved. He had starved his body, frozen it, beaten it, allowed it to become crusted with filth and grime. But his mind was cheating. Whenever he let it free from perpetual prayer, it thought of Guinevere. And his tired, battered, emaciated flesh would respond with longing. He pounded his fists against the wall. Would nothing but death release him?

St. Illtud paused in his evening rounds. Poor Sir Lancelot! He set his jaw. This wouldn't do any longer. He was demoralizing the boys. It irked him considerably to admit defeat, but it was obvious that the traditional methods of rendering the body subservient to the spirit were not going to work here. He squared his stooped shoulders and went to the hut.

Lancelot stood respectfully as Illtud entered. The saint stepped back a pace. This was definitely not the odor of sanctity.

"My son," he said sadly. "I have meditated long on your problem and I have come to the sorry conclusion that you cannot remain at Llanylltud Fawr. You have done everything I have told you. You have been an obedient student, St. Anthony and St. Simon would be proud of you. But your inner turmoil is just too strong." He coughed repeatedly as Lancelot moved closer. "As I was saying, too strong to be in close contact with the young minds and souls entrusted to my care. In short, you are frightening the little ones."

Lancelot sank down, his head nearly resting on his knees. His worn voice, even more than his appearance, smote the old man.

"What am I to do, then? Where am I to go?"

"Perhaps your salvation lies out in the world after all, my son. We must have faith that there is a reason for everything. You may find when you return to Camelot that you no longer have any feeling for the Queen but that of friendship."

He stopped as Lancelot's eyes fixed his.

"Perhaps not. But you must continue. If you remain as you are here, you cannot hope to live much longer and that will not help you. You will have died for love, not religion. Please, Sir Lancelot, go back! Take up the search for the Grail again. Your suffering may have been enough to earn it. If you no longer have the heart for that, might you consider going back to your father's land?"

"Banoit? I don't even remember where it is, only that Meleagant's father, Claudas, conquered it long ago, when he killed my father."

"One of the young men here is named Bors. He says that he is connected to your family in some way. He has told me that there is a fortress in the mountains of Banoit that has lain abandoned since your father died. There are those who would be joyful if his son came back to it. Bors has offered to accompany you there. He has no vocation for the priesthood. He has been promised to the daughter of an old friend and is eager to go home and begin the secular life. Shall I tell him you will go?"

"Yes." A little more strongly, "Yes. I would like to see Banoit. I wonder if there is anyone still alive who remembers my father. But first I suppose I should wash and trim my nails and beard."

Illtud clapped his hands. "Good! I mean, I'm sorry I couldn't help you, but there is more than one path to salvation. You may find yours in Banoit. Now, it's not the regular night for bathing, but I'm sure that we can arrange something for you. I'll send Father Eulogius to shave you and cut your hair. No, no, he won't mind at all. He does all our tonsuring. His great-grandfather was barber to the proconsul. No, it's not too late. He'll still be praying in the church. Don't worry about anything, Sir Lancelot. I feel we've failed you here. We can, at least, help prepare you to return to the world."

Two days later, a pale and gaunt but very clean Lancelot left Llanylltud Fawr. His sword and shield, tarnished by neglect, hung from Clades' saddle. Bors, a cheerful young man of well-educated morals, rode next to him. For the first few days, Lancelot drifted within himself, speaking little, ignoring the land around them. Then he started to straighten. His hands began to curl as if they remembered the feel of the sword. One night, he took it from its scabbard and, with a corner of his spare wool tunic, began polishing it.

He spoke to Bors without looking at him, the fire glowing between them.

"I have never seen anyone from Banoit at Arthur's court, Bors. I didn't know there was anyone of my family still there."

"We are not easily destroyed, kinsman. But we do not go to Camelot. Arthur is not our king. We owe tribute to Meleagant from his father's defeat of King Ban, but he learned long ago not to intrude upon us too far. He is not of our tribe and he can no more truly conquer us than the Romans could."

"Arthur is High King for all of Britain, for everyone. He pays no attention to the old tribes. He has united the whole island south of Hadrian's wall. Under him we are one people," Lancelot insisted.

The young man sighed. Illtud had taught him not to contradict his elders. But Lancelot should know what Banoit was like, today.

"Arthur should pay attention to the tribes, kinsman. In the mountains, in the North, even in Cornwall, they are uniting again. The bonds that hold us to our clans are more important to us than any idea of 'country' some outside ruler may try to impose on us. If Arthur had called us in the name of his ancestors, we might have answered. As it is, he is nothing to us."

"Nothing to you but the dam which is holding back the Saxon invaders!"

"We haven't heard that the Saxon wants to try to tame our mountains. We can fight off the Irish slavers without help. Banoit does not need another foreign king. But Lancelot, we *do* need a king of our own blood again. You are all that remains of the line of King Ban." He leaned forward. "We would follow you."

Lancelot felt his head spinning. His first reaction was a wild excitement. This boy was asking him to become a king. A king like Arthur! He would give commands and others would rush to obey. He would . . . Then he thought of Arthur's face, the lines of care and weariness. He thought of the long nights Arthur spent working out strategies, answering complaints, while Lancelot slept, or sat with Guinevere. How lonely his friend was, even at the Round Table, where all men were considered equal. No, in one thing only did he wish to be like Arthur. Being King of Banoit would take him even farther from that. He was not intended to rule others. How could he be?

"Bors, I cannot even rule myself," he laughed apologetically.

"Very few men are saints such as Illtud," Bors replied. "Banoit would not ask of you what the Church asks. In the old days, if a man wished a woman who belonged to another, he would buy her."

Lancelot rose, his naked sword ready to strike. Almost too late, Bors saw that he had overstepped himself. He drew his knife and scrabbled to get up.

"I'm sorry! I apologize! Truly, it is none of my affair. I only meant that a king who leads his people well would not be condemned for his private matters. Banoit will support you, Sir Lancelot, whatever you do. You are one of us! Please, forgive my hasty words. I don't know anything about it!"

Lancelot halted. He was short of breath, just from anger. That frightened him almost as much as the anger itself. Shaking, he returned to his place by the fire.

"Arthur is my leader. I am sworn to him. He is also the best friend I have, the one man who accepted me without question, from my first day at Camelot. Don't speak to me about this anymore!"

Bors had no intention of doing so. Even after months of

self-denial, Lancelot was far more imposing than he realized. Timidly, Bors ventured an assurance.

"We would still be honored to have you among us, kinsman, in any way, for as long as you wished. And, if you ever need us, we will be at your side. I give you my word."

Lancelot got up again and went over to Bors, who tried not to shrink back. The knight knelt and held out his hand.

"Forgive me, kinsman. I had forgotten that I am here now by your kindness and that I am going to Banoit by your charity. In this you both honor me and show me my most grievous faults. I give you my hand in friendship now. Will you take it?"

"Gladly, kinsman! Gladly!"

There was a rumor of spring in the air when they came to the river. The struggling sun touched Lancelot's hair, making the silver in it gleam. They stopped to rest and eat before making the ford. While waiting for Bors to finish, Lancelot stretched out on a warm slab of stone from which he could see the brown, teeming water as it tumbled by. The reflected warmth was like a smooth hand on his back, pressing at his sorrow. He had followed Bors like a whipped dog. He could not go on and he dared not go back. The Grail had been no more than a symbol; he had wanted answers. Now he felt there were none. What had gone wrong? He had been the shining sword of Arthur's court, the man who was the best of all the knights: just, honest, strong. Everyone told him so. He was the Right which must always conquer evil, the one who would save the world.

He was tired. Dear God! He was so tired.

He thought at first it was a trick of the light on the water, a bird swooping low. He rose onto his elbows. It did not vanish. Coming up the river, under billowed silk, was a boat from the land of dreams, a boat that ought to sail the stars. From it he heard the sound of laughter and singing. He wondered if they were friends of his Lady of the Lake, come out of the ocean to visit her. He smiled. It called him back to the simplicity of childhood. Then, as it drew nearer, his brow creased in puzzlement. The music sounded uncommonly like a drinking song popular at Caerleon the winter before last. And the voices . . .

He was instantly on his feet, hollering and waving at the approaching craft. Against all reason, it veered toward the shore, and from the tent Galahad's head popped out.

"I told you it was his voice!" he insisted to someone inside. "Father! Come and see! We are going to find the Grail!"

Behind him, Lancelot heard Bors' whistle of disbelief.

Lancelot could not move. The face of his son had been illuminated in a way that both exalted and terrified him. The Grail! Could it be that he was being given another chance?

Inside the boat a hurried debate was going on.

"Galahad," Claris insisted. "I was sent only for you and your companions. Sir Lancelot was not mentioned. Therefore, he can't be worthy of the Grail."

"Of course he is!" Galahad assured her. "He's my father!"

"He *must* be worthy; he's the one who brought me to Camelot," Percival added. "I would never have found the castle the first time if Sir Lancelot hadn't helped me."

"I see. And what do you say, Sir Palomides?" the woman asked.

"Lancelot is a good man," the wanderer answered firmly. "And he is my friend."

"Then we must let him come with us," Claris decided, worriedly tugging at a stray lock of hair. "The final decision will be made at the castle. But I don't think, Galahad, that it is the Grail that your father truly wishes to find."

On the bank, Lancelot was waiting breathlessly. Bors stared first at the boat, as delicate and ephemeral as a butterfly, and then at the face of the man next to him, transfigured by joy.

"You can't mean to trust your life to that thing!" he exclaimed. "It will break apart on the rocks further upstream! That is . . . Sir Lancelot, it's riding against the current; how does it do that?"

Lancelot didn't answer. Galahad was on the deck again, dancing his impatience to be with his father. As the boat came no closer to shore, he leapt from the side into Lancelot's open arms, knocking him over.

"Why, Father! You used to catch me like that all the time!" Galahad chided when they had righted themselves. "Are you well?" he added, when he had studied him more closely.

"Yes, my son! God Almighty! When did you become a man?" Lancelot cried. The boy's gentle eyes looked out at him from a mature face. No, not exactly, for the barest aura of blond beard was only beginning on Galahad's cheeks. And yet he had an air about him that comes only with long years of understanding.

Galahad laughed, a sound so young and innocent that Lancelot thought his first impression had been mistaken.

"I have been learning to work with my hands, Father, instead of fight. You have no idea how much more wearing it is. Percival says it has aged him to senility."

"I didn't know you had a son, Sir Lancelot," Bors interrupted. "Your heir would also be welcome at Banoit."

Galahad bowed as Lancelot introduced them.

"Banoit?" he considered. "I would like to see it, but I can't, you know. The boat is waiting for us. It is taking us to the castle of the Fisher King. Will you come, Father?"

"Yes, of course, if they will have me. I don't know if I can climb aboard, though. I've grown weaker and it does not seem to be coming near enough to let me step on."

"I will help you. Come, take my arm. Haven't your shoulders borne me far greater distances?"

And Galahad lifted his father over the rapids and set him steadily onto the deck. Bors started to make the sign against evil and then stopped. The boy's feet had not touched the water, surely a use of old magic, and yet Bors found his hands spread instead, palms up, and he was filled with a longing to follow.

"May all the gods protect you, kinsman!" he called. "And should you return from this voyage, remember that you will always have a home in Banoit!"

* * *

Inside the tent, Lancelot fell into a healing sleep that may have lasted hours or days, for all he could later remember. He had caressing dreams that were mostly made up of song and pale mist. Now and then there would be a clear image of Guinevere as she had been that day in the forest and he felt once more the surge of freedom they had known then. Once he knew he was with Arthur, as they crept through the brush, hunting pheasant. His friend was pointing at something and grinning, but Lancelot couldn't see what it was. The rest was hidden in the cool, green fog.

Slowly, he became aware of the world around him. It was twilight and he was alone in the motionless boat. He jumped up in panic. They had gone on without him!

He pulled on his boots and pushed his way out of the tent.

The boat was moored at a wooden pier on an island in the river. On the pier stood Palomides, Percival, and Galahad. They were watching as a procession approached them. The faces of the people were glowing in the torchlight. Men and women alike wore long robes of white. Around their shoulders were cloaks of brilliant red and gold. Suddenly, Lancelot was afraid. He wanted to join the others, but could not make his feet take the leap onto the pier.

Galahad turned to him and held out his hand.

"Come, Father. They are going to bring us before the King."

Lancelot took a deep breath, and jumped.

They were led into the castle, just as Percival had described it.

In the Great Hall, they were brought before the couch of the Fisher King. He was wizened and weak from his endless agony, but he extended his hand in welcome to them.

"You have returned, son of my son," he greeted Percival. "And you have brought the one whose coming we have awaited so long. Well done!"

Palomides stepped forward and knelt to the King.

"I have searched my whole life for that which you serve," he told him. "I beg you to let me stay among you."

The old man lifted himself up on one elbow. He smiled.

"Sir Palomides, you are deserving of more than that. Oh,

steadfast pilgrim! If you survive the watch, you will be given what you most desire."

Lancelot stood apart from the others. He hoped his presence would somehow be overlooked. But the King beckoned him nearer.

"Sir Lancelot, it is not such a dreadful thing to be no more than a man. From your weakness has come our hope. It is true that your son is the knight of the *Siege Perillous*?"

Lancelot nodded.

"We had feared he would never come. For this gift, you will be allowed to keep the watch also, Sir Lancelot. I cannot tell you what will happen then. The result lies in the Grail alone."

All this time Galahad had been paying more attention to the designs along the walls and floor of the hall than the formalities. In the silence, he realized that it was his turn to be introduced. He stepped up to the couch. His face changed.

"Sir!" he cried. "You are wounded. How awful! Who has done this to you? I will avenge you. What must I do?"

A great sigh of release came from the servitors but the King silenced them with a gesture.

"Come closer, child. You have already begun. But there is no warrior for you to battle. I was wounded by my own pride and for it my people and my land have suffered. There has been no death and no new life here since I was struck down. But now you have come. Already I feel stronger. But wait! I keep you all standing when you are in need of food and rest. Claris! Take our guests in to dinner."

The three older men ate the exquisite food absently, all waiting for the procession Percival had described. Galahad seemed to have forgotten about it and chatted happily to Claris and the King.

At the end of the meal, there was another breathless silence as the procession passed through the hall. But it was not exactly as Percival remembered it. First came Cundrie, her hideous face now covered by a veil. On the silver patens she carried were piled grain and fresh fruit. Behind her walked the man carrying the spear, a trail of blood in his wake. Lastly came the boy holding the covered Grail. The light from it shone through the cloth and outlined the veins in the boy's hands.

Galahad watched, puzzled. "That is the Grail, Sir?" he asked the Fisher King.

"Yes, and I am its guardian."

"But what is the Grail for, Sir? Whom does it serve?"

"The questions!" the King cried joyfully. "At last!"

The pealing of the bells vibrated through the hall, overpowering the shouting and laughter from the Grail servants. Cundrie threw off her veil as her beauty was restored, and the Fisher King rose from his bed, his strength regained. Galahad watched in amazement, totally unaware of his part in the transformation. For how could mere words cure a people? He laughed and danced with the others, happy for their sakes. Now Percival could forget his guilt. But still Galahad yearned to see the Grail uncovered. Could they take the cloth off now?

The Fisher King, gasping from the unaccustomed activity, sat down beside him.

"You were thinking that you still wished to know the answers to your questions?" he asked Galahad.

"Yes, Sir," the boy answered.

"I, too, Sir," Palomides added. "I rejoice in your recovery, but you are but the guardian of the portal which is opened by the Grail, are you not?"

"Very astute, Sir Palomides!" the King nodded. "You have studied the mystics well. And now you wish to cross through that door? You also, Sir Galahad?"

"More than all the world!"

"You are very young, it seems to me. Fortunately, it is not my choice. You must go to the tower and watch for three nights running, one night for each window. Then you will learn if you may be given what you seek."

"And what of Sir Lancelot?" Palomides asked.

The Fisher King shook his head. "He may watch with you, if he wishes, but somehow I doubt that his way to the other side will be so easy."

So, while Percival remained below to learn about his new

role as heir to the Fisher King, the other three ascended the staircase to the top of the tower. There they found only a bare room with windows looking north, west, and south. The wooden planks which made up the floor were warped with age and damp and creaked at their step but Lancelot judged that they would hold. They set their blankets at the center and composed themselves to watch.

Lancelot took the southern view, and all night long all he saw was the twisting fog. Once in a while, it would press against the thick glass and seem to shape itself into a face or a limb, but then it would dissolve and float away. From the gasps of amazement Palomides and Galahad were uttering, it was clear that the other windows provided better views. But the next night, at the window Galahad had used the night before, he still saw only mist.

The final evening they dined again with the Fisher King. Although he had been healed, his skin was pale as night-grown flowers, and he was too weary to eat. Galahad sat beside him and took his hand.

"What is it that weakens you so?" his voice was high with concern. "Can no one help you? I thought you had been cured, now that you have found Sir Percival again."

The old man leaned his head back against the cushions and closed his eyes. His transparent hand patted the boy's arm.

"You will understand soon, child. I *have* been cured. I'm free now to leave this ancient body and seek my master. I have no more pain and only await the signal to go. Then my grandson, Percival, will become the guardian, and m~y he be a wiser one than I have been."

The three knights climbed the stairs for the last time. Lancelot watched the other two racing ahead of him, eager for whatever wonders they had been watching before. He dragged his left foot up another step and forced the right one to follow, slowly, slowly until he reached the top.

They each took a new window. Galahad laughed and Palomides sighed happily. Lancelot resigned himself to the enigmatic mist.

It was still there, swooping and blowing outside the window as if a storm were raging. Glittering ice crystals blew past. Lancelot shivered, although the tower was sealed and warm. Despite his determination to see out the watch, he blinked more and more slowly. His head nodded, then jerked up. What was that, a reflection?

He turned around, but saw only Galahad and Palomides, each engrossed in their visions. He leaned closer to the window. There was an image there, distant but in bright colors: a boy, the center of loving attention, petted and adored. The fog became the diamonds and thin silks of the Lady's palace. Lancelot saw himself, spoiled and precious. He watched the image flow as he began to understand guilt and become obsessed with giving himself pain to compensate for the voluptuous pleasure of the immortals. Then he saw King Arthur's brave, pure knight, arrogant at being the best, proud of his piety and, at the same time, disgusted at his own pride. Lancelot writhed as the too-accurate images of his own life appeared in the window. In them, he rushed out again to save the kidnapped Guinevere, sure that only he could accomplish the deed, and watched as her scorn showed him the truth of his motives. The madness that followed was as blurred as his memory of it, only a naked, wild man, living by instinct, not reason. It was superseded by the face of Guinevere, transformed during his illness from an idol for him to adore and serve to a woman who needed to give love as well as take it.

She was not a goddess and he was not a saint. And he needed her more now than ever before. He closed his eyes and the window went blank. From far away, a mighty gong sounded and the tower shook with its resonance.

He felt Palomides and Galahad tug gently at his arms, bringing him to his feet. He saw with alarm that there was a door in the formerly blank east wall. It was of carved and polished ivory. A locked bolt of gold was drawn across it. In Galahad's hand was a golden key.

"Do you hear it, Father?" the boy asked softly.

Lancelot shook his head.

"It's time for us to go, my friend." Palomides put his arm

on Lancelot's shoulder. There were tears streaming down his face. "Please, when you get back, tell King Arthur that I never found such honor or honesty in any man as I found in him. He led me to this night. I have no words for my gratitude."

"But, Palomides, I'm not going back. I'm going with you!"

"You can't, Father." Galahad was weeping, too, but for those he loved who must be left behind. "Not this way. You must return to tell them that the quest is ended. You must help my mother, Guinevere. She will understand but not accept this. It hurt so much to leave her when I knew she would need me, so you have to be with her, instead. I love you both, and I promise that I always will. Father, I'm sorry. They won't let you through the portal, not yet. Please, say farewell without grief."

Lancelot swallowed. "I can't. I will miss you both too much. But I understand now how foolish I have been in my search. I only marvel that I was allowed to come this far."

"God loves his fools, too," Palomides laughed. "Or why else would we be here? Now, come, Galahad. It's time."

Galahad inserted the key in the bolt. The lock fell open and Palomides lifted the golden bar. The door opened inward and they entered.

Timidly, Lancelot approached. Instead of the drop outside the tower, he saw a large, clear room, with vaulted ceiling and stone floor. It was empty except for an altar at the far end. On the altar was the Grail, still covered with its crimson cloth. Taking hands, Palomides and Galahad moved toward it.

From behind the altar came a voice.

"In wisdom and innocence, joined by selflessness and love, you have come to me. Therefore come forward and partake of my reward and be with me from this day forth, welcome in my mansions."

The light from the Grail increased and a form appeared. The brightness was too great for Lancelot to make it out. As the two knights reached the altar, the cloth was removed and a blinding radiance filled the room. Lancelot was thrown back by the force. It pierced not only his eyes, but his whole body. There was a roaring in his ears and a great trembling in his limbs. It enveloped him a moment and then, suddenly, was gone, leaving Lancelot alone in the dark tower, shaking and blind.

Chapter Fourteen

"Gawain! Psst! Gawain!" Risa beckoned from the doorway of Guinevere's tower. Gawain looked about for a few seconds until he noticed her hand curling out of the shadows.

"Risa! How nice," he said as he slipped through the door. He gave her a semi-passionate kiss for old times' sake. "We haven't done this in years."

She pushed him away, but fondly. He had been one of the best of her lovers.

"Never mind that. I need to talk to you about Modred. Can we meet somewhere?"

"Without everyone knowing? I doubt it. That's the only bad thing about being back at Camelot; there's no private corner for an assignation."

He leaned against the doorpost, smiling as if chatting, but his mind had gone cold serious. He had found out from Risa long ago why she continued to let Modred into her bed.

"Have you discovered something?" he asked her.

"I can't tell you here, but yes, I think so. Oh, Gawain, how can I make them believe me?"

"I don't know. It frightens me how Modred has wound himself around Arthur. Even Guinevere likes him. We have to find some certain proof. He has to be made harmless. But now is not the time to go to Arthur with suspicions and no proof. With the news coming back from the Grail knights, he won't be willing to hear anything about treachery at his own table."

Risa nodded. With spring had come rumors, then messengers, then slowly, some of the Grail-seekers themselves. Tired, worn, jaded by what they had seen and done, they were no longer the brilliant, gleaming knights of Camelot.

Sagremore had tried to stop a feud between two families over their sheep and found both sides turned against him. They hadn't wanted justice. They had wanted victory and the annihilation of their enemy. He had been attacked in his bed and his horse and armour stolen. They had dumped him, unconscious, by the roadside, where he lay all morning as nervous travelers averted their eyes from his body. He was finally recognized by a trader who cared for him in the hope of a reward from Arthur. Sagremore now sat always with his back to the wall, watching, his hand never far from his knife.

The Irish knights, Cunorix and Ebicatos, returned with tales of monsters in the North and a tree of hanged men, tortured and left by the local lord to die and rot in the rain and wind.

"There were dragons in the waters and *bansidhs* leering from the smoke. Giants roam the countryside, stealing children to eat and maidens to ravish. They laugh at Arthur's laws. We spent our time in combat and never saw breath of the Grail."

But everyone knows how the Irish tell tales.

Perredur came back, but would tell no one what had happened to him. A month later, his wife took their children and returned to her father. When her family pleaded to know why, she answered only that she could not live with what looked out of his eyes.

Others were dead or had wandered out of Britain, obsessed with the search. And no one had heard anything of Lancelot, Percival, Palomides, and Galahad.

It was not a time to bring bad tidings to Arthur, especially if they were about his new favorite.

Gawain put his arm around Risa and tilted her face so that he could see clearly the lines around her eyes and mouth. She grimaced and turned away.

"Risa," he said softly. "Bolt your door tonight."

"Dear friend, I wish so dreadfully that I could. But he has some plan for my Lady Guinevere and I must discover it before he can harm her more. Watch out for her, Gawain."

"You know how little use I am, Risa. But I promise that anything that can be done by day, I will do. We can't let my baby brother destroy all that Arthur has built."

After he left her, he went in search of Gaheris. Agravaine was still at Tintagel and Gareth was no use where Guinevere was concerned, but this was a family matter and he needed to talk with one of his brothers.

He found Gaheris in the scriptorium, deep in conversation with Father Antonius.

"So, you see," Gaheris summed up. "If there is no dual nature in the personification of Christ, then the sacrifice would have no meaning. He must be primarily man, not god."

The priest shook his head firmly. "Certainly the gods of my childhood were more human than I in their tastes and foibles. But that is why it seems essential to me that Christianity divorce itself from any claims of the flesh, particularly in the godhead."

Gawain yawned. He wondered how long this would go on. Father Antonius heard him and yawned in response. He looked up.

"Oh! Sir Gawain! Were you looking for me or your brother?"

"Gaheris, if you don't mind. Although I would be delighted to eat with you this noon and discuss your views on transubstantiation."

Father Antonius blinked and then laughed. "Don't worry,

Sir Gawain. I never discuss religion when I'm eating. I'll see you then. Good-bye, Sir Gaheris."

Gaheris stood politely until the priest had left the room.

"Couldn't you wait? I had almost got him to admit I was right."

"It didn't sound that way to me. Anyway, you know you'll just be at the same arguments tomorrow. I have to talk with you now."

Gaheris sighed. "If you've come to me about Modred again, don't bother. I think you're imagining it. Arthur seems to have made a real change in him. He's a lot nicer than he was at home."

"But what about all those rumors about Guinevere? That she's practicing witchcraft to stay young and that she's responsible for Arthur's not going out and conquering the clans?"

"What about them? I haven't heard Modred say anything against her. And you must admit that she doesn't age. She looks as young as Aunt Morgause and we know that *she* doesn't look that way naturally. Maybe there's something to it."

Gawain let loose a sharp expletive which hit Gaheris squarely in the jaw.

"All this theology has turned your brain to mush, boy. Guinevere doesn't care if Arthur battles the clans, the Irish, the Saxons, or the whole damned Roman army, if that's what he wants. And, until Galahad comes back, I don't think she'd even notice if the war came to the walls of Camelot, as long as it didn't get in the way of her view of the road. And as for her looks, well, nothing wicked ever wore a face like that. Witchcraft! The whole thing is mad!"

Gaheris gathered up his sheets of vellum and put away the ink, quills, and sand. Apart from his own nonviolent nature, he knew better than to pit himself against his older brother.

"You know more about her than I do, of course, and you're probably right. But there is something going on here, and it's the Queen that people are wondering about."

"Idiots! Modred's behind it. And I'll wager that Aunt

Morgause is behind him. Satan smiled the day she was born and she must have given him some good laughs since then. How can you even think Guinevere could traffic with evil?"

He stormed out, breathing in the sun-warmed air in an attempt to expel the cold fear that was building in him. What kind of spell were they weaving that even Gaheris felt its power?

Now that they were back at Camelot, Guinevere was too busy to realize the change in the people around her. Lydia was in childbed again and her tasks needed doing. Even after more than twenty years, Guinevere still knew little about the day to day running of the King's household. But she tried to appear as if she did. Letitia, having been raised to be a stolid Roman matron, was ready to organize cooks, potboys, weavers, woodsmen, washwomen, and scrubbing drudges into a smooth unit and really did most of the planning and checking, but she deferred to her aunt in public. Privately, Guinevere longed to return the whole mess to Lydia and go back to her books and quiet evenings. But she was grateful that, at least, she was too occupied to worry so constantly about Galahad. In the bustle of the kitchens and the laundry, she sometimes even lost the gnawing hurt of Lancelot's rejection.

Being out among the people of Camelot helped their attitude toward her, too.

"Poor thing," the third cook whispered to the laundress. "She doesn't know a roasting spit from a pot hook, but she's trying."

"And her that worried about little Sir Galahad, too," the laundress clucked. "I do think she's lost color this past year, and weight, too. Her bones stick out right through her robes."

"That's so. I'll see to it that she gets an egg and honey-mead posset tonight. With those lords from Armorica coming again, we can't have the Queen looking like a starved rabbit."

Modred went to spend a few weeks with his aunt, Morgause. She gave him a tongue-lashing about letting sentiment get in the way of destiny and reported that Meleagant, Ligessauc Longhand, Gerontius of Dumnonia, and Fergus of the Dal Riada would join with him if there were a valid excuse to set against Arthur.

"But you had better be sure that Meleagant lives long enough, because his son, Sir Dyfnwal, is committed to Arthur. Cissa of the Saxons will only continue as he has done so far. He will harry anyone other than traders within his lands and keep those on his borders from coming to Arthur's aid. But beware of him! Like Maelgwn, he will be more than willing to wait while you do the work and then sweep in and conquer the victor while he is still weak."

"There will be no chance of that, dear Morgause, if you keep to your work."

"I can only do so much, Modred," she snapped. "You seem to think that the daemons and old ones are like dogs to be whistled for. I was able to poison the air in London so that men's minds were set on trails of suspicion. But that took skill and time. And I couldn't work with nothing. There was already envy there and resentment, carefully disguised. I only gave it form. You must do some work, yourself. Start collecting your bishops and saints. We should let the Christians do the hardest part. That will save our strength for . . . better things."

Modred reached across the thick, lush velvet and pulled her against him.

"They say that the exercise of absolute power is the greatest physical arousal there is. That's why the emperors soon became jaded by the usual offerings. But I wonder how it would be if the two were combined."

She stretched her arms over her head, reaching toward the ceiling, seeing beyond it to the culmination of her striving. Her breath came more quickly. Modred gave a short laugh.

"Exactly, my dear. Just what I had in mind."

The hills were emerald with the first leaves of summer. Guinevere's roses had unfolded in the morning sunshine and released their perfume into the air of Camelot. Wildflowers scattered themselves throughout the grass and bees skittered among them, too busy to be bothered with stinging. Lydia was up again and the new baby could be heard protesting her absence at frequent intervals.

"Come out and look, Arthur!" Guinevere called from the balcony. "You'd think the world had been made afresh last night. Forget those Armoricans and come riding with me today. They only want you to give them soldiers. I don't remember them sending any to you when you needed help."

"Hush, my dear!" Arthur came out and gently laid his fingers across her mouth. "They sent me no aid because I asked for none. But, in the past twenty years, hundreds of their sons and daughters have come back to Britain and settled the empty towns and villas that their fathers abandoned. It's only right that we give what help we can now that those Merovingian Franks are snapping at their lands. They might not need help if we hadn't taken so many of their youth."

"They were glad enough to be rid of younger sons then," Guinevere sniffed. "And you know how many of them just came back to dig up the coins their ancestors buried when they fled."

"Guinevere." He looked at her and she smiled sheepishly.

"You're such a *nice* person, Arthur. I don't know how you do it. Now, will you be even nicer and come riding with me?"

"I can't, my dear. But I'll get plenty of riding in the next few days. I've promised to accompany our guests on their way back to London, at least for the first day or two. On the way back, we'll do a little hunting. I've a craving for the taste of wild boar."

"Very well. I'll see if Gawain wants to go riding, or Brisane or one of the other ladies. But don't spend all day in that dark hall. Days such as these are too rare to waste."

Brisane was being fitted for a new pair of shoes, and the other ladies were occupied for the good of their families, their bodies, their souls, or all three. It occurred to Guinevere that they often were, recently. So Gawain and Guinevere set out alone through the maze to the gate of Camelot and down the road to the West.

"Guinevere, wouldn't you like to go the other way for a change?" Gawain asked. "You've been up this road as far as time allows every clear day for weeks."

She gave him her most innocent glance. "Don't you like this road?"

"As well as any other, I suppose. But you don't fool me. This is the road they went down when they left and someday, you think, you'll find them coming home again."

He said it in a kindly voice, but it brought tears to her throat all the same.

"Are you laughing at me for my foolishness?"

"No, dear Auntie. I'm weeping with you for your steadfast hope."

"There must be news of them someday; they can't have . . . oh, Gawain! Look! Look!"

They had reached the top of a hill. Below the road twisted as it followed the river Cam. Gawain shielded his eyes and tried to see what made Guinevere sit as if frozen, her arm locked outstretched. There was no one on the road but an old man, probably a priest on his way from Llanylltud Fawr. Odd horse for such a man to be riding, probably given him by some grateful lord whose sins he had absolved. Funny, he thought he'd seen that horse before, and the way the rider sat him . . .

"Gawain! Can't you see him? Please, tell me he's really there!"

"I see a man in hermit's robes riding a white horse. Is that . . ."

But he didn't get a chance to finish. She had dug her heels hard into the horse's flank and was galloping down the hill, screeching at the top of her lungs.

"Lancelot! Lancelot!"

Gawain started after her.

"Guinevere!" he called. "Don't be a fool. That couldn't be Lancelot!"

The man had stopped and was watching Guinevere's descent. Her hair had come undone and was billowing behind her. Her arms were bare and she had kicked off her riding boots as soon as they had gotten out of sight of Camelot. He made no move, even to pull off his hood, as she rode up to him. But as she came alongside and made to slide down, he reached out and lifted her so that she hung from his neck, her feet hanging in the air.

"You came back, you came back!" she sobbed as he kissed her. "Don't ever, ever leave me again, Lancelot. No matter what!"

"Never!" he promised, as she looped one leg up and across Clades' back so that they faced each other. She put her arms about him inside the robes and the hood fell back. For a long minute she simply held him, feeling the beat of his heart against her ear, as individual to her as his voice. Then she looked up.

"Oh, my darling! Your hair!"

He ran his hand through it. "I know. It went gray at Llanylltud Fawr and white . . . later. I have not grown wiser, my dearest, only old. Can you still love me?"

"For all my life and more," she told him. Her lips pressed against his throat and chin and mouth. "As long as my soul wanders the universe, it will search for yours."

Gawain had been minutely studying the leatherwork on his bridle. Finally Lancelot noticed him. The arm that wasn't holding Guinevere went out to him.

"Gawain? Are we still friends?" he asked.

"Just because you left me at the castle while you went on?" Gawain clasped Lancelot's hand with a grin. "Wait until you hear how that story's grown!

"Anyway," he added in an altered tone, "I think your journey was a harder one than mine."

"Yes, but it was my own doing that made it so. And I was rewarded far beyond what I deserved. Guinevere, my love, why don't you get back on your own horse before we get to the watch tower?"

Guinevere held him more tightly. She had forgotten everything in the joy of meeting: Camelot, Arthur, all the slippery glances and sly tongues. His hand rested on her hair. She raised her face from his chest and kissed him again while Gawain searched the sky for signs of rain. Then she slid down and hoisted herself back upon her horse. She fumbled for a scarf to cover the disarray of her braids. Gawain slipped her boots back on and tied them.

Arthur was in the courtyard, pointing out the finer sights to the Armorican visitors, when they arrived. He waved them over.

"And who is this?" he started to ask. Then he stopped. "Lancelot?"

Lancelot dismounted and bowed to his King. Arthur's face lighted in an incredulous grin.

"Lancelot!" He grabbed his friend in a great bear hug. "You've come back. I can't believe it. We thought you'd left us for God."

"I found I make a poor saint, Arthur. Will you take me back?"

"Take you back? Of course! I'd have never let you leave. I can see you have a tale to tell." The two men's eyes met and Arthur nodded understanding.

"Gawain, will you take Sir Lancelot to his quarters and help him settle his things. When you are ready, come to our rooms. Guinevere and I will want to hear your news there. Won't we, Guin?"

She started. "Yes, of course. If you gentlemen will excuse me, I must make myself presentable for dinner."

Somehow she managed to walk casually to her door and mount the stairs. It wasn't until she had washed her face and changed her clothes that it came to her what Lancelot might want to tell them privately.

"Galahad."

She started to shake so hard that she had to sit down, gripping the chair arms until her own could be still.

"He knows and now I have to know, too. Oh, my child, my beautiful Galahad!"

She bowed her head, shutting her eyes to hide her terror. Her fingernails cut crescent slivers into the dark wood.

Chapter Fifteen

He told them late that night. It had been essential to good
manners that they remain with their guests throughout the
evening's entertainment. Guinevere had eaten and drunk and
smiled when they seemed to be saying something they
thought amusing. She must have been enchanting, for King
Hoel's emissaries were not inclined to retire until quite late.
The stars were wheeling toward morning when Lancelot finally told his story, the feeble glow of the coals in the brazier
casting the only light. They sat on the couch in the anteroom, Guinevere in the middle, as Lancelot faltered through
his tale, his voice still filled with awe from what he had been
allowed to witness. Arthur could feel Guinevere's stillness as
she listened. It was as if she were drawing all the life in her
body to one small space, but to hide from her grief or contain
it, he didn't know. He wanted to put his arm around her but
was afraid she would shatter at his touch.

Lancelot's voice flowed in the dark.

"I stayed with Percival until I could see well enough to
travel. I don't think the world will ever be clear to me again.
There is a mist around things now, unless they are very close.
I'm afraid I won't be any good at the hunt anymore."

"It doesn't matter," Arthur murmured.

Lancelot took a deep breath. "I'm sorry, Guinevere. I said
I'd bring him back, but I couldn't. He found the Grail, you
see. He doesn't belong here anymore. He's gone on."

"I know." Her voice struggled to break from a whisper. "I

knew the day he left. He never belonged in the world. He was a gift, just like . . . like my . . ."

"What, dear?" Arthur stopped her quavering hand.

"I don't know . . . Nothing. It doesn't matter."

"He was happy to go," Lancelot went on. "Palomides is with him. I've never seen anyone so joyful."

"I know. I wouldn't have let him go, otherwise. Both of them were meant for this. Galahad was always more than this imperfect earth could bear. But God is being terribly selfish to take him for Himself. Couldn't He see how much I wanted my child? Didn't He ever wonder how I would survive without him? I loved him more than anyone in the world. God must be very wicked to take a child from his mother like that. Whatever use could he be in heaven?"

She bent sharply and suddenly, huddled over her knees, her face covered in the red silk. It darkened like fresh blood as it filled with her tears. Her body convulsed as she tried to draw breath over her sobs. Lancelot looked at Arthur.

"I dreaded this. I don't know what to do. I shouldn't have come back."

"There was nothing else you could do, Lancelot. Would you rather she never knew?"

Arthur put a hand on his friend's arm. "You're very tired and it's nearly dawn. Go to bed. I'll give her some warm mead and make her sleep. There's nothing more we can do."

Lancelot wiped his fingers over his eyes in a movement that was becoming habitual. He threw his head back and sighed deeply.

"I know. Yes. I need to rest. Good night, Arthur."

"Good night, Lancelot. Welcome home."

As soon as he saw Lancelot, Modred knew that his opportunity had finally come. First, he sent a raven to Morgause with the news.

"And if you stop even once on the way," he threatened it, "I'll have your young in pastry for dinner."

The bird squawked understanding and flapped off at once.

"Now to see that Arthur's men go with him tomorrow and

mine stay behind." He frowned as he plotted. "And the bishops are meeting at Cirencester next week. Yes! It can work! She's the key. Whatever Arthur does, he'll lose. And I will be ready."

He was brimming with hilarity at dinner that night and Arthur, wracked by sorrow and worry for Guinevere, was silently grateful to him for covering up his own inattention. He thought again how sorry he was that he couldn't acknowledge the boy openly. Modred was a son a man could be proud of.

Guinevere spent the night curled into a ball in the farthest corner of the bed. She had not changed her dress or combed out her hair. She didn't move and by that Arthur knew she wasn't asleep. But she wasn't aware, either. He didn't know where she had gone or how to get her back. And he had to put those blasted Armoricans on the road to London as if nothing were wrong. Perhaps he should leave Gawain and Cei behind.

"Don't worry about her," Risa counseled. "I saw her mother the same way when the Saxons killed Matthew and John. It's their way of waiting until they can bear the pain. Lydia and I will take care of her. There's nothing you can do."

"Well, Lancelot will stay, at any rate. King Hoel's men don't know him and he can't see well enough to hunt." He looked at his wife, only the curve of her back visible through the blanket. "I was a fool to let anyone go out after that damn Grail! All it's given us is despair. You heard about Galahad?"

"Yes. Gaheris and Father Antonius are debating now whether we should mourn for him or set up a shrine and rejoice."

"Rejoice? Are they mad?"

"I have no idea, my Lord," Risa said testily. "They say he is in heaven now beyond doubt, and no one should grieve for that."

"Don't tell Guinevere that," Arthur warned.

"Hardly. But at least she knows!" Risa forced back the lump in her throat.

Arthur remembered. "I should have asked you. There's been no word of your boy, then?"

"The last we heard, Bedivere and Domin had crossed the wall and were heading into Pict lands. I don't know why. That was last fall."

"Damn," Arthur commented. Risa nodded. Then she shook herself.

"You should be down in the courtyard now. I can hear the horses and the voices of the men. Don't worry," she repeated. "Someone will stay with her until you return."

"I'll be back as soon as I can," he promised. "No more than four days, no matter what."

Guinevere didn't stir as the riders clattered beneath her window. She didn't hear the shouted greetings and good-byes or the horns as the gates were opened and closed. She remained coiled into herself, seeing nothing, her mind empty of memory and pain.

It was late the next morning before she roused. Risa and Lydia were talking together. They weren't discussing her but some new herb to add to their almond milk which was guaranteed to erase wrinkles from the skin.

"You can feel it almost at once," Lydia was saying. "It sort of chills and pulls your face smooth. Of course, it doesn't last very long, but you look years younger while it does."

"Do you have to say some sort of spell over it while you crush the herbs?" Risa asked.

"No, silly! This isn't magic. It's just the property of the herb. It comes from some old medicine book of the Greeks."

"Fascinating! Well, I think we should try it."

Guinevere's body loosened. She unwrapped herself on the bed. Risa jumped up and bent over her.

"There, that's better, my Lady, dear. Just have a sip of this now. You'll be feeling better soon."

The drink had been kept hot on the coals and it stung bitterly as it went down.

Guinevere made a face at it.

"Are you sure you didn't say a spell over *this* concoction, Risa? It tastes very strange."

"Only a little one, dear. Nothing your own nursemaid wouldn't have used."

Guinevere was sure of that. Charms and spells had been lullabies to her nursemaid. Still, she took another sip. There was something in it that eased the jagged pain inside and let her breathe again. She gave Risa a grateful smile.

"Galahad won't be coming back, you know," she said.

"They told us." Lydia came to the bedside, too.

"It hurts very deeply. Lots of people I loved have died, but it never hurt this much. I think I need to lie here and cry for a long, long time. Would you mind going now?"

Lydia and Risa looked at each other. She sounded reasonable. That was a bad sign, but what could they do? They kissed her and brushed her hair out of her face and left.

"I'll have some soup sent up to you," Lydia said firmly before she closed the door. "And I want you to finish it all."

Guinevere eased herself out of bed. She changed into a nightshift and splashed rosewater on her face. Then she picked up a small ivory box from her dressing table. She took it with her back to her bed where she sat with her knees up to her chest under the covers. Slowly, she opened it. In it were three baby teeth, molars, and a soft curl of golden blond hair. It was the same shade as her own, but short and springy. She ran her fingers along it then gently closed the box. She held it in both hands, pressed to her breast. Then, she cried.

Lancelot was sitting crosslegged in the chapel, his head bowed more in sleep than prayer, when Gareth came to him.

"I'm glad you came back, Sir Lancelot," he said formally. "I suppose that means that you succeeded at Llanylltud Fawr. So now we can go on like before. Arthur says that the clans in the North need someone to show them who's in charge. We could set out that way next week and be back before the snow, I'll wager. Everything will be fine, now that you're cured of the Queen."

Lancelot lifted his head. He hadn't quite followed what Gareth was saying.

"Oh, hello, Gareth. Good to see you again. What was that about Guinevere?"

"Oh, nothing. The ladies say she's up in her bed now, crying herself ill because of Galahad. Isn't that ridiculous? Galahad was a hero. He found the Grail. He won! She never did have much sense. Well, we're rid of her. I'm glad you're not tangled up in all that. There've been some strange stories going around about her. You escaped just in time."

He leaned against the wooden pillar, smiling. He was unprepared to have Lancelot rise all in a motion beside him and grab his shoulders hard.

"Gareth, what are you talking about? Who's with Guinevere now?"

"I don't know. No one, I guess. Lydia is feeding the children and Risa is off somewhere with Cheldric. His nose has been out of joint since she took up with Modred. I guess while he's gone, she's making it up to him."

Lancelot didn't care about Cheldric's nose.

"She shouldn't be by herself. What's the matter with them?"

He released Gareth and hurried out. Gareth sat in the dusk for a while, suspicion growing in him that Lancelot's cure was not yet complete. In that case, it was up to him to see that his idol came to no harm.

There was an empty bowl on a tray outside the door but no one in the anteroom when Lancelot entered. He knocked on the chamber door.

"Please, I'm fine. I don't need anything. I just want to be alone. I'll be fine in the morning, I promise." She sounded controlled, but only barely.

"Guinevere, may I come in?" He knew he didn't need to identify himself.

The door opened and she was in his arms.

His fingers caught in the disheveled mass of her hair and jerked her head back. He looked into her red-rimmed eyes and forgot every vow he'd ever made. Without a word, he turned and barred the door.

Late that night, the guard on duty let in a group of men dressed in priests' robes. It was irregular but they had a pass token from Sir Modred, and Sir Sagremore and Sir Perredur came to the gate and vouched for them. The guard had meant to save the token, in case he was questioned, but in the morning it was gone and Sir Modred denied ever issuing it.

Guinevere sighed and nestled more securely against Lancelot's body. His fingers traced a spiral across her cheek and down her neck.

"He was our son, wasn't he, Lancelot?" she asked.

"Yes. Only ours."

"It won't ever stop hurting, will it?"

"I don't see how it can, but we can keep him always in our hearts. As we hold each other."

Her arms went around him again.

"I couldn't have borne it to lose you both."

"He knew that. I wanted to go with him. But I realize now that, if I had crossed the portal, I would have had to come back for you, however long it took."

"I would have been waiting at the gate."

They lay quietly awhile, tired, but not willing to lose each other in sleep. The candlelight flickered over them as if leaving a benediction.

The door below them slammed and there was the crashing of a score of booted feet. Lancelot sat up, automatically untangling his legs from the blankets.

"What is it?" Guinevere's voice shook.

"Nothing good. Where's my sword?"

"You left it in the anteroom."

He swore at himself. "All right then, here, throw this on!" He scrambled into his trews and was fumbling with the cords when the pounding came on the door.

"Open! Vile witch and seductress! We know you have your paramour in there! Open and face the King's justice!"

"The King? Arthur wouldn't . . ." Guinevere stopped in bewilderment.

"Of course not," Lancelot snapped. "Don't unbar the door. Blast! There must be at least a knife in here! Hurry! They've got an axe! Do you think you can climb down the trellis?"

She went out to the balcony and peered down. A cry went up.

"There are men down there, too. Lancelot, what's happening?"

"Treachery. I can't fight them all and they know it, but I can hold them off. You must get away."

"Where? Who are they? Why are they calling me those names!" She was becoming hysterical.

He stopped his frantic search and held her. He was more frightened than he had ever been in his life, but he had to calm her. The axe was splintering the door; in another moment, they would be in. His brain was spinning. He wished someone had trained him for a situation like this. Gawain would have known. How could he have left his sword out of reach! Idiot! Their only hope was that the noise would waken others and someone would come to help.

The bar split under the axe and the door crashed open. Three men jumped at Lancelot, their weapons raised. He spun Guinevere away from him and picked up a small table to shield himself. He thrust it at them, so that they swung at it, hacking off the legs. He thrust again and the first attacker caught his sword in the wood and had it flipped from him with a jerk that snapped his wrist. Another swung at Lancelot and found himself sprawled on the floor.

Guinevere cried out, but he couldn't see her in the melee. He was being pushed toward the balcony. The third man knew his business and, despite his efforts, Lancelot could not trick him into making a sudden lunge which might take him through the air and send him over the rail. The roses were at his back. He looked down. There was only one man there now, with a horse. There was nothing for it. He would have to jump.

Lancelot took a deep breath and threw the table at his

adversary. At the same time, he leapt from the balcony, catching himself on the thorny vines on the way down. He landed hard, his naked chest and arms scratched and bleeding. The man knelt over him and he swung.

"No! Wait! It's me, Lancelot!" Gareth dodged the blow. "I've brought Clades. You've got to get out of here or they'll kill you! Hurry!"

"But Guinevere! I have to save her! Help me, Gareth!"

Gareth pulled him up and pushed him toward the horse. "No! There's nothing you can do. Don't worry, I heard them talking. They're not going to hurt her. They're taking her to Cirencester for trial. If you don't go now, you won't be able to help her at all! Please, Lancelot! Believe me. There's nothing you can do. You'll only make it worse for her. Now! They're coming!"

Lancelot had mounted. He leaned down to Gareth. "All right. But you get to her. Tell her I'll be back for her! Do you understand?"

"Yes, of course. Lancelot! Please!"

He slapped Clades' rump and the horse sped off. Lancelot knew the gate would be locked and aimed for the lower fence overlooking the practice field. He leaned over the horse's neck and whispered fiercely.

"You're a magic horse, my Clades, and you're as young as ever. You can do it."

Clades tossed his head in agreement. He galloped up to the wall and, with a mighty leap, cleared it with inches to spare. By the time anyone could mount to follow him, he was through the maze and deep into the forest.

In her confusion, Guinevere only knew that he was away and safe. She was furious at these men who dared to break into her bedchamber and tie her with coarse ropes. But as long as they could not harm Lancelot, she wouldn't worry. They were mad, of course, with their talk of witchcraft and trials. Arthur would see to them. She told them so.

"Arthur can do nothing about it, Witch," the leader laughed. "We're taking you to the Bishops and St. Caradoc. And don't try to set your sorcery on us. We've all got cold iron next to our skins. You won't be working any more magic on King Arthur, either. Britain will be a strong power again, once you're destroyed."

He would have continued, but Guinevere had given him one incredulous stare which had turned his knees to jelly and then she had fainted.

"There," he said in triumph. "I knew the iron would work. Hurry, men. Get her down and tied to the horse. We'll get to the Bishops and let God take care of her kind!"

Chapter Sixteen

"How could you just let them take her!" Arthur roared to the assembled group. "What kind of men did I leave to guard Camelot?"

He pulled off his muddy boot and threw it on the floor with reverberating force. The terrified guard inched forward and knelt cringingly before the King.

"We didn't know what to do, my Lord. The men had a pass and Sir Sagremore and Sir Perredur were there to admit them and left with them. We thought . . ." he swallowed. "We thought that it was done with your knowledge."

Arthur scrutinized the faces around him; frightened, alarmed, curious, some even secretly gloating. Of course with his knowledge. They had even hoped it was true that he had set a trap for Guinevere and Lancelot. Is that what Guinevere believed? Was that why she had not called for help when they brought her through the compound? Is that why Lancelot had vanished? The other boot hit the wall. How dare they have so little faith in him!

"Get out!" he ordered with a sweep of his arm. "Get out every one of you! If any harm comes to the Queen through this, I'll have you all flayed, I swear it!"

They fell over each other shoving to get through the door. Arthur rubbed his temple and exhaled slowly. Only Cei and Gawain were left in the room. Arthur looked at them and shook his head.

"Will someone tell me what in hell is going on?"

As much as they could, they did, Gawain only omitting his suspicions about Modred. Arthur listened with escalating fury.

"Whatever Lancelot and Guinevere have done is no one's business but mine. The Church has no right to interfere, and they know it."

Gawain agreed. "It's more than that, much more. Someone has woven a net of lies and half-truths around Guinevere, and I was too stupid to see how thick they had grown. They are also saying that she practices sorcery."

"Nonsense! And even if she did, what of it? Most of the people in Britain try a charm now and then. Merlin certainly worked unmolested."

"They may have thought him too powerful to challenge."

"All right, what's the penalty for sorcery, then?"

"Under Roman law, if she confesses, twenty-five gold coins."

"Someone is trying to destroy my wife for twenty-five gold coins?"

Arthur was growing increasingly bewildered. Cei put a hand on his shoulder. In the past few hours he had gathered enough information to make him very much afraid. As Gawain had said, the net had been woven by a master. He didn't understand, yet, all the possibilities involved.

"That's if she confesses and repents. If she does not confess and is found guilty, the punishment is excommunication, branding, and exile."

"No man would dare!"

"Wait! That is just the beginning. The bishops at Cirencester will try her for pagan sorcery, but now the word has gone out that a civil tribunal will also meet, and there the charge will be treason."

Arthur looked from one man to the other.

"This can't be," he said finally and firmly. "It makes no sense. Who would conceive such an accusation and who would believe it?"

No one answered but he could feel the fear from the other two. Arthur looked around for his boots.

"We leave for Cirencester tonight. I will have this madness ended at once."

Cei stepped in front of him. "You can't go, Arthur. You must stay here. Anything you do to try and save her will only convince the people that the charges are true. What man would let himself be cuckolded and then not wish to see the woman punished? Only one who had been bewitched. They will believe it if you go."

Arthur stood. "If we were not closer than brothers, Cei, I would have run you through for saying that."

"I know," Cei grimaced. "That was why I had to be the one to say it."

They glared at each other a moment, then Arthur closed his eyes and rubbed his aching head. Gawain reached out to him, grief-stricken but bound to add his say.

"And if *you* go to Cirencester, dissolve the courts, and bring Guinevere back, what will that do to the system of laws and justice you've had us working on all these years? You've promised the people that no man, not even the kings or the bishops, can be above the law. Are you now excepting yourself?"

Arthur looked from one to the other, anger warring with incredulity in his eyes. He slammed his fist on the table.

"I wish I had never led an army or read a law or ridden more than a day from my own hearth. I wish I had let Britain be overrun by barbarians and that I had left all of my fine knights to butcher peasants in their own happy ignorance. I wish I had never cared about anyone, that I had looted the churches and raped and burned and taken whatever I wanted.

By all the gods that ever laughed at man, I wish I'd been born without a soul!"

Gawain and Cei sat on the floor at his feet. They couldn't bear looking down on him.

Gawain broke the long silence.

"Whatever happens, Arthur, we won't let her be harmed. You know that. Cei and I will leave today. I'll have them tie me to my horse again rather than waste time. We'll be there in a day and a half."

"It will be all right, Arthur," Cei added. "No one could look at Guinevere and believe all the nonsense they're saying about her."

"No, of course not." Arthur did not relax. "But if any harm comes to her at all, those power-hungry 'saints' and greedy kings will find that I have not sunk into my dotage yet. I will chase them into their warrens and burn them out to face my sword."

"If any harm comes to her," Gawain said grimly, "we will be at your side until the last one of them is destroyed."

Except for burns on her wrists from the ropes, Guinevere was not uncomfortable. They had not spoken to her on the hard ride to Cirencester and had served her with fear. Even Sagremore and Perredur, whom she had thought were her friends, stayed as far distant from her as possible. When she caught their eyes, the look in them made her feel shaky and cold at the pit of her stomach.

"This is ridiculous!" she told herself sternly. "I am the Queen. Moreover, I am a daughter of Rome, of a Christian family, bred to reason and to rule. They are mad or enchanted but they know better than to hurt me. Arthur will not let them. Soon, someone will come and rescue me; someone always has. I need only to be calm and wait."

She told herself this again and again, during the long ride by day and the fearful silence by night. She remembered it when they brought her into the town and the few remaining citizens stared at her as if she had been a rare bird, captured for their astonishment. When she was taken to a room and the door barred she sat down on the bed and composed herself to wait.

When a guard brought her some food, she thanked him and calmly informed him that she would need water to wash with, a clean robe, and the services of a maid to attend her.

"I . . . I . . . don't know about that," he stammered.

She smiled.

"Of course it must be difficult to provide for so many in the town, when the streets have been nearly empty for so long, but perhaps you could ask?"

"Yes, of course." He bowed. "Perhaps my wife . . ."

"If she could lend me a robe and some hair clasps, I would be grateful." Guinevere smiled again.

An hour later, there was a timid knock on the door and a woman entered, followed by a servant carrying a steaming kettle of water scented with mint. They were followed by a shoemaker with a selection of sandals and another woman whose arms were piled with a rainbow variety of cloth. Guinevere showed no surprise. This was the way she had always been treated. People were so kind! Perhaps things hadn't changed so much after all. Now, as long as Lancelot was safe, everything would be all right.

In the town, however, there was consternation bordering on chaos. Only St. Caradoc had known the real reason for the meeting of the holy men of the church. The others thought that it was only an unhappy coincidence and their reactions were many and varied.

Dubricius was cautious when asked about the charges.

"I did hear something about it last winter," he admitted. "Some say that the King would never have entertained Saxons at his table if the Queen had not influenced him. Since her brother took a Saxon wife, they assumed it was her doing. But I never heard she was that fond of those heathens in spite of the gossip. I don't know. We must have more proof before we condemn a woman of such high status."

"Have you seen her?" Bishop Teilo asked. "I have heard that she does not age and that her beauty is a temptation to any man who dares look at her. The proof may lie in the accused herself."

"She has not changed much since I first saw her, well over twenty years ago, but she has not had the cares of motherhood or the burden of toil to wear away her youth," Dubricius hedged.

Caradoc overheard them and spoke across the room in the penetrating tones of one who often preaches to the stones. "Time touches us all, to remind us that we are but mortal and decay is the fate of our bodies. To go against that is to go against God's design."

Dubricius quelled a desire to clap his hands over his ears. These country ranters! He turned back pointedly to Teilo.

"I will wait until all have spoken and we have questioned the woman before I decide if she is a sorceress and if she has committed any evil through it."

"Adultery isn't evil enough for you, Dubricius?" Caradoc rang out again. "London has tainted the purity of your faith, I fear. Well, there will be enough evidence to convince even you."

"If that is so, I will not flinch from my duty," Dubricius answered wearily. "But I, for one, would prefer not to discuss the matter until we convene, tomorrow."

He did not wait for a reply but returned to his rooms.

Modred was waiting there.

"I apologize," he began. "I just rode from Camelot with Sir Gawain and Sir Cei. King Arthur has sent us to be the Queen's defenders."

"He wishes her defended, then?"

Modred avoided the older man's eyes. "He does not believe she has done anything that is anyone's affair but his own. He says there is no truth in the gossip of witchcraft and treason. He is very angry but will abide by the good sense of the tribunal."

Dubricius concentrated, trying to find a hidden meaning in Modred's words.

"He will not intervene, even if she is sentenced to excommunication and death?"

"Arthur told me that the laws are just and all must obey them."

"So!" Dubricius thought. "He believes her to be guilty but will not condemn her himself. Perhaps there is some truth in all the wild rumors."

Aloud he only murmured that it was a rare man who would not use his office to go around justice.

"My . . . uncle is indeed a rare man. If he were not the King, I think he might have been called a saint."

"Your loyalty commends you, Sir Modred. You may tell the King that he can trust me to be true to his laws. Now, would you like some wine before you go?"

"No, thank you. I must speak to many more people tonight and, if possible, visit the Queen."

"They won't let you do that, I'm afraid. Sir Sagremore was terribly shocked when he discovered that she was holding a sort of court in her cell, so that he has forbidden anyone to see or speak to her. Her meals are lowered from the roof to the window in a bag. They are afraid she will work her enchantments on the guards and escape."

"Idiot!" Modred snapped, then recovered himself. Perhaps it was just as well. "I find it difficult to believe that a being that powerful could have been captured in the first place. Clearly Sir Sagremore was overzealous."

Dubricius had thought so himself, but there was a question in Modred's voice that made him wonder. It was true that she had not been imprisoned a day before people began to arrive with gifts and comforts for her. Was it just that she was loved by the common people, or did she have some unnatural influence over them?

He pondered the question long after Modred had gone.

Sir Perredur had told Guinevere that the next morning she would be taken to the center of town, past the forum to the Basilica. There she would be questioned by the bishops and saints, and witnesses would speak for and against her. He held iron out before him at arm's length to keep her away. Guinevere had watched him with sad wonder, but said nothing. What could be said?

She lay on her narrow bed that night, wrapped in the soft woolen blankets the guard's wife had brought. He had looked fearful, and she hoped they had not punished him. There was no sound in the rooms around her. Her lamp had been taken away. For the first time in her life she was alone in the dark. She put her back to the wall and stared into the moonlit room. Her eyes drooped and she dozed. It seemed in her twilight state that she could hear music from somewhere, singing by many people, with melodies that chased each other round and round in complicated patterns until she grew dizzy trying to follow them. Only once before had she heard anything so exquisite.

"Dear Geraldus," she murmured in her sleep. Then she sat up with a shock.

The moonlight quivered around the sitting forms of two men. One was slight and laughter shone in his eyes. His hands were waving in the air, in time to the music. The other man was taller. He was younger than Guinevere remembered but still as imposing. He watched her with the same look of annoyance that he had always shown in her presence.

"I should have warned Arthur before I left," Merlin said. "I always knew she would bring him ruin."

"She hasn't done anything. You know that or you wouldn't be here," Geraldus chided. "Hello, Guinevere. I've missed you. How do you think we've improved?"

He indicated the choir.

"Geraldus!" Guinevere reached out her arms to him. "I knew you didn't die, but no one would believe me."

"I shouldn't have left my body behind," he admitted. "But I don't seem to have missed it."

"There is a shrine to you now. People say you work miracles."

He squirmed. "Not really. I cured two cases of tone deafness. These things get exaggerated."

Merlin cut in. "You can gossip later. Guinevere, they are going to condemn you at this trial."

"No, of course not. Arthur won't let them."

"He can't stop them, and if he tries to rescue you, he'll destroy everything I worked for."

Guinevere stared at them. "You came here to tell me that I'm going to have to let them kill me?"

"No, Guinevere." Geraldus smiled with eagerness. "We came to take you back with us. You can live with us here until the end of the world."

He held out his hands to her, but she drew back.

"Is Galahad with you?"

Merlin tapped his foot impatiently. "Of course not. What would he do here?"

"Then can Lancelot come with me?"

"I doubt it. He couldn't stand the comfort."

"Then why should I come?"

"Because if they come for you in the morning and you are gone, they will say that all the charges about you were true, but it will be over. There will be no trial, no accusations, no chance for anyone to criticize Arthur. He can possibly recover from the shambles your adultery has made of his life and of Britain. And if you had ever done anything for the good of anyone else, you would know this was the best and only way."

Her lower lip trembled. "Geraldus?"

"You belong with us, dear," he said gently. "You were never meant to stay so long in the mortal world. You're like me, neither one nor the other. It's so beautiful here. You'll soon forget."

"Forget! But I can't forget! I don't want to! What if I went back to Arthur and swore never to see Lancelot again, ever?"

"Child, you still don't understand."

"I don't believe you, Merlin. First of all, no one can condemn me for a treason I haven't committed. This is Britain, not some lawless waste. But even if they did find me guilty, if I went with you, it wouldn't be as you said. There would always be talk that Arthur or Lancelot had freed me and that I was still alive somewhere, brewing horrible potions, no doubt, to destroy my enemies. No, I won't go with you. I'll stay here, and if the tribunal says I'm guilty, then I'll die.

Merlin stood; his look showed his complete disgust. "The one time in your life you make up your own mind and you choose the wrong answer. We can't force you. I saw in you from your childhood the seed of disaster. I should know better than to try to change what must be. Come, Geraldus."

The musician kissed his fingers to her tenderly. "Don't be afraid, Guinevere dove. He doesn't know the future. Everything may turn out well. I'm proud of you, dear. But we will miss you here. Listen for us!"

They were gone. The moon was higher and the rays slid onto the wall, outlining the ancient stones. Guinevere pulled her feet back onto the bed. Her mouth was dry but the water ewer was empty. She wrapped herself up again. What had she done? Those awful men couldn't mean to kill her, could they? For the first time, she was afraid.

Chapter Seventeen

Guinevere's belief in the kindness and reason of the people of Britain was severely battered during her 'questioning' and trial. The first day she sat in the Basilica with the holy men while they set her recitations of dogma and creed. She had been taught well and had read widely, so she was able to answer with no difficulty. Despite the tendency of her questioners to argue the answers among themselves, she felt it went well and began to hope it would soon be over.

The following day was different.

They put her behind a fence of iron grillework. St. Caradoc began the morning with a speech of two hours which set the stage for the rest of the trial. Slowly she began to realize that Merlin had been right. No one was going to be able to convince her inquisitors of her innocence, for the saint was using their own sympathy toward her to convict her. With this fear growing in her, she stared at him with the horrid fascination of a rabbit mesmerized by a snake preparing to bite as he shouted and gestured toward her, sending gusts of odor from his unwashed robes.

"You see her before you. Look at her, my brothers! Look closely. What do you see? A child, almost, just setting out on her adult life; an innocent flower just creeping from the bud. Yes. We look at her and see freshness and sweetness and transcendent beauty. I've watched you all when you speak to her. You are kinder, gentler, protective. You can't believe that this fragile, delicate creature could possibly have evil in her. And last night you went to your rooms and dreamed of her."

He sneered at them. Guinevere reeled back coughing as he thrust his finger at her, waving the fetid cloth of his sleeves even closer. From the back of the long Basilica she could hear Gawain start to interrupt and someone shush him. Caradoc went on.

"From this you should know what this witch can do. She hides behind her beauty; she lures us with smiles and guileless eyes. And just as she plans, just as King Arthur and the unfortunate Sir Lancelot were trapped, so she intends to trap us! But I can see past the flesh into the hideous soul beneath. God has given me the strength to resist her wickedness, and now I exhort each man among you to pray that the temptations she sends to torment you be thrust out! Yes! Even now I see doubt on some faces. Her magics are still at work even in this holy place. But think, my brothers, think of your sisters and wives and mothers. Yes, especially think of your mothers. I see you young men with lust in your eyes. And yet this woman who excites you is older than your mothers. How can that be, without sorcery?"

He went on and on in his most flamboyant style. Guinevere stopped listening. It made her queasy. In the back, Gawain seethed and longed simply to hit that haggard face as hard as he could. It would be a relief to crush the man's skull. Cei put a hand on his arm.

"No one will believe this," he muttered. "We'll make them see. It would be easier, though, if she hadn't been caught with Lancelot."

Gawain leaned his head against a pillar and closed his eyes. Modred had to be behind this, he and Aunt Morgause. But how could he convince anyone? And how could he stop them? He wished his mysterious father had thought to give him brains to match his strength.

In the afternoon, Guinevere was surprised to see the guard who had stood outside her room come forward to speak. His wife had continued to send her small offerings of flowers and bread, and she became hopeful. But when she smiled at him, the guard looked away.

Caradoc approached. "You are Sevilis, of this town, are you not?"

"Yes, Sir," the guard answered. "I was assigned to keep watch over the Queen. I mean, the prisoner."

"And you came to me last night with some information. Will you tell it to my brothers, here?"

Sevilis nodded and turned so that he wouldn't have to look at Guinevere as he spoke.

"I have, myself, taken the duty of spending the night watch outside the prisoner's door. Last night, I overheard her speaking to someone in the room with her."

"Had you let anyone in?" Caradoc asked with suppressed excitement.

Sevilis bridled. "Of course not! I know my duty! I sent for my second-in-command to wait while I went around to the window. It is on the second floor and there is another guard below. He swore no one had entered. I climbed alone to the window and saw the prisoner. She was talking to two ghosts! I swear it!"

He added this as an outcry arose. Sevilis wiped his brow and went on.

"They were terrible beings, full of smoke and fire. As I watched, one of them rose and floated toward the window. I am ashamed to confess that in my fear, I lost my grip and fell to the ground."

Dubricius came up to him and fixed the guard with a skeptical glance. "Are you quite certain that is what you saw? Two ghosts? How did you know that's what they were? Perhaps it was only a trick of light on a mirror or a wall hanging. Why should you assume they were spirits of the dead?"

"I'm not lying, Lord Bishop," Servilis said earnestly. "I know what I heard. That was why I had to look. Capiam will swear to it also. She called one of the ghosts by name! She called it Merlin!"

The noise in the church was deafening. The guard passed by Guinevere and paused.

"Forgive me, my Lady," he muttered. "But it's true, you know it is. We can't have that sort of wizardry anymore in Britain."

In the midst of this revelation, old King Meleagant arrived and was helped up to the podium by Caradoc. He leaned heavily against the wood as he told of how Guinevere had charmed his servants and family and even his doddering father during her captivity in their castle.

"You all know the tale; it's been sung often enough," he said bitterly. "Arthur and I made a bet for my allegiance. I captured her and would have kept her for the time we set. My castle has never been breached by honest means. The gate is guarded by spirits and the only other entrance is by a bridge of a fine-honed knife. No man could have crossed it, yet Sir Lancelot did. And then, when he appeared, ragged and bleeding all over my floors, she wasn't even grateful. She must have had her own plans to spirit herself away. She screamed at him and mocked him and drove the poor man mad. It made me sick to watch it."

He gave Guinevere an ugly glance and resumed.

"And now they say she lured him to her, in spite of her cruelty to him before. What man would let himself be so used? I'd not let a woman, a human woman, do that to me. There's evil in her!" he cried, waving his hands to ward off her spells. "Don't set her free to do more harm to innocent men!"

"No!" Guinevere cried out. "It's not true! Please!"

Dubricius stood and addressed her gently.

"Were you kidnapped by King Meleagant?"

"Yes, but . . ."

"And did Sir Lancelot cross the sword bridge to rescue you?"

"Yes." More subdued.

"And what happened then?"

Guinevere hung her head. "I called him a fool for taking such a risk. It was only a wager! Arthur would have come. That was all! It was not his job to save me. I didn't know my words would affect him so."

Dubricius nodded and sat down again. But Caradoc leaped up.

"How did you know Arthur would come? Had you provided him with amulets against spirits or charms to cross the sword?"

"No!"

"And what about Merlin?" Caradoc probed. "Will you also say the guard was lying? Or will you admit that the wizard Merlin came to you in your cell?"

"It was Merlin, but he's not a ghost; he only wanted to help me!" She started to say more, but was silenced by the wall of horror and fear before her. She covered her face. It was no use. She had sealed her own fate.

Cei was completely frightened by the end of that second day. He had listened to the timid attempts by Dubricius and Father Antonius to defend the Queen and seen how their own words had been turned against them; how her own words were condemning her. The murmurs of the men as they left the Basilica were full of confusion and not a little fear. If they found this woman innocent, might they not be accused the next day of being in her enchantments or, even worse, in collusion with her? And, though she refused to admit to sorcery, by her own words she had seen the greatest magus in

· 167 ·

Britain, vanished these ten years past, appear to her in a locked, guarded room. It seemed very bleak. Cei went to find out what Modred had learned from the civic leaders who would make up the tribunal.

Modred was well pleased with the attitude of the townsmen. They were tired of paying taxes for protection from the Saxon and Irish. They didn't believe there was any more danger from them. Arthur had not expanded Britain's hegemony on the island since the battle of Mons Badon. He was growing old and his influence was ebbing. The towns had not recovered in the way he predicted.

"It's no use your trying to sway me, Sir Modred," a lean, lantern-jawed merchant insisted. "Maybe she's the cause of our weakening and maybe she isn't, but since he married her, Arthur's done nothing but talk and send us laws and levies. And we don't think much of a man who does nothing when his wife makes a fool of him. In the oldest days, when the King grew weak they would have said it was time for a sacrifice."

"Now, my friend!" Modred exclaimed in mock-horror. "You can't mean to go back to those barbaric, pagan times! We have the great Roman culture surrounding us now, laws and customs of civilization."

"Maybe so," the merchant shrugged. "But we had rules then, too, and I can't see that her baths and forums and fine laws did Rome any good. Maybe our great-grandfathers should have kept up the old ways as well as the new. I've heard what Meleagant and the holy men have been saying. There's something wrong at Camelot and she may be the cause. I'll hear the testimony, but I think, if the priests believe her evil, I'll agree to whatever they say."

Modred repeated the conversation to Cei.

"They all say the same," he added. "Arthur has given them peace, but they've grown used to it. The prosperity he hoped for isn't coming to them. It can't come without the trade that we had in the days of the empire. They need someone to blame and they've found her. I've done my best, but it looks very bad for Guinevere."

· 168 ·

As he said this, he was swept by such a feeling of relief and elation that he had to sit down and bury his face in his hands to hide it. Cei patted his back awkwardly and rubbed his own eyes with his knuckles.

"You've tried, Modred. I don't think you've slept three hours straight since we got here. The only thing left to do is get Arthur. He's the only one who can stop them."

"If he does, he may be faced with civil war," Modred cautioned.

"Are you saying we should let this rabble have Guinevere? Do you know some of the things people are saying should be done?"

"Yes, but I may be able to get them to stick to Roman law. In that case, the worst they could do to her would be to brand her with the mark of a sorceress and exile her."

"Modred, we're talking about Guinevere!"

Modred rose. "And I'm talking about Britain and keeping what my . . . what Arthur has created. Don't you see? If we can get them to take out their anger on her, she can be sent away someplace and Arthur can get on with making Britain whole again."

Cei stared at him.

"Gawain was right about you, Modred. How can you even think of such a thing? Arthur would never allow his wife to be used like that. You sound as though you believe those slanders."

"And you've forgotten that Guinevere is not exactly innocent." Modred was tired and his temper frayed. "She acted the whore with her husband's best friend in his own bed. Arthur knew about it for years and did nothing. Would you have stood for that? Maybe there is something to the charges!"

Cei felt icy with doubt and fear. Without another word, he opened the door and left.

The cooling evening air made the sweat on his forehead clammy as he stumbled back to the room he shared with Gawain. He had to get back to Camelot, to see Arthur, to talk to Lydia, to try and find some sanity again. And there wasn't time.

The next morning Guinevere stood outside the Basilica with her chin high and her eyes blank as St. Caradoc announced that the priests and bishops had come to a conclusion.

Guinevere, Queen of Britain, was to be condemned and excommunicated by the church for the use of sorcery.

That afternoon, a civil tribunal convicted her of treason.

Numbly she followed her guards back to her cell. They circled her at spear length and kept their eyes averted. The day had turned cloudy and she shivered in her thin summer gown. All the people of the town were in the street, staring mutely as she passed. She looked into their faces and shrank inside herself as she saw the quick flickering of their fingers to ward off her magic. In the courtyard of her prison, she heard weeping and wondered if it were for her sake. But it couldn't be that bad. Surely tomorrow they would see reason. Surely in the morning she would awaken at Camelot. Galahad would barge in with a hurt bird he had found and they would nurse it. Then they would play tag in the meadow with the other children and Lancelot would come with Gawain and chase them all with mock-lion roars. She lay down on the narrow bed and closed her eyes. Tomorrow it would all be just a nightmare, fading with the moon.

Gawain looked toward the setting sun and swore loudly.

"I haven't much time today, Cei. We've got to do something before I fall asleep again!"

Cei paced the room in sharp, jerky paces. "What do you suggest? Every time I open my mouth, I'm accused of being under her influence. We're lucky these madmen haven't locked us up as well!"

"Then let's rescue her! They are fools, all of them, and, if we can just get her away from here for a few months then Arthur can show them just how insane this whole thing is!"

"I don't know." Cei sat down wearily but his feet still continued their nervous tapping. "I've been lost ever since we got here. Your brother, Modred, nearly has me convinced that the only way Arthur will win is to let Guinevere be punished."

"Modred is a conniving weasel!" Gawain stated. "I'm sick of hearing him praised. He never did anything in his life that wasn't for his own good. They're talking of branding her with hot iron, Cei! I've even heard rumors that they're weaving a wicker basket for her!"

Cei was puzzled. "Why would they do that?"

"You were raised in a Roman household or you'd know. It was the old way to pacify the gods. If you won't help me, I'll save her myself, or try to. I . . . I . . . ahhhhahh, blast!" He yawned and fell into bed as the last rays of sunlight vanished.

Cei looked at him for a long minute. With people like Gawain in the world, it was no wonder he was having such trouble convincing anyone that Guinevere was no witch. He knew how Arthur must be chafing at Camelot. He would be more than furious when he found out what had happened. If they did not save Guinevere, Cei felt uncomfortably sure that Arthur would keep his oath and twenty years of patient work would be destroyed. He had sent relay messengers every day. Why was there no response? Had they been waylaid or was Arthur coming himself with his men-at-arms? Cei kicked Gawain's bed in irritation, but the golden head only burrowed further under the blanket. With a curse, Cei flung on his cloak and stepped out into the growing darkness.

The town was silent. The forum was empty. All the curious and taunting citizens had gone home. In the Basilica only the eternal flame still burned. Cei tried to approach the house in which they were holding Guinevere, but he was turned away by the guards. Finally, he retraced his steps back to his room and his lonely bed. Sighing, he wished for Lydia again. She would know how to deal with madmen.

In a large room at the last remaining inn in Cirencester, the bishops, saints, merchants, and landholders sat in a wary group and tried to decide what should be done with the Queen.

"By Roman law, she still has the right to final judgment before the King. If he wishes to forgive her, we have no further say." Father Antonius spoke up boldly, knowing that he was the youngest man there.

Caradoc snorted and would have rebuffed the priest, but Dubricius raised a hand to quiet him and gently explained the problem.

"She has been convicted of influencing Arthur. How can we allow him to stand in judgment on her? We don't know how long her spells last."

"Do you all really believe this?" Father Antonius looked pleadingly at his elders.

This time Caradoc would not be silenced.

"I knew from the time he refused to accept my protection of Ligessauc Longhand, someone other than his proper advisers was controlling him. Now we know who it is. Now we know why Arthur has chosen to trade with the pagan invaders instead of sweeping them back into the sea."

"I am sure that if we send her into exile, to Armorica, perhaps, Arthur will soon be himself again." Dubricius faltered.

"No," Caradoc spoke firmly. "She must be utterly destroyed. Nothing must remain of her tainted flesh."

"What are you saying?"

"That her unholy body must be burnt entirely."

"We are Christians, Caradoc. How will her soul rise on the day of judgment if her body be lost?"

"Her soul, if she ever had one, will have its chance to escape from the flames. It may be the only chance. Her obscene body will pay the price so that her soul may be free."

"You mean burn her *alive?*"

The saint nodded.

Father Antonius was appalled. "That is barbaric! Even our pagan ancestors abandoned that hideous form of sacrifice years ago. No one will allow it."

He looked around the room for confirmation. St. Illtud's face was considering, Bishop Teilo's grave but resigned, Meleagant's positivly gloating.

St. Illtud spoke with hesitation. "It may be the only way to save poor Lancelot. If you could have seen the struggle he made to free himself, you would know the power of this woman's sorcery. I, too, think it barbaric to burn her. But to save a man's soul, I will agree even to that."

Father Antonius pushed back against the door.

"This cannot be the Christianity I was taught! What sort of men are you? I will not be a part of this. You must hold the torches. I will be at her side. You will not deny the Queen a confessor."

"My boy," Dubricius soothed. "Of course you must do your best to help her. We don't forget that you have been in her household and under her influence for years. When this is over and you're free, you'll understand."

"Never!" He found the latch, opened the door, and stumbled out.

Dubricius shook his head. "I can't believe how far this went without our knowing. Yes, I agree also. The Queen must burn."

Chapter Eighteen

"I don't know how you did this, Modred, but I'll see that you pay for it. Don't ever doubt me!"

Gawain's voice was low in the crowded forum but his outrage could not be contained even by the need for secrecy. His hair coiled and sparked out his fury. Modred noted it and smirked.

"Be careful, Brother. In the mood here today, you, too, will find yourself tossed into the flames from which you came."

Gawain spat on the ground at his brother's feet. "You

could have been the best of us all, Modred, but you chose to follow Aunt Morgause in her blind need for revenge. Why should any of us have cared what Arthur's father did to our grandmother? What does it matter? They're dead now."

"Every family must have its little traditions," Modred replied. "I wouldn't speak so openly, Gawain. You know how Morgause likes to eavesdrop."

He laughed again at the change on Gawain's face. Morgause might very well be perched on one of the eaves, attending to their conversation. Gawain clenched his fists but did not raise them.

Around them the townsfolk scurried by. It was Saturday afternoon and the execution was set for Monday. Caradoc and his cohorts had arranged for it to be as soon as possible in order to carry out the sentence before the ardor of the people could dim and before Arthur could arrive to stop them. Cei, stunned by the horror of it all, had gone with Father Antonius to try to see Guinevere. Gawain had decided to make an unauthorized visit later, to assure her that he would not let her be killed, whatever the consequences. How could anyone have believed all that nonsense! Over Modred's shoulder he caught the curious, fearful glances of the people. What kinds of ugliness lurked in them that they would want to destroy a beautiful, innocent woman? What did they think her death would give them? He had no answers. He only knew that it was through Modred's machinations that it was happening.

"How could you do this to Arthur now that you know him?" he asked sadly. "You know what this will do to him; his grief and anger will destroy Britain."

"I don't think so." Modred stared directly into Gawain's eyes. "She is only a woman, after all. He may take revenge on Meleagant and the bishops, but that will mean he'll have their property to give to those who help him. He may even remarry and beget a son."

Gawain leaned away in disgust. "I see. You don't know Arthur after all. If you planned on playing Merlin to a boy-king heir of Arthur's, you can forget it. He won't look at another woman. It's more likely he'll die of grief."

Modred smiled. In his face Gawain saw the confirmation of his accusations. He backed away but Modred caught his sleeve.

"You can tell anyone you like, Brother, but you won't be believed. Every man here will swear I have spent all my time in efforts to save the Queen. No one will weep more convincingly when we bring her ashes back to Camelot. You still think you can save her, don't you? I thought of that, too. The pyre will be lit in the hour before dawn, 'when evil is weakest,' and when you are still trapped in your unnatural sleep. You see? You are defeated, Gawain. Go back to Cornwall. Agravaine will take you in. You can live out your remaining years in safety, a curiosity of the house. But if you continue against me, well, think how vulnerable you are in the night."

With a contemptuous snort, Modred turned and left his brother. The remaining townspeople made a wide circle to pass Gawain as he stood there, too angry to move, lest he smash whatever or whomever came near him. Finally he took a deep breath.

"I will not let you win, Modred," he muttered. "And Guinevere will not be the sacrifice to your ambition."

Cei was back when Gawain returned to their quarters. In the past week Arthur's seneschal had grown gaunt and pale. He sat on the bed and leaned against the wall.

"I can't believe it. They wouldn't let me in, and Father Antonius had to invoke the right of a confessor before they would let him through. What am I going to tell Arthur?"

"Don't give up, Cei. You did all you could in the face of this madness. I know I can rescue her. I'll take her back to Cornwall with me. She won't die!"

"Gawain! I know how strong you are, but the town is full of warriors brought by Meleagant, Fergus, and the others. You can't defeat them alone."

"He won't be alone!" Gareth spoke from the doorway. "Caet and I have come to help you."

With a glad cry, Gawain grabbed his brother and hugged him.

"I never thought I could be so glad to see anyone! How many men did you bring? Is Lancelot with you?"

Gareth pulled away in embarrassment. "Only the two of us came. We left the day before yesterday. Arthur doesn't know about the verdict, yet. Isn't Lancelot here? I haven't seen him since the night Guinevere was taken."

"No, at least he hasn't been seen. Arthur didn't send you? Why are you here then? Of all people, I'd think you would be the last to want her rescued from the flames."

Gareth sat down. "Thank you, Gawain. What sort of man do you think I am? I know, I said she bewitched Lancelot, but I didn't mean *really*. I couldn't spend all those years with our aunt and mother at Tintagel and not know the smell of sorcery. I don't like Guinevere, but I won't let her be killed. For whatever reason, she is precious to Lancelot and I'll do whatever I can to help you."

Cei turned to the other man. "Caet? What are you doing here? You have no stake in this. You're not even a knight."

He meant it kindly, to give the man an excuse to go, but Caet's eyes flashed.

"No, I'm not. I'm only the son of a slave who might have been a king if the Romans had never come to Britain. Now I breed the horses and see that they're ready when you gallant warriors ride forth. I have no stake in this but that woman they mean to burn. You've all forgotten whose family owned mine. I saw her the day she was born and I've loved her almost as long. Even now, I'm the one she comes to when she's homesick, when she's lonely. All these years I've watched her, worked in the stables, just to be near her. I ride better than any of you and I can wield a sword well enough. I will die for her. Will your prejudice deny me that?"

He glared the other three down. Cei held out his hand.

"Welcome, Caet. We need your help. Your fidelity is worthy of knighthood. Sir Sagremore and Sir Perredur have shown what they thought of Arthur's trust. There will be empty places when we return if you wish to be considered."

Caet sat down heavily for such a small man. The bed creaked under him.

"If we return I will think about it. Has anyone thought of a plan of attack? We are only proposing to cut our way through a thousand people, sweep up Guinevere, and ride off. I think it will take some organization."

Cei groaned at hearing it so baldly put. The four men put their heads together and tried to think.

The sun hung like a great red eye on the horizon outside Guinevere's window. From the town came the clanks and calls of the evening meal. Pale and still, she lay on the narrow bed. Her gold hair was loose on the blanket, spilling to the floor. Her hands fell at her sides, limply open in a state of resignation. Her breath was slow as in sleep, but her eyes stared at the ceiling. Guinevere was waiting for feelings to come. Logically, she told herself, there should be fear or hurt or violent rage. Monday before dawn, strange men with lustful eyes were going to take her down to the forum, put her on a wicker throne and set torches into a pyre beneath her.

Father Antonius had wept as he listened to her simple confession; the many sins of omission and the one of love. His head had rested in her lap as he sobbed his grief and fury at his inability to make the bishops believe in her innocence. Her hands had been cool on his burning cheeks.

"You are absolved of guilt in this," she had told him, and he had gone away comforted.

Even then she had felt nothing but a wistful pity for the young man. She thought of Galahad and a tear slid from the corner of her eye. She wondered softly if Lancelot were safe and hoped he would remember her promise to wait for him, even at the gates of hell. She thought of Arthur and managed a brief ache of regret. He deserved a better wife, one who would have pampered him and loved him unasked and given him a long line of children to rejoice in. But for herself, she had no emotion left.

The music surrounded her but she didn't turn to look for

the singers. Dear Geraldus! Perhaps she should go with him. Would the shame for Arthur be any the less if she simply flew away into the night? But an eternity without Lancelot, even in Eden, would be torture. She smiled thanks and shook her head. The music stopped on a mournful high sough. There was a creak at the door, the smell of pork simmered in fresh cider. She closed her eyes. There was no need to bother with food anymore.

"Guinevere, sit up, old girl, and eat a bit of this."

"Gawain!" Her fingers stretched out as he lifted her hands and pulled her from the bed. "How did you get in here?"

"I bribed the guard. I had no idea how cheaply they come. Now, come on. Take a bite. You'll need all your strength. Your rescue party will need any help you can give."

"Rescue! Oh, no, Gawain! Don't try it!" Guinevere dropped the spoon he had just handed her.

"Guinevere! We have to. We can't let those slimy obscenities kill you!"

"But Arthur, they'll go against him, even send armies if he keeps me. Meleagant has been looking for an excuse for years."

"Do you think that matters to Arthur?" Gawain picked up the spoon, wiped it on his tunic and handed it back. "He's ready to sweep them from the earth with his own hands simply for the pain they've caused you already."

She stirred the meat seriously, her attention fixed on the bowl.

"But what about the pain I've given him, already? You know better than anyone what I've done to him. Perhaps I am as wicked as they say. I don't think I mind dying so much, if it doesn't hurt too badly. It seems easier than facing my poor Arthur again."

"Guinevere." Gawain nearly shook her in exasperation. "They are going to *burn* you. I have it on very good authority that it will hurt a great deal. And think, also, of what it will do to everyone else, both those of us who couldn't save you and those who think death is your only salvation. Especially those! What if this becomes a custom, a standard way of dealing with people who follow the old gods as well as the new. You've seen how easy it is to accuse and how hard to deny. We can't let them start believing they can rid themselves of enemies merely by crying 'heresy' and 'treason'! Think of all those other innocent victims!"

Guinevere gave a crooked smile. "You always did tell me when I was behaving thoughtlessly. Very well. I would not want to be so inconsiderate as to die so that Caradoc can continue spouting his venom against truly innocent people."

"I knew you would be sensible. Now, there are only four of us, so you must be ready to act quickly. This is what you must do . . ."

The morning was thick with mist. Cloaked shadows appeared and vanished through the columns of the forum. Caradoc leaned from his window and cursed the witch who must have conjured the weather to make it harder to light the flames.

"I don't suppose," Dubricius ventured timidly, "that God might have created the fog to keep us from committing this act?"

Caradoc's answer was unbecoming a man of the church.

"Have the guards around her doubled!" he yelled to a soldier in the street. "Let no one come near her until it is over!"

Dubricius shook his head doubtfully and went to find St. Illtud and Bishop Teilo, who were already beset by the same second thoughts he was having.

"I should have been stronger," he thought. "Or am I just being swayed by the charms of an evil woman? I wish I could tell!"

In Guinevere's room, the guard's wife was helping her into the simple white robe of the penitent which Caradoc had decreed she must wear.

"This linen is too thin, my Lady," the woman was saying. "You will be cold on a morning like this."

Guinevere could not keep from laughing. "You needn't worry, good woman. My inquisitors have arranged to warm me well enough."

The woman covered her face in the fabric. "Oh, my Lady!

Forgive me! How could I have been so tactless! Those wicked, wicked men!"

Guinevere smoothed the material against her waist. "You mustn't say that. Someone might hear you."

"If it weren't for my man and my children, lady, I'd shout it from the top of the Basilica steps. It's an evil thing they've planned this day."

Guinevere was cheered by the championing but something compelled her to admit, "But I was unfaithful to my husband."

The guard's wife put her hands on her hips. "Were you, now? Well, if they burned every woman in Britain who had a lover on the sly, there wouldn't be a tree left on the island to cook a meal over or a woman left to do the cooking. It's those saints with their preaching of celibacy. It isn't natural. It turns them mad. And it's you, poor dear, who must pay for their madness."

She clucked and commiserated over her until the soldiers came. Then she gave Guinevere a hug and traced an old symbol on her brow. "Excuse the liberty, but your own aren't here to do it for you," she said and left, weeping into a corner of her shawl.

One of the guards tied her hands behind her back. The rope was drawn around her wrists and looped into her palm. She grabbed it as she had been told. Caet stepped back into file.

They put her in a cart, symbol of the lowest criminal, and she shrank back from the shame of it. Then she remembered how, years before, Lancelot had endured the same ignominy for her sake alone and she held her chin higher. She had laughed at him then, for going so far beyond what was necessary to rescue her from Meleagant. It had all been a game, but no one had told him. Perhaps somewhere now, someone was laughing at her. She prayed that Lancelot was safe now, and far away. The cartwheel hit an old boot in the road and jolted her against the side. Her unbound hair caught in a split in the wooden railing and she couldn't get it untangled. Another guard jumped up and pulled it out. The procession stopped until she was standing again. Did she dare try to slow them down with something else? Guinevere wondered how long it would be until dawn. Could Gawain manage to wake in time?

Faces swirled out of the fog and vanished again. Voices echoed against the stones as the cart lurched into the forum. The thin robe was damp through and plastered against her body. Guinevere was acutely aware that she was as near naked as never mattered, and the knowledge reminded her of some of the other remarks the guard's wife had made about the motives of St. Caradoc and Meleagant. She swallowed hard to keep from being sick.

They lifted her onto a crude wicker chair set on a wooden platform. Piles of brush and logs were stacked beneath and around it. Guinevere smelled lamp oil and her hope that the fire would refuse to light died. The crowd pressed forward. How could four men, one not even wakeable, get her safely away from this mob?

Caradoc stood in the Basilica portico out of the wet. When the cart had been removed, he came forward, his eyes fixed on Guinevere's body. He had planned on making a long sermon, excoriating this woman piece by piece, but Meleagant had reminded him of the necessity for the flames to be searing her by the first gleam of the sun, so he hurriedly climbed the makeshift ladder to the platform and faced his victim. His breath came faster.

"Do you repent of your wicked and lascivious scheme to pervert our High King Arthur and, through him, all Britain?" he bellowed, bending over her chair and thrusting his face against hers.

Guinevere pulled back. "The wickedness is in your heart, not mine," she whispered. "God knows it, whatever you do."

He stiffened and his lips grew taut. "We shall see if He knows it well enough to save you."

As soon as he reached the ground, he grabbed a torch from the nearest guard and thrust it into the pyre. Flames leapt up and spread, sending sparks across the forum as well as onto the platform, where they landed and sizzled on Guinevere's wet robe and hair. Frantically, she worked to untangle the slippery and swollen rope around her wrists. Smoke surrounded her. It billowed so that the people below her were obscured. Her eyes were running and she couldn't breathe. Somewhere beyond she could hear shouting and the sound of a horse, hooves beating on the stone of the piazza. Where was Caet? Where was Cei?

A man in priest's robes climbed onto the pyre. Just as she had on the road, Guinevere recognized him at once. His hood fell onto his shoulders, uncovering his white hair, now dusted with ash. Without speaking, he grabbed her and thrust her into and through the scorching smoke and flame. Guinevere screamed as a flaming brand landed on her foot. They kept going. She felt herself pushed onto Clades by Caet. Lancelot landed behind her and they forced their way through the crowd. It had been no more than half a minute since he rode in.

Some made way to let them pass, but a contingent of soldiers beat their way toward them, swords and knives out. Guinevere leaned far over Clades neck to give Lancelot all the room he needed to fight them off, but it didn't seem possible that he could escape them all.

From the other side of the forum, Gareth realized the danger.

"He needs me!" was his first thought and he shoved aside everyone in his way to reach his idol. He brought down two of the attackers as he neared Lancelot's side.

Lancelot could see only the flash of the swords as they came at him. The growing blaze made them glitter like the stars he would never see again. He knew which direction he had to go and hacked his way toward it as best he could. Someone called his name and another blade swung at him. He jabbed back and felt his sword connect with a human body. He gave a twist and it came out again as he turned around to face the next enemy.

Guinevere saw the sword enter Gareth and the look of surprised anguish on his face as he fell.

"Gareth! Oh no! Dear Lord, not for me!" she cried.

He saw her in the moment before she was swept away, before the crowd passed by him. He gave one last adoring gaze at Lancelot and then back to Guinevere. He shook his head. His lips moved.

"Don't tell him!" he mouthed. Then Clades forced a path for them out of the forum and they galloped down the road, out the southwest gate, past the amphitheater to freedom.

Behind them, the sun was rising.

In the dust and smoke and spilled wine, Cei and Caet found Gareth.

"He's still alive!" Caet cried. "Help me get him back. Here, take this. Let me get my tunic off to stop the bleeding."

They covered the hole but the blood continued to pour out. They managed to drag Gareth as far as the grass outside the forum. He was making a noise now, high-pitched like glass on metal.

Gawain hurried up from one direction and Modred from the other. Despite all differences, the blood-bond was in them, and they knew when their brother fell. Gawain knelt at Gareth's side as Caet told him what he had seen.

"Lancelot!" Gawain wailed. "How could he do it? Gareth is his own man!"

Gareth's keening ceased and only long ragged breathing came from him. He reached out to his brothers.

"Don't . . . blame . . . him," the dying man begged. "It's me . . . Just too damn . . . inconspicuous."

Pounding toward the forest and safety, Guinevere prayed that she had been mistaken or that Gareth might have survived. Lancelot clung to her with one arm and she leaned against him, lost tears filling her eyes.

Oh, my dearest, she thought. Will you still want me when you discover the price you just paid?

Chapter Nineteen

Many weary and fearful days later, Lancelot brought Guinevere through the mountain passes to the tiny land of Banoit. She was wearing a worn robe over the white shift, her face hidden far into the cowl. She had no shoes and no other clothes. The burn on her foot was refusing to heal although they had wrapped it in wet cloth with a piece of wheat bread over it to draw out the infection. So one leg froze and the other burned as they climbed farther from Arthur's realm.

"It should have been I who was hurt so," Lancelot moaned as he changed the cloths and noted the spread of the redness. "It was I who loved you first."

"And it was I who called you to me." Guinevere winced and then sighed as the cool bandage touched her foot. "My love, you can't suffer for everyone. My guilt is as great as yours, greater, because I do not repent. I regret the pain we've caused, the hurt we've left behind. That's all. I can never be sorry for loving you."

They had taken refuge one night in an abandoned villa. It had been fortified in some recent time, but that had not been enough to protect the owners. They had fled the invaders only to be taken by Irish slavers. The peasants in the area had taken stones and wood but no one wanted to live among the ruins. The hypocausts had gone out and the pipes were clogged with silt and weeds. The place frightened Guinevere. She would have preferred a drafty shepherd's hut to this obvious reminder of vanished Rome. There were ghosts waiting just out of her vision. Their faces were those of her ancestors.

She moved closer against Lancelot. He thought he understood. In the dim light, he noticed the crumbling plaster, the mildewed frescoes, the fallen tiles. The place looked like his conscience.

"If that pilgrim was right, tomorrow we should reach the castle of my cousin Bors," he told her. "It's the only place I can think of where we might be safe. But it won't be what you're used to."

Guinevere smiled as she gazed into the dusk. "One summer I lived in the mountains with a hermit couple. We had a stone hut and raised chickens and bees. Gaia made me help cook and wash and weed. It was beautiful and quiet. I was happier then than I have ever been since. I think it was the last time I was ever completely happy; except when I've been with you. Lancelot, is it so dreadfully wrong to be glad that we're together at last?"

He was still for a long time.

"I don't know any more," he answered at last. "It can't be right that our happiness should come from such disaster but I can't feel sorry that we have no choice but to flee together."

"And you promised, Lancelot. You promised you would never leave me again."

They arrived at the castle looking like mendicants, and the guard did not want to admit them. Lancelot humbly accepted the rebuke and turned to go but Guinevere threw back her hood and looked at the man. The gate was opened.

Bors greeted them with delight and took them at once to his brother, Lionel, who was king.

"He will be so excited that Ban's son has returned at last!" Bors told them.

Lancelot was worried, though.

"How can he be pleased?" he asked. "We have nothing but my horse and sword and the clothes we wear. We may have pursuers close behind us. I could be bringing ruin to his door."

"It doesn't matter," Bors assured him. "We are a family, a tribe. Our own are more important than any outside realm.

Lionel will defend you even if you have come to challenge him for the kingship."

"But I don't want it!" Lancelot protested. "I only want refuge for myself and the Queen."

"Then there will be no problem at all." Bors led them into his brother's hall.

Lionel rose to greet them. Guinevere saw the resemblance in their faces and the way they stood. The man before them could have been Lancelot's younger brother. As they approached, he noticed Guinevere's limp. Immediately he came forward and offered her a chair. He seemed not to see the dirt or the roughness of her clothing. Perhaps it was because she did not consider them important. Beneath any disguise or indignity, she was still a queen.

"You are very kind." She smiled wanly. "I am tired and the traveling has made it difficult to treat my hurt properly. I would be grateful if you have a healing-woman who might look at it for me."

She looked up at Lancelot.

"I will leave you to explain to your relatives why we have come and what we need. I will do whatever you decide."

Lionel called out a name that Guinevere didn't catch. A woman hurried forward.

"Lean on me, dear," she said, in the sort of kind, accepting voice Guinevere was used to. "We'll have that looked after and I'll see what I can find you to wear."

Guinevere sighed with relief. Perhaps the universe had not gone totally insane after all.

Cei and Gawain brought Gareth's body to Camelot.

"He would want to be buried here, I think," Gawain told Arthur. "Father Antonius says we can put him by the chapel. Will that be all right with you?"

"Yes." Arthur could barely be heard. "How could this have happened? Not to Gareth. He worshipped Lancelot."

"It was so confused and the fog and smoke were so thick." Cei faltered. "We tried to help but we didn't know he was coming. Everything went wrong. I'm sorry, Arthur. I blame myself."

"Modred says we must avenge our brother," Gawain began.

"But it was an accident!" Cei interrupted. "You know that! You heard Gareth. He didn't blame Lancelot!"

Gawain waved him aside. "I know that! I don't blame him, either. But Gareth is dead by Lancelot's hand. Family honor demands that Lancelot pay for Gareth's life. It's my duty to challenge him. I'm sorry, Uncle. After what you've been through, you'll think I'm purposely trying to hurt you. But it must be this way. It always has been. All the laws of Rome can't cover the rules we've lived by for centuries. Family honor comes first. My poor mother spent most of her life trying to teach us that. I didn't realize until now how important it was."

"But how can you fight Lancelot?" Arthur pleaded. "He's your best friend."

"I can't let it matter," Gawain sighed. "I can't change the code we live by. And what of your own laws, Arthur? Lancelot defied them when he rescued Guinevere. Your laws demand that you destroy them both. Will you do that? Or are you as weak as the northern lords say?"

"Gawain!" Arthur rose, his face twisted into a form Gawain had never seen on anyone human. Cei stepped between them.

"Arthur! Please! Look at him! He's not telling you what he wants to do. He saying what the rest of Britain will say."

Arthur fell back. He picked up the small ivory box that Guinevere had left when they took her away. He ran his fingers across the ridges of carving.

"I don't give a damn anymore about what they say. What did they ever care for me? Well, they'll soon have the war they want and see how weak I am. I made a treaty with King Hoel of Armorica and he's asked me to fulfill it. The Franks are moving against him; they grow stronger every year. He wants me to join him next spring, as soon as the crossing is safe. I'll bring every fighting man I can spare. Not knights, just soldiers; men who can fight and loot and win. Meleagant will like that, and Maelgwn and Fergus. The bishops can declare a holy war. Everyone should be happy at last. Won't that satisfy them? Do I have to send you to kill our best friend, too?"

"You don't need to send me, Uncle." Gawain stressed the title. "I must go. Someone from the family must avenge Gareth and I'm the only one who has a chance of doing it. I don't want to. I wish I could leave them in peace wherever they've gone, but I can't. If I don't challenge Lancelot then everyone will know that the Lords of Cornwall do not protect their own. Then Agravaine could be killed or Gaheris or even you, Arthur. You are of our family, too. Would you want your death to go unavenged?"

"But what of my law!" Arthur pleaded.

"Will you invoke it, then? I will submit to it if you mount a search for Lancelot. Bring him back to be tried for the murder of Gareth. Do you think he would resist? That will prove your law is greater than the tribes, that you can punish crimes against them all, without the rivers of blood we have known. Can you do it, Arthur? Don't look at me that way, I know what I'm asking. He's my friend, too, and Guinevere is closer to me than a sister. Tell me no. Let me go alone to find them while you prepare your army to cross to Armorica."

Arthur stared at the straw on the floor a long time. Nothing had been changed in the short time Guinevere had been gone. The shattered table lay where Lancelot had thrown it and the touseled blankets still shouted their testimony of guilt. He tried to strengthen his anger. But he kept remembering the day he had first shown Merlin the plans for Camelot. "A city of God and man," he had called it. He had known how close to the surface the old tribal feelings were. That was one reason why he had been determined to build a place entirely new, not of Roman or Celt, but of his own. He had thought he could join both peoples together with his laws. He had let them try Guinevere under those laws even though it was clear that she was being used to hurt him. They had twisted his own honesty to shame him and make him a fool in the eyes of those he must lead. Gawain was right. The people would call him weak, some for allowing the trial, some for letting Lancelot and Guinevere escape. Whatever he did, someone would castigate him.

His law said he should go after them and bring her back. The laws of the tribes told Gawain he must fight his closest friend. Why should either one of them take any heed of laws that sent them against the beliefs of their hearts?

Because that is the only hope of peace that we have.

Arthur raised his head.

"Cei, send out couriers and spies to find out where they have gone. In the spring, before we sail to Armorica, I will come with you, Gawain, and see that the King's laws are upheld. But no more talk of treason. I want that scotched immediately. Guinevere will pay the fine for adultery and then, if she will come, I will take her back *as is my right under the law*. Will that satisfy everyone?"

Cei sighed. "Probably not, but it should quiet them at any rate. By the time we return from Armorica, it will be simply another story. Frankish gold will stop the mouths of many who might criticize. Now, Arthur, will you please let Lydia send the women in to clean this room?"

King Lionel gave Lancelot a fortress that backed onto the side of a mountain. He offered servants and food in return for the teaching Lancelot could give his men in battle techniques. The living quarters were in ill repair and drafty, and Guinevere immediately caught a cold which did not aid the healing of her burns. She spent her days in bed or lying near the fire feverishly twisting her hair into knots. Finally, the day arrived when the healing-woman came to Lancelot.

She was a young woman with strong features and large, competent hands. They were clasped together, reddening as she explained to him what must be done.

"The inflammation has gone too far. I must cut into the foot to let the poison out. I may cut the muscles used in walking so that she will always have a limp. But if I don't try, she will surely die."

"Why do you even ask me, then?" Lancelot wondered. "Do you think a slight lameness matters against her life?"

"No." The healer twisted uncomfortably. "It's only, she was so perfect. I have never seen anyone before who had no physical flaws. I couldn't destroy that without your permission."

"Do whatever you must to keep her alive!" Lancelot shouted. "What do I care for scars?"

"Then come with me." The healer regained her authority. "You will have to hold her while I do it."

Guinevere screamed once and then lost consciousness but Lancelot felt the knife with all the intensity of his empathetic soul. He sobbed over the limp figure in his arms, begging the gods to give the pain to him and free her. The healing-woman, hands covered with gore, gave him a disgusted glance.

"There," she announced as she wrapped the last bandage. "Now she will most likely recover. If you can control yourself, you may carry her to the bed. Odd, she looks so fragile, but the muscles were tough as an old hen's. Well, can you lift her or must I call the guard? Some sort of warrior you are, to fall apart at the sight of a bloody knife."

Guinevere came slowly to awareness. Lancelot watched her by night from a pallet on the floor. She slept most of the time, only rousing to drink or eat a thin gruel. The women came in each day with fresh linen and cleaned her. Finally, one morning, she was able to drag herself from the bed on her own. When she came back, she knelt by Lancelot and cupped her hands about his face. He woke with a start. She smiled at him and he looked at her as if she were resurrection morning.

"All these years," she chided, "I have dreamed of waking up with you beside me, and now I find that you prefer the floor. Lancelot, come to bed."

"But, you are so weak!" he protested.

"I will become stronger if you share your warmth. Please don't argue. Just bar the door."

He had never been able to refuse her anything.

The snow came early to the mountains. Guinevere watched it settle into the valley with a glorious feeling of peace. They had fashioned a crutch for her, an old man working the stick into marvellous lines of birds and beasts. The top they had padded with lamb's wool and linen. She clapped her hands in childish delight when it was presented to her. In a short time she was able to maneuver the passages and stairs with considerable skill. The healing-woman was not surprised.

"Tougher than she looks," she told her friends.

With the mountains too dangerous to pass, they put the outside world from their minds. At least, they never spoke of it. They ate at Lionel's table and entertained him and Bors' family at theirs. They played games with the children and laughed at the tricks of the resident juggler. They made love far into the night and learned that one could laugh in bed, too. As long as the snow lasted they pretended that life would go on that way forever.

One day Bors found Guinevere crying over a crocus in bloom.

Chapter Twenty

The spring wind rustled the tent flaps of Arthur's camp. It was too early for any but the sentries to be about, but inside the commander's tent, marked only by the ensign tied to a post in front, Arthur lay awake. The birds were being obnoxiously cheerful, and he cursed them for their happy ignorance of his state.

Nothing had a right to delight when he was saddled with so much. On top of his own grief and sorrow, goads in the forms of Meleagant and Maelgwn had been added. They had insisted on accompanying him to Banoit. Of course it was to support him. Meleagant even had some justification, since Banoit was his by conquest. Their gloating presence was enough to send him to the edge of murder, but he would not let them see it. Maelgwn had no stake in the matter at all except his eagerness to pick up the pieces afterwards and attach them to his realm. His excuse was that he could send his men as nonpartisan intermediaries. That was all Arthur needed. An hour alone with Lancelot and Guinevere could have settled everything but there was no chance of that.

Modred, Gawain, and Gaheris slept in their own tent. Arthur had hoped that Gawain could be convinced to stay behind and let the law work. But the bonds of family were too strong. Agravaine sent word that he was unable to leave Tintagel but Gawain should, of course, take his place in avenging Gareth. Even pious Gaheris agreed. The only compromise Arthur had been able to forge was that only Gawain should fight Lancelot. The issue would be decided by single combat.

How deep the family ties went was shown to Arthur again when he asked Constantine to accompany him to Banoit.

"I can't, Sir," Constantine had said in surprise. "Queen Guinevere is my wife's aunt and she was fostered by my mother. You wouldn't expect me to stand against her."

"But she's *my* wife!" Arthur answered in exasperation. "And everyone expects me to stand against her."

"That's different, Sir, you understand that. If she had sinned against her family or truly committed treason against you, then I would be the first to lay a sword at her throat. But in this, I must either stay away or defend her. You don't need me there, anyway, and Sir Cei needs help with the provisioning of our army. Let me stay with him. Don't be angry, Sir. My father says it was like this even when the Romans ruled. Actually, he always felt that Rome disintegrated when the great families began their internecine battles. If a man's kin won't stand with him, who will?"

Constantine grinned. "Of course, Father's ancient now and has some odd quirks. He even has this strange belief about your nephew, Modred—insists that he's the incarnation of Uther Pendragon. He can barely see, of course, but he swears that Modred even moves like Uther. Ridiculous ideas the old get."

He took his leave, whistling cheerfully. Arthur listened to the tune fade away, feeling that someone had dropped a block of ice into the pit of his stomach.

When Meleagant's couriers arrived Lionel went immediately to Lancelot.

"We'll defend you to the last man," he swore.

Lancelot shook his head. "That was what my father did and the last man died. Tell them I will fight their champion for the Queen's honor. That way we can settle the matter without destruction."

Lionel turned to the courier. "Tell your message to him, just as you did me," he commanded.

The courier saluted and then recited from memory, "To Lancelot of Banoit: We call you to account for thwarting the King's justice, for the act of adultery, and most especially for the willful murder of Sir Gareth of Cornwall. Will you submit to trial by combat to prove your innocence?"

Lancelot turned pale. "What is he talking about? Gareth? What happened to Gareth? How could they think I killed him? Guinevere, tell them they're wrong."

Guinevere couldn't look at him. Lancelot grew cold.

"I couldn't have killed Gareth," he whispered.

"He was in the crowd, trying to help you," she faltered as realization flooded him. "You didn't even see him."

"You knew?"

Tears choked her. "I saw him fall. I hoped he still lived. He didn't blame you, I'm sure of it. There were so many people and the smoke was so thick."

"Oh, my God!" he wailed and threw himself on the floor, pounding the stones till his fists were bloodied.

Lionel took the messenger outside. "Tell King Arthur that Lancelot will meet with his champion. I will have him ready."

The courier looked doubtful, but it wasn't his business to wonder, so he saluted again and returned to the camp.

Guinevere was kneeling next to Lancelot when Lionel returned.

"Help me!" she begged. "He'll hurt himself. He wants to hurt himself."

Together they got him to a chair and forced some wine into him.

"It wasn't your fault, Cousin," Lionel insisted. "Such things happen in battle. Don't give way to despair. You must be ready tomorrow to meet their champion."

"I don't care. If I killed Gareth then I deserve to die. Let them take me."

Lionel made Lancelot take another gulp from the cup.

"If you do that, they'll take the Queen, too. It's admitting all guilt. I have heard that King Arthur would be willing to take his wife back if you proved her innocence in combat."

"But everyone knows we've spent the winter together!" Guinevere protested.

"Don't ask me for logic. That's what I was told. Arthur doesn't want to punish anyone, but he has to save face. You know him. Does it sound like a trick?"

Lancelot shook his head. "Arthur has no deceit in him. Guinevere, if I fight this man and win, will you return to Camelot?"

She fumbled for her crutch and pulled herself over to the window. Across the valley she could see the white of the tents in the setting sun. In one of them Arthur waited; patient, kind Arthur, who had never asked anything of her but the love she couldn't give. She had hurt and humiliated him in a way she would not have treated a vicious dog. But Lancelot!

"How can I leave you? Tell me! What should I do?" she pleaded.

"I can't," Lancelot sighed. "I can't even decide for myself."

Guinevere leaned against the rough wood of the window frame and tried to think. Merlin was right. She had never made a decision in her life. It had always been done for her.

She had never even felt the need to deny herself anything, for no one had ever held back anything she wanted. She couldn't decide now! It was too hard! It wasn't fair!

"If I go, will that end the fighting?" she asked Lionel.

"They say so," he told her. "It probably will. In a few weeks, most of the soldiers in Britain will have gone to Armorica to defend it against the Franks. Everyone, I think, would be glad to have this resolved by then."

She set her lips and exhaled. She closed her eyes. She opened them. The situation hadn't changed.

"All right. If Lancelot fights Arthur's champion and wins, I will return to Camelot."

"And if I lose?" Lancelot wanted to know.

"Then she must be turned over to the King's justice, whatever that may be."

"It doesn't matter, Lancelot. If you lose, nothing matters." Guinevere hobbled back and, standing behind him, put her arms about his neck. "We were never going to be parted again, and now we have only one night left."

Lionel took the point and excused himself. On the ride home, he worried about Lancelot. Would he make an effort to defeat the champion? Everyone knew he was the best of the knights and the most skillful at arms. He had shown his students this winter that he had lost none of that skill. But could he win if his heart wasn't in it? Lionel knew Meleagant would be there. Lancelot had to win, if only to salve the pride of Banoit. They had to make Lancelot see that. It wasn't just for himself and Guinevere that he would fight, but for the honor of his kin.

The moon had risen in their window and drifted farther across the sky, trailing stars behind her. Guinevere saw each one staring at her curiously, but with no malice. To Lancelot they were only a smear of light against the blackness. Together they waited for the last dawn they would share.

"You should sleep, my love," Guinevere murmured. "You need to be strong tomorrow."

"I'm rested enough," he told her. "I'll sleep when it's over."

She shuddered and he drew her closer, her ear against his heart. The slow beat went through her and calmed her.

"It was a lovely winter," she said.

"The most wonderful of my life," he agreed.

"Will you hate me for going back to Arthur?"

"Will you hate me for letting you go?"

She settled more firmly across his chest. "I won't really be gone. I know better now. And your promise is unbroken. You will never leave me again."

"Never."

They were quiet for a while.

"Lancelot?"

"Mmmm?"

"Tell me, just once more, about Galahad."

"Galahad was ours, only ours. We made him with our love and there was only love in him. He went joyfully into the light. His last words to me were of concern for you."

"We could not be evil and be loved by Galahad."

"No, we could be weak with humanity, but not evil. He would have known."

"My beautiful, golden boy!" She smiled. "Yes, they can never make me repent my love. The sky is lavender now; the clouds are turning pink and gold. Soon, someone will call us. Sleep a little, while I hold you. Nothing can harm us here."

An area had been staked out on a level field not far from Lionel's castle. There was room enough for the traditional combat on horseback first. But no one believed it would end with that. It would come to hand-to-hand fighting, with short sword and dagger. Meleagant surveyed the area with a pleased smile. A good day's entertainment. With luck, not only Arthur would be discomfited. Those stiff-necked lords of Banoit could use some embarassment. He'd never bothered with Banoit before; it was too much trouble to do more than send for the tribute each year and count it to be sure he hadn't been shortchanged. When he returned from Armorica, he'd have to investigate it. There wasn't land enough in Gaul to provide for all his bastards. Banoit might be a good place to dump a few. Meleagant rubbed his hands together. Sir Modred was right. After all these years, matters were finally working out his way, and most of it was Modred's doing. There was a man who knew how to get things done.

Gawain banged his sword against his breastplate at Arthur's tent.

"I'm ready, Uncle," he stated, as Arthur came out. "But first I have to meditate for an hour or two. After that, you can begin the speeches and reading of the charges and the rules and so forth. Then, after lunch, we can begin the duel."

"After lunch?" Gaheris had come up to hear this. "Don't be stupid, Gawain. You know you begin to weaken after lunch!"

"The days are growing longer. I'll be strong enough," Gawain answered calmly. "Will you allow me time for meditation, Uncle?"

"If you insist on it, Gawain. It's your right. Do you feel you need it?"

"To do what I must do? Yes."

"Then I will tell the others that we meet at the field in an hour and a half."

Guinevere dressed herself carefully. Lancelot helped her weave her hair into a crown and drape the veil over it and across her shoulders. Then she helped him into his armor, seeing that the padding under the mail was even and that none of the metal pieces sewn onto the leather were angled to scratch him. She laced up his boots and tucked his pants in before making the last knot. For a moment, she knelt at his feet, struggling with her tears. Then she held out her hand to be pulled back up.

"Are you sure you want to be there?" Lancelot asked worriedly.

"I couldn't sit alone here and wait," she answered. "That is not my kind of cowardice."

There was a knock at the door.

"Lionel and Bors are here to escort us." Guinevere reached for her crutch. "Do I look all right?"

Lancelot had to laugh. "Like a proper matron on her way to Mass."

"Good enough." She gave him her hand. "One last time; I love you."

"To the gates and beyond, Guinevere, I love you, too."

When Gawain saw Guinevere being helped down from her horse, he ran to her, just as he had always done. Bors saw him coming and drew his sword. Guinevere stopped him.

"Bors, it's Gawain! He's been my friend since we were children." She held out her arms to him and he swung her around in the old way. When he set her down, she stumbled against him and held out her hand for the crutch. His face changed at the sight of it.

"What happened to you?"

"It's all right, Gawain. It's almost healed; then I can get around with just a stick. Lancelot, look! It's Gawain!"

Lancelot's face lit up. "It's good to see you. Why are you all girded for battle? Have you come to be my second?"

Gawain dropped his hand and stepped back.

"They didn't tell you yet, did they? I'm your opponent. I'm sorry, Lancelot. I have to do this. I owe it to Gareth. Why did you have to kill him?"

"Oh, no!" Lancelot was at the breaking point. "They can't make us do this! I won't! Kill me now and get it over with. I can't stand this anymore!"

"Why did it have to be you, Gawain?" Guinevere demanded.

"He was my brother, Guinevere, and I wasn't particularly kind to him while he was alive. I owe him something now. I'm the only one in the family who could give Lancelot a fair match. Everyone knows it. I had to agree. Believe me. This is the best way."

"But you did nothing! There is no reason to punish you!" she refused to accept it.

"It doesn't work that way, Guinevere. Gareth did nothing wrong. That couldn't save him."

"Look at Lancelot! No matter who wins, you'll have killed him."

"I know that, as he will destroy me."

"Oh, Gawain! This is not the way life is supposed to be!"

"Guinevere, this is no time for philosophy. Just give me a kiss and say you'll forgive me, whatever happens."

"Of course." And she did.

He smiled at her in the old way, as if going off for a day of hunting.

"Good-bye, Auntie! See you in the morning."

They waited through the preliminaries, the speeches, the explanations. Father Antonius prayed for the truth to shine forth and for justice to triumph. Then Bors led Clades to Lancelot. When he had mounted, Lionel handed him his shield and spear.

"Remember," they urged. "Don't let Meleagant see Banoit defeated again."

Modred handed Gawain his shield.

"Better you than me," he smirked. "Don't trip on your own sword."

"Why couldn't Lancelot have killed you?" Gawain replied.

They missed each other on the first pass, to loud booing from the crowd. On the second, their spears rang on the shields with a screeching clash that set men's teeth on edge. The third time, both spears broke. They drew their swords and circled each other.

"Are they speaking?" Maelgwn asked. "I don't trust them not to make some alliance out there."

"They are my knights," Arthur told him. "They won't, whatever it costs."

"Then they're fools. I would."

"I know." Arthur folded his arms and stalked away.

Gawain overbalanced in an attempt to slice through Lancelot's bridle and fell, pulling the bridle and Lancelot down with him. There was some confused whacking until they righted themselves, then they seemed to settle down for an afternoon of thrust and parry.

"Oh God!" Meleagant complained. "This can go on for hours. Where is the boy with the wine jug?"

It did go on for hours. With every stroke, Guinevere felt the jar run through her bones. Her hands were clenched so tightly that the fingers were numb. If only they could end it, one way or the other. Anything to have it over!

Gawain felt the sun settling lower on the horizon, drawing his strength down with it. He knew Lancelot was aware of it, but wouldn't take advantage. Gawain's arm moved more slowly and he nearly missed countering some of the blows. Lancelot eased in his attack. Gawain knew better than to believe his opponent was equally tired. Lancelot was waiting, hoping to start again in the morning when Gawain would be at his peak and impossible to defeat.

"I won't let you do it!" he muttered and, closing his eyes, stepped into the blade coming toward him.

He gasped as the steel went through him. He had thought it would feel like fire, but it was more as if he had been hit by something massively heavy. He tried to get his breath but blood was rushing into his lungs and he could only gag on it.

"Gawain!" Lancelot screamed, dropping his sword and scooping up his friend. "Gawain, why? You could have killed me in the morning!"

Gawain smiled and beckoned Lancelot closer. He brought his friend's ear close to his mouth.

"I know," he hissed. "That's why I had to die tonight."

He tried to smile reassurance, but coughed and gagged on his blood instead. Lancelot tried to raise him, to staunch the wound, to do something that would bring Gawain back. Nothing helped. Lancelot gave a shriek of anguish and brought his sword up to drive it into himself. But Bors was too quick for him and wrenched it away. Deprived of even that release, Lancelot began beating on himself, until his kinsmen restrained him.

Gawain heard Lancelot's sobs and the cries of the people watching as they rushed to him. Someone, Guinevere, he thought, took his hand and tried to hold him back from death. He felt her fingers and then felt nothing. Nothing at all. It is a noble death, he told himself, so why am I so afraid?

The sun blazed upon the metal in his armor with a fury unusual at the end of day. Gawain felt life flow from him and waited for the darkness. But it wasn't getting darker, but brighter, and the touch of coldness that had frightened him was being replaced by intense warmth.

"No, not that!" his mind shouted. "I can't have been that wicked! Damn it all, it's just my luck. So, come for me, Satan, if that's what I have earned. Your fires will be nothing so dreadful to me."

Suddenly he heard the sound of deep, friendly laughter, the sort that made one grin and look around for the source. Gawain was not amused.

"It figures. Even in death there's something funny about me. Can't I even be left a little dignity?"

The laughter grew louder. The light surrounding Gawain coalesced slowly until he saw before him a man. His eyes opened wide with awe. It was as if his own radiance had been magnified a thousand times. The apparition was huge with great, muscular limbs and hair as wild and living as unchecked flames. The man put his hands on his hips and laughed again.

"My son, my son!" he bellowed. "What do you want with dignity? There is a universe to play in for those of us who can enjoy it. Come with me. I'll show you all of it. By day, we will drive the chariot across the sky of this little earth, but by night, ah my son, what wonders I can show you."

"Then mother didn't lie!" Gawain said in astonishment as his father took his hand and they rose together high into the air.

Apollo laughed once more. "No, my son. You were an experiment of hers that went farther than she intended. A foolish woman, to conjure me into her room. But I think she enjoyed her mistake. A fine mistake you are, Gawain. I claim you for my own. Come, lad, the universe awaits!"

And Gawain went, without a backward glance.

Chapter Twenty-One

It seemed to Guinevere that a many-armed monster had captured her and was dragging her remorselessly away, separating her from Lancelot and from Gawain. She could just make out Lancelot's white head above the crowd as he was drawn away by his cousins. He was making no resistance. Poor Lancelot! He must be numb with shock. He would need her when it wore off. He would need her and she wouldn't be there.

Finally and roughly, she was deposited in Arthur's tent. There was no one there. With painful steps, she made her way to the narrow bed and dropped upon it, too worn to cry anymore. She thought of Gawain and wondered where his soul had gone. How good he had been to her! God couldn't let him suffer. Caradoc would say he was a pagan and damned, but Guinevere was beginning to suspect the same was true of Caradoc.

It grew dark and still no one came. She could smell meat roasting but she wasn't hungry. The taste of bile was in her mouth. There were cries from farther away, but not, she thought, of anger. There were no sounds of mourning. Did no one care about Gawain?

It was very late when Arthur came in. He lit the oil lamp on his table, his back to her. His hands rustled the scrolls as he pushed them aimlessly aside. Finally, he faced her.

"Gaheris is taking Gawain back to Cornwall. We leave at dawn for Camelot. I have been told that no one will attempt to harm you again. The bishops were frightened by the intensity of St. Caradoc's vituperation. As long as you stay quietly at Camelot or Caerleon, they will not mention your trial again. Lancelot"—he paused—"Lancelot will stay here in Banoit. He has sworn never to see you again in my lifetime."

Guinevere's lip trembled, but she nodded. Arthur went on.

"The things that have been done to you, Guinevere, have been because you were my wife. Men who wanted to destroy me used you and your . . . association with Lancelot. I should have realized how powerful they were. I didn't understand in time how much they resent me. I ask your forgiveness, Guinevere. You are the last person on earth I would want to suffer because of my dreams. I'm sorry, Guin."

During his speech, she had listened in mute astonishment. Now she fell upon the bed, hiding her face in the sheets.

"How can you?" she sobbed. "After all we did to you, how can you apologize to *me?* Oh, Arthur!"

Gingerly, he came near and patted her on the back. She righted herself at once and, grabbing his hand, held it in both hers.

"It was my stupidity, my own willfulness, that caused this. Now Gareth and my dearest friend, Gawain, are dead because of me. How can you take me back to Camelot after what I've done?"

He leaned her head on his shoulder and rocked her for several minutes before he answered.

"I love you."

She clung to him, saying over and over, "I'm sorry, I'm sorry, I'm sorry."

He went on, "You see, it's my pride, too. I knew about Lancelot for years. I could have let you go, but I was too selfish. I didn't want to give you up. You are my weakness; my enemies know it. This was my fault, you were not to blame."

All at once something in her snapped. She sat straight up, anger pouring forth.

"I'm sick of guilt, Arthur. I won't hear of it again. And I

won't let you take it all upon yourself. I'm to blame for loving Lancelot; you're to blame for loving me. Lancelot is to blame for every sin since Cain killed Abel as far as he can see. We're wallowing in it. It's enough. I can't go back to Camelot in sackcloth and ashes. And I won't let you waste away or throw yourself on your sword because you're a human being. None of us are blameless. I've apologized and so have you, and Lancelot is probably beating himself with branches right now unless someone has the sense to stop him. When you come back from Armorica we can start again, but with no more talk of guilt and blame. People weren't meant to live so. Can you remember that?"

"Yes, my dear." He took her by the shoulders. "I'll remember. We won't talk of it anymore."

She slept on his cot that night with him rolled up in blankets on the ground beside her. She woke early but without the energy to get herself up. Looking down at him, she noticed that the stubble on his cheek was nearly white. There were new lines on his forehead and, in repose, the furrows from nose to chin were deep.

"When did we start to grow old?" she wondered. "And why is it happening to everyone but me?"

She felt her face, searching for the dents and ridges that must surely be starting. But there was nothing. It upset her.

"I don't like it. I don't want to be left behind."

The journey back to Camelot was hurried. Ships were waiting at Portsmouth to take the army to Armorica. Apart from rapturous and tearful reunions with Lydia and Risa, Guinevere was almost lost in the confusion. There was no time for acrimony or explanation. There was too much work to be done. Guinevere simply resumed her place on the balcony, her walking stick beside her and the ivory box in her lap.

Old friends called up greetings to her and Durriken, the poet, took to sitting with her.

"This is the only safe place for a noncombatant," he assured her. "It also makes a wonderful stage. My harp and I would be quite safe from harassment up here. The dining hall can become quite dangerous if I select the wrong story or if a new one doesn't please."

"You are welcome to use it whenever you like," Guinevere told him. "I have always enjoyed your tales. Perhaps tonight you could recite the one about Gawain and the Green Knight."

"But, Queen Guinevere! I hadn't planned ever to sing that again! It wouldn't be respectful to his memory. I have been working on something else for him entirely, a lament for a fallen warrior. It will be stirring and martial, to remember his great strength and valor."

Guinevere leaned on the railing, considering. "Well, he was strong and valorous. No one would deny that. But he was also loving and funny, and he had the most amazing talent for getting into ridiculous situations. I don't want that part of him forgotten. Don't you think he deserves to be remembered for more than the ability to uproot trees and knock over walls?"

"Yes, but so many of the stories deal with adventures of a . . . uh, lewd character."

"He told them himself," Guinevere insisted. "They made us laugh. Please don't stop telling them."

"As you wish, my Queen," the poet replied. "The exciting and eventful tale of Sir Gawain and the Green Knight."

He strummed his harp to keep the meter, and occasionally the rhythm would switch from chant to song. Guinevere nodded; yes, that was Gawain. Brash, sure, good-hearted, rather overeager to please a lady, always dreaming of glory. She hoped that he would be remembered that way.

The night before they left, Arthur called Modred into his rooms. Guinevere was down with Lydia, helping to make one last inventory. As he did in private, Arthur greeted his son affectionately.

"Sit down, lad. I want to speak with you. You have been very generous about being left behind on this expedition. I know how much you must want to go and fight with the others."

"That's all right, Father. I understand. Someone must keep an eye on Britain while you and the others are gone."

"Quite right, although most of the troublemakers are going with me. Nothing like the smell of loot to make men settle their differences. But I don't leave you without some forces. You own handpicked troops have offered to stay with you. That speaks well for your ability to create loyalty."

"Thank you, Father."

"Now, I need your help with something else. This is a great adventure we are undertaking. Despite everything, I have at least brought Britain to the point where we can go to the aid of our cousins without fearing that our own homes will be destroyed in our absence. Even though I've failed in other areas, I am proud of that."

"As you should be." Modred felt that he was supposed to make some comment here.

"Yes. Now, I am an old man by most reckonings. I may not return from Armorica. I may not even survive the crossing. There is still so much work to be done that I can't leave without naming someone as my heir."

Modred's heartbeat quickened. He tried to keep his breathing even.

"You shouldn't think of such things, Father. You're still strong and healthy."

"But death comes to everyone, when we least expect it. I've been thinking about this for many years now, but I was unable to face it. Now, I've decided. There is only one man whom I believe has the wisdom and skill to continue with my dream. That is Cador's son, Constantine."

"Constantine!" Modred's jaw dropped. "He's not even your kin!"

"But he's of the old blood. And his wife is granddaughter to Leodegrance, who was one of the most respected men in Britain. More than that, he believes in Camelot, in our ideals. I want you to help him, Modred, to support him after I'm gone. You've made friends with many factions and you can lead them to him."

Modred's mind was working fiercely. How could the old

goat do this to him? His own son! Constantine was a plaster cast of a man, fit only to put in front of a public building. How could Arthur be such a fool!

Aloud, he said, "He's a fine man, Father, but perhaps not strong enough to keep the tribes in their place. Another man, more skilled at diplomacy . . ."

"But that's what I want you to be there for, Modred. I've seen to it that when I die my private possessions will go to you, apart from a few things for Guinevere. I thought you might sell some of them and get your own land, since I can't leave you any property openly. It would be an act of self-lessness on your part to wait until Constantine is secure in his kingship, before you go. And, I've another favor to ask."

"Anything, Father," Modred said between clenched teeth. What did he want now? For him to clean out the privies before Constantine used them?

"Since Constantine will be with me in Armorica, it is all the more important that you stay behind and take care of things while we are gone. Don't worry. I expect the campaign to last only the summer. Especially, I want you to watch out for Guinevere. She hasn't recovered yet from her ordeal. Take good care of her. Don't let anyone hurt her."

Modred had brightened considerably during this speech. He stood at the end of it and placed his hand on Arthur's shoulder.

"Of course, Father. It will be an honor to serve you in any way. And Queen Guinevere would be a concern of mine in any case. Then will you announce your selection before you go?"

"I have. I've told you and Constantine, of course. When the time comes, you will be the one to let Britain know. If I do survive the war, then next autumn I can proclaim my choice to all the lords and kings. I'm telling you now, just in case. I rely on you."

"You honor me, Father." Modred bowed and let Arthur grip him in a bone-crushing hug. Well, the old fool did still have his strength. Thank the gods he had not let anyone know his plans. If the arrest of Guinevere had proved a disaster, this would not. He had all spring and summer to establish himself, and there were multitudes of dangers to a king crossing the sea to wage war. He would be willing to wager that Arthur would not survive the campaign.

The army left in a blaze of trumpets, waving pennants, and dancing horses. It took most of the day before the last soldiers marched through the gate and disappeared around the bend in the road.

Guinevere stood with Risa, Lydia, Brisane, Tertia, and the other women, all waving and smiling as if this were a holiday.

"This is worse than the Grail," Brisane muttered through her grin. "At least then we assumed they wouldn't be fighting."

"I know," Lydia answered. "I feel like my mouth is starched in this position. How can they be fooled by it?"

They were finally gone. The last flutter was shaken out of the scarves and the women went back to the hall, empty of all but children and old men. Even Durriken had gone, to play the army to glory. Guinevere wanted desperately to be alone in her room in peace. She started to go that way when she was struck by a thought. What if the other women felt that way, too? Perhaps she should stay and share in the talk and the pretending. It was very thoughtless of her to assume she was the only one who was tired and worried.

Reflected from nowhere, a sunbeam shone in her eyes. For a second, she thought she heard two men laughing.

Gradually, life settled into patterns, summer progressed as usual. Guinevere began to spend more time with the other women. The snide glances and sudden whispers did not reappear, for all her notoriety. She felt a real friendliness from the women of Camelot that they hadn't extended before. It puzzled her enough to ask Risa.

"It's simple enough," she replied as she folded summer gowns. "You've lost a child and you've lost a lover. Now you're one of us."

"But don't they condemn me for Lancelot, for poor

Gawain's death? Don't they believe with the saints that I tried to destroy Arthur?"

Risa snorted. "Of course not! Sorcery, nonsense! No one credited that. And, as for Lancelot, well, there are still some that say you betrayed your husband. But most of them know what it's like, married as the family says, never mind if he's fat or feeble-minded or prefers little boys. I think some were jealous of you, to have it both ways, a kind husband and a handsome lover. But even those don't fault you now. You paid, and each woman thanks her own private deity that it didn't happen to her. Don't think they pity you. It's not that at all. It's more that they finally realize that you're not just the Queen, and a bit spoiled, too. You've suffered as much as any woman; now we can be kin."

Guinevere took this as truth, for Risa understood these things. She wondered if she ever would. When she got back to her own rooms, after Banoit, the first thing she had done was to find her mirror and hold it close to her face. Arthur was aging, Lancelot was older. Risa was a grandmother now, and looked it, despite the herbs and almond milk. Was it true that she had escaped what comes to all mortals?

The eyes that stared back at her were variable gray-green, as always. There were no lines on her forehead, but she thought she saw a few tiny ones at the corners of her eyes and mouth. She had to examine her face intently to find them, but they were there. She was almost relieved.

So there was the promise that someday, she too, would grow old. It was not a prospect she had thought to contemplate before, but now that Morgause was here for Guinevere to study, aging looked better and better.

Morgause had appeared a few days after the army left. Modred greeted her with guarded enthusiasm, the rest of Camelot with undisguised astonishment.

She was like a woman stepped out of legend or the wickedest days of Caligula and Nero. Everything about her breathed color, from her hair to the huge black and brown dogs that followed her everywhere. Next to her Guinevere was bland and the fashionable Brisane hopelessly drab. Her ability to manage men and beasts was watched with an envious awe, but rumors of her other talents caused rowan branches to appear hanging over doorways and cradles. *That* was a sorceress, make no mistake, and no one was fool enough to want to tangle with her.

The precautions and wardings amused Morgause. She laughed about them with Modred in his room as they plotted the final coup that would give them the power they had yearned for for so long.

"I wish that Morgan could see you now, Modred," she crooned. "She thought you'd rejected her completely."

"I did. The old whore made this even harder for me. You know how I feel about your petty *vindicta*."

"What did you feel when Gareth died, and Gawain?"

Modred squirmed. "Nothing, nothing at all. They were fools."

"So are you if you ignore the blood ties. I never cared about avenging our mother's rape by Uther. But you can't ignore the bonds; they're part of the weaving that holds all things together. Arthur has tried to ignore them with his laws and artificial justice. Even the Romans were smarter than that. They gave the power to the families who had always wielded it, as long as there was order and prompt payment of taxes. In return, Rome gave its civilization. Arthur believes that veneer is enough. But what survived were merely Romanized Cornovii and Dumnonii and all the other tribes of Britain."

"Morgause, I am very tired of history lessons. I'll write my own, thank you. 'Modred, High King of Britain, Conquerer of the West.' That's what the bards will sing of and the scribes copy into their books. When Arthur and Rome are just shadows, it is I who will be exalted."

"Wonderful." Morgause was not impressed. "I will believe you when it's all over and you sit in the King's chair at the Round Table."

* * *

The summer days were long and sultry at Camelot. It was hotter than anyone recalled. The baths were kept cool all day and the sound of children splashing and calling overlaid all others. Guinevere found her balcony too hot and spent most of her time near the women's quarters, where there was often a breeze. It looked out on the northern wall and the forest, so that was how she missed the messenger.

She only knew about it when the wailing started. Risa bade her sit still while she ran to see what it was about. She came back almost at once, her face wooden with shock.

"Oh, my Lady dear," she cried. "News has come from Armorica. King Arthur is dead!"

Chapter Twenty-Two

Modred was a model of kindness and sympathy in the days that followed. Guinevere knew they could not have borne the news without him. Even Risa admitted he was wonderful at calming the panic felt by everyone.

"But I still don't trust him," she insisted. "A man who is cruel in bed won't be kind anywhere else. Anything he does will be for his own good, not ours."

"Risa, he has given of his own wealth to so many people. What can he hope to gain from that?"

"Just what he has gained, my Lady. Your admiration."

Guinevere refused to listen. Even if Morgause made her nervous, Modred had never been anything but kind and gentle to her, even in those horrible days at Cirencester.

Risa drooped in the unusual heat. She was tired and not willing to continue the debate.

"All right, believe what you like. I don't know why you won't listen to me, though. I know that man and he is evil. He'll do his best to destroy us all."

Vainly, Guinevere tried to get more details of Arthur's death. Had he drowned, been killed in battle, or fallen ill? What of the rest of the men? Was Cei safe? Lydia was thin and sleepless with fear. What of Constantine? Letitia was pregnant now and had been sent home to her mother and grandmother for care. Why did no other word come? Wouldn't Arthur's body have been sent home with a guard of honor, even if the war went badly?

Something odd was going on. Guinevere told herself she was being foolish, that Risa's feelings were affecting her too. But why did no one else come back from Armorica? And who were those men who came by night and left before dawn? From the cool darkness of her perch, she had seen them, forms only, taken at once to Modred's rooms.

Then they came by day. The children brought the first warning.

"Saxons!" they screamed as they raced through the gates. "A whole Saxon army on the road! Mother! Mother!"

They sat for a moment, paralyzed by terror, each clutching a child. Then they ran for the towers to see for themselves. Guinevere limped behind, half supported by Lydia.

"I can't climb the ladder," she snapped in irritation. "What do you see up there?"

Brisane called down, "Sweet Mother, it's true! There must be a hundred of them!"

Modred had heard the noise and come running.

"Come down, all of you!" he yelled. "There's nothing to worry about! Come down, no one is going to hurt you!"

"But the Saxons . . ." Guinevere began.

"They aren't Saxons; they're Jutes."

Guinevere looked at him strangely. "I see. That makes a difference?"

"Of course. They're here to protect you. I've hired them. Now, come down!" he shouted again.

Guinevere was not to be put off. "What do you mean *you* hired them? For what reason and with what right?"

"They're *foederati*. Arthur took all the men worth anything to fight the Franks. He left us nearly defenseless. The Jutes are willing to defend us for land and gold. They have no love for the Saxons."

"But who are we in danger from? I've heard no rumors that the Irish or the Saxons are near."

"You can't understand such things, Guinevere." Modred spoke indulgently. "It's my duty to see that Camelot is safe."

"Don't you think you ought to wait until Constantine returns before doing anything so sudden?"

Modred whirled around. "What do you mean. What about Constantine?"

Guinevere was bewildered. "But Arthur said that he told you that Constantine was to follow him as King. You're to be seneschal, like Cei."

"That's a lie!" Modred's face grew red with fury. "I am to be King. I *am* King now! Arthur always meant me to be his heir. Constantine is just another minor lord. Arthur wouldn't even have considered him to take over at Camelot! I am King! Do you understand?"

She thought she did. Terrified, she nodded.

"Good." With an effort, he calmed himself. "I don't want to hear about this again."

Then he strode briskly toward the waiting army.

Guinevere stared after him, her mouth open in horror. "He's gone insane!" she thought. "Dear Lord, we've all been left in the charge of a madman!"

The next days seemed to prove her right. More and more soldiers came to stay at Camelot, and Guinevere began to fear for the safety of the women and children. Modred said the men were there to protect them but there had been more than one attempt to break down the barred doors of the women's quarters. She conferred with Risa and Lydia, but neither one could think of a plan.

"You see now, don't you?" Risa spoke with sadness.

"Yes," Guinevere admitted. "I wish I had believed you."

"We must do something, though." Lydia tried to keep panic out of her voice. "My Enid is nearly twelve now, and the way they look at her terrifies me."

Guinevere looked at them. "I'll go to Modred," she decided. "We are worth nothing to him. Perhaps I can convince him to let us go."

"But where?" Risa demanded. "Most of the women have only empty lands to go to, where they would be no safer than here."

"They can go to my family at Cameliard. My sister-in-law, Rhianna, is there and we still have our own men-at-arms along with all the peasants and farmers in the country around. Now, what can I say to make him let us go?"

Modred seemed more amused than angered by her request. "Why should all the women wish to take their children and leave Camelot? It's lovely here, don't you think? And so well protected."

"It is the protectors we fear, Modred," Guinevere replied. "If you are, as you seem to be, preparing for war, then all those children and babies will only be in the way. Also, your soldiers may be Jutes and they may be friendly, but they look like Saxons to us and they look at us like something they expect to get as a battle prize."

Modred laughed at her indignation. "You are as closeminded as the rest of your race. They are only men, with wives and children of their own. You're worrying about nothing."

"Nevertheless," Guinevere said firmly. "I want to take our women and children away from here."

He sat at his table a long time, considering her. He etched something in the wood with his belt knife. Her foot was hurting dreadfully, despite the cane. But she wouldn't back down. She continued glaring at him until he spoke.

He smiled. It was not a warm and friendly expression. "Very well," he said slowly. "The women and children may leave Camelot if they wish. But it would look very inhospitable if no one remained. I wouldn't like that. I think I would like to propose an exchange."

Guinevere was wary. "Of what sort?"

"There has been talk that I have usurped Arthur's place. People who don't know the truth might become difficult. I don't want that to happen. I think you should remain behind here at Camelot."

"All right."

"As my wife."

"What? That's impossible. I'm Arthur's wife."

"Arthur is dead."

"I need more time to mourn."

"You can do it after the wedding."

"I can't walk!"

"You won't need to."

"I'm old and barren."

"You're only six years older than I am, and despite your infirmity you look much younger. As for your childlessness, you might be mistaken. At any rate, I have bastards enough. I have no prejudice against them."

"You can't be serious."

"Oh, yes. Our marriage would quiet the accusations. I would hear no more about Constantine if you gave my rule your approval."

"There must be another way!"

"Not one that would amuse me as much. Make your decision, Guinevere. Marry me and you can send all the women and children wherever you wish. Defy me and the army gets what it wishes. It's a fair trade, don't you think?"

He waited, his expression pleasant, as if offering her the choice of an apple or an orange. Guinevere felt sick. She closed her eyes, but the nausea didn't go away. With a groan, she lurched over to the window and vomited, retching until her stomach was empty. Calmly, Modred walked over and handed her a cloth to wipe her mouth.

"Does that mean yes or no?" he asked.

She gave him a look of contempt.

"If that's what you want, I'll marry you. But not until word comes from the head guard at Cameliard that all the women and children of Camelot are there and safe. I want to hear it from him and no one else."

"Done!" he said, and flipped his knife into the floor at her feet where it stuck, quivering.

She didn't tell the women why she was staying behind and their relief was so great that they asked no questions. It took only a day for belongings to be packed and stowed in carts for the journey. Lydia promised to send word as soon as they arrived.

"Then you come join us, dear. I worry about you here, alone."

"Risa has insisted on staying with me. We'll be all right," Guinevere answered. She couldn't believe she was saying these things. When had she become brave? Or was it just that, without the men she had loved, nothing really mattered any more.

When they had gone, she told Risa of the bargain. Risa gaped in horror.

"You can't do it! He's a monster!"

"Would you have wanted me to keep your children here?" Then she bit her lip. "Is he so very cruel?"

"Oh, my poor lady! He can be; he knows how to hurt. But don't you fear. I'll get a knife to you for the wedding night, if I die for it."

"A knife! It's so awful that you want me to kill myself?"

"Don't be foolish, my Lady; I want you to kill him."

Aulan came two weeks later and reported that everyone was fine and Rhianna and Letitia were delighted with all the company. Letitia, by the way, had had a boy, whom they wanted to call Arthur. He left the next day, but did not return to Cameliard. Instead, he rode for Portsmouth faster than if he had been chased by demons.

Morgause was not thrilled by Modred's intended nuptials.

"Why are you bothering with her? Take one of Maelgwn's daughters and cement the alliance."

"Are you jealous, dear Aunt? Don't worry, I won't neglect

you for her. This should please you above all people. Just think what it will do to Arthur when he hears of it! The deepest cut."

"Don't tell me you're doing this just to hurt Arthur," Morgause sniffed. "You're fascinated by her."

"Perhaps. There's something about her. You should have seen her when they led her to the pyre. She looked like a goddess."

"And you've decided to worship her?"

"Maybe. My father's wife. That's very appealing, rather the final nullification of his existence. I have his country, his castle, and his wife. Arthur no longer exists."

Father Antonius came to Guinevere when he heard of plans for the wedding.

"Are you sure this is what you want to do?" he asked. "I won't perform the ceremony if you're being forced into this."

"I have to do this, Father. I have sworn to." She took his hand. "And I will tell you why, but as a priest, you must never let anyone else know or something terrible will happen. You must promise."

"Of course." So she told him. His eyes were wet when she finished.

"I will do what I can to help you. No, don't worry, I won't say anything. But there are things I can do without speaking, at least to guard your immortal soul."

"Thank you, Father. Good night, then."

"Good night, my Queen."

Modred had announced the betrothal at once and had a bridal gift of a necklace of moonstone and gold delivered to Guinevere. Her acceptance of it would seal the marriage more than any rite. She held the ponderous thing in her hand, dreading the thought of it lying around her neck.

"It's a slave torque," Risa said in disgust.

"He must have known how I loathe things around my neck. I never wear anything but the pearl Caet sent me when Arthur and I were married. Oh, Risa! Must I take off Arthur's ring?"

"Modred hasn't sent you one for the betrothal. Perhaps he won't notice. Guinevere, dear, there must be a way out of this. Look at yourself! You've lost weight, you haven't slept, and you have a rash on your arms that's pure fear."

Guinevere absently scratched at the rash.

"If I thought he'd just kill me, I might resist him. But he has threatened to destroy everything I have left. Anyway, I'm tired. Risa, in my life I've been kidnapped by vengeful Saxons, a game-playing king, and fanatic saints. Good people have died for me. Always, I waited for someone else to come and get me, like a parcel. Arthur, or Lancelot, or Gawain. Arthur and Gawain are dead and Lancelot is in Banoit and probably has no idea of what's happening. This time no one is going to come, and I have to survive the best I can. I can't grab a sword and fight my way out. I made a trade using the only currency I have."

She leaned back, her eyes closed. Her skin was so pale that the veins in her arms showed clearly through the rash, like blue lace. Risa knelt beside her and held her tightly. My poor Guinevere! She doesn't know! What can I do? How can I save her?

There was nothing to do. Modred's men were all around them and even their dinner knives were confiscated after every meal. Modred, for reasons astrological, had chosen the ides of August for the wedding. The day was hotter than ever, the sky clear and angry, the sun striking every exposed surface relentlessly.

Risa clasped the hated necklace on over the red-and-gold silk tunic. She draped the veil over Guinevere's head and tied her sandals.

"Modred doesn't want anyone to see me limping," Guinevere said dully. "He's sending a chair for me, with bearers. A curtained sedan chair! I'll feel like a fool."

"I knew he was working up to declaring himself emperor," Risa sneered. "You'll be dripping wet in that box."

She was. Modred handed her down from it and then had to wait while she regained her balance. He made as if to help her into the chapel, but it was more as if he feared she would somehow manage to get away, even then.

Father Antonius rushed through the Mass, stumbling on the old Latin and dropping the chalice after mixing the water and wine, so that he had to start again. Finally it was over. Modred had huge casks of beer opened for the soldiers. Morgause kissed Guinevere coldly. She gave Modred one also and whispered loudly, "I'll be in my rooms later tonight, dearest."

Guinevere fervently hoped Modred would be there, too.

She tried to stay at dinner as long as possible, but with a laugh echoed by his friends Modred swept her up and carried her to her room. He deposited her on the bed and began to remove his clothes.

"Hurry up!" he told her. "I'm not interested in waiting."

She made one last plea.

"I'm your uncle's widow, Modred. How can you do this? It's like incest!"

To her astonishment, Modred began to laugh so hard that he collapsed into a chair.

"Guinevere, you can't know how little that means to me! Incest is an old family custom. It's a pity you can't ask my mother. She knew all about it. Arthur, too. Your good and precious husband wasn't above getting a son on his own sister. Shall I tell you his name, or can you guess?"

She shrunk away from him in horror. For some reason, she knew he wasn't lying.

"Dear Lord! You tell me you're his son and you expect me to lie with you? I'll never let you touch me, Modred, never."

"That's all right my dear. I like rape."

He blew out the light and came to the bed.

"I won't scream," she told herself. "He won't make me scream and he won't make me cry."

She struck out at him, but he only grabbed her arm and twisted it high over her head. He took her other arm and held it hard against the bed. Then he pushed his knee between her legs, oblivious to her writhing.

"This is going to be fun," he said, his eyes glittering. "For you, Father, all for you."

Guinevere's mind went numb as ice. She could only think, over and over again, "Stop him, please, somebody stop him."

But, as she had expected, nobody did.

Chapter Twenty-Three

It was a ragged and exhausted man who stood before Arthur at his camp in Armorica scarcely two weeks after his departure from Camelot. Aulan had never been across the sea and the new land he was in frightened him. But he knew that such a tale had to be brought at once and personally for anyone to believe it. Even then, it had been hard to make the King understand.

"Modred?" he repeated. "But he's my . . . It can't be! I trusted him! There must be some other explanation. What of the messengers I've been sending back each week? And the ones he's sent me? When do you say you first heard of my death?"

"Almost two months ago, Sir," Aulan replied. "There's been no word that I know of since then. At least, that's what the Lady Lydia told me."

"Lydia! She's safe?" Cei broke in.

"Yes, at Cameliard with all the other women and children. Only Queen Guinevere and her maid stayed behind."

Cei let out a long breath of relief. Arthur leaned forward.

"I have received a message from Modred every week since we left. The last one came only yesterday. Is the man still here, Cei?"

"No, he asked for a fresh horse and left this morning, with our letters."

Arthur chewed the corner of his mouth. "How can this be? It's too hideous to be true."

Aulan was impatient in his fear. "Please believe me, Sir.

All Britain believes you to be dead and by your wishes or no, Sir Modred has filled Camelot with hired soldiers and, when I left, he planned to marry the Queen. I came here only hoping to find Sir Cei or Sir Constantine and beg them to come back with me to fight him. You can't know how I felt when I saw you here, alive."

"Yes. I understand. But Modred! Gawain always warned me, but it didn't seem possible. Of all the men I trusted . . . And Guinevere! How could she marry him?"

"Risa told me, Sir. You mustn't blame the Queen. She did it to save the others. They were scared still when they got to Cameliard, partly of the soldiers but also, some of them told me, scared of something bad at Camelot. They didn't know what, but they didn't want to stay there. They felt like they were being trapped inside it."

The color drained from Arthur. He looked a hundred years old.

"Cei! Get all the men loyal to us together at once! Tell them we are leaving for home tonight! Constantine! Find King Hoel and explain the situation. Tell him I'll meet with him later today. We can't leave him stranded."

"Sir Constantine?" Aulan stopped him. "It may not be the time, but you might want to know that the Lady Letitia gave birth a little over a month ago."

Constantine stopped. "Letitia? She's all right?"

"Was when I left, Sir," Aulan answered, dropping into the vernacular. "And the baby, a fine big boy. The whole tribe of 'em's so proud, you'd think they invented him. She says he has your ears and I'd have to agree, if you don't mind my saying it."

Constantine rubbed his ear with a slow foolish grin. Then he remembered his mission.

"Thank you! Aulan, is it? Thank you!" He left at a run. They could hear him hollering the news to his friends on the way.

Arthur, watching him go, felt as if someone were turning a knife in his gut.

"Yet a new life is wonderful," he told himself. "Another

generation to carry on. Someone should have a son to be proud of. I have to stop Modred. Even if everything in my own life is ruined, he has to be vanquished for their sakes."

But the knife kept turning.

As soon as Modred left the next morning, Risa crept in. She found Guinevere, half hysterical, huddled on the floor. She crouched down beside her, pushed the hair back and began sponging off her face. Guinevere moaned and tried to bury her face again.

"I know, darling, I know," Risa murmured. "Let me help you, dear. A wash is what you need first and something clean to wear. I'd take you down to the baths but it would mean us having to pass all of them, staring at you."

"No!"

"Of course not. We won't leave here. I've brought you food, too. Here, Guinevere dear. I won't leave you. He doesn't know how I feel about him. Come, dear, give me your arm. That's right. I'll take care of you. There'll be bruises there. My poor dear! That wicked, wicked man!"

"Oh, Risa," Guinevere sobbed. "I tried to stop him. I thought I could get away. I didn't know I was so weak! No one ever hurt me before!"

"Hush, hush! I know, dear. But listen to me. I sent Aulan for help. You've got to hold on. I know they'll come."

"But they didn't come!" Guinevere's voice rose.

She started crying again, and Risa just held and rocked her until she quieted. She kept up a litany of cursing, starting with Modred and what she'd do to him and surging out to include all men for all time. Her fluency was so amazing that Guinevere was shocked into silence.

"Risa?" she asked after a long time. "This has happened to other women, too?"

"Yes. Over and over."

"How do they survive?"

"Some don't," Risa answered shortly, still too full of hatred to consider her words. "Some are killed; some kill themselves. Some go mad. But you won't," she added quickly. "You're stronger than that. You can survive."

"Can I? I never felt less strong in my life. That's even worse than the pain. It was knowing that there was nothing I could do! And he'll be back again, tonight! Risa, I think I'm going to throw up again."

When she had finished, Risa sponged her face and neck once more. There was a look on Guinevere's face she'd never seen before. Risa clenched her teeth. She had been with her lady since they were children and she had always been filled with awe and a little envy at the way life had managed with no apparent effort to keep her safe from evil. Not even barbarian Saxons could harm her. How could the gods have abandoned their favorite? Risa felt sick, too.

Guinevere was quiet a long time. Until she spoke, Risa thought she might have fallen asleep. When she spoke, it was haltingly, but with growing determination.

"All my life I've been protected; I've been loved. Someone always took care of me. Risa, help me! Teach me how to take care of myself."

"My Lady, dear, it's not your doing. We never wanted you to do for yourself. When we were girls I used to watch you, how you walked through a room. Everyone's eyes would glow, not just from the beauty of you, but from something about you. We always knew you were special, like a secret we all shared. When visitors came to Camelot, they might not think it very different from their own castles. But we always waited and whispered among ourselves, 'Wait until they meet our Queen!' And when they did, we laughed behind our hands, because you were so much more wonderful and shining than anyone they'd ever known. We didn't want you to worry about little things. It was enough that you just were."

Guinevere laid her head on her maid's shoulder. "Even if that once were true, it isn't now. I don't think I want it to be."

Risa thought a moment. "No, perhaps you wouldn't. But you will need all the belief that kept you so special. If we're ever going to stop that Modred, it will have to be because we're stronger than he is."

Slowly, Guinevere straightened. "I'm afraid of him, more than I've ever been of anything. But I won't ever let him know it. If I never submit to him then he can never defeat me."

"But you musn't let him hurt you anymore, Guinevere!"

"Risa, I don't see how I *can* be hurt any more."

Despite the heat, the room felt cold to Guinevere as she waited for Modred to return that evening. She had refused to come down for the evening meal and play hostess to his mercenaries. The sun had barely gone down when she heard his step. She closed her eyes and prayed for courage.

Modred opened the door and found Guinevere reclined on her couch, studying a commentary on Vergil. She didn't look up. Her fingers trembled as she turned the page.

In three strides, he was at her side. He picked the codex from her hands and dropped it on the floor. He seated himself next to her, pressing his chest against hers and bringing his face too close for her to avoid.

"Are you ready to come to bed willingly with me, Wife?" he sneered.

"No." She couldn't believe she had said it without any sign of terror.

He got up, pulling her with him.

"Then we'll play again, as we did last night, and again until you understand that I am now your master."

"You aren't, Modred, and you never will be."

Her tone stopped him in blind fury. There was no bravado or contempt about it, just a simple declaration of fact. He took out his knife.

"I don't want to mar your looks, pretty Queen. Your ornamental value is great. But I don't value it so highly that I'm afraid to destroy it."

"I don't doubt you, Modred, but it will not change the truth." She spoke calmly, trying to keep her eyes from the gleaming knife.

He held it to her throat. It was warmer than she had

thought metal should be. She thought of Risa and something not quite a smile crossed her face. "I hope I'm something more than my looks, after all," she thought in tired despair. "It appears that soon I'll find out."

For that moment, she really stopped caring what Modred would do to her. She knew that when he hurt her she would care vividly, but not just now.

She met Modred's fierce glare. She waited.

He could sense the relaxation in her body. He looked into her eyes and what he saw there bewildered and frightened him. The Saxon Aelle, and Meleagant, and even Caradoc had seen the same thing, and none of them had understood it. Even though she was barely aware of it herself, Modred knew that there was nothing he could do to her that could reach what she was, and, after everything, the mysterious essence that was Guinevere would remain. The others had called it witchcraft but Modred knew it was nothing he had ever encountered before, and in that moment he knew she had won.

He threw the knife deep into the wall.

"Damn you, woman! Damn you!" he said with deep intensity. "I'll be back, don't think I won't. I'll find a way to destroy you yet!"

He slammed the door so hard that the lamp rattled on the table. Guinevere slumped back onto the couch, feeling that she had just stopped a hurricane with a toothpick, and totally astonished to find herself still alive. She heard him pounding on another door and the creak as that door opened. She sighed in relief.

"I know he'll be back," she thought. "But at least not tonight."

Sometime later she heard screams coming from Morgause's room. She couldn't tell if they were of pleasure or pain, nor did she care.

Morgan le Fay was deliriously happy under the Lake. She was pretty again and desired. There was no need to work and no nasty children to bother her with their demands and ingratitude. Everything was beautiful, rich, and luxurious.

Even the food was good. She wished she had found the place years ago. How she had wasted her life! If only she had known, she would never have spent all those years in a futile struggle for power over Arthur.

She stretched out on the warm grass in the sunshine. How perfect it all was. It did not occur to her to wonder how the sunlight penetrated to the Lady's country below the Lake. She yawned. Idly, she thought of the sons she had left behind: Agravaine, Gawain, Gaheris, Gareth, and Modred. She sleepily forgave them for running off to Camelot and abandoning her. She had the satisfaction, at least, of knowing they were actively perpetuating her image back in the other world.

"I ought to look in the mirror sometime and see how they're doing," she mused. "I wonder if any of them has managed to give me some legitimate grandchildren yet?"

After a time she got up and wandered toward the Lady's pavillion, where the mirror was kept. It was a new invention. The Lady had grown tired of getting her news of the outside from chance travelers and unreliable waterfowl. So she had set all her people the task of creating a way to peek into the land above. After several mishaps, the mirror was perfected. Its range was only south of Hadrian's wall and it couldn't see across the ocean, but it was novel enough for the Lady to sit and watch it by the hour. Morgan found her at it and made her request to see her sons.

"Ah, Morgan!" The Lady drew her into a nearby seat. "Yes, of course. I must say the past few months with you have been fascinating. Let's see, tell me their names and I'll try to focus on them."

Agravaine was no trouble. He was still at Tintagel. He had just married a local girl, far below his station, who was a genius at organization. They were devoted to each other and Morgan's lip curled in disgust at the domestic harmony. Gaheris was with Arthur in Armorica and could not be seen. But the waves against the rocks showed the place he had last touched in Britain. Gareth's name only produced gray mist in the mirror and, upon asking for Gawain, they were rewarded by a blast of light that left black and gold spots dancing before their eyes.

"What does it mean?" Morgan asked as she blinked repeatedly.

"I have no idea. You have a most intriguing family, my dear," the Lady answered. "We should ask Torres. He keeps up with the happenings in your world."

Torres had been raised with Lancelot under the Lake and had spent some time with him in the early days at Camelot. But the rigors of outside life had not appealed to him and he had returned. For nostalgia's sake, however, he had kept aware of the happenings at Camelot.

He came when summoned, but reluctantly.

"Things are in dreadful confusion up there, Lady," he told them sadly. "Gawain and Gareth have been killed by my milk-brother, though not through malice."

"My Lancelot killed her sons!" The Lady was not interested in believing it. "Lancelot, who couldn't bear the thought of offending someone's feelings? A murderer? Nonsense!"

"I told you it was confusing. Arthur is still in Armorica, if the geese are telling the truth, but he is hurrying back to Britain and should be here within the month. Your Modred, Morgan, has taken the country for himself and is preparing to fight Arthur for it."

"Then he is dead too," the Lady announced. "I'm sorry, Morgan. I hope you weren't fond of him. That sword I gave Merlin for Arthur is enchanted. He'll never lose a battle with it."

Morgan was reeling from the shock. Two of them dead and Modred about to be vanquished? Yes, now that she thought of it, she discovered that she did still care deeply about her sons.

"What do you mean about the sword?" she asked.

"Oh, it was one of those trick things they made before the floods," she answered without interest. "It made combat so much more interesting. It was the sheath, really. As long as the wielder of the sword carries the sheath, he can't bleed. He can be cut, of course, but it will heal fairly quickly. You see the advantage it gives. A man could be stabbed right through the heart and the blood wouldn't even notice. It would continue in its course. They were very popular in those days. I can't believe Arthur was such a great warrior that he never discovered that."

Torres frowned. "Everyone knew there was some magic to it, but he never said what. I don't suppose he'd want it well known."

"No, I suppose not." The Lady looked at the sky, a uniform blue without clouds. "I think I'll go see how Adeno is doing. He took down all the diamonds in my chambers and was replacing them with sapphires. Did you find out all you wanted to, Morgan?"

"Yes . . . yes, thank you."

"Fine. It must be nice to know the people up there personally. It makes it more interesting, I would think. Lancelot is all I care about and he's just off in some drafty castle, suffering again. That boy can be very tedious."

She wafted away. Morgan grabbed Torres before he could go, too.

"Torres, I've got to get back up there, just for a night. How do I do it?"

Torres tried to release himself. "Now, Morgan. You can't do that. You know the rules."

"Don't talk to me about rules, Torres. I know you go up whenever it suits you. Now, tell me how or I'll be sure the Lady knows all about your secret jaunts."

Torres looked around. There was no one in earshot.

"For only one night, you say. You're sure? You'd have to come right back."

"Why would I want to stay up there?" she argued. "I just left some business unfinished and I have to take care of it."

"All right," he said slowly. "Tell me when, and I'll see that you get away."

"Thank you, dear. It won't be for a week or so. First I have to get a scabbard made to fit Arthur's sword."

Chapter Twenty-Four

Arthur landed at Portsmouth and, without pause to rest, forged toward Camelot. The news of his arrival swept through Britain and new men came every day to convince themselves of his existence and to fight at his side. The reverence in their faces was unmistakable. It annoyed Arthur a great deal but Cei could do nothing to help.

"I've told everyone that you were never dead at all; that it was a lie of Modred's. It doesn't seem to matter. They think you've been resurrected."

"That's blasphemy, Cei!" Arthur cried in exasperation. "I won't have it!"

"I don't see what we can do about it, Arthur. They don't want to believe anything else."

"All right." Arthur gave up. "What have you found out about Modred?"

They were seated in the best room that the wayside inn could offer, but it was small and poorly ventilated. The room was sweating as badly as the people in it. Cei absently chipped pieces of plaster from the wall with the toe of his boot.

"It's worse than we thought," he said. "This is not a sudden idea of Modred's to take advantage of your trust. He's been laying the ground for it for years. He has his own mercenaries—Jutes he's promised land to. He has support from the kings in the North, too, and St. Caradoc has been preaching in his favor, for what that's worth."

Arthur scowled. "And how does the good saint get around his abduction of the witch, Guinevere?"

"Modred is saving her soul," Cei replied tersely.

Arthur's knuckles were white and his teeth clenched with anger but he made no comment.

Cei continued. "If he decides to withstand a siege at Camelot, we might be there all winter. You made that place too well, Arthur. There's no way we can storm it."

"Then we'll have to force him to come out to fight," Arthur told him.

"I don't see how." Cei reviewed the land in his mind. "He has all the advantage there. If he came out, the armies would be even."

"He will, though. He'll have to face me to kill me, and that," Arthur suddenly knew with piercing clarity, "is what Modred wants most."

Guinevere knew that the activity inside Camelot had increased, that there were more drills and mock battles. Every day new people arrived; more Jutes and Dal Riada and possibly other Irish from the tribes settled in the west. But she didn't know why. She had more than enough hours to spend in wondering. Most of the time she was alone. She only left her tower to attend Mass or, after dark, to bathe. But every moment of the long, broiling weeks she spent gathering resistance and courage. She fought for dignity and endurance. Modred did not give up. Every few days he would appear again, unexpected and cruel. Sometimes she felt she was made up of nothing but terror. But her pride or her anger or something else she couldn't name kept her from allowing him to master her. She wouldn't comply and she wouldn't beg, though sometimes he forced her to cry out in sudden pain.

In her struggle, everything else grew blurred and distant. She buried her grief for Arthur and her yearning for Lancelot. It was only by keeping the most minute watch on every aspect of her mind that she could hope to survive. She had no idea what month it was. She had early on lost track of time. Outside the furious sun scoured Camelot without pity. Timid clouds evaporated under its glare. The summer seemed very long.

Risa came every day with food and sanity. Father Antonius prayed and was outraged that a divine hand had not immediately struck down Modred where he stood. Then he decided that the Lord intended him to do something more active, so he started planning. But how could they escape and where could they go that Modred wouldn't seek them? The priest thought of Sir Lancelot but dismissed him. Antonius couldn't lead Guinevere from physical into spiritual danger. Another few days of this, and he might be driven to it, though. That monster had bruised the poor woman's face so that she could barely open her mouth to receive communion. Father Antonius wished for the first time that he had learned to fight before he had consecrated himself to peace.

When the news finally reached them, it took Risa several minutes of exclaiming before Guinevere came out of herself far enough to understand. The first reaction she had was irrational anger. If Arthur were still alive, how could he have let this happen to her? The feeling swept over her swiftly and was gone. But it did its work, shaking her to full awareness.

"Risa," she stated. "We have got to escape from here and find him."

"He's coming here, my Lady, dear! Soon, I think. Those filthy saints visiting from Gwynedd are preparing to sneak out tonight. They have no intention of being martyred for Modred." Risa squeezed her hands. "So we need only to wait. He'll get us out."

Guinevere pulled away. "No. That man will use us as hostages. Arthur must be free to destroy him! We are going to get away from Camelot on our own. Father Antonius, too."

"But how?" Risa was thrilled to see her so determined and alert but it seemed impossible. Camelot was full of armed men.

Guinevere set her lips. "I don't know yet." She paced her room. She had done it so much that she was able now to walk without the cane, although the limp would never quite vanish. Then her eye fell on the little ivory box containing Galahad's baby teeth and curl. She picked it up. Everything else she could abandon. This must come with her. She remembered when Galahad had found it for her, just after he came to live at Camelot. It had been brought by a merchant from Egypt with a load of pottery. She had not even noticed it at first among all the painted cups and plates and bowls. It had been insignificant among so many. Only someone like Galahad would realize its simple beauty and pick it out from the mass.

"Risa," she said suddenly. "I think we should go to the chapel for religious instruction. We have neglected the welfare of our souls during our trials."

"What?"

"Hurry! While they're still eating. The guard downstairs speaks some British, doesn't he? Tell him it's the eve of a holy day for us. Ask him to help me across the compound."

"Guinevere, I don't know what good . . ."

"We are going to become saints, Risa, if we get there in time. Go on! I'll follow as quickly as I can. Send the guard up for me. No one should become suspicious if I'm escorted."

She left her room carrying only the little ivory box. On the bed, twisted until the rings broke, lay her betrothal necklace from Modred.

Father Antonius knew he would have to do an onerous penance for what Guinevere was suggesting. The bishops were very strict about violence, especially against a brother religious. But he was still so angry with them all for being too weak to defend Guinevere that he thought he would enjoy himself while he was sinning. It would be a relief to knock some heads together.

"Providence must be on our side," he announced after checking the courtyard. "That silly St. Olanidd left only two men to watch their belongings while all the others went to fortify themselves for the journey. This heat is a blessing, too, or they would never have decided to travel by night. Risa, can you get those two to come into the chapel?"

Risa smiled. "If they're still men, I'll bring them, even if I have to lure them with the promise of cool ale, rather than

· 232 ·

my warm . . ." Guinevere looked at her. "I mean, certainly, Father Antonius."

When she left, Father Antonius grinned sheepishly at Guinevere. "I know this is deadly serious," he said, "but I have this feeling of elation all the same. I must be as wicked underneath as my old teacher believed. To take delight in the prospect of damaging a fellow priest!"

Guinevere took his arm. "You don't need to damage them seriously. Just long enough for us to get away. You can beg their forgiveness later."

"Don't worry, I'm not backing down, just reconsidering my vocation."

"Please do it later, Father. They're coming."

Risa led the men in, laughing and talking. She might not be young any more but she had not forgotten the art of being charming. She never once looked over their shoulders as Antonius and Guinevere came up behind them and brought the stone slabs down on their heads. They crumpled like empty clothes. When they awoke, they were certain that only the wrath of God could have struck them so unexpectedly and deservedly.

In the cooling twilight, Father Antonius offered to walk a while with the departing saints. His conversation was so provocative that no one noticed the two slighter hooded figures among them, one leaning on the other's arm.

Arthur was alone in his tent when Cei came to tell him that a hermit had arrived who wished to speak with him in private. In the depths of his misery, Arthur failed to notice the barely suppressed excitement in Cei's voice.

The night was moonless and the tiny lantern gave little light. He knew her by her hands, the short and practical fingers that she had always hated. He was afraid to say her name, though, lest she vanish. She stood for a minute by the doorway. Then she pulled back the hood.

She turned her face away at once, but he saw it. He grew very still.

"I had to come see you, Arthur," she explained, still staring at the tentskin. "To let you know I was not with Modred. I wasn't sure if you would want to . . ."

"Guinevere!" Very gently, he touched her cheek and drew her face to his. She looked at him and all the tears she had refused to shed came spilling out. She stumbled against him and continued sobbing on his shoulder.

"I left you with him!" he accused himself. "I trusted him for the most illogical reason in the world. It was my stupidity that did this to you."

She tried to regain control. She had not come to bring him guilt. She had had enough of that. She groped at the belt of the hermit's robe.

"Arthur," she begged, still on the edge of hysteria. "Do you have anything I can wear instead of this? I can't stand it another second."

"I'll find something," he told her. "Wrap yourself in this blanket while I go see. Here, let me take that out and burn it."

"No," she said abruptly. "I mean, I'll hand it out to you."

Arthur looked hurt. "I'm sorry, I didn't think you would mind my seeing you."

"Oh, no! It's not like that!" She closed her eyes. "I hate to have anyone see me now, even you."

"Guinevere, give me the robe."

She took a ragged breath and gave it to him. She winced at his gasp of shock and grabbed frantically for the linen. She couldn't look at him. It must disgust him horribly to see her so cut and bruised. How ugly she must be!

"Oh, my love," he choked as he wrapped her tenderly and carried her to the couch. "Until tonight, I've been grieving that Modred has forced me to fight him. Despite all he has done, I didn't want to hurt him. Now I can kill him in cold vengeance and smile."

"I'm glad of it, Arthur, although it's an awful feeling. I think that is the worst thing he did to me, I never knew how to hate before. Now it eats at me. I want him destroyed. Oh, Arthur! Don't go, yet! Please stay with me. Hold me; talk to me. I just need to feel safe again."

He stayed with her, cradling her in his arms with her face hidden on his chest. Slowly her breathing grew more peaceful, and finally she slept. He put her down with bitter reluctance. Her hair gleamed in the lamplight. He blinked rapidly to stop the blurring of his eyes. Then he knelt and kissed her before gingerly picking up the discarded robe and leaving the tent.

Guinevere didn't wake when Morgan slithered in, pulled Excalibur from its sheath and replaced the sword in the new one she had brought. She vanished as quickly as she had come. No one saw her at all.

Risa had explained to Cei what had happened. She was looking for Cheldric, her most faithful lover, when Arthur found her. He thrust the robe at her.

"Here," he commanded, "have this burned."

"King Arthur," she pleaded running after him. "Don't blame her."

Arthur stopped. "Blame her! What are you talking about? In the morning, I want you to take her to the hill overlooking the river, the one they call the glass tower. There is an old temple there where the two of you will be safe until it's over. If we win, someone will come for you. If not, well, if not you will have to decide for yourselves what to do. Risa, take care of her, please!"

He strode on. Risa felt a bit piqued. "'Take care of her.' Haven't I always? I did the best I could," she muttered, "while he was off at his wars. And she was the one who got us out of Camelot. Ah, well, poor man! It must be awful for a king to feel helpless, and I'll wager anything the sight of my dear battered lady must have undone him."

She held out the robe at arm's length. Her own had already gone into the fire. "Those saints must all be mad. Three days in one of these filthy things is enough penance for any sin!"

Arthur did not look undone, but grimly determined, as he made the rounds of his army. Cei walked just behind him, afraid to do more than give short answers to questions equally short. The men were ready, seasoned but not worn by their weeks in Armorica. Frankish gold shone from some of their arms. They were satisfied with themselves and looked forward to looting more tomorrow. But most of them would have fought for Arthur's sake alone. Arthur sighed. He knew that they were here for love of him, but how much more wonderful it would have been if they had been willing to fight for his laws and his dreams.

"Idiot!" he told himself. "Only martyrs fight for ideas. I asked too much of them. But it would be nice if there were one man left by my side who still believed. Not even Cei understands. He is here because he is my milk-brother and we are closer than kin. And the others, because I am their king. I was a fool to think I could change the way things have always been."

His self-pity was interrupted by a commotion. The guards were leading a man on a white horse across the camp. They had taken his sword and his hands were tied behind his back. He made no resistance.

"Lancelot!"

The man looked up at the sound of his name. "Arthur. I came when I heard what had happened. I beg you to let me join you. My eyes are not good anymore, but my arm is as strong as ever. Send me into the fray first. That way I won't harm my own side. But please let me fight!"

"Untie him!" Arthur ordered. "Why did you come, Lancelot? Even if we win against Modred, Camelot will never be the same. The Round Table is ended. We're too divided to ever unite Britain again."

"I won't believe it, Arthur." Lancelot dismounted, rubbing his wrists, and fell into step with Arthur out of old habit. "We would all be speaking Saxon now, if it weren't for you. You taught the people of Britain that it is possible to live by one law. Not even the Romans could do that. They had different rules for everyone. Even more, you've showed me what a king ought to be. I couldn't stay rotting in Banoit if I could help you. Will you have me, Arthur?"

"Yes, Lancelot. Of course! Who else would I want at my

right hand?" Arthur paused, then went on. This wasn't a time to perpetuate old bitterness. "Lancelot, Guinevere was able to escape from Modred. She's here now. Would you like to go see her?"

Lancelot stopped, then looked away. Arthur's generosity always shamed him. "Thank you, but I made a promise and it would be better if I kept it. Don't let her know I was here."

"All right, but if I don't survive this battle, Lancelot, I want you to remember that your vow dies with me."

"If you don't survive, old friend, then neither will I. Where do you think we will fight?"

"There is a field by the river Cam, not far from here. If Modred brings his men out, then that is the most likely place for us to meet. He'll try to drive us into the river. We have to keep him from returning to Camelot. My men have their orders. Those on foot will circle through the woods and try to cut off his retreat. The knights and other mounted men will attack him face on. It seems too simple to work, but there is nothing else we can do."

Lancelot ran over the plan in his head. "I remember the place. We used to have picnics there with races in the grass. It makes this whole thing even more like a nightmare, to be killing men in Camlann field."

The clouds were thick over Britain the next morning, dark and lowering, but unable to rain. Modred looked at them with pleasure and wondered if Morgause had conjured them up. It was easier to fight under gray skies, cooler, with less chance of being distracted by reflection off shield and armor. He had fought with Morgause the night before. She thought it was stupid to leave a fortress to fight in the open.

"Stick to your sorcery," he told her. "Warfare is my business and I know what I'm doing. We're stronger than he is now. After a siege, it might not be true. He'd have all winter to gather new forces while we would remain trapped in here. Trust me in this and be ready to welcome me back."

"I suppose I can expect you, since you let the Queen get away," she sneered at him, jabbing at a lock with her comb.

"You were a fool ever to take up with her. I should have left you then. No, don't sputter more excuses. I don't want to talk to you."

He had thrown one more razor-cut remark at her anyway and left before the dish hit the door. She wasn't in a good mood.

Looking at the sky that morning, he decided that she must have forgiven him. It was going to be a fine day, and, at the end of it, there would be no question as to who ruled Britain.

"You wouldn't give it to me, Father," he whispered to the wind. "You kept it from me out of shame. Your incestuous bastard. You could have avoided this. But I will take my rights just as I took your city and your Queen. I will stand on your body and proclaim myself your heir."

Then a chill passed through him, a sense of the sickness destroying him. Briefly, he longed for warmth, for a friendship he would never have.

"Mother!" his mind screamed in anguish. "Look what you've done! Are you satisfied now? Why did you drive me to this! You never should have made me!"

Chapter Twenty-Five

Guinevere and Risa followed Cheldric up the tor. At the top was a tiny stone temple, dedicated to Lugh and Apollo, sun gods of two peoples. It was near dawn, time for the priests to welcome the god, but the priests had died out fifty years before and the day was one that wanted no greeting. Fog and shadows made the landscape alien, ignored by the guardians of men. If the scorching summer had not dried the bogs between Camlann and the tor, they might never have arrived at the top. As it was, they turned the wrong way and had to retrace more than once before they reached the overgrown road leading to the sanctuary.

"I should be down there," Cheldric muttered. "Even with one arm, I could do something."

"Go on back then," Risa goaded him. "We're perfectly safe up here. If you're lucky, you can run into Modred's men in the fog and kill them all by yourself. Then we can go back to Camelot and clean it out before the King gets home."

Cheldric had known her too long and too well to pay attention. "I have my orders," he stated. He squatted on the ground by the old temple, his back to the eastern wall. "Can't see a damn thing down there."

He sounded worried. Guinevere sat a little away from them. She had wakened in semi-darkness to find Arthur still asleep on the ground next to the couch. Even rest could not erase the weariness on his face. She had lain watching him, memories and regrets filling her mind, until Cei's call awakened him. His eyes opened, saw her, and lighted with pleasure. She leaned down and kissed him.

"Remember, my love," he told her just before she left. "We've done with guilt. Whatever happens today, you'll not forget that we've forgiven each other everything. We did the best we could according to what we knew at each moment. I sacrificed you to my dreams."

"And I sacrificed you to my desires," Guinevere answered. "I wonder why we humans are allowed to go blundering through our lives. So many things I should have known but learned too late! I wish this were our wedding dawn."

"So long ago!" Arthur sighed.

"I was never unhappy because of you," she went on. "I have always loved you, since the day you kept my brother, Mark, from running away from us in his despair. You are the kindest man I've ever known."

"And I've told you ever since then what you are to me." He raised her hands to his lips. From outside the tent came the rattle of armed men preparing to set out. Without turning his eyes from her, Arthur reached for his buckler and fastened it over his shoulder. Excalibur was cold against her leg as he kissed her good-bye.

And somewhere, buried in the mist below, the battle had begun.

The Lady of the Lake regarded the wretched woman before her with scorn.

"If you break my laws, you must expect to suffer," she told Morgan with disgust. "You've done more damage today than you'll ever know. Or perhaps I'll see that you do know. That would be a lovely codicil to your punishment. Don't sniff!"

"I can't help it!" Morgan retorted. "I caught cold on the way back here. I don't care what you do to me. It was your magic in the first place that meant to kill my Modred. All I did was even things out."

"And you thought I'd never know. Well, I might not have if I hadn't been looking for my Lancelot. He's there now with King Arthur. If your mischief results in his being killed . . ."

She couldn't think of anything dreadful enough.

"Can't you stop it?" Morgan pleaded.

"Of course not! What happens up there has nothing to do with us. Interfering in their quarrels will only destroy us all. But my poor, foolish Lancelot! Adon, get my boat ready. We can at least be there at the end. If he survives, perhaps at last I can convince him to return to us. You're coming too, Morgan le Fay. I want you to see what your precious son has caused."

For Arthur, once it began, the fight at Camlann blended in with all the other battles, starting with the first skirmishes nearly forty years before, through that awful, long day on Mons Badon to the recent encounters with the Franks. He hacked, slashed, cut, ducked, parried, wiped his face, slashed again, swore and thrust over and over throughout the cloudy morning. He could feel Cei on his left and Lancelot on his right fending off other attackers. For a moment, there was a silent space; he grabbed his waterskin and drank deeply. Someone yelled that Modred had ambushed the men sent to cut him off. Arthur shouted to Caet to find out what had happened and report back to him. Then a group of warriors made a rush at him, axes swinging at his horse's legs. Most of them were cut down by the archers but two got through and Arthur was busy again; thrust, hack, jab, parry, duck, slash, slash again, and again, recoil as an arrow hits the shield, hack, jab, parry, swear . . .

Cei was swept away from him. Lancelot stayed close, swinging with a maniacal steadiness at all who came near. Arthur tried to see what was happening. Were they winning? He could hear Constantine exhorting his men. There were no lines; both sides were in a jumble, little clusters locked together in single combat not aware of the turn of battle. Sir Dyfnwal was hurrying toward him, his horse leaping the bodies strewn about like last night's feast. Arthur kicked the chest of another attacker and went to meet his knight.

"Father's men are siding with Modred!" Dyfnwal panted. "They are still in the woods, but will join him soon. Give me some men to meet them, Lord. There are many who will desert when they know they have to fight Meleagant's heir. Even Father will think twice before attacking his only legitimate son."

"You'll fight your own kin?" Arthur asked.

The boy lifted his chin proudly. "You are my kin, Lord. The men I will fight are your enemies. I have no duty to them."

"All right, take Sir Cunetrix and his men and do what you can to stop Meleagant. And thank you, lad. Good luck!"

Lancelot had formed a protective barrier while Arthur talked with Dyfnwal. Arthur moved in to help him. They were coming closer to the river. Were they pushing Modred's men there or being led that way themselves? They had broken through the foot soldiers and were encountering the horsemen now; Arthur noticed among them his own renegade knights and hoped none of them had the conscience to face him. Then the crowd opened and Arthur saw Modred.

Curiosity or fear or a sense of drama made everyone draw away from the two men. Quiet rippled outward until every man on the field was still, staring, waiting.

Arthur felt a horse beside his. Lancelot reached out.

"Arthur, let me, or Cei."

Arthur shook him off. "It's not your affair. I created this . . . problem. I must take care of it."

Unconvinced, Lancelot backed away only a few feet. Therefore, he could hear some of what passed between Arthur and Modred, although it was several days before he understood any of it.

Arthur steeled himself as he rode slowly toward his son. He suppressed an irrational thrill of pride at the strength and bearing Modred showed. A king could be proud to have such an heir beside him. There were no flaws in Modred's body or his brains. The curse of his parents' sin had been put on his soul. Then Arthur remembered what he had done to Guinevere and his resolve increased.

"Modred, will you surrender to our justice?" he shouted, so that all the field could hear.

Modred answered just as loudly, "Father, you gave me no justice! I claim what is mine by right!"

They were closer now. Arthur spoke only to his son. "Why? I trusted you as I would have no other!"

Modred trembled. "You trusted me as you would a tame dog. If you had named me yours, I would have become one and followed you to your death. Together we could have conquered the world. But you preferred your childish morality. Now the only way I can receive my patrimony is on your grave. What you wouldn't give me, I will take."

"Including my wife?" Arthur asked bitterly.

Modred's smile was a rapier. "Guinevere? She came willingly enough. After an old man like you and a clod like Lancelot, she was thrilled to have me in her bed. Shall I tell you what we did?"

Arthur knew he was being goaded to strike, and he didn't care. He drew Excalibur, knowing that it would protect him. He had never needed it before. His own skill had kept him from ever receiving more than a scratch. But today he was glad to know he could attack in fury. Modred was not caught off-guard. Arthur's blow was deflected by his shield, but the force of it surprised him. The old man wasn't as feeble as he thought. Modred settled down for a long fight.

Arthur felt the cut without much interest. He'd been cut before. They were fighting hand to hand now, having pulled each other down from their horses over an hour before. He wished he knew how late it was but the clouds gave no indication of time. He raised his guard and struck again. It was a few minutes later that he realized that he was bleeding, not seriously, but bleeding all the same. He stared at the spreading red stain in shock. Excalibur had failed to protect him, how could that be? Modred lunged again and he swerved and jabbed with his knife. This move threw him off balance. Modred saw his chance. His sword passed through Arthur's body, between the rings of his mail and into his spleen. Blood poured out.

With his last strength, Arthur grabbed Modred, pulling him down with him. Modred's face gloated an inch from his.

"You're dying, old man!" he hissed. "I have it all now! You couldn't destroy me; I'm part of you."

"Yes, my son, you are. And that part I will cut out!" As his eyes glazed over, his last sight was the horror on Modred's face as Arthur's knife entered his heart.

With a wild cry of grief, Cei raced across the field as he saw Arthur fall. He tore Modred off the fallen king and ran his sword through him, oblivious to the fact that Modred was already dead. Then he bent over Arthur and gave a wail that could be heard all the way up the hill of glass to where Guinevere and Risa waited.

The sound of it passed through Arthur's men and sent them into a frenzy as they renewed their battle. As he saw men come forward to carry the bodies off, Constantine raised his sword and led his section forward again. His commands were choked with tears but all around him understood. Modred's men, driven only by fear for their lives, began to fall back.

Lancelot could not believe what had happened. How could

he have let Arthur die? What right had he to still be alive? With total disregard for tactics or sense, Lancelot threw himself into the battle. Not far from him, Cei had remounted and was doing the same thing, calling down curses on Modred's soul as he went.

They laid Arthur on a bed of animal skins on the bank of the river Cam.

Father Antonius bent over the King. He thought there was still a pulse, weak, but there, and hurried to administer last rites before it was too late. As he mumbled through the ritual, he saw Arthur's lips moving, following the prayers. He leaned closer.

"Excalibur," Arthur whispered. "Merlin said, throw it."

"I don't understand." Father Antonius paused in his work.

"Excalibur," Arthur said more faintly, "must be returned."

The priest looked at the sword. He had no idea what to do with it.

"Yes, of course," he promised. "I'll see that it's returned."

"That won't be necessary!" a woman's voice said behind him. Father Antonius jumped and nearly fell into the river.

There, floating easily against the current, was a boat of polished wood with silken sails. In it were four women, all heavily veiled. The one who had spoken held out her hand to be helped ashore. Dumbly, Antonius helped her.

The Lady knelt at Arthur's side. She ran her hands over the wounds and shook her head.

"This is your doing," she snapped at one of the other women. She put her hand in Arthur's and willed life to stay in him while she spoke.

"King Arthur, I can cure you, but not here. Come with me under the lake and you will be well again. You can live with us forever."

At first there was no response. Had he heard her? Then, with great effort, Arthur shook his head.

"No," he whispered. "Not live forever. Tired . . . so very tired. Just let me sleep."

His breath came out with a rattling sound and Father Antonius feared he had died. He tried to move the Lady away so that he could finish his work, but she pushed him aside.

"Very well," she said. "He shall have his wish." She put a hand on his forehead. "Sleep, poor weary man. I will take you to a cave in my land where you may sleep until your spirit is healed. That is the least I can do for you."

The men watching dared not make any protest. They had all heard legends of the Lady of the Lake and some hoped that she would take Arthur with her for a while and return him, alive and young again. These helped her wrap him in blankets and lay him on the boat. Before it sailed away, the Lady called to them.

"Tell Lancelot what I have done," she ordered them. "Tell him he has only one more chance to come with me. Otherwise, he must face the mortality of men."

As the boat slid downstream, the clouds opened to send long fingers of light onto it, making both the boat and the water sparkle so brightly that men's eyes were dazzled and no one could tell when the craft vanished.

From the hilltop, Guinevere saw the boat shining, its sail billowed with conjured winds. She didn't know what it meant, but the beauty of it gave her sadness and hope. It took away the cold sickness that had filled her at the unearthly wail they had heard only a few minutes before.

But it was hours before they saw the figure trudging up the hill to tell them that Modred's men had been routed, and Constantine, son of Cador, was now King of Britain.

Guinevere didn't want to go back to Camelot. She couldn't stand the thought of seeing it again, after Modred had desecrated it. But Constantine sent horses and escorts for her. Their leader was Caet, the horsemaster. He had a bandage wound around his head and was truculent with her from the start.

Guinevere didn't know it was because he was so shaken by the change in her looks.

"King Constantine needs you at Camelot, to prepare the

place for his wife's return. You've never hesitated to tell me my duty; this one is yours."

"Caet, haven't I had enough?" she asked, her green eyes melting his resolve. "I want to go home and grieve for Arthur alone. Constantine doesn't need me to establish himself. Arthur told everyone the night before Camlann who his chosen heir was."

Caet dropped his formal pose. "You have to go, Guinevere. Do you want people saying that you were in league with Modred? One look at you would prove them liars. And there will be those who try to take advantage of this to declare Constantine a usurper, or, at the least, to challenge his control. You represent the old order, the peace of Arthur. Come help him."

"But there are others. Cei, for instance."

"Cei died protecting the men who recovered Arthur's body." Caet was formal again, but the hurt was evident. "The messengers sent to Cameliard to bring back Letitia also carry news of those lost."

"Oh, poor Lydia, what will she do? All those children!" Guinevere wanted to cry for them, but she found she had no tears left. So her only alternative was to capitulate. "Very well. I'll come with you to Camelot. But as soon as everything is settled, I want to go home."

Guinevere thought that seeing Camelot again would be too painful to bear, but the first person she saw at the lower gate was Father Antonius, his hands outstretched to welcome her. While her escort went about their business, the priest took her at once to the chapel.

"He's been here since the battle ended. I persuaded him to wait and see you before he left."

The wooden door creaked open and, in the half light, filtered through the narrow glass windows, Guinevere found Lancelot. Very likely he had been praying again, but weariness had overcome him and he slumped against the wall, head thrown back in sleep. Quietly, Father Antonius left them.

She stooped to kiss his forehead and his eyes opened. She

sat down beside him and took his hand. He leaned his head on her shoulder with a sigh.

"I couldn't even die for him, Guinevere. They fell all around me, and when it was over I wasn't even hurt."

"I'm glad of it, my love. Would you want me to lose everything?"

He straightened and looked at her closely through his fading eyes. His fingers traced the bruise on her chin.

"We made all the wrong decisions, didn't we, Guin?"

"Not all." She kissed him again. "Father Antonius says you want to leave soon."

He put his arm around her and they settled together with the ease of long practice.

"There's no place for me here, Guinevere. At Banoit, I'm a doddering relative, at Camelot, a relic. I don't know how I could have grown older and still understand so little. Living here only reminds me of the friends I killed, of the ones I couldn't save. I want to make a pilgrimage, to Rome, I think—Jerusalem, if I have the strength. There must be someone, somewhere, who can explain my life to me."

"My poor dearest love." Guinevere smiled sadly. "Perhaps somewhere there is."

"If I go, will you be all right? I know Constantine wants you to stay here. I can't leave if I think you might be put in danger again. I may never forgive myself for letting you go last spring."

"Was it so little time ago? I feel so much older now." She stopped his cries of self-reproach. "Yes, I will stay here for a while, if they think they need me. But I can't live here the way we did before. That was a different time, and I was someone else. My father left Cameliard to me and my brother, Mark, if he ever comes out of the mountains to claim it. It's my own place, and when you come back that's where you may look for me."

"Are you angry at me for going?" Lancelot asked.

"You'll never leave me. I know that. I need time alone now, too. Right now, I can't bear the thought of being touched again, even by you. We can't just go back to Banoit as if nothing ever happened. Someday, perhaps, there will be a better time again. Lancelot, it won't make sense to you, but horrible as this summer has been, I discovered something amazing. All my life, I've waited patiently for someone to come along and rescue me. But with Modred I knew no one could. And I stopped waiting. After all these years, I finally rescued myself! So you see, I need you now only by right of love. I always will. But I want so much to find out what else I can do, all alone."

Lancelot didn't understand, exactly, but he felt the exultation in her and it worried him, even while he rejoiced that she wasn't crushed by her misfortunes.

"When I come back, though, you won't turn me away, will you?"

She laughed and rubbed her nose against his cheek. "Silly! Loving you is something I do very badly alone."

Guinevere refused to return to her old rooms at Camelot. They were for the King and Queen, she insisted, and took up her lodging in the rooms reserved for visiting delegations.

She was astonished at the change in people's attitude toward her. She was no longer a wicked adultress, a pitied martyr or even a household treasure to be petted. Suddenly, she was a matriarch, a dowager queen. People asked her advice. They listened to her opinions. They stood when she entered and gave her the softest cushions. How very strange!

"This is how my mother is treated!" she exclaimed to herself. It was pleasant to be respected as someone who knew all the answers, but Guinevere felt something wrong in it. She didn't feel like a matriarch. She didn't know all the answers. And she definitely did not want to spend the rest of her life telling stories of the old days of Camelot. The sight of the Round Table, with Arthur's name still glowing, but without him and Gawain and Cei and Gareth and too many others, was painful to behold. She let them spoil her for a few months, wintered with them at Caerleon. But, when all the women had returned and Letitia proved an able mistress of the house, there was no reason for her to stay.

The morning of her departure, she found Caet at the gate

of Caerleon, holding the reins of his own horse as well as hers. She was surprised, but pleased.

"What are you doing here? I thought you had to train the new men-at-arms."

"They can train themselves," he replied shortly. "It's about time we were going home."

Chapter Twenty-Six

The first few years after Guinevere came back to Cameliard were quiet ones. She returned to the room of her childhood, with its narrow bed and animal mosaic on the floor. The changelessness of it helped her to put aside the intervening time and concentrate on letting her body and spirit heal. She helped her sister-in-law, Rhianna, supervise the farmlands about the estate. She cared for her mother in her slow decline and final illness and knew the peace of letting someone she loved go gently. And slowly, carefully, she was finding out at last what Guinevere could do.

The outside world didn't vanish. Messengers came from Constantine and Letitia every few weeks. Sometimes Guinevere went to see them, especially after they left Camelot for good. Too many people complained that it was too haunted for anyone to live comfortably there. Also, while the country didn't collapse, many of the kings, such as Maelgwn of Gwynedd, Ida of Northumbria, and Vortipore of Demetia, took advantage of the confusion after Camlann to declare themselves once again free of any government but their own, especially in the matter of taxes. Only Dyfnwal, now King, sent the tributes. Constantine retreated to Dumnonia, where only Agravaine's friendly Cornwall lay at his back. From there he could still control a large part of Britain. Through him, Arthur's laws and Arthur's treaties continued.

She was at the court when Gaheris left for Armorica, to train for the priesthood. He promised to send any books to be copied to her first, so that she could read them before passing them on to Illtud.

"And if I hear word of Sir Lancelot, I'll send that also," he promised.

"It's kind of you," she told him. "But don't worry. I know he is well, without word of him."

"He's been gone three years now," Gaheris warned. "How can you have such faith?"

"It's a long walk to Jerusalem and back." She smiled. "And we are making it together."

Gaheris left wondering if anything the bishops would teach him would help to explain the mysticism at home. He could hardly wait to tell them about Gawain.

Guinevere believed that she was managing her lands, but actually her role was more subtle. Rhianna ran the household, as she had done for twenty years. Caet had taken over the organization of the farms. He inspected the horses and sheep, gave the final approval on planting times and work owed to the villa, and went to Portsmouth to bargain with the traders for wine and silk. On the land where his grandfather had been born a slave to the Romans, Caet was now almost the lord.

The first time a woman came to the door, asking for help with a sick child, Rhianna prepared to go without mentioning it to Guinevere. But the woman had wrung her cracked, red hands and begged that "the Queen-Lady" come too.

"But we can't bother her about this, Paedden," Rhianna scolded her. "Guinevere isn't such a one to have to mess herself with illness."

"Please! The old ones say she has healing hands!"

Rhianna was growing annoyed, and only sympathy with

Paedden's worry kept her from speaking sharply. At that moment Guinevere came in.

"I thought I heard voices. What is it?"

"Guinevere, this poor woman thinks that somehow you can help her son. He has a sweating fever and she's afraid he's dying. I've tried to tell her . . ."

"But if she thinks I can help, shouldn't I try?" Guinevere asked. "Anyway, you do too much, wearing yourself out whenever there's sickness. At least I can learn what you do, in case you need help. I've read our medical books, of course, but I've heard each illness is different and not every recommended treatment always works."

Rhianna looked doubtful and Risa made Guinevere tie up her hair and wear clothes that could be burnt afterward, but she went.

It was a simple hut of stone and wood, built a hundred years before and maintained by each generation. It had only one large room, partitioned into smaller ones. The hearth in the center warmed everything and a hole in the roof provided ventilation. The walls were clean with whitewash and decorated with bright wool winter blankets and long chains of onion and herbs. Rhianna set about making a hot emetic to administer. Guinevere went to the bed.

The boy was about nine years old. His brown hair was tangled wetly on his forehead and neck. The large brown eyes were glazed with fever as he tossed himself wildly in delirium.

"Mama! Mama!" he called, unable to realize that his mother was next to him.

"He mustn't thrash about so! Galen is clear on that." Guinevere tried to hold him, but he jerked in her arms. "Hush, dear, hush. You'll be fine. Rhianna is making you some medicine. Just lie still, it will be all right."

She put one hand over his forehead and absently began to croon an old song from her childhood. Almost immediately the flailing arms relaxed and the boy's eyes closed.

Paedden felt his head. "He's sleeping natural!" She burst

into tears. "I knew you could save him! You knew the old words! How can we ever thank you!"

"But I just held him a moment," Guinevere protested. "I didn't do anything."

"What did you sing to him, then?"

"Nothing, just an old song of my nurse's. She sang it to me when I caught a winter chill. It was only a children's song."

Paedden's face lit up. "A children's song! As if I didn't know the oldest language when I heard it. My grandmother always told me that Flora was teaching you. Why else would the high priestess of the goddess Epona be serving a Christian family? She must have taught you all the old charms and spells. You needn't fear. I won't give you away to the priests. You've saved my son today. Anything we have is yours."

"Thank you." Guinevere was still puzzled. There were mysteries from her childhood about Flora, memories that never made sense and gaps that she could find no memory for. "But it would be well to give him the medicine, too."

"Of course," Paedden agreed. "The Lady Rhianna's potion will keep the fever from returning. But it was your hand that healed him."

Rhianna was silent on the walk home. Guinevere thought she was piqued at being ignored. She tried to apologize. Rhianna laughed at her.

"The boy is getting well. What difference does it make how it was done? If Flora had taught me her spells, I wouldn't need to spend each spring and fall boiling down these smelly weeds."

"You mean you believe it? Was Flora really high priestess?"

"Of course. Everyone knew that," Rhianna answered. "I remember Matthew telling me of a time he and your other brothers sneaked out on solstice eve to watch the sacrifice. My, was she angry!"

She stopped suddenly, remembering that Guinevere was not supposed to know about her nurse's other life. But that was years ago. What harm could it do now?

Guinevere didn't notice, she was considering. "As far back as I can remember, Flora sang those songs to me and taught me the finger plays and hand games that went with them. But she never told me that they were anything but rustic charms. I thought they were just to amuse me."

"She had only sons and grandsons, you know, like Caet," Rhianna said thoughtfully. "She might have decided to make you her acolyte." She did not add that rumors hinted Guinevere was also meant to be a sacrifice. A long time ago, she repeated to herself. Flora was only ashes now.

"Perhaps she died too soon to tell me. I was only fourteen at the time. I don't remember it well. Rhianna," Guinevere decided, "perhaps I should learn more about healing."

"It's often very ugly, Guinevere."

"That's all right. I think I've had enough of prettiness for this life."

And that was how, when the plague reached Britain, Guinevere was one of the first to be sent for. But, before that, came the Book.

The Book was not one sent by Gaheris. A trader brought it to Britain and showed it to Caet.

"I can't read but numbers," he said with regret. "But they're saying on the other side that this Gildas fellow gives them all hell-fire. All those kings, you know, and even the bishops. There's supposed to be lots in there all about their sinful ways. You couldn't read me a bit, could you?"

Caet had to admit that his reading wasn't up to the convolutions of Gildas, but he brought it back for Guinevere.

It chanced that Father Antonius was visiting when he returned, and he and Guinevere were both delighted by the prospect of something new.

"*De Excidio et Conquestu Britannae,* 'Of the Destruction and Conquest of Britain.' That's a rather premature title, don't you think?" Guinevere said in amusement. "Who is this Gildas?"

"A man I was at school with, I'm afraid," the priest admitted. "He is older than I am, of course. He studied first with St. Docca. He went to Armorica years ago."

"That must be why he thinks he can survive castigating every important person in Britain," said Guinevere as she thumbed through it. "My Lord! Look what he says about Vortipore's daughter!"

She riffled forward a few pages and her amusement became grim. "How dare he! The sanctimonious slanderer! How can he make up such things! He accuses Constantine of murdering boys in church, and of adultery and 'vulgar domestic impieties.' Oh, he'd never get away with that in Rome! He'd be sued and executed for calumny before the first copy was finished."

But, in spite of her disgust, Guinevere went to the beginning and read the book through. She couldn't understand how Gildas could have gotten so many facts wrong about decent people like Constantine and King Cuneglasse, who had married one sister to please his father and, after his death, divorced her, happily for both of them, to marry the sister he had wanted all along. Yet, when he spoke of Maelgwn and Vortipore, she relished knowing that their crimes were only what she had suspected.

"He does have a way of making one feel the depths that these men have fallen to," she admitted. "Listen to what he says about Maelgwn: 'Why art thou foolishly rolling in the black pool of thine offences, as if soaked in the wine of the Sodomitical grape?' It seems a fair question."

"Read what he says about the priests," Risa demanded. "Of course, he doesn't mean you, Father."

"Oh, he goes on about them for pages and pages, all about simony and gluttony and throwing their poor devout mothers and sisters in the street so that they might 'familiarly and indecently entertain strange women.' I wonder what school of rhetoric he adheres to?"

Father Antonius was not so amused. "His words remind me of Caradoc. Obviously Gildas believes he has never sinned. Or perhaps he is hiding his own stained soul by heaping rebukes upon others. There are abuses in the Church in

Britain. We know that well. But to insist that we deserve a second flood as our mildest punishment and to berate the entire country as another Sodom is not a responsible act!"

"You're right, Father. I'm sorry I laughed," Guinevere apologized. "But I can't believe that anyone will take this book seriously. Why, hardly anyone will ever read it. The Latin is very flowery and he does make mistakes in grammar. Can you see Maelgwn spending an evening listening to this?"

"I suppose not," the priest admitted. "But I did see how eagerly you and the other ladies here went through it."

They had the grace to be ashamed. "For a young man, you are very astute, Father Antonius," Rhianna laughed. "Very well, what is the penance for enjoying seditious literature?"

But the book was not ignored. More copies found their way into Britain and excerpts of it were read aloud in court and church. Some priests found Gildas' copious quotations from the Bible perfect for sermonizing, and spread the condemnation of rulers among their people. "Britain has kings, but they are tyrants!" became a catch phrase that prepared listeners for lurid denunciations to follow. Vortipore was furious, and had the bishop who preached the book in Demetia poisoned. He didn't care particularly what was said about his daughter, but he wasn't having any baseborn cleric tell him to "turn from his sinful ways with a humble and contrite heart."

Maelgwn, on the other hand, thought the whole thing a great joke. He had chapters read every night at dinner and roared loudest at the parts about himself.

"Say that again," he commanded the reader. "That part about 'hot and prone, like a young colt coveting every pleasant pasture.' Ah! Wonderful how this Gildas uses words. I think I should like that on my tombstone."

The winter was certainly livelier because of it. In spring, the interest died down, as the more mundane concerns of planting and sheep-shearing and raiding a neighbor's land took precedence again.

Guinevere was in her mother's garden, thinning the lettuce, when one of the new servant girls came running.

"My lady, come quick!" she begged. "There's a man at the gate with Saxon hair and British eyes who says he's your nephew. The guards want to kill him but I thought I'd better tell you first."

At the gate, Guinevere found a young man standing beside his horse with an air of unconcern. He was not fazed by the naked swords a few inches from his stomach. He greeted her with a smile which told his patrimony at once.

"Aunt Guinevere! Father warned me not to expect a royal welcome, but I hoped for a little better than this."

"Put your weapons away, Mauric and Hom. This is my brother's son," Guinevere told the guards, who still looked suspiciously at the man's hair. "It can't be Matthew; you don't look old enough."

"No, I'm Allard, Aunt. I was afraid that if I gave that Saxon name, your men would slit my throat before you could be fetched. I have a letter from father with me, if you doubt me."

"A letter from Mark! Oh, that's wonderful! But you look just like he did at your age, at least in your face—just as I remember him before he went to war. Now, you must need to tend to your horse and wash and so forth. I'll read this while you're being settled. Grisel! Show my nephew to the corner guest room, please. You don't need to be afraid. He's really family."

As soon as he left, Guinevere unrolled the letter. It was written on a piece of lambskin, poorly scraped. Mark was not a frequent correspondent.

> My dearest sister:
> The news of our mother's death only just reached me. I grieve for her, and now find I can forgive her for her bitterness toward my wife. I have no desire, however, to return to my birthplace. I will die and be buried here in my own land. Matthew has married and wishes to remain here also. If my parents did not request that I be denied my share of their lands, I would like to

deed them to my second son, Allard. He has always been eager for tales of Cameliard and the old
days of Britain. He is an able man, whom I have
sent as my agent before to various parts of Britain.
He speaks Saxon as well as British and reads a little. I have not told him of this plan. Let him stay
with you awhile, and if he seems to want to remain, find him a fair portion to settle on. In this, I
trust your sense of honor completely.

Mark

Guinevere read it over several times. It was the first she
had heard from her misanthropic brother since she visited
him fifteen years before. He must have struggled with his
pride a long time before writing such a letter. Of course,
Allard did have the right to part of his grandparents' estate,
but a Saxon! Even though he was only half, his bright blond
hair and solid build were so obvious. And the fear and hatred
of the Germanic invaders went deep throughout all Britain.
If she gave him his patrimony, it was quite possible that the
peasants on the land would revolt. Yet she couldn't deny him
his right.

The best thing to do was wait. Let Allard spend some
weeks with them. Perhaps he would decide he would be happier with his mother's people or back in the mountains. She
could even hope that somehow the people of Cameliard
would learn to accept him. But it was a fragile hope.

After washing and changing Allard returned, full of enthusiasm.

"Your baths are still working!" he said in amazement. "I
thought most of the pipes north of Aquae Sulis had burst and
never been repaired. This is just as my father told me. Do
you have time to show me more?"

"Of course, Allard. Your Aunt Rhianna is away now, but
she'll be back this evening. Until then, we can explore wherever you like."

"Well, if it's not too much trouble, I'd like to see all of
the house and the chapel and the tree one could climb from

the stable roof and the cave where the wine is stored and the Round Table was hidden. Oh, I've been told all the old stories!"

"I would have thought my brother would never have mentioned any of that to you. He wanted to forget all of us."

Allard shrugged. "I don't know any of the reasons he left here, but he does love the place. He's told me all about it. Now I almost feel I'm coming home."

The look he gave Guinevere was so familiar and friendly that she made up her mind then that he must stay.

"I think, Allard, that it may be true. Welcome home!"

Chapter Twenty-Seven

"My mother says it doesn't matter if he's the Lady Guinevere's kin; he's still half Saxon and I'm to stay away from him," Grisel said decidedly to her friend, Cafdd. The two girls were sitting in the anteroom, waiting for Guinevere to finish bathing.

"Well I don't care what your mother says," Cafdd retorted. "He's friendly and handsome and I've heard it said he's going to build his own villa over by the orchard. When the mistress dies, he's likely to be lord here, and I'm not going to give him cause to want to turn me away."

"We'll be old women before she dies, Cafdd. She's older than my grandmother, who's white and toothless and wrinkled as a dried apple, but does she look it?"

Cafdd sighed. Her hands were already rough from the washing she did, and her skin was starting to line from the sun and wind.

"The aristocracy do seem to keep themselves up longer than folks like us."

Grisel thought it was something more than birthright, but she didn't have a chance to say, for Guinevere called them then to brush her hair.

Allard was not only clearly delighted with Cameliard and its surroundings, he was also very useful to it. He had grown up among his father's sheepfolds and knew as well as anyone how to shear. He understood breeding techniques enough to hold his own with the old shepherds and showed them a new treatment for the summer coughing, which killed so many of the lambs. He won respect from them, despite his strange looks. Before June was well begun, Guinevere had decided to deed him a section of the property. She had proper legal decrees drawn up and notarized by the priest, sending them both to court and to the Bishop in London. Allard was given a copy for his own at a banquet in his honor. He held the thick document as if it were an eggshell, not quite believing that it made him officially part of this place he loved so much.

"You may find, Allard, that it's now a part of you," Guinevere cautioned. "You shouldn't thank me. This is your father's portion you hold now."

"I'll care for it well. I promise, Aunt." He could hardly finish his meal. He wanted to take a torch out and pace off his section, filling it already with flocks and fields and a villa like this one his many-times-great grandfather had built.

Guinevere was pleased. He would see that the old ways were kept up, as well as he understood them. The things her father worked to preserve were safe for another generation, at least. Arthur would have been happy, too. If only he could have known. Constantine was holding order in Dumnonia and even the other kings, though they had abandoned Arthur's dream of unity, still called in need on his justice. Modred had destroyed Camelot, but not the dream. She wished Allard could have known Arthur. He would have been one who believed.

Allard threw himself into organizing and improving his

land. He begged Caet to let him go along on the next trading journey.

Caet looked up sourly into Allard's face. The lad was thirty years younger and a head taller than he was. He combined, both in looks and temperament, the best of both his races. Caet knew that, if he lived long enough, one day he would be taking orders from this man. He shook his head. There had never really been any hope. The day of the Celt was long over.

He made the best of it. "Yes, come along. I can tell you who to deal with and where to get the best price for your wool. They say that the Eastern Emperor, Justinian, is mad for British hunting dogs. Have you thought of raising them, too? And when we go to the tavern, keep your mouth shut. It's better if they think you a dull wit at first. Later on you can dazzle them with your highborn dialect."

They returned in the middle of July with fine cloth, wine, glass beads wrapped in thick cloth, peppercorns, and fever.

Caet fell ill on the road home and it was a panic-stricken Allard who carried him into the villa.

"He woke up one morning complaining that the light was too bright and that it kept moving; then he seemed better, but quiet. By noon the fever was on him. I don't know how he kept his seat, but he wouldn't let me stop. Then, last night, that swelling started in his neck; there's another under his arm. What should I do?"

He looked like a bewildered sheepdog, holding his charge.

"Take him to his room and undress him for us," Rhianna ordered. "Cafdd, send your brother for a bucket of cool water. Then come for Caet's clothes and throw them in the midden. How do you feel, Allard?"

"Fine. I don't understand it. There wasn't any sickness in Portsmouth while we were there."

"Well, go to the baths and be sure you wash yourself all over. Then send your clothes after Caet's."

Guinevere came in soon after.

"Is he very ill?" she asked. "I can't remember him ever

being sick, even when we were children. Flora wouldn't have permitted it."

"I wish she were here now," Rhianna sighed. "I've never seen anything like this. These swellings are hard and hot as if some horrible creature is growing inside him. I'm going to try to bring the fever down. Sing to him, dear. If anyone will respond to that, it's Caet."

Guinevere leaned over the bed and placed her hands on either side of his head. Softly, she hummed the ancient words and from deep in her Christian heart, she prayed that his pagan goddess would spare him.

His eyes opened and she thought he knew her. "You're home now, Caet. We'll take care of you. Just rest and get well."

He smiled at her in wonder, then looked over her shoulder with awe-stricken eyes. "I tell you, Lord Arthur," he said loudly, "it's not your Virgin, but the goddess Epona. There! Look! The celestial horse, her guardian, stands behind her!"

Startled, Guinevere turned around. But there was nothing there.

Caet had collapsed back onto the pillow.

They worked over him for three days, but nothing seemed to help. He began coughing blood, the first time spraying Rhianna, who was bending over him. On the last day, strange red blotches came out on his chest and face, and the next morning he died in Guinevere's arms.

She held him a long time, not believing he was gone. He had always been like a shadow to her. Except for the years of her fostering and the early part of her marriage, he had always been there, quietly waiting, never intruding. When she had needed something special done, she had gone to Caet. He had taken the blame for her childhood pranks. His death made her feel that there was suddenly a cold wind blowing on her unprotected back.

"My poor friend," she wept. "I never knew you as I should have."

Because it was summer, they buried him at once, with little preparation. With him went the small leather bag he had carried all his life. It held only a pagan charm and three strands of golden hair. Allard looked down on the small coffin and shook his head.

"It seems a man like that would need a bigger piece of earth to hold him."

They burned the bedclothes and washed themselves thoroughly that night. After dinner, they sat out in the atrium and watched the stars. They spoke very little, still numb from the strange and ugly thing that had struck Caet. Rhianna got up to go first.

"How sweet the air is tonight," she said. "There must be some flower in bloom I never noticed before."

Guinevere took a deep breath. "I smell nothing different. Perhaps it's just the change from being in the sickroom so long. You wore yourself out, my dear."

"Yes, I do feel tired. But the scent is so strong. How odd that you don't notice it. Good night, everyone. Tomorrow, I must start on the making of the brine to preserve the vegetables. Everything is ripening at once and we are sadly behind."

By the next morning Rhianna was delirious, calling for her mother and Guinevere's long-dead brother Matthew. In rare lucid moments, she complained that her head ached dreadfully and begged for water. They gave her potions steeped with herbs and applied cool cloths to her burning limbs. Nothing helped. By the end of the day, her nose began to bleed and they couldn't stop it. In the hour before dawn, she died. When they uncovered her, they found the same small red blotches on her as on Caet.

Guinevere looked at Risa; her hands were shaking.

"What is this thing that has come down on us?" she asked in a dazed whisper.

Rhianna was buried in the family section, next to Guinevere's parents. Father Antonius was away, so Guinevere read from the Gospels over the grave.

"Rhianna should have had more honor than this," she worried. "We must have a stone made as soon as possible."

But that was to be a long time. That afternoon the serving

girl, Grisel, fell ill, and then two of the stable boys. Guinevere found herself too busy to feel anything but fear and frustration. She did all Rhianna had taught her and used the pagan chants as well as Christian prayers, but nothing made any difference. One after the other, they died.

"We must send someone to Constantine," she told Allard. "He has to know what's going on here. Perhaps someone at the court knows what this is and how to treat it."

"I don't know the way, but if you make me a map, I'll go," he offered.

"I don't know. You seem healthy. I would think that if you were going to get this, you would have by now. I don't want to send this horror anywhere else. Yes, you should go."

But before he could, the poet Durriken arrived. When he got to the gate, the guard called down.

"You don't want to come in here! We have a plague upon us! Deliver your message and go!" he warned.

"Dear God, no!" Durriken cried. "You may as well let me in, man. It can't be any worse than what I just left."

Guinevere greeted him sadly. "You shouldn't be here. Every day someone dies of this hideous illness. There is nothing in my books about it, nothing in the lore. It seems we can only wait and bury. What news do you have of the court?"

Wearily, Durriken sat in the chair she brought and sipped some ale. He took a long time about it. Finally, with a deep breath, he gave his information.

"This evil plague has swept through Britain, my Lady. They say it is the same Black Death that was in Constantinople four years ago. The trading ships may have carried it here from Iberia. No one knows what causes it or how to stop it. The sorrow is great in Dumnonia. Hundreds have died, including the King's first-born son."

"Little Arthur!" Guinevere cried. "Poor Letitia! How does she endure it?"

"Not well. She is concerned for the two younger children and wanted them sent to you, but it seems that there is no place safe now." Durriken took another deep drink. "People are saying that this is a judgment on Britain for our contentiousness and sin, as was foretold in Gildas' book."

"I can't believe that," Guinevere retorted. "What sins could that little boy have had on his soul?"

"Not his, Constantine's. Like the son of Pharaoh in Exodus. Since the child's death, the King has locked himself in the church. He prays and fasts and weeps constantly. No one can convince him to put aside his grief and resume the government. He is even talking of renouncing the throne and entering a monastery."

"That's insane! What will happen to the country?"

Durriken leaned forward and lowered his voice. "My Lady, if this plague continues unabated through the summer, there will be no country to matter."

Guinevere thought of all the new graves, too many to be contained in the old cemetery. They were taking the bodies to the fields, now, and putting them in common graves. There wasn't time or energy to dig them individually any more. Of the thirty or so people attached to the villa, twenty-two had died and dozens more among the farmers and shepherds. There would not be enough people to bring in the crops this year or care for the sheep. And, if they slaughtered animals to bring down the herd size, there were not enough people left to eat the meat before it rotted. Durriken had reported that in Wroxter there was no one left alive. Bodies lay on the side of the road and no one, not even looters, had the courage to enter the town.

"I don't care," she said firmly. "Someone will survive. It's cowardice to abandon our duties now. Constantine can't destroy what's left of Arthur's order just because his son has died. I have no patience with that. Oh, Durriken, I'm sorry! You're tired and I've kept you here so long. Forgive me! Cafdd! See if you can find a clean room for Durriken and something to eat. I must go, now. Risa was taken sick last night."

The lump in Risa's neck was already huge and burning. She tossed on her bed, her hands clutching at her own throat. Even through the stupefaction caused by lack of sleep and the

sight of constant pain, Guinevere felt wrenched unbearably
by the agony Risa was suffering. She wiped the maid's face
and neck, swallowing her horror of the swelling. Risa
grabbed her hand.

"My throat!" she sobbed. "It's choking me! Cut it out,
Guinevere, please! I can't breathe!"

"Risa, I can't!" Guinevere looked with revulsion at it.

"Help me!" Risa cried. Then she fell unconscious.

Guinevere sat there, staring at Risa's neck. Sometimes
those things had burst open on their own, spewing out a
stinking viscous liquid. "I couldn't do it," she told herself.
"I'm not used to such things."

Risa tried to scream again, but only coughed hoarsely.
With streaming eyes, Guinevere drew her knife. She held it
in the candle flame until it glowed. She put a dish at Risa's
neck and prayed to anyone listening.

"Please let me do this without killing her!"

Then, before she lost courage, she plunged the knife point
into the swelling. There was a disgusting noise and then a
gush as the liquid poured into the bowl. Guinevere set it on
the floor and wiped the cut clean. Then she staggered out of
the room and fell in a dead faint outside the door.

When she awakened they told her that Risa's fever was
down and she was breathing clearly. She was going to live.

They tried the cutting with others. Sometimes it worked,
sometimes it was too late. They learned that once the red
marks appeared, early or late in the illness, nothing more
availed. As summer waned, so did the plague. By early autumn, there were no new cases. The rains began and seemed
to wash away the contagion with them. Travelers were seen
on the roads again, bringing news of the rest of Britain. It
was hard for Guinevere to understand what they were saying,
her world had shrunk so in the last few months. One pilgrim
did catch her attention.

"We can be grateful that old King Arthur went to aid the
Armoricans," he stated. "They took in our refugees and even
sent help in the worst days. If we had turned our backs on

them, they'd have ignored us in our need. He was a good man, the old King. Would there were any like him now."

She treasured the man's words. "You see, Arthur! It didn't die with you, like a candle in a storm. Your light still shines. I won't let them forget. I promise."

Slowly, they learned what had happened elsewhere. Gwynedd was hard hit. Maelgwn and most of his court had died. Whole towns, like Wroxter, were inhabited only by ghosts. It was thought that the British population had been cut by a third. The Saxons were untouched. No report came of any cases of the plague in their villages.

"You see," people told each other. "That Gildas was right. We're being punished for our sins."

Wandering monks preached the same thing and swore that only through prayer, repentance, and a life of self-denial could Britain be saved. Strict monasteries were founded. Great lords and ladies rushed to join them, leaving worldly property behind. One day, word came from Letitia that she was returning to Cameliard permanently, if they would take her.

She arrived a few weeks later, weak and thin, with her two remaining children. She was hard and angry. It was several days before she would tell them why she had come.

"He's renounced the crown, the land, our children, and me," she told them, her voice shaking with bitterness. "He's left his cousin, Vortemir, to run things as best he can and gone into a monastery."

"Constantine!" Guinevere wouldn't believe it. "But he's coming back, of course."

Her niece stared at her blankly. "If he does, I won't be there waiting. But I don't think he'll leave it. He blamed himself for little Arthur's death and then for all the others and for not being King Arthur reborn. He left us gold and jewels and alone. So, I've come back. When my children are old enough, I'll try to see that they get their patrimony. But now we're defenseless. Will you let us stay?"

So there were children again at Cameliard. Guinevere showed them her old hiding places and taught them to swim in the baths. They quickly forgot the horrors of the summer past. Their presence discouraged others from dwelling on it. Under the snow and rain, the graves sank and blended into the landscape again.

In the spring Allard came to Guinevere with a suggestion. He hemmed a long while, rather defensively, before he came to the point.

"There aren't enough people here any more, Aunt," he pointed out. "We need people to settle and work the land. I want to go to the Alemanni living on the coast and offer them a chance to live here."

Guinevere looked at him suspiciously. "Alemanni? I remember Arthur had a treaty with them. Aren't they a kind of Saxon?"

"No, Aunt. They're a kind of Alemanni. The languages aren't too unlike but it's a totally different tribe. They've been here a few generations and know something about the way we farm and raise animals. They won't just hunt and fight as the Saxons do, but they can fight, if we need them, and I think we will."

"You want *foederati* at Cameliard?" Guinevere was outraged.

"Now Aunt." Allard backed up a few steps. "Not hired warriors, settlers, with wives and families. They're Christian now, you know. There was an Irish missionary among them a few years ago. That's more than most of the peasants here are."

"I don't know. I have to think about it," Guinevere hedged. "We've had the same families living here for three hundred years."

"Then it's time for new blood," Allard insisted. "Please, Aunt Guinevere. Let me bring a few of them here. We must have more people or Cameliard won't survive."

"Well . . . only a few, though, two or three families to start." She felt he was right, but hated the idea anyway.

He kissed her excitedly. "Thank you, dearest Aunt. You won't be sorry. I'll see that they are model tenants."

"I'm sure," she replied. "You know, you didn't need my

approval. You could have put them on your own land without saying anything to me at all."

"Yes," he answered. "But that wasn't the way I wanted to
do it."

She felt very comforted.

The Alemanni were greeted with apathetic distrust. They
cleaned out houses from which whole families had died and
began to till the land. Under Allard's guidance, they gradually blended in with the natives. The adults never gave each
other more than wary acknowledgment, but watching the
children together, Guinevere could see that the next generation would be as much a blend as Allard. She wondered if
Arthur would approve. His walls had been built to fend off
the invaders. In the rest of Britain, there was no sign that
anyone else was welcoming the Germanic immigrants. Still,
she was reminded more and more of the early years at Camelot when she saw the new tenants and the old together.

Another year passed and another. Allard built his villa and
went north with an invitation to Lydia to spend her last years
with her old friends. He brought back regrets and her youngest daughter, who was not afraid of Saxons. Guinevere received her with joy.

She was busy and useful. She was happy. But every morning she watched the road and wondered how many steps one
took to Jerusalem and back.

Chapter Twenty-Eight

After the plague, the remnants of the British aristocracy
who did not enter monasteries withdrew deeper into the

mountains and the peninsula. Saxon, Angle, and Jutish new-comers flowed into the forsaken land. Where a number of people remained, there were battles, but not great ones as in the first days. The British loathing of the Germanic immigrants never abated, and they refused to send missionaries or envoys to "barbarians." Intermarriage with the Franks had brought Christianity to some Saxons and the land of Britain itself had changed them, drew them into herself and away from continental relations.

They tried to conquer Cameliard, but Allard and his Alemanni settlers joined in the defense and a treaty was made and hostages exchanged.

Guinevere found herself in charge of five Saxon children, terrified of the strange world they had been sent to. Their grandmothers had told them that the old Roman buildings were full of ghosts. The first day, they refused to enter the villa.

"They can't spend the next seven years camping in the atrium," Letitia said in exasperation. "We'll have to drag them through and show them there are no spirits."

"I hate to frighten them even more," Guinevere worried. She got down on her knees and reached out her arms to the youngest child. She racked her brain for the little bit of Saxon she had learned.

"*Leof cild,*" she began. The little girl started, then cautiously touched a lock of Guinevere's hair.

She smiled. "*Swa swa Mama,*" she said.

"Yes!" Guinevere was pleased. "Just like Mama's. Now, *Comst! In hus na grimlicum gastum.*"

The children looked doubtful. Guinevere repeated, "*Na grimlicum gastum!*"

"What are you saying?" Letitia asked.

"I think I'm telling them we have no ghosts, but I'm not sure," Guinevere admitted.

"Well, let's try to get them inside again and find out. I hope they learn good British soon. I'll never get my throat around that guttural language!"

"All right," Guinevere agreed. "Oh, what is it, Leofric?"

"My Lady, there is an old, blind monk at the gate who has asked about you."

"Oh? Did he want to talk to me?"

"No, Lady, but Aulan thought you should be sent for. He gave me no reason."

"Very well, I'll be there in a moment." Guinevere looked at the guard. "Leofric, how close is your language to that of these children?"

"I can understand them a bit, if they talk slowly."

"Good. Then go with Lady Letitia, please, and try to make it clear to these poor babies that we are not sending them inside to be devoured by monsters, but to wash and eat and put their belongings away."

She hurried to the gate, a hope growing in her. Her lame foot dragged as she tried to go faster. The hope flamed into certainty as Aulan hurried to meet her, pointing to a figure sitting patiently at the gate.

"He didn't give his name, but I knew him," Aulan told her. "He only asked for news of you. I made him wait until you could come. I hope that was right?"

"Of course. Thank you, Aulan, thank you!"

As they came closer, the pilgrim's face turned at the sound. How worn he was! The winds of sea and desert had furrowed his face, but not stooped him. So many years! Guinevere struggled to control her trembling as she laid her hands on his shoulders.

"A long journey, Lancelot," she whispered. "Did you find your answers?"

He took her hands in his, conscious that they were not alone.

"I only found more questions, Guinevere," he answered. "The world is filled only with questions."

"Not here, my love. Here there is sunshine and quiet and children discovering that, in my house at least, monsters are not real. Stay with us . . . awhile?"

"Yes, I dreamt of it, all the way to Jerusalem and back."

She led him to a guest room and ordered that food be

brought to them there. While they ate, she told him of what had happened in Britain in the years he'd been gone.

"And have you discovered what you can do?" he asked wistfully.

She laughed. "Some of it. I can help in a sickroom and play with children and, maybe, I can hold people together. I never knew that was a talent before, but I've worked all these years to keep Cameliard, just my own corner of Britain, safe and well. It may be selfish to preserve what I love, but it was as much as I could do."

"From the babble of tongues I heard as I journeyed to your door, you've accomplished a miracle."

She pushed her tray aside and came to sit next to him. He finished his cup, then touched her face with his fingers.

"My eyes dimmed slowly until I finally realized that I could tell nothing more than light and dark. Constantinople was only a blue and gold blur, and Jerusalem a blending of browns. It didn't really matter. They could not have outshone the Grail. But I would give so much to be able to look at you now."

"It's better that you have only memory, my love." She kissed his palm. "I've grown old. Feel the wrinkles in my brow. My skin has faded and my hands are mapped with veins.

"And your hair?" he asked, as he pulled out the pins and unwove it.

"Gray, almost white," she lied, tears in her throat.

"It feels as beautiful as ever. Oh Guinevere!" He buried his face in her neck. "I've missed you so dreadfully. Stay with me tonight!"

"I never meant to do anything else, my dearest."

She lifted his face to hers and kissed him slowly. He drew her more closely against him, sliding her robe from her shoulders. She shook it off.

"I forgot to tell you, Lancelot, my own. Loving you is what I can do best."

*   *   *

They lay awake in the early morning dusk, Lancelot's head cradled in the hollow of her shoulder and her breast. Guinevere sighed and felt all her muscles relax for the first time since Gawain's death. Lancelot chuckled.

"My dear, you are purring like a kitten."

"I feel like one, warm and lazy. Do you think we could just spend the rest of our lives in this bed?"

"Mmmm, what would your household think of us?"

"Probably that we were too old and feeble to get up. They are all so young! Even Risa is gone now. I hope she finally knows what happened to her son. We never heard a word of him."

He absently let his hand drift across her body.

"Are we really the only ones left, Guinevere?"

"Nearly, I think. Agravaine died two winters ago and Lydia last summer. Gaheris, they say, is a bishop now, in Iberia. We have outlived our time, my darling. To most men today we are nothing more than legends."

"Then hold me tightly, Guinevere, before even our memory fades."

He stayed a month. They both knew from the first that he couldn't remain forever. Too much had changed, and too much of the past was still with them. Lancelot told stories of his travels to wide-eyed listeners, and they begged for tales of Camelot and Arthur.

"Please," the children begged. "Lady Guinevere will tell us nothing, not even if the songs the poets sing are true. Did you really walk a flaming sword over an abyss to rescue her? Did Arthur really kill a hundred men in one battle? Did the wizard Merlin build Camelot overnight? Lady Guinevere laughed and laughed when we asked her that."

"I can't tell you about that," he insisted. "Camelot was finished before I came there. Be content with what the poets tell you. What I remember does not belong with their songs."

The night before he left, they didn't sleep at all.

"They built the monastery on the tor of the sun god. It overlooks Camlann and what remains of Camelot, so it will be good that I can no longer see. The monks will take me in as a lay brother," Lancelot explained. "I know better now than to make impossible vows."

"Do you think you'll find peace there?" Guinevere asked, smoothing his hair.

"No. I found it here. But there's a stubborn part of me yet that longs for redemption. I don't want to be left behind in purgatory when you ascend to heaven."

"My darling fool! You still believe that happiness must be sinful!"

"Only my own, Guinevere."

"Someday, I'll teach you how wrong you are." She kissed him again and they said nothing coherent the rest of the night.

Although she appeared much younger than she was, after Lancelot left, Guinevere felt older. Being with him again had showed her the gap between her old half-Roman world and this vibrant one of eager newcomers. She had accomplished what she wanted. Arthur would not be forgotten, nor, she believed, his dream. Her home was safe. It had even become a refuge. After Allard finished building his villa across the valley, she deeded hers to the church as a house for women who needed protection. Many were relieved to know there was a monastery just for them, where they could be free to study and work without male supervision. The management of the house and lands fell to Letitia.

Her hair never lost its gold and she took to covering it. Her pale eyes and translucent skin made the contrast too startling. Occasionally, Lancelot would send word. Only that, a word. But it was enough. She was simply biding time, and the world around her grew less and less important.

Late one winter night she was in her childhood room, reading the poems of Ausonius. She heard the singing very clearly and smiled. Geraldus was at her side.

"Have you come again to ask me to come to your country?"

"This is the last time I can ask, Guinevere."

"Really? Oh, Geraldus, how wonderful! I've waited so long! I only hope Lancelot will follow me soon!"

"Guinevere, please. You don't know what waits for you out there! Our land is beautiful and filled with magic and music. It's where you've always belonged. We even have a unicorn."

"A unicorn!" Memory filled her eyes. "Of course, how could I have forgotten all these years. My other self, it was, when I was a girl. But no, not even for my unicorn. I've grown up, as far as I can in this life. It's time for me to see what else there is. And I promised Lancelot. He can't reach the gates and not find me there."

Geraldus sighed and reached across the narrow gap between them, kissing her good-bye.

"I didn't think you'd change your mind. I hope it's all you want it to be."

"If Lancelot is with me, it will be."

His choir sang to her one more time, a song very much like the prothalamium they had made for her wedding day. Dear Geraldus!

Guinevere looked with longing into the growing dawn. She thought she saw Gawain's face framed in the clouds. "Galahad is gone to some holy place where I may not be allowed to follow. Arthur, they say, will never die, poor dear. But I have made a promise to Lancelot and with all my heart, I want to keep it. If Lancelot is not in paradise, then I might as well be damned. Thank you, Geraldus," she called to the fading singing. "But death seems very wonderful to me. Give my love to everyone left behind."

Letitia found her later that morning, her face turned to the window and her eyes wide open as if in delighted surprise.

They put her in a sarcophagus made for one of her ancestors, wrapped in her brilliant hair and with Galahad's curl tucked into her hand.

Letitia took the message to Lancelot herself. His tears slipped quietly through his gnarled hands as she told him.

"I should have felt it," he muttered. "But she still lives in my heart. I don't understand."

"Poor old man," Letitia said to herself.

The monks thought the news would kill him, but Lancelot could not will himself dead. Later the Lady of the Lake tried to make him come home to her, threatening him with eternal youth, but he laughed in her face.

"That was my third offer, Lancelot. Take your humanity and rot in it!" she screamed at him.

"There is nothing I want more," Lancelot answered. She vanished in a puff of fuchsia smoke, which quite unnerved the monks working outside.

He took her words as a gift. That afternoon he complained of a fever and chills, and a week later he finally died.

When they heard of Lancelot's passing, the women of Cameliard took Guinevere's coffin to Glastonbury.

"We promised her, Lord Abbot," the abbess, Elfgifu, insisted, with a melting glance. "She was to be buried again with Sir Lancelot. Please allow us to fulfill her last desire."

"*Brother* Lancelot renounced all earthly desires when he came to us in his last years. We cannot permit such blasphemy as to have his paramour laid with him in the grave."

"What harm could they do there?" Elfgifu's face was innocent, but the abbot sensed her mocking.

"It grieves us terribly," she continued, "that you won't let us lay our poor lady to rest. We have labored in the time since her death to create fine offerings to give the monastery at Glastonbury, for the peace of her soul, of course. Fine altar cloths, exquisitely wrought candlesticks of silver, gold patens, and a relic which was brought to our lady while she was Queen and which she always kept in this carved ivory box."

"What is it?" The abbot sniffed greedily at the hoard.

Elfgifu opened the box, but only for a moment. "Baby teeth from John the Baptist and Saints Peter and James, saved by their mothers and lovingly preserved. We felt they should rest in the chapel over our lady's grave."

The abbot relented. "Very well. Perhaps she was not so wicked as the tales say. Some of them do tell that she was kind to the poor and needy. But we will not let them lie side by side; her bones must rest at his feet in an attitude of submission."

Elfgifu looked at Letitia, who shrugged. "All right, we agree."

So they put her bones, still wrapped in her golden hair, at Lancelot's feet and buried them both in a sealed lead coffin.

Legends grew up about the place, as about Arthur and Merlin and all the knights of the Round Table, until they obscured the truth like ivy on a wall. A generation later, a monk of Glastonbury reasoned that if the woman buried by the chapel were Guinevere, then the man with her must be King Arthur. He had a lead cross carved to that effect and placed it above the grave. In time, it came to be believed. Then for many years the grave was forgotten and new buildings and new monks came and only the poets remembered the tale.

In 1184 a fire raced through the monastery. In the extensive clearing out and rebuilding, the association of the monastery with Camelot was recalled. In 1191, while digging a foundation for a new chapel, the cross was discovered to great excitement.

It read: HIC JACET INCLITUS REX ARTURIS IN INSULA AVALLONIS SEPULTUS CUM WENNEVERIA UXORE SUA SECUNDA.

"Here lies the famous King Arthur, in the isle of Avalon buried, with Guinevere, his second wife."

Why the cross said second wife, no one knew, unless the monk knew Modred was Arthur's son and that Guinevere was not his mother.

When the coffin was opened, the bones of a large man were found, with those of a woman curled at his feet. In the sunlight, something gleamed from her and the monks saw a single strand of hair, the color of gold. One monk leaped into the coffin, grasped it and held it up. It was caught by the breeze and crumbled to dust in his hands.

King Henry the Second and his wife, Eleanor of Aquitaine, had the coffin taken in state and buried in a great tomb in front of the high altar of Glastonbury. It remained there until the Reformation, when it was destroyed and the bones were scattered.

Arthur, still dreaming under the lake, neither knew nor cared about the matter. Guinevere heard of it and laughed. What difference did it make? For at last, she and Lancelot were together and free to spend eternity wandering joyfully among the stars.